BLACKBIRD

TOM WRIGHT

CANONGATE
Edinburgh · London

Published in Great Britain in 2014 by Canongate Books Ltd,
14 High Street, Edinburgh EH1 1TE

www.canongate.tv

1

British Library Cataloguing-in-Publication Data
A catalogue record for this book is available on
request from the British Library

ISBN: 978 1 78211 324 9
Export ISBN: 978 1 78211 355 3

Typeset in Century Oldstyle MT by Palimpsest Book Production Ltd,
Falkirk, Stirlingshire

Printed and bound in Great Britain by Clays Ltd, St Ives plc.

For my accomplices; you know who you are

Forget then. Forget now. Any story that matters begins and ends everywhere and everywhen.

Tori Ogwyth Marsh

The broker, the coker, the midnight toker, the woman thought. Confederacy of dumb-asses, she thought. Organ meats wall to wall. Sneezy, though – Sneezy had his assets, she had to admit. And even Grumpy wasn't exactly a dead loss – especially in the hot tub, where he could hold his breath longer underwater than anybody in the group – as long as he's got his blow. And his little blue pills.

On the other hand, she didn't much like this recent tendency of hers to relent, to start cutting people slack, anytime a little snow blew in. She looked across the den to where Bashful, naked as a baby like everybody else, sat slouched back in the grey loveseat, absently twiddling a lock of her blonde hair and gazing off into the middle distance. The sight of those bouncy little bare boobs ignited a momentary glow of need in the woman, not quite hot enough to compel action but nice all the same. Shaking off the thought for now, she rolled the archaic but still satisfactorily crisp thousand-dollar bill she kept for just this purpose into a slim straw, inserted one end into her right nostril, touched the other to the line she'd just built on the jade coffee table, and tooted up. Her own private reserve, not the street-level Bisquick these morons always brought.

1

'Phone,' groused Grumpy as he walked in from the kitchen.

'I'm busy,' she said.

'Yeah,' he shrugged. 'Lotta that goin' around. You seen my shorts?' He tossed her the phone.

She caught it and said hello as she stood, realising with satisfaction that she was now a comfortable minimum of two lines past caring where her own clothes were or what anybody thought of her nakedness.

'Who is this?' she asked the phone. 'How'd you get this number?'

She listened for a moment, glancing at Grumpy with a frown.

'Well, believe me, she and I'll be having a little come-to-Jesus meeting about that tomorrow.' Another frown at Grumpy, who turned and wandered off toward the bedrooms. 'So, what's this about, Bone?'

By now some of the others were looking at her. She walked out onto the deck and slid the door shut behind her, noticing the absence of stars in the sky. The air out here was humid against her skin and had a restless, overcharged feel.

She looked around at the trees and down toward the dim light-haze of the town. 'It'll cost you a lot more than that, Bone,' she said. 'But I'm listening.'

Which was true – it was her trade, and she was good at it. Switching the phone to her other ear, she glanced up at the sky again. 'Make it an hour and a half,' she said. 'Do you know where my office is?' She looked in through the glass door at her companions, listened a moment longer, then said, 'Okay,' and thumbed the phone off, unaware that the decision she'd just made meant, among other things, that she wouldn't live to see the end of the coming storm.

ONE

Dr Deborah Serach Gold died on the cross sometime during a night of freezing rain mixed with sleet in late October of my last year at Three. It probably wasn't the worst thing that happened to her that day, but it had been over two decades in the making, and there's no doubt lives could have been saved if anybody here had known that at the time. How many of them actually should have been saved is a fair question, but one I have no answer for.

An hour or so before the call came I had stood up to stretch and was looking down Broad Street through the rain from my window on the third floor. The year was winding down fast and although yesterday had been almost balmy, the cutting edge of winter in the form of a hard blue norther snapping with ozone had blown in during the night. Now, with the front past and the rain falling vertically, I watched the coloured umbrellas tilting and weaving along the sidewalks, trying to remember which Disney feature they reminded me of and wondering what it was about them that made the day seem darker rather than brighter.

A couple of pigeons on the ledge under the window fluffed themselves like partridges and cocked their clown eyes fearlessly at me. Three storeys below them the wet red bricks of the street had an oddly clean look in spite of the cigarette butts and miscellaneous crud rafting slowly along the gutters. A Tri-State October, my window a membrane between contradictory realities: out there the run-up to Thanksgiving and then Christmas; in here a sky of buzzing fluorescents that never changes, and no such thing as a holiday.

This is Three – a block square, lunar grey, four storeys high – smelling of pine cleaner and trouble, with a faint, permanent aftertaste of scorched cotton. If you could burn it down by setting fire to mattresses and jailhouse scrubs in the fourth-floor cells it would be long gone. The structure itself moans when the east wind blows, and people say it looks like the Ukrainian embassy in Bumfukkistan. It goes by various names, officially the Tri-State Public Safety Complex, TSPS in newspaper headlines, Tea-sips or Oz to some of the bureaucrats and jailers and the Magic Forest to others. The assistant DAs, probation and parole officers and judicial clerks, stuck with the spaces under the southern friezes where the birds congregate, call the place Pigeontown in polite company and Birdshit Central among themselves.

But it is unique, with its footprint in three states and housing three separate police departments, all here on the third floor overlooking Broad Street's pre-Depression store-fronts going to seed and beyond those the dark railyards held over from the steam age. From my window I could see the northeast corner of Texas, a hundred acres or so of Arkansas and, at just the right angle, a thin slice of Louisiana. For people who see symbolism in buildings, thinking of this one as a watchtower is not much of a stretch.

Back at my desk, three quarterly reports behind and

ignoring for the moment the twenty-tens waiting to be signed, I punched the monitor's power button. But instead of the in-house website, what materialised on my screen was the chess game I'd started yesterday and then forgotten about. Hearing footsteps behind me, I turned and saw Detective Danny Ridout critically eyeing the screen. He was an actual cowboy and looked it, a semi-pro steer wrestler with a chest and arms like a collection of boulders under his red Wrangler shirt. Spending every minute he could out in the weather under a cowboy hat had left him with a complexion that shaded smoothly from dungeon-white along his hairline to a kind of baked mahogany at the jaw and neck. He studied the board over my shoulder. Deciding to try a move before shutting the game down, I grabbed the mouse and moved the cursor over to my queenside rook's pawn.

'Wouldn't do that, boss,' he said.

I looked back at him. 'Okay, Red Ryder,' I said, 'what *would* you do?'

'Go for the bishop trade.'

'Didn't know you played.'

'Chess club president my senior year.'

I had learned the game, or at least learned how the pieces move, at around the same stage of life, on the endless dogwatches of seventh-period study hall at General Braxton Bragg, but even if we'd had a chess club I was pretty sure I never would've made president. But I did eventually get good enough to win most of the games I played, except when the opponent was Coach Alonzo 'Jesus Wants You to Light Up That Scoreboard' Bubner, who was doing a better job of making a halfback of me than a chess player.

Coach believed the cornerstones of victory were the

running game on the football field and the knights at the chessboard. The running game thing made sense to me, but the knights were a headache. Their attack is indirect – a combination of one and two squares at right angles to each other in any direction – and they can't be blocked by intervening pieces. But understanding this isn't the same thing as being able think ahead four or five knight moves, which is what it took to stay in the game against Coach Bub.

Then suddenly I saw, precisely superimposed on the chessboard, a brilliantly clear image of Bragg Field back in Rains County, where I'd played football for Coach, as it had looked from the visitors' end-zone stands, top row centre, the stadium brightly lit but completely empty and silent. As I watched, the overhead lights began to go out in rapid succession – each leaving an indecipherable hint of an afterimage too brief and faint to register on the retina but somehow imprinting itself directly on my brain – and then the lights beyond the stadium, a wave of darkness rolling outward toward the horizon in every direction, leaving the world in a cold, starless nothingness deeper and blacker than any night.

But intense as it was, the image had no staying power, dissolving almost immediately to leave me staring at the chessboard behind it. All my life I'd had what my grandmother called a 'touch of the Sight', beyond ordinary intuition but rare, unpredictable, and almost always short of useful clairvoyance, and I assumed I'd just been touched. But as usual I had no idea what it meant. I sat for a minute, thinking about it and waiting for my heart rate to subside. Nothing occurred to me.

Then, remembering that as usual lately I'd skipped breakfast this morning, and wondering about the relationship between blood sugar levels and a runaway imagination, I found a couple of fairly crisp singles in my billfold and headed for the break room. Finding it deserted, I walked across and stood at the window for a minute watching the rain from a new angle. It seemed to be coming down harder now, and though I couldn't hear anything through the thick double-paned glass I actually thought I could smell it, the two facts seeming, for no reason I could put my finger on, strange and wrong to me.

I pulled the knobs for a couple of candy bars, poured coffee into a Styrofoam cup and picked up a copy of the *Gazette* somebody had left on one of the small Formica-topped tables against the wall. No surprises here: everybody supporting the proposed new rehab facility and halfway house as long as it wasn't in their neighbourhood, evangelical commandos in a sweat over sex education and *Huckleberry Finn* in the high schools, Louisiana Quarter politicians angling for a cut of the new highway bill. A tenth anniversary retrospective on the unsolved rape and murder of a local eleven-year-old named Joy Dawn Therone, the coverage then transitioning into a rundown of all the uncleared murders and disappearances of girls and young women in this part of the state over the last thirty years. I folded the paper and pushed it across to the other side of the table.

Then the vision of Bragg Field returned, this time superimposed only on the background of the break room and persisting as an accurate replay of something that had actually happened. Now the stands and the field were no longer dark but rocking with life and light and sound inside the cold grey roar of the rain soaking the county and threatening to drown out the marching bands and the screams, cheers, whistles and air horns from the stands, never letting up from the kickoff to the last play. Our Homecoming game, the field now nothing but a hundred yards of churned mud and turf, the District championship and our shot at the State title on the line, and time running out on us. We stood in a ragged, dripping circle, eyes on number 16, quarterback Eldrew Cleveland Dasbro, brutally forcing himself to stand straight in defiance of the two cracked ribs that would show up on the x-rays after the game.

'Red Hook Toss?' he gritted through clenched teeth at Johnny Trammel, who'd just brought the play in from the sideline. 'Are you shittin' me?'

Johnny, my closest friend at Bragg, was a magician. He'd played Dr Prestidigito in the drama club's fall presentation, and I'd seen him make all kinds of things appear and disappear – the coins from his collections, golf balls, even on one unforgettable occasion a gerbil that had first vanished, then somehow gotten out of Johnny's coat pocket and down the neck of Janie Cochran's sweater. But, as quick and elusive as he was, Johnny could never pull the Red Hook out of the hat, not in conditions like these, or against the kind of speed the Hawks' defensive end had. We were down seven points with two and a half minutes left in the game; this was the only shot we were going to get. Johnny shook his head miserably.

But Daz was through with bullshit. 'Okay, listen up, you lesbians,' he said. 'This here's your higher power telling you Fake Twenty-two Boot Right is what Johnny-boy said, and that's what we're gonna run on these limp-dicks.' Winking at me, he leaned aside to spit through his facemask, flinching and showing his teeth at the movement, then clapped his hands to break the huddle. Then as he stepped in behind centre I saw him do what he'd always done when

8

he had to – send his pain to some other dimension and become an uninjured version of himself, nothing now to show he was hurt but the blood on his hands.

At the snap I feinted left toward the line as Johnny blew by me to wrap his arms around Daz's phoney handoff, Daz sideslipping back from the line with the ball still on his hip in a perfect bootleg fake, me kicking out and swinging downfield through the right flat and Daz floating the ball over my shoulder with flawless touch. I cradled it in twenty yards downfield, just out of the corner's reach, and a few seconds later I was in the end zone, bringing us to within a point of the Hawks. We went for the two-point conversion and got it, me going off-tackle this time, nothing fancy, just hitting the hole as hard as I could. We were up by one.

Our kickoff carried to the back of their end zone in spite of the downpour, and four hopeless plays later the Hawks were done. Daz took a knee a couple of times and the District championship was ours.

The coaches all agreed that if he could stay healthy Daz was a sure thing for a major college scholarship, and would probably go no later than the middle rounds of the pro draft, but as it turned out he was a dead man walking. Halfway through a season when it looked like the Aggies' were on their way to the Cotton Bowl, Daz on the roster as the freshman second-string quarterback, he would crash head-on into an eighteen-wheeler out of Beaumont while driving the brand new Audi an alumni dealer had let him 'borrow', his death instantaneous.

The memories popped like bubbles when Ridout stuck his head in the door, holding up his right hand splayed like a chicken's foot. 'Cueing Squarepants in five,' he said.

'I thought it was your turn?'

'Nope. We traded back when you took the girls to Sea World.' He disappeared, leaving behind a suggestion of Stetson aftershave on the air.

A former Texas-side chief had come up with an idea he called Conference Day, designating a media room where the departments announced toy drives, made excuses in high-profile murder cases, warned against drunk driving and issued tactical lies. My old partner Floyd Zito had called it the Officer Squarepants Show, and the name had turned out to have legs. This morning Channel Six wanted a two-minute spot on the dangers of burglar bars.

By now the Tri-State sky had darkened to the colour of wet slate, the rain still steady and hard, beating silently at the window and branching down the glass in miniature rivers. I looked at the candy bar I'd just taken a bite of. I couldn't see anything wrong with it, but it had no taste. I tossed it in the trash, checked the time and headed for my rendezvous with the cameras.

When I stepped into the media room the reporter rose from the metal folding chair she'd been sitting on and walked over to meet me. I knew her from a couple of past interviews, a thin, tense woman named Mallory Peck with a big arrangement of black hair and a parsimonious smile. As Mallory stuck out an icy little hand to shake, a production assistant wearing tight, scruffy jeans out at the knees and a Soundgarden T-shirt appeared from somewhere with a makeup kit, tilting her head as she approached, assessing the angles and shadows of my face with an expert eye.

Mallory said, 'So, Jim, ready to reach out to the masses?'

I was about to answer when I saw Ridout making his way toward us from across the room, wearing a crooked little grin of defeat as he cocked and fired an imaginary six-shooter in the air. He tipped his head toward Chief Royal's office as he joined us, Mallory smoothly transferring her attention to him, saying, 'Well, looks like I get the bull rider instead.' Her smile notched up a few watts as she inventoried Ridout's muscles.

'Steer wrestler,' he corrected, his own expression brightening. 'Bull riders are those crazy-eyed little dudes that walk crooked.'

'Mallory, Danny,' I said. 'Danny, Mallory.' I headed for OZ's office.

Nobody who'd worked out of Three for more than a day would have misunderstood Ridout's six-gun gesture, which harked back to OZ's thirty years with the Texas Rangers, an outfit founded by characters who hunted their man until they got him and didn't talk much about it; silent, fearless, incorruptible men who never complained, never explained and never quit. Superstitious nineteenth-century border bandits and Comancheros, watching them ride alone through the true valley of the shadow of death, the only law in a quarter of a million square miles of the most dangerous ground on earth, called them demons.

The hunt that had made OZ the Big Gun had ended on a hot, windy afternoon in Starr County, where he'd faced down four Mexican dope dealers in the middle of the street, he with the .45 Colt Single Action Army revolver he still carried as a duty weapon, they with their nine-millimetre automatics. They took their shots, he took his. One of their thirty-three cut a clean hole through the crown of his grey Resistol and another ended up in the heel of his left boot, but OZ, ignoring their fire and working left to right, took out all four of the shooters with consecutive heart shots.

The people who'd known him longest said he could tell you the names of these guys and every other man he'd killed, except for the two he referred to as *Mal Tiro Uno* and *Mal Tiro Dos*, who'd floated away on the Rio Grande by the dark of the moon without having told anybody who they were.

OZ operated without organisational charts or middle management. There were no file trays, staplers, pencil cups or tape dispensers on his desk, just his phone, a computer monitor, a picture of his late wife Martha, and the calendar blotter in front of him. He kept his files in his head, and to him 'accessories' meant his Colt, his saddle and his hat.

I found him sipping coffee from a plain white mug as he watched me from across his desk – pink, clean-shaven jowls, what was left of his silver hair standing out in leprechaun tufts above his jughandle ears, sky-blue eyes as hard as tungsten. Behind him the walnut panelling was covered with photos of famous fellow Texas Rangers and other old-time lawmen, Hall of Fame Dallas Cowboys stars and big-game guides.

I walked over to the nook where his coffee machine stood and sniffed what was in the carafe. It smelled better than dishwater, so I poured some into a plastic cup from the tray next to the machine, settled back in the black leather chair in front of OZ's desk and took a sip.

OZ said, 'You done anything to get sideways with our city fathers that I don't know about?'

'Don't think so, why?'

'Got a call from Dwight Hazen this morning.'

'The city manager? What did he want?'

'Could be something, could be nothing,' OZ said. 'He's jawin' about a civilian review board, for one thing. Which is a piss-poor idea on a good day, and there ain't no good days.'

I shook my head, imagining a dozen petty bureaucrats micromanaging the department and fighting over the microphones at press conferences as they tried to position themselves in terms of sound bites, headlines and voting blocs. Calls to abolish the use of Tasers, demands for budget increases to buy more Tasers, new automatic weapons and sniper rifles to go with them, pleas for a return to God, detailed suggestions for rewriting the Constitution.

'Then the *cabrón* got goin' about you and that old graveyard collar,' he said. 'Wanted to know how I thought you were dealin' with your "issues", whatever the hell that's supposed to mean.'

I heard three quick taps behind me, recognising them because they were the same three I routinely got at my own office door. Like OZ, I usually kept all of my phone's mechanical and musical noises disabled, admittedly a hardship for Bertie, the head secretary, who was constantly having to huff her way back by shank's mare to tell me to pick up.

At OZ's grunted invitation, Bertie stuck her head in the door. 'Line four,' she said testily. 'For Lieutenant Bonham.'

She glanced at my right hand, frowned at the square of grey sky showing through OZ's window, then returned her gaze to me. I looked down at the hand myself as I stood to reach for the phone, made myself stop clenching and unclenching it, and raised the handset to my ear.

It was Wayne Gaston with the Crime Scene unit. It sounded like he was out in the rain, meaning he must be at a scene somewhere. He said, 'How about lookin' at some evidence with me, Lou?'

13

'What have you got?' I asked.

There was a silence, then, 'Uh, that's kinda what I'm askin' myself right now – '

'Can't you send me a shot with your phone?'

'Sure would like to have you take a look in person.'

'Not to jump to any conclusions here, Wayne,' I said, biting back the unexpected impatience I felt edging into my voice, 'but can I at least figure on somebody being dead?'

'Eyes-on, boss,' was all he'd say.

TWO

I loosened my tie and unbuttoned my collar, trying not to limp as I crossed the squad room to grab my gun and get a car. No new business on my desk, just the twenty-tens on a grill-fork stabbing at a family reunion out on the white end of Burnsville Road, and the potshot a one-legged combat vet on Maple Hill may or may not have taken at his neighbour's cat last night with his AR-15.

I checked the Glock's chamber and magazine, slid the weapon onto my belt and went looking for Mouncey. I never drove when I went out on a call if I could help it because I wanted to see everything I'd otherwise miss by rolling up on the scene and parking the vehicle myself. There was general agreement at Three that Mouncey operating a motor vehicle was at least a metaphorical felony in itself, something along the lines of criminal assault against time and space, but she was always my first choice as a driver because she never had to ask where anything was, got us there fast, and up until now had always given the other traffic enough time to get out of her way. I found her at her desk picking through the old maids at the bottom of the bowl for the last few kernels of popcorn, and asked her to get us a car.

She made the call, checked her own .40 and pulled on her tan leather jacket. 'Where we goin', Lou?'

'Wayne's at a scene.'

'What he got?'

'He wants to surprise us.'

Ten minutes later we were out of the garage and headed north in the rain, which had lightened a little for the moment but was still falling steadily from a sky that now had taken on the look of heavy oilsmoke. Mouncey was decked out in tight pressed jeans and a lavender turtleneck under the leather jacket, with rings on every finger and what looked like a quarter of a pound of gold hanging from each earlobe. Her hair was piled up in ringlets that flashed with opal-coloured highlights. I knew that if we were out chasing leads or doing interviews there'd be nothing grabbable attached to her ears and nothing at all on the fingers of her gun hand, but on this call she was dressed for working inside the tape.

The plastic ID she'd just used a corner of to winkle out a popcorn hull stuck between her incisors said Mouncey, Jacquanda S., Detective II-CID, but everybody called her M. She didn't look much like police, but she had been a major-crimes detective for almost ten years and earned three commendations for things she'd done while being shot at, two of the shooters having had to settle for obituaries.

Looking over her outfit, I said, 'You put me in mind of a fleeing felon.'

'The job just a day gig,' she said. 'Nights, I out perpe-trating.'

The passing landscape of miscellaneous storefront busi-nesses started phasing into classier re-zoned conversions, upscale shops and finally older homes set back on spacious lots under mature oaks, sweetgums and longleaf pines, surrounded by acres of tailored, unseasonably green lawns with automatic sprinkler systems. Maybe money didn't buy happiness, but it bought lots of grass.

M said, 'How the single life treating you, Lou?'

Listening to the dull cardiac thumping of the windshield wipers for a minute, I took in a deep breath and blew it out along with the half-dozen bullshit answers that had occurred to me. I wasn't much good at casual social lies and hardly ever wasted time or energy on them any more.

'I don't seem to be very good at solitude, M.'

'Like to see the man that is,' she said. 'Y'all just be layin' around suckin' Bud Lite till you stufficate under all them dirty socks and pizza boxes.' She looked at me with some expression or other for a couple of seconds before deciding to go directly for the throat. 'Seen them two girls of yours waiting for they ride after school yesterday,' she said. 'Both of 'em lookin' a little floopy, Lou.'

The only replies that came to mind were defensively self-serving and useless, and I didn't respond. Knowing Mouncey would have used one of the tac frequencies to talk to somebody on Wayne's crew as she was bringing the car around, I said, 'Get anything at all from out there?'

'Uniform name Hardy catch it and buzz Wayne,' she said. 'Call from a pre-pay, sound like a white lady, most likely local, but wouldn't give 'em no name. Crime Scene up there a half-hour now. It that field across the interstate, west side the tracks.'

I visualised the area, which I remembered as being mostly deserted, and started pawing around in my pockets in search of camphor.

Noticing this, Mouncey said, 'Told me this a fresh one, Lou.'

I stopped pawing and said, 'Any civilians at the scene when Wayne got there?'

''Bout a bo-zillion of 'em, way he carryin' on. Man just cain't handle people jackin' with his clues. I told 'em leave ev'thing like it is till we get there and e'body stay sharp cause the Man on his way.'

'Why the hell'd you do that?'

'Keep they sphincters tight,' she said. 'Discipline crucial, got a outfit like this one.'

Humming a tune from 'More Than A Woman', she swung left through the red light at Hancock, setting off a massive chorus of horns and squealing brakes, made a hard right under the trestle and took Springer north between the lake and the wooded railroad right-of-way to the zigzag below the double bridges of the expressway.

Coming out from under the vaulted concrete, we rounded the curve under a high billboard and saw what looked like every patrol car, fire truck and EMT unit in town parked at random angles along a quarter of a mile of the access road shoulder and out across the field wherever the ground was solid enough, their red and blue roof lights twinkling.

'Be a good time to stick up the town,' Mouncey observed. 'Protectors and servers all out here gawkin'.'

We rolled to a stop next to an Arkansas-side pumper and Wayne's Crime Scene bus, and I climbed out. A hundred yards away at the edge of the pines and assorted oaks on the low bluff above the tracks several dozen uniforms along with city councilmen, courthouse civilians, off-duty fire-fighters and EMTs – basically everybody in town who had a scanner – were milling around and trying to look involved.

Seeing Dwight Hazen among them surprised me a little, but I didn't take time to analyse the feeling. Outside the yellow tape the media people, bristling with cameras, microphone booms and lights, stood around in knots and cliques looking restless and surly.

They swarmed me as I bent to duck under the tape, video cams, flashing still cameras and microphones converging a few inches in front of my nose, all of them demanding information and comment. Sticking with the rule that when you know nothing, that's what you should say, I tried to look reasonable and trustworthy but kept my mouth shut.

The temperature felt like forty or so by now, with no wind to speak of, the rain still fairly light but coming steadily. Low streamers of mist drifted over the uneven yellow and brown weed-fields surrounding the site, almost obscuring an abandoned-looking storage warehouse a quarter of a mile to the west, leaching the colour and depth from the mixed hardwood and pine woodlands to the north and giving them the look of an old oil painting. If you didn't know about the country club and the upscale suburbs beyond the trees you might think the scene was completely rural, but we were actually almost half a mile inside the city limits.

As we worked our way up the slope toward the gathering under the trees, Mouncey picking her way along behind me like a deer, trying to keep the mud off her lime-green platforms, I caught sight of Wayne, suited out in white Tyvek, nitrile gloves and a surgical cap. He saw my wave, broke away from the group and came over to meet us. He was a tall, slightly awkward, middle-aged, east Texas country boy with a strawberry-blond moustache, wire-rimmed glasses and a flash-mounted Nikon hanging from a strap around his neck, like everybody else on his crew. To him the proposition that you could overspend on photography gear, or that there was any such thing as too many pictures, would have been nothing but crazy talk.

'Howdy, M. Howdy, Lou,' he said, a drop of rain hanging from the tip of his nose. Stripping off one surgical glove, he stuck out his big hand and we all shook. 'Y'all ready to join the workin' stiffs?' He tried with no success to kick some of the clingy red clay off the surgical booties covering his size-thirteen Noconas.

I took the gloves he handed me, pulled them on and looked around at all the people who thought Do Not Cross applied to everybody but them. Hazen and a younger man who looked like a staff gofer or maybe an intern of some kind were working their way toward us, Hazen locked in on me with a grim, concerned expression, the rain plastering a couple of spitcurls of dark hair to his temple. I had once heard somebody called 'Joe College at forty', and it wasn't a bad description of Hazen except for being maybe five years low. The assistant, a sort of scared-looking, unfinished version of the city manager in a dark suit that I thought would have looked silly out here even if it wasn't plastered to him like wet tissue paper, glanced uneasily back and forth between Hazen and me, trying to decide which flag to salute.

'Uh, Lieutenant, I thought I'd get your take on this – ' Hazen began.

'Yes, sir,' I said, wondering what it was about him that irritated me so much. 'I'll be happy to give you that as soon as I know something. Right now I'd appreciate it if both of you would wait behind the tape.'

20

Hazen looked at me with a questioning expression, like a man who's not quite sure he heard right, took in the kind of breath you do when you're about to give somebody an attitude adjustment, but then apparently had second thoughts. He glanced back at the reporters, made a show of shrugging and flashing his let-the-man-do-it-his-way smile, then retreated, the gofer hopping from one weed clump to the next behind him until they reached the tape and stooped inexpertly under it.

Turning back to Wayne, I said, 'So what have we got?'

'I'll show you,' he said, leading the way toward the medium-sized possum oak at the centre of what was left of the gathering, which now consisted mostly of Wayne's crew, a dozen or so uniforms and a few EMTs waiting for their cue.

'Don't worry where you step along here,' Wayne said. 'We did all we could with the ground, but you know what that's worth when it's already trompled to pieces before you get to it.'

I'm not sure what I'd expected, but this definitely wasn't it. The oak's lower branches had been hacked away with a heavy-bladed tool, probably a machete or axe, and what looked like a six-foot length of four-by-four had been lashed to the trunk with coarse-fibred rope to form a cross-beam. Pinned by two thick bridge spikes driven through the wrists, with several loops of rope binding the arms to the beam, was the corpse of a woman, head fallen forward as if she were looking down at us with dull eyes as we stood before her slack body. All my life I'd heard of corpses having expressions of horror or pain on their faces, reflecting the manner of death, but the job had taught me better. The only expression death leaves the dead is indifference, and that was all I saw in the woman's features now.

Stepping in for a closer look, I could pick out individual drops of rain refracting the light like jewels in her dark hair. A strip of silver duct tape that had apparently been placed across her lower face had been pulled back to expose the bloody mouth and chin. A torn and bloodstained ecru cashmere pullover sweater still covered most of her torso but she was naked from the waist down. The insides of her thighs were black with congealed blood. Her feet had been turned to the side and a third spike had been driven through the heels and deep into the wood of the tree trunk. More blood had run down from the arms and feet to form a black puddle in the wet grass.

Wayne said, 'Them spikes up there at the top went through between the radius and ulna just proximal to the carpals on both sides and didn't cut either one of the radial arteries, even with all the struggling she did.'

Looking up through the rain at the dead, grey face, I said, 'I know her.'

All eyes came to me.

'It's Deborah Gold.'

'The psych doc?' said Wayne.

I nodded absent-mindedly, thinking about Jerusalem thieves, Texas psychologists, and dying hard. Dr Gold had been a department consultant at one time, mostly doing the pre-hire psych screening of new applicants, and she and I had a history.

Mouncey squinted as she took another look at the face. 'Believe you right, Lou,' she said. 'Look like some hard miles on her since then.'

'Yeah,' I said. 'Especially the last few.'

22

'Be damned,' Wayne said, squinting up at the empty eyes.

Lying in the weeds not far from the base of the tree I saw a pair of expensive-looking alligator shoes which, by reason of living mostly with women all my life, I knew were the kind called pumps. Bloody earlobes and grooves around three of the curled fingers meant the victim must have been wearing jewellery, which the killer had apparently taken while she was still alive. The hands themselves were fairly slender and long-fingered with what looked like a clear lacquer covering the well-manicured nails.

Something about this thought caught at me. I stepped in for a closer look at the hands, seeing no significant injuries anywhere other than the wrists. I thought about the hundreds – maybe thousands – of crucifixes and images of Jesus on the cross that I'd seen in my life, filing the question away for later.

'Now look here,' Wayne said, gloving up again. He reached up and placed one thumb against the corpse's forehead to push the head upward and back, and with the other prised open the jaw to reveal a mass of bloody flesh and clotted, curly hair.

I shone my pocket flashlight into the cavity. 'What is this?' I said. 'Doesn't look like any tongue I ever saw.'

'It ain't, Lou,' he said. 'Matter of fact, I don't think her tongue's even in there.'

I turned to look at him.

'Then where it at?' Mouncey asked.

'Question of the hour,' Wayne said. 'First thing we did was grid the area out about fifty yards around the site and all the way down to the road and the tracks over there, but

23

no luck so far. We'll keep opening up the circle if we don't find it.'

'So,' I said. 'What's this in her mouth?'

Wayne cleared his throat. A quick glance at Mouncey. 'Believe that'd be her snatch, Lou,' he said.

'Law,' said Mouncey, bending down for a look at the bloodied groin. 'Wait by the river long enough, e'thing in the world gone float by.' She straightened up and looked at me. 'How you figure it, Lou? We lookin' for Romans or what?'

Wayne gave her a strange look, then turned back to me, saying, 'There was some camouflage netting wrapped around her when we got here. That's it in the evidence bag over there.'

Keeping to the grass tufts as best I could, I excuse-me'd my way around the tree through the cops and EMTs, the pine needles, dead leaves and bracken looking mostly undisturbed behind the tree, at least out to a distance of a yard or two.

Joining Wayne and M again, I looked closely at the wrists and the spikes that had been driven through them. The heads of the big nails showed an impressed waffle pattern.

I said, 'What leaves a mark like this?'

'Framing hammer,' Wayne said. 'Most likely a California.'

I glanced at him.

'Daddy was a carpenter,' he said.

Working at the horse farm as a kid, I thought I'd swung every kind of hammer there was. I knew about framing hammers, but the idea of individual state models was new to me.

I said, 'What makes it a California?'

'Longer handle, straighter claws. Wider face with check-ering, like you see there.'

'And she was alive when she was hung up here,' I said, leaning in and shining my light on the sleepy-looking eyes, seeing no sign of petechial haemorrhaging. The visible skin of her face, hands, belly and upper thighs was pale as boiled pork, but the lower legs and especially the feet had darkened to a plum colour. It looked to me as if she had died with enough blood left to keep her alive at least a while longer. 'How cold did it get last night?'

'Right around freezing, per the Weather Service guy. That'd be airport temps, which I'd guesstimate might run a degree or two higher in a spot like this, with all these conifers around.'

I said, 'Time of death?'

'Full livor with coag,' he said. 'Max rigor by the time we got here. Say at least four hours ago, probably not over twelve. Best I can do for now.'

Meaning she was probably still alive when the weather front came through. I tried to imagine dying like this, in the cold rain with blue-white lightning strobing the sky and thunder shaking the earth.

'So, what the hell was this about?' I said.

Wayne cleared his throat again. 'Been hoping you'd tell me,' he said. 'All I know is, something's not right here, Lou.'

'That true,' observed Mouncey. 'Lady got dead all over her.'

'That's not what I mean,' Wayne said.

'Then what do you mean?'

'I mean this just ain't natural.'

Mouncey snorted again, moving up for a closer view of the face, narrowing her eyes. 'Maybe them Romans figure she a Saviour or something.'

Dropping the flashlight back into my pocket, I looked at Wayne.

'Uh, well, okay,' he said. 'Correct me if I'm wrong, but the whole show took a hell of a lot of figurin' aforethought, and nobody does something like this for a pair of earrings.' He removed his bifocals and shook off the beads of rain. 'Which'd knock out robbery and random.' Back on with the glasses. 'Leavin' us with personal and premeditated. No immediately lethal wounds that meet the eye. Anybody's guess what the actual COD's gonna turn out to be.'

'How many doers are we thinking?' I said.

'Well, the beam's six feet long,' Wayne said. 'It and the woman together are gonna weigh a little south of two hundred pounds. She was bound to be thrashing to beat hell on top of that – no one guy's gonna manage it. Even two'd be a stretch.'

Mouncey folded a stick of Doublemint into her mouth.

'And while we're amazin' ourselves,' said Wayne, 'there's this.' He produced a little zip-lock evidence sleeve containing what looked at first like an irregularly shaped silver button a half-inch or so in diameter but actually turned out to be a crudely struck, heavily tarnished coin with some kind of profile on one side and a standing figure on the other. Taking it from Wayne's hand, I felt an odd heat through the clear plastic.

'How'd it get so warm?' I asked, thinking Wayne was right; there was an eerie wrongness here, one that somehow wouldn't let itself be pinned down.

Wayne frowned. 'Didn't feel warm to me.'

Mouncey touched the coin with her fingertips. 'Feel like pocket temperature, Lou.'

I shook my head. Maybe I had a fever or something.

Already knowing the answer, I said, 'What kind of coin does this look like to you, Wayne?'

'Had to guess, I'd say Roman.'

One of Mouncey's eyebrows went up.

Wayne shrugged, looking a little embarrassed, the way he always did when confronted by something beyond his rational understanding.

'"The footprints of a gigantic hound",' I said.

'Huh?' said Wayne. Mouncey stared at me.

'My grandmother said that sometimes. It's from Sherlock Holmes – means something strange that you can't explain.' I held the coin up to the light. 'Doesn't look like this thing's been in the dirt long.'

'Wasn't in the dirt at all,' Wayne said. 'One of the techs found it by her shoes, just layin' there in the leaves and litter.'

I handed the coin back to him. 'Show me where it was.'

He stepped over and indicated the spot, a couple of feet from the base of the tree and maybe eight inches from the nearest shoe.

I stared at the coin, trying to make sense of it being here instead of in the ground somewhere in the Holy Land, or maybe Europe. But for some reason the strangeness didn't seem to run very deep, as if the situation made some kind of non-logical sense to me.

'How they carry they money anyway, them little dresses they wore?' wondered Mouncey. She shook rain off the fingers of one long pink-palmed hand.

'Who?'

'Romans.'

'Maybe they kept it in those tin hats with the bristles on top,' Wayne said thoughtfully.

I said, 'Could her connection with the department be what got her killed?'

Wayne looked up at the dead face for a moment, then shrugged. 'Nothing here to tell us, Lou,' he said. 'But that would have been a good while back, and it don't sound like she was ever real tight with the job anyway – all she ever actually did was them screens, right? You feature anybody dreaming this up because she kept him off the job with a bad report?'

I nodded, but my mind was somewhere else.

'How about a whole chariot-full of 'em get together and dream it up?' said M. 'Be like a focus group.'

'And still wouldn't tell us anything about the coin,' I said.

'Crime provide more of a challenge for our mind this way,' Mouncey philosophised. 'Too easy, we apt to fall into sloth.'

I turned up my collar and walked a loop around to where the techs were examining the ground, what was left of my knees screaming at me in the wet cold. I thought some more about dying out here alone in the night, the interstate roaring with cars, vans, SUVs, eighteen-wheelers – all those safe, dry bubbles of warmth less than two hundred yards away but for Dr Gold as unreachable as the stars. I'd read somewhere that on the verge of death everybody prays if there's time, but I wasn't sure how the author got his infor-mation. I wondered if Gold had given up, maybe even welcomed death, releasing her spirit to whatever eternity she thought was waiting. Or had she died saying the *Shema*, still trying to hold on, praying for her life?

Shema. An image of the word floated up in my consciousness, and behind it came *Aleha ha-shalom*. Then – before I could slam the door on it – a face. I stood still and took a couple of deep breaths, then walked back to where Wayne was watching M try to shield her notebook from the rain with her body as she wrote in it.

I said, 'Wayne, you might as well go ahead and bag her as soon as you're done here.' I glanced back at the milling reporters. 'These guys will be in trouble if they don't get some close-ups and quotes, so how about you give them a few?'

'Anything special you want left out?'

'Let's hold back the missing jewellery, the shoes and the coin. Don't give them anything they don't already have about the mutilation, and don't say "crucifixion" or "Jewish".'

By now it was well past noon, and I thought about Danny. We'd planned to meet at the Auction Barn steak-house for their once-a-month skillet lunch special, but my appetite was gone, and I had at least one good reason for not expecting it back any time soon.

THREE

Like a lot of things that had completely and permanently changed my life, it hadn't seemed like much at the start: the day after Braxton Bragg's Homecoming – I'd just walked into the Skillet, looking back when I thought I heard somebody call to me and almost bumped into a girl I didn't recognise under the orange and white GO TIGERS! banner spread across the wall.

'Hey, you're number twenty-two, aren't you?' she said, holding out her thin warm hand to shake. 'I'm Kat Dreyfus. I watched you play last night!' I could see the name Katherine engraved in flowery loops on the gold ID bracelet she was wearing. In her loose-fitting khakis and baggy white cotton sweater, she looked like a little girl lost in her big brother's hand-me-downs. But there was nothing little-girl about her clear, bottomless sea-green eyes, shining black hair, and lips that looked almost as if she were about to blow me a kiss. 'It was hard to hear the announcer,' she said, 'but it sounded like he was calling you Jay Bonham.' Her accent was strange, like something from a movie, the sound of far places and unknown worlds.

'It's James, but everybody calls me Biscuit,' I said. 'Where are you from?'

'Boston.'

'Sorry I didn't see you last night.'

'You had other things on your mind,' she said. 'Come on, sit with us.'

At the table she introduced me to Ronnie Geddes, a pale, thin-faced guy about our age with curly blond hair and very little to say, and Father Beane, a redheaded man in his thirties wearing jeans and a white polo shirt, probably a tennis player, I thought – or maybe in Boston it was squash or something.

'Father Beane's our supervisor,' Kat said. 'He's a Jesuit.'

He was cheerful-looking, but I could sense that under the surface he was sure of himself and had a certain kind of controlled toughness, his eyes intelligent and quick. I had the same thought I always had about Roman Catholic priests: how could their job mean more to them than sex? Which probably tells you something about the state of my knowledge at the time.

He reached out to shake, saying, 'Pleased to meet you, Biscuit. That was some unbelievable running you did last night.' His hand was soft but strong.

'Thanks, Father.'

'Call me Al.'

We talked football and the playoffs for a while until the waitress came with her order pad and a paper bag full of carrot tops and apple trimmings, Saturday being beef stew and apple pie day at the Skillet. She took my order for a Coke, stuck the pencil in her hair and went back behind the counter while Kat eyed the sack.

'Any scholarship prospects?' asked Al, sipping from his drink.

'Yes, sir. A couple of scouts have been down.'

'Where are you going to college?' Kat asked.

'TCU, probably. How about you?'

'I'm already enrolled, at Wellesley. But I'm taking my first year off for this.'

'What's this?'

'VISTA,' said Rick, looking at Kat with some expression or other.

She said, 'It's to keep poor and black kids in school down here, get people registered to vote, help them find better jobs, stuff like that.'

'Where are you staying?'

'Zion Hope Church.'

Zion Hope was the little black COGIC church out toward Spoon Bottom on Elam Road, where the pastor, a retired felon whose name I remembered as something like George Washington Hooks, could be heard from at least a quarter of a mile away when the windows were open and he was in the spirit. Visualising white faces scattered through Spoon Bottom like dimes in a dark pool, I said, 'We're cooking out tonight – why don't y'all come over?'

Al shook his head. 'Too much paperwork, I'm afraid,' he said. 'Anyway, I've got a meeting at eight.'

'Thanks a lot, but I think I'll pass,' Rick said in an accent from somewhere farther west than Boston. Halfway smiling, he looked me up and down in a way that made it clear he and Kat were not together.

Kat was watching me and thinking, her ocean-coloured eyes seeming to radiate a delicious heat at me.

'It's just me and my folks,' I said. 'We're gonna barbecue burgers out at the horse farm.' The Flying S was really more of a ranch, but it was called a farm because we grew crops on it and because its main purpose was breeding quarter horses.

'Horse farm!' Kat said. 'That's what the scraps are for, the horses! Hey, c'mon, Al, how about it?'

Al looked at Kat, then me, thinking it over. Finally he nodded to her. 'Bed check at twelve,' he said.

My old sunblasted red and used-to-be-white Ford pickup sat at the curb just outside the Skillet, the antenna lopping over a little and the rear fender rusted through in a couple of places. I walked to the passenger side, kicked the back corner of the door with the heel of my boot and opened it for her. Sliding in behind the wheel, I cranked the engine and we rattled up through the gears and out to the Lone Oak road, heading north toward the farm and my family.

Now, turning my collar up against the rain, imagining I could still smell the old Ford's permanent bouquet of gasoline and exhaust fumes after all these years, I tried without much success to picture Dr Gold as part of a family, or as anybody's wife. But I knew she had been; the last I'd heard she was married to a guy who owned a local data-services company called QuikCom. After a few seconds his name came to me: Andy Jamison.

The rain actually seemed to be getting colder, and the body looked more bedraggled than ever, causing me to wonder if this was going to create any additional problems at the autopsy.

Again remembering my lunch date with Danny Ridout at the Auction Barn, but still having no appetite, I called him to ask for a rain check.

'That must be what the learned among us refer to as a "wisecrack",' he said.

'It was a waggery.'

'Naw, you're thinkin' of a whim-wham there.'

I went around checking the name tags of the uniformed cops I didn't know until I found Hardy, Jason L. and asked him what he'd seen when he got here.

He glanced over at the body with a focused but not self-important expression, organising his recollections. 'Naturally the first thing I noticed was her, just like she is now,' he said. 'I gloved up and checked for a carotid pulse, but it was obvious there wasn't gonna be one. About a dozen civilians milling around, so I was thinking no footprints that would do us any good, but I herded them back anyway and went ahead and secured the scene. All the tyre tracks I could make out down there were accounted for by the vehicles present, and the vehicles were all accounted for by the onlookers. That's basically it until the geeks and suits got here.' He glanced down at my street clothes and cleared his throat in embarrassment. 'I mean – '

'No problem,' I said. 'I'm undercover. Any other thoughts?'

'Well, I looked inside all the vehicles the best I could without touching them, but I didn't see anything.'

'What were you looking for?'

He shrugged. 'Nothing in particular – a bloody knife maybe, rope, tape, maybe a mallet or some big nails – just anything that looked interesting.'

I nodded. 'Anybody volunteering theories, talking like a cop, trying to posse up with you?'

'No, sir.'

'How about anybody hanging back, watching the crowd instead of the body, antsy, looking flushed or too pale, anything like that?'

'No, sir. When I was looking into the cars I'd give it about a five-count, then turn and check the crowd. Nothing looked funny.'

I wondered if I'd been anywhere near this smart when I was starting out.

'Hear anybody say anything at all that made you take notice?'

'No, sir.'

'Okay, Jason, you know what we need now?'

'Yes, sir, I think so,' he said. 'A clean twenty-ten.'

'Which means – ?'

'Lawyer-proof,' he said. 'I can get it to you by end of shift.'

'But first, I think this woman's husband is Andy Jamison, the computer guy, and I need somebody to find him and make the notification. You ever done that?'

'Yes, sir, once.'

'Then you know how it goes. If you're going to get anything interesting in the way of a reaction, it'll be when he opens the door and sees the uniform or when you hit him with the news, so stay alert. Pay attention to whether he wants to know what happened, when, where and why, or tries to talk you out of it really being her – all that stuff. If he doesn't, he's probably our best suspect. Either way, don't act like you suspect him of anything, don't get spiritual with him and don't say you know how he feels. Just keep it simple and make sure he's okay before you leave.'

'Yes, sir.' Hardy nodded and headed back downslope toward his cruiser.

By now Hazen must have lost interest in my take, because he was nowhere to be seen. I looked around the scene one last time, as usual not wanting to walk away for fear of missing something. But I knew Wayne and his people were too good at what they did for that to be a legitimate worry.

'Okay,' I said, stripping off the gloves and stuffing them into my jacket pocket. 'I'm going back to Three and get the paperwork started. Let me know if anything else turns up.'

Mouncey moved to join me. 'First time I ever seen you do that, Lou.'

'Do what?'

'Send a kid blue to get first look at the old man.'

'Maybe he's not the usual kid blue,' I said, but my mind wasn't on the conversation. I was wondering exactly how crucifixion causes death and how long it takes to kill the victim.

'So you be workin' this one youself, boss?'

'Yeah, I think so,' I said as we headed down the way Hardy had gone. 'I wouldn't want to fall into sloth.'

Then I remembered Coach Bub again, a man who was never troubled by hesitation or self-doubt, and wondered what his advice would be if he were here. After that I thought of my friend Jonas McCashion, a history teacher, and the reason was no mystery. The title of his most recent book was *The Blood Imperative: Barbarity Through the Ages,* and I intended to track him down for a free consult.

FOUR

But between meetings, returning calls, catching up on scheduling and reports, getting a file started on the Gold homicide and trying my best not to think about going home, I managed to forget about Jonas that afternoon.

And for whatever reason – maybe wanting to feel useful, maybe just wanting some air – I'd gone ahead with my decision to work lead on Gold's case. Glancing at the board, I settled on Mouncey and Danny Ridout to help with the interviews. One of the reasons I wanted Mouncey was her uncanny way of making people feel they needed to explain themselves to her. I had no idea how she did it, but it made her one of the two or three best interviewers I'd ever known. Danny, on the other hand, had those big, innocent, disappointed eyes that just kept closing in on liars until they finally lost heart and gave up the truth. He and Mouncey had a weird chemistry of some kind that made them a good team, and they usually got results, but sending them out together was also good for a few laughs.

Next I called Max Karras' office to book an appointment for a consult with him later in the week, taking the first hour he had open. However, thanks to all the time I'd spent chitchatting while I waited in his outer office, I knew all about his secretary Andrea's kids, her marital problems, and her never-ending war against weight gain, and we were pals. She didn't hesitate to rat Max out, telling me he'd just had a cancellation and was playing online poker.

'How much time has he got?'

'About half an hour. Want me to get him for you?'

When he picked up I said, 'Bill me for a session, Max. I've got a case I want to talk to you about later, but right now you're on my clock.'

'What's going on, Jim?'

'These days everything pisses me off,' I said.

'Okay, fast out of the gate, like always,' he said. 'Any other depressive signs?'

'Nothing tastes good.'

'Okay, we'll get to that, but first tell me what's happening with you and Jana.'

'I don't know, Max,' I said. 'She's still gone. I guess I'm just hoping she doesn't learn not to care any more.'

'And the girls?'

'Taking it pretty hard,' I said. 'How are kids supposed to feel when their parents break up?'

'I'd say it's a little early to call this a break-up. Aren't there still some options short of that?'

'I'm not really sure. Maybe it's Jana you should be asking.'

'So you're still blocked about the Flying S offer. What was it, fifty-one per cent?'

'Yeah,' I said. 'Me running the place, Dusty and Rachel retiring on the other forty-nine percent.'

'Begs the same old question: why are you still in town talking to a therapist about it instead of out there on your horse?'

'I'm working on that, doc,' I said. 'Somehow I just can't get it to feel like the thing to do.'

Max grunted but said nothing.

'And I keep getting these flashbacks – '

'To what?'

'Braxton Bragg. Football. All kinds of stuff.'

'Kat?'

'Yeah,' I said. 'Kat.' I stared off into my memories for a minute, wondering why Max was asking about her . . .

That Saturday – the day we met – the first thing Kat had said as we climbed into the Ford to head out to the farm was, 'Pretty neat truck,' adjusting her feet among the empty Dr Pepper cans, Snickers wrappers, chemistry and social studies books, and general clutter on the floorboard. 'How'd you know where to kick the door?'

'It's always been the same place.'

But eventually came the question I considered myself unqualified to answer: 'What are your folks like?'

'It's just my Aunt Rachel, Dusty and Gran Esther,' I said. 'I work for Dusty on the farm after school except when I've got practice.'

'So it's like Rachel and Dusty adopted you?' she said. 'They sign your report card and send you to the dentist and make you pick up after yourself?'

'Pretty much.'

'Do you have any brothers and sisters?'

'Just my cousin LA. She's really Rachel's daughter, but she's always been more like a sister to me,' I said, wondering if this sounded as inarticulate to Kat as it did to me. 'She doesn't live with us.'

'LA?'

'Short for Lee Ann.'

'Pretty name,' Kat said. She looked around at the countryside, drinking it in, everything new to her. 'How come she's not here too?'

I thought of saying something about how a house usually isn't big enough for two drunks, sober or not, but I didn't, instead deciding the main truth in short form might actually leave me less explaining to do later. 'Things aren't really okay between her and Rachel,' I said, 'on account of what her stepfather was doing to her.'

Kat stared at me for a minute and swallowed dryly. 'You mean he – '

I had just looked blankly at Kat for a couple of seconds, trying to think of a good way to answer her, which must have been answer enough, because she'd nodded once and turned her face away.

'I never really know what to say when somebody asks about that, Max,' I said. 'Which makes me feel like it's always coming up. I'm not sure why I think I've got to make people understand, unless it's that my family doesn't seem to make any damn sense at all, at least to me, if you leave that out.'

'What does Lee Ann think?'

'She says secrets like that are toxic, and we've swallowed enough of them for ten lifetimes.'

'Point well taken,' Max said. 'How did Kat's visit go from that point?'

A couple of minutes after our non-conversation about LA, Kat and I turned into the drive and under the archway of the farm's white-painted wrought-iron entrance gate, heading up the half-mile drive to the house. Rounding the curve, I

40

saw Rachel's green Volvo under the big loblolly behind the house and Dusty's blue GMC longbed parked beside one of the tractors farther down toward the barns. I coasted into my usual spot next to the Volvo and crunched to a stop on the gravel.

'Geez, what a beautiful house!' Kat said, gaping at the fieldstone, cypress, glass and slate construction overhung by two dozen huge old oaks, the long gallery and the iris, tulip and jonquil beds Rachel had planted along the southern slope of the yard.

We found Rachel at the bench in the potting shed, wearing jeans and an old red canvas shirt, sleeves rolled up to her elbows, a lock of hair down in her face. She squinted against the smoke from the Pall Mall dangling from her lips as she carefully broke up the rootball of the ivy she was re-potting. The air in the shed was dusty and cool and spoked with coppery sunlight angling through the latticed sidewall.

'Hi, Aunt Ray,' I said.

'Hey, doll,' she answered without looking up. 'What's goin' on?'

'I want you to meet somebody.'

Rachel brushed the hair from her eyes with the back of her hand as she turned to face us, then took the cigarette from her mouth. 'Well, would you look at this,' she said. She stabbed the cigarette out in a jar lid on the bench, wiped her hands with a cloth and reached out to shake with Kat. 'Hi, my name's Rachel,' she said. 'I'm the farmer's wife.'

'Pleased to meet you. I'm Katherine Dreyfus, but I go by Kat.'

'And a yankee at that,' said Rachel. 'Where'd Biscuit find you, honey?'

41

'At the Skillet,' said Kat. 'I watched him play last night. He was terrific.'

'Oh, yeah, he's that all right. Hell of a game, wasn't it? But the more yards he gets, the harder it is to make him do his homework. Come on in, Kat. I'll introduce you to Esther and get you something to drink. Biscuit, tell Dusty we've got company, will you?' Tossing me a wink, she took Kat's arm as they walked up the arboured flagstone path toward the back door of the house. 'So, where you from, girl?' I heard her say as they disappeared from sight.

I found Dusty currying Mariel, a pregnant four-year-old Janus mare, in the paddock beside the first barn. Mariel and I were good friends because she trusted the way I saddled and handled her, and because I hardly ever forgot her treats. Waggling an ear, she eyed the sack I was carrying. Dusty glanced at me. 'Say, podner, what's up?'

'Not much. I brought some company.'

'Who is it?' He stuck the comb under the stump of his left arm, picked up the towel and ducked under Mariel's neck to take a close look at her offside eye, which had been crusting a little.

'A girl I met,' I said. 'Her name's Kat. She's from Boston. I invited her for supper.'

'Sounds good,' he said. He wiped at the corner of the mare's eye and she tossed her head impatiently. 'Hope they like hamburgers in Boston, 'cause I think we're out of scrod.'

'I'll cook tonight,' I said, holding out a couple of carrot heads for Mariel and watching her take them delicately with her soft lips.

'Doubt it'll get you out of doing dishes.'

'I know. I'll still clean up.'

'Then it's all yours, cookie,' he said, tossing me the comb

and towel. 'Put those up while I take her in and get her some oats, then we'll go up and meet your friend.'

'Sure,' I said, handing him the sack.

'Oh, yes, my dear, yes!' Gran Esther was saying to Kat as we came in. 'Boston was a completely new universe for me – that cold, cold wind, but history simply everywhere, such wonderful museums, the moon coming right up out of the sea – I can see it now, just like it was yesterday!'

Aunt Rachel was slicing tomatoes and onions at the breakfast bar, listening to the talk and smiling her absent little eavesdropping smile as Dusty and I got out of our boots in the entryway. I washed my hands at the sink beside her, then ripped open the two packages of hamburger she'd set out. Dusty had poured a cup of coffee and carried it around the open counter into the den, where I heard him say, 'You must be the young lady from Boston.'

'Yes, sir,' Kat said, rising to walk over and shake his hand. 'I'm Kat Dreyfus.'

'Call me Dusty,' he said. 'You eat hamburgers?'

'Quick as a mousetrap.'

'Miss Dreyfus is on a journey of conscience,' Gran Esther said, sipping her tea. 'She's helping the black people and the other poor folks.'

Something caused me to shiver slightly as I worked spices and chopped onion into the meat. When that was done I padded out to the patio in my socks to get the fire started. The air was cool, the sun low and red beyond the oaks. An owl hooted sadly somewhere behind the house. Dumping charcoal into the grate, I saturated it with starter fluid and rummaged around for matches. When I had the fire going, I walked back inside where Rachel had the hamburger fixings laid out on plates along the counter.

43

She said, 'How's it feel to be so far from home, Kat?'

'It's beautiful here,' Kat had said. 'Especially at night. I've never seen so many stars. Compared to the city, it seems so peaceful and safe – '

As I tried to describe this part of the conversation to Max now, the words died in my throat. After a silence he said, 'Y'know, Jim, you're dealing with some pretty knotty abandonment and mortality issues here – could that be what all this is about?'

'Sounds like something LA would ask.'

'Mmm,' said Max. 'We're lucky to have her.'

He was right. She'd gotten me in to see him after diagnosing my depression a couple of years ago, and the two of them had been a hell of a tag team, having me surrounded before I could think of an evasion strategy. But I'd liked and trusted Max immediately because he was a smart guy, obviously not a bit afraid of whatever was wrong with me, and entirely unimpressed by my suffering. The first thing he'd said to me after introducing himself was, 'So, Jim, how's it feel to piss on your own grave?'

Now: 'Sounds like Kat and your folks really hit it off from the start – '

I said, 'That was then – '

'Humour me,' he said. 'Where did things go from there?'

Kat and I had been seeing each other every day since the District game, and I'd proudly introduced her to Johnny, the miserably envious Daz, and pretty much everybody else I knew. We rode the far places of the farm in Indian summer, past grazing Brangus and Charolais and sunning brood mares watching us with patient eyes, under windmills that creaked like cellar doors in their tireless turning, through woods as high and silent as cathedrals, across pasturelands where the wind ran through the grass in waves that chased and overran and re-crossed each other until they lost themselves in the hills.

On a golden Saturday afternoon we let the horses graze as we lay back under the old willows by the Far Pond listening to the goggle-eyes take insects from the smooth surface with little smacking sounds. Pale peach and ivory coloured clouds piled on themselves to the highest reaches of the sky, and the gently sloping bluegreen fields stretched away endlessly into the long afternoon. The heartbroken call of a dove drifted across the water from the cottonwoods along the opposite shore, and swallows dipped, climbed and turned in the cooling air.

Without opening her eyes Kat said, 'It's really sweet being out here. How far are we from the house?'

'About three and a half miles.'

'Wow. How much of it is the farm?'

'Everything you can see from here. A little over nine thousand acres.'

'Must be a lot of work.'

'Sometimes.'

Pointing to the cupped brown nests in the dry cattail stalks fringing the shallow end of the pond, she said, 'Did blackbirds build those?'

'Yeah, redwings,' I said. 'Soldier-birds, some people call them, because of those little stripes on their shoulders.'

'We have them back home,' Kat said. 'At least I think they're the same. But I've never seen them up close like this – they're beautiful.'

45

'They say some of the Indians thought they called people away from life, like "Time's up", off to the Happy Hunting Ground or something.'

'Then we better not listen.'

Kat played classical guitar, and sometimes brought her Ibañez along on our rides. She'd make up songs about things that caught her attention along the way, like the one she called 'What Colour Is Time?', about the green hills around us and how long they'd been there, waiting and watching for other colours to come.

Another time she told me about having a nanny named Estrella from Guadalajara when she was a little girl, and asked me in perfect Spanish how I learned the language.

'Mainly just hanging around with the hands – a lot of them are from Mexico,' I said. *'Porque lo preguntas?'*

'I've heard you and your family talking to them,' she said. *'Es una lengua hermosa. Es un mundo hermoso aqui.'*

And she was right. I looked away across the fields and valleys, thinking about how beautiful it all was and wondering why I'd never seen it like this before.

She made a couple of tuning adjustments on the guitar, strummed and chorded randomly for a while, then found her key. 'There's about a thousand versions of this one,' she said. 'See if you've heard it like this – Estrella used to sing it to me sometimes, like a lullaby.'

Ay, ay, ay, ay
Canta y no llores
Porque cantando se alegran,
Cielito Lindo, los corazones.

46

Este Cielito Lindo
Lindo Cielito que canto aqui
Viene de la huasteca cielito lindo
Solo por ti

Que tu estas dentro
Tierra de las aztecas
Cielito Lindo, que Dios nos hizo
Son esas tres huastecas
Cielito Lindo, un paraiso.

She laid the guitar beside her on the grass and said, 'Do you think that's really true?'

'That God made us? I don't know,' I said. 'Maybe just the good stuff.'

'Do you hate black people? Or poor people?'

'No, why would I?'

'I thought I was supposed to be mad at the rich white people down here. I thought there was some kind of conspiracy or something, and everybody was in on it. It was like, here are the good guys and there are the bad guys over there, and you can tell the bad guys because they're white and they have growly teeth.'

'You've met a lot of people around here,' I said. 'What do you think now?'

She shook back her hair. 'I don't know,' she said. 'All I can say, I haven't met any bad guys yet.'

Now Max said, 'Was that not your last ride with her?'

At first I couldn't speak.

'Jim, are you still there?'

'Yeah, I'm here.'

47

'Wasn't that your last ride with Kat?'

Finally I said, 'You know it was.'

'And you're telling me all that was then, and this is now?'

FIVE

I finally got around to Jonas an hour or so after I got back to what used to be home, the three-bedroom on Lanshire where I slept at night and where the emptiness was like an icicle through the heart. On the way, thinking maybe I needed a sugar and caffeine hit, I had stopped for a cappuccino at Starbucks, but ended up grinding my teeth and throwing it savagely at the ArkLaTex Realty sign in the front yard as I crossed the drive toward the door. Just the thing to show the neighbours what a stable guy I was. Then for my self-imposed act of contrition I walked humbly over and retrieved the cup, thinking, for no reason I recognised at the moment, of Father Joe – José Carbajal, senior pastor at Sacred Heart downtown – gone now but bright in memory.

Father Joe walking into the fellowship hall, finished with confessions for now and carrying another six-gallon bucket of pancake flour to the kitchen, setting it on the end of the counter and lighting a small cigar. It was a freezing Saturday morning toward the end of my first year in Traverton, and I was standing elbow to elbow with Jonas McCashion, flipping all-you-can-eat pancakes for the Kids' Roundup Ranch in Bowie County.

'I thought this place was smoke-free,' said Jonas.

'*Que es peor que la que,*' the priest said, rolling up his sleeves, the cigar cocked at an obstinate angle in his teeth. '*Es de la reserva privada de Fidel.*' He grabbed a spatula. 'Let's feed these *paganos hambre.*'

Jonas and I went back to our conversation about women, snow geese and incoherent Texas governors, already on our way to becoming good friends. I was what he called dismated, a circumstance he was unwilling to let stand. He introduced me to a former neighbour of his, a ceramic artist named Jana Stiles, and his instincts turned out to be dead-on.

Because without Jana I'd have had no story that could be whole. I still saw and smelled and felt the exact moment when it began for me: the CCR concert in Baton Rouge – our third date – midnight, cigarette lighters held high all around us in the dark, Fogerty and his latest line-up doing a long, sweet reprise of 'Who'll Stop the Rain?' and Jana, deep inside the music, swaying against me, leaning over and taking the lobe of my ear lightly in her teeth, growling softly.

When I lost her it was for reasons I should have understood then but didn't even now, a fact that joined forces with many others to make me wonder how the hell there could be enough room in the known universe to accommodate all the things I didn't understand.

One thing I did get was that most of the women I'd loved had been John Fogerty fans, and I remembered him from about as far back as he went. When it came to dancing Rachel had been more country-western than anything else, but couldn't get enough of Fogerty's early stuff, like the Blue Velvets version of 'Have You Ever Been Lonely?'.

In fact, that was what had been playing on the kitchen radio the first night I'd been the designated cook on one of Kat's visits. That had given me full control of the operation, which meant steaks all around. It was the first time I'd been trusted with that many rib-eyes, but I brought it off without a hitch if you judged by all the compliments and the almost complete absence of leftovers.

When the table was clear, Dusty had said, "Fraid y'all are going to have to hold the fort without Ray and me tonight. We're goin' boot-scootin' at the Palomino with Liz and Doc.'

'How nice,' Gran Esther said. 'You two have a good time – you've earned it.'

With Dusty and Rachel on their way, Kat and I were doing the dishes. 'Where's the Palomino?' she asked, her hip warm against mine.

'Greenville,' I said, lowering my voice a little to keep Gran Esther from hearing. 'It's a couple of hours each way. They usually stay the night in town.'

Kat smiled, passed me another handful of knives, forks and spoons.

'Here, let me help with that,' said Gran, carrying a couple of stray saucers she'd found in the living room over to the sink.

'No, ma'am,' I said. 'We'll have this done in no time. How about some hot chocolate or something?'

'Come to think of it, hot chocolate would be very nice, dear.'

Kat quickly dried her hands, saying, 'Let me make that for you, Mrs Rhodes. Biscuit can show me where everything is.'

Gran said she was tired and decided to take the chocolate

to her room. 'Goodnight to both of you,' she said, 'and God bless.'

What Gran called her room was actually a good-sized apartment at the far end of the house, and once she was in for the evening she never came back out. Kat watched as Gran closed the door behind her.

'You've got a great family, Biscuit,' Kat said.

'Yeah, I know,' I said. 'Want a beer?'

'You can do that?'

'One or two on weekends as long as it's just around here. Dusty thinks beer is good for your constitution.'

'How does Rachel feel about it?'

'She doesn't drink. And she doesn't say anything about anybody else's drinking either. Calls that taking other people's inventory.'

'My Uncle Marty says things like that. He's in AA.'

I just nodded.

'Well, she seems like a pretty terrific lady to me.'

'She is now.'

I opened two Lone Stars from the fridge and handed Kat one of them as we wandered over to the stereo.

Flipping through the tapes, Kat picked one up and said, 'Judy Collins, great.' She took a drink of Lone Star and looked around the room's wide hardwood floors scattered with area rugs. 'This room was made for dancing, Biscuit. Think Gran would mind?'

'She takes out her hearing aid when she goes in at night,' I said. 'She'll never know.' I pushed the tape into the player, and we rolled back a couple of the rugs and lowered the lights. Kat slipped her penny loafers off, took my Lone Star and set both bottles on the counter, then came back and held her hand out to me as the music filled the room. I buried my face in her hair, smelling her skin and her summery perfume, her soft breasts lightly pressing my chest and her hips moving smoothly against mine.

After a few more numbers she lifted her mouth to mine, kissing me deeply as we danced, her hands on my waist.

When we finally broke the kiss she said what I'd been trying to think of a way to bring up: 'Show me your room?'

When I opened the door to my room and switched on the light Kat glanced around. 'Hey, you're not too messy for a guy, Biscuit – and your own bathroom! Wow!' She walked over for a closer look at the framed picture on my dresser next to the cracked red coffee mug bristling with pencil stubs and dried-up ballpoint pens. 'This must be Lee Ann in the middle,' she said. 'Who are the other two?'

'My grandmother and Dr Kepler.'

'Dr Kepler?'

'She was a professor, a friend of ours,' I said. 'She didn't have any family or anything, and she kind of adopted us.'

'What happened to her family?'

'Her parents and sisters died in a concentration camp in Poland,' I said. 'Now she's dead too.' I stood gazing at her image, feeling its familiar dark energy, like a permanent, warm, almost undetectable push against my skin, and wondering why I couldn't stop saying things that made me sound even stupider than I actually was.

For a while Kat just stared at the picture in silence, something changing in her eyes. She swallowed hard, touched her fingers to the glass. '*Aleha ha-shalom*,' she said softly. '*Baruch dayan emet*.'

I was about to ask what this meant when she pulled my mouth down to hers and kissed me again, her breath coming faster. She stepped back, looked at me for a while without saying anything, then walked over to the door, closed it and thumbed the lock.

Taking a deep breath, I unlocked and opened the front door of my house and stepped inside, bracing myself against what I knew I was going to see, which was nothing. Or maybe I should say everything, but all of it exactly as I'd left it this morning. Until Jana took the girls and moved to the big cedar A-frame behind her gallery off Border I hadn't understood that inanimate things could die, that all those atoms could stop their quantum dance at once and something as full of energy and purpose as a house one day could become only a shell the next, a replica of life like the detailed husk a cicada leaves behind when it moults.

It wasn't that I denied being mostly responsible for what had gone wrong between Jana and me, or that I didn't understand what she was saying about the job. And for her it went beyond the fact that her brother had been killed in the desert, or that her cop uncle had been murdered by a couple of skinheads on the street in Houston. It really came down to her being through with the locker-room police culture that still hung around me like cigar smoke when I got home from work at night, the gun I put on my belt every morning – to her nothing but an ugly black killing tool – the constant anxiety, the midnight calls. She wanted no more bagpipes playing 'Amazing Grace' or white-gloved honour guards firing blanks at the sky as somebody with colourful medals and

54

high rank handed young widows or widowers in sunglasses their tightly folded American flags. And outweighing all the rest of it put together, the half-ounce of copper-jacketed lead in the form of two nine-millimetre bullets that wouldn't have had to be cut out of my body if I'd had some other job.

Her solution was direct and uncomplicated: take the fifty-one-per-cent deal Rachel and Dusty had offered us on the Flying S in Rains County, move out there and run the place, and let them take off to find out what the rest of the world looks like – something they'd been dreaming of for the last fifteen years. But the terms didn't really matter, because for Jana the question of where we'd be going was a non-essential detail; what she cared about was what we'd be leaving behind – a folded flag of her own.

But nothing about Jana was simple. She'd been an accounting major but cared more about natural fibres than bottom lines. She had killer instincts at poker, but kids lost in stores ran to her on sight. She called herself a 'pretty good potter', the real-world meaning of which was that she was an at least moderately famous artist, a ceramicist exhibiting in galleries from one end of the country to the other.

Maybe it was being an artist that made her so contradictory. But whatever gifts she had, she wanted to share. One of the most vivid memories I had of her went back to a Saturday morning years ago, our daughter Casey still in her yellow footie pyjamas, an icy rain falling steadily beyond the windows of the breakfast nook where she sat at the table with her colouring book, Jana standing beside her, watching in silence, her face soft and radiant with undisguised pride.

My eyes stinging as the already-dead house somehow found a way to die a little more, I was suddenly filled with a pure, brilliant hatred of the echoing emptiness banging against my eardrums and sucking the oxygen from the air.

Mutt, my personal cat, came pacing silently in from the hallway. He was mostly black, with two barely visible tan markings above his eyes that gave him a permanently surprised expression, and he stopped and stared at me now as if I were the last thing he'd expected to find in here. Jana had taken him along when she and the girls moved out, thinking he was more attached to them than to me, but he'd run away the first day. Then three days after that I'd found him sitting on the front doormat, licking a curled paw and ignoring me. He'd somehow made it almost six miles across town to come home, probably using up several of his spare lives on the way.

As cats go, he wasn't a bad roommate – no clawing the furniture, keeping me awake at night or spraying in the house – but he reminded me so much of Jana and the girls that I sometimes had to work at not resenting him for it. On the other hand, right now I was glad to have the company of another conscious being.

'Ahoy,' I said.

He gave no sign that he heard me.

The thought of other conscious beings brought to mind the only Dallas phone number I didn't need to look up. I grabbed the phone and punched it in.

'Dr Lee Ann Rowe's office,' said LaKeisha.

'This still group night?'

'That you, Lieutenant Bonham?'

I said what I always did: 'Call me Jim.'

'Yes, sir,' she said. 'It is, and she should be out any second. I'll put you on hold. Enjoy the music.'

The next thing I heard was a slow instrumental version of 'Satisfaction', strings and light brass, which I enjoyed as much as I could.

Thinking about LA as I waited – as always trying to edit out the memories that underlined my own failures and selfishness, my inability to prevent what had happened to her – I argued myself around to the position that this call was justifiable, that I wasn't going to kick up any dust from the past that she couldn't deal with, that she was probably tougher than me anyway, and certainly no longer had any need for my protection. If she ever really had.

Then, thinking some more about families, I looked up at the pictures on the wall: Jana in front of the fieldstone fire-place at the Flying S; Gram, my grandmother Miriam Hunnicutt Vickers, who'd raised LA and me after everyone else ahead of her on the depth chart had defaulted – a wise and beautiful woman, battered but never broken by a world that didn't deserve her, looking sadly into the lens from among the tomato plants in her garden; and my own daughters, Casey and Jordan, on horseback, the November sun backlighting their hair against a background of red and gold leaves.

But images of Deborah Gold's dead flesh began shouldering their way back in, her half-shut eyes gazing emptily down at me through the icy rain, her viciously violated body already gone cold on its way to rejoining the soil.

Then the soundtrack transitioned to 'Circle of Life', taking me smoothly back through time to an evening with the girls not long after the separation, the three of us sharing a tub of popcorn and watching a movie about cartoon animals having conversations and singing songs, Jordan saying, 'That's pretty dumb,' not carping, just thinking out loud. 'They'd be eating each other.'

A huge sigh from her sister Casey. 'It's a *meta*phor, you dink.'

'I think you mean fable, Miss Hairball.'

All her life Casey had been what Jana called an 'easy upchuck', like a cat, throwing up for any reason, or no reason. When there was a purpose it was usually evil – to duck chores, an exam, or some adverse social situation – and it had earned her the nickname Hairball. She was a little sensitive about it. 'Well, just up yours, Little Susie Einstein,' she said, giving her hair a sulky toss.

The soundtrack clicked off. 'Speak, troop,' LA's telephone voice said. 'Start by telling me you're not relapsing.' I imagined her leaning back in her desk chair, sporting one of her two main looks – denim and boots that would look spot-on in a boardroom, or a serious suit in toned-down colours that she could wear to a dogfight without raising an eyebrow. Not much jewellery or makeup, probably no high heels – you don't paint extra stripes on a tiger. Of course with her the concept of a hairstyle had never had any actual meaning because no matter what she or anybody else tried to do with it, she still ended up with the same dark, unconquerable mop that our grandmother had said always looked freshly dynamited.

'Hi, girl,' I said. 'I'm fine, but I need your wisdom.'

'Some things never change,' she said. 'How's your appetite?'

'Not too bad,' I said. 'But junk food has kinda lost its taste.'

A brief pause. 'How long since you've been fishing?'

'I don't know – quite a while.'

'But you've still got the boat?'

I said, 'Yeah. And tackle. And a fishing licence. I just don't go.'

'What's your weight?'

'One-seventy-five.'

'Still a light heavyweight. How well are you sleeping?'

'No way to know,' I said. 'I'm always asleep at the time.'

'Give.'

'Okay, I've waked up too early a few times since the last time we talked.'

'What are you calling a few?'

'Four.'

'Talked to Max about it?'

'Yeah, some. He gave me a couple things to think about.'

'But you haven't talked to Jana and the girls about the farm.' Not a question.

'Would you believe it if I said I was working on it?'

'No,' she said. 'But I'd believe you think you are.'

'Maybe the problem's not really knowing where I belong.'

'I saw how you were when you were working the place that last year, troop. Nobody could belong there more than you. Except maybe Casey and Jordie.'

I looked again at the pictures of the two of them on the wall. She was right; both were natural riders, as much at home on horseback and in the open country as birds in the air. If anybody belonged out there it was them.

'Yeah, they'd be great with it,' I said. 'What worries me is how they're handling the separation. I'm taking them out for lunch tomorrow, probably to the marina. I know it won't fix anything, but I really need to spend some time with them.'

'The main thing they need is for you to keep being who you are – the guy they can count on, who loves 'em like a rock. So who're you sleeping with and how long has it been?'

With therapists there are certain constants, one of them being that you've got to account for your sex life.

'It's still Jana when it's anybody,' I said. 'It's been three weeks. Why?'

'Because I hear skin hunger in your voice,' she said, awakening new images of Gold's violated skin in my mind. 'You need more human contact.'

'Okay,' I said. 'But first, question number one: what's the difference between a hallucination and a vision?'

'Sometimes nothing, but generally you call it a hallucination – meaning it's a symptom – when you're nuts,' she said. 'A vision is just an experience. Why?'

I described what I'd seen on my computer monitor, and the memories that went with it.

'Sounds like flashbacks,' she said. 'Anything happen lately that took you back to the farm or football or anything like that?'

'Not really,' I said. 'I mean, I see Johnny now and then, but that's about it. Losing Jana and the girls might have triggered something, but I can't really think of anything else.'

'You haven't lost Jana yet,' LA said. 'And you'll never lose the girls. But your brain's working on something. Give it a little time – things like that come when they're ready.'

'Okay,' I said. 'Thing number two is a murdered psychologist I want to talk to you about.'

'Wow,' she said. 'That's hittin' a little close to home,

troop. But I don't know how much I can help with something like that. I'm no criminalist.'

'But you're kind of smart,' I said. 'And you know a bunch of psychology words.'

'Okay, Bis, let's hear it.'

I said, 'This woman used to do our employment screenings. She was hung up in a tree.' Hearing myself, I realised how weak and obtuse this sounded. If I wanted to keep my communication skills anywhere above rock bottom I needed more interaction with people who had the kind of mind LA did, though I wasn't exactly sure where to find anybody like that.

'Hung up how?'

'She was crucified.'

There was a short silence as LA processed this. She said, 'Any religious connection?'

'Like what?'

'Like she was about to blow the whistle on some monsignor for embezzlement, a child-abusing cult, anything like that?'

'Not that I know of,' I said. I outlined what we had so far, including the anatomical switch the killers had performed. I'd been worried about this part, but the non-negotiable standing price of a conversation with LA had always been the naked truth or nothing.

'Jesus, Bis, that's some pretty incredible rage – but at least I'd say it eliminates most of your likely suspects.'

Seeing no way around having to admit I didn't get it, I said, 'What do you mean?'

'Not trying to play junior detective here, but this sounds too complicated for plain sexual sadism. And I'd bet your killer wasn't her husband, or her lover. The killing was some kind of punishment, no doubt about that, but this isn't the kind of anger you get when a guy's wife or girlfriend cheats on him at the Christmas party or runs off with the tennis pro. When a man is mad enough to murder his woman, if he doesn't shoot her it's usually either spur of the moment, where he goes for the face or neck, or else it's a premeditated thing like an insurance killing and he'll try to make it look accidental. Or hire a guy to fake a burglary.'

'Doc Stiff,' I said.

'Explain that.'

'A homicide detective I knew. Used to be a biology teacher. His thinking was, the hotter the blood, the sooner and simpler the killing. He called it the Index of Passion. Not saying these doers kept a cool head exactly, but this took thinking and planning and patience.'

'Doc sounds like a pretty smart guy,' she said. 'Anyway, your bad guys went to all that trouble for *some* reason. Any messages around the body, or on it?'

'No note, no anonymous calls, no hieroglyphics carved on her chest,' I said, watching Mutt groom himself. 'Wayne found a Roman coin, but there's no telling how it got there or if it had anything to do with the killing.'

'A *Roman coin*?'

Suddenly Mutt came to attention. He looked first toward the back door, then the garage entrance, the fur along his back standing up, his eyes huge. Hearing nothing myself. but catching his mood like an instantaneous virus, I said, 'Hold on a minute, LA. I'll be right back.' I grabbed the Glock and a flashlight, checked to be sure there was a round in the pistol's chamber, and slipped out the front door. As I waited for my eyes to adjust I listened carefully to the night. I hadn't expected to hear crickets or cicadas at this time of year, but even taking that into account it seemed unnaturally quiet out here. I started working my way slowly around the house, staying as deep in the shadows as possible. Nothing in front, nothing in the driveway, nothing anywhere around the house that I could see. I stood motionless again, listening, hearing only the menacing rumble of a Harley somewhere in the middle distance, and behind that the faint hum of the interstate that could only be heard from here on a quiet night. I switched the flashlight on and made a non-stealth circuit of the house. Still nothing.

Back inside, I picked up the phone, saying, 'I'm here.'

'What happened?'

'The cat spooked,' I said.

'Only you would have a watchcat. What spooked him?'

'Don't know,' I said. 'Maybe some colleague of his dropping by. Coyotes come through sometimes, but usually not before three, four in the morning.'

After a short silence LA said, 'I don't like the sound of that, Bis.'

'Yeah, well,' I said. 'Where were we?'

'The coin.'

'Right – the mystery coin. Wayne says it hadn't been in the ground.'

'So it got dropped there recently,' LA said. 'Meaning you can't rule out that it was your bad guys who dropped it. And if they did – '

'If they did, it was probably on purpose – '

' – so why? What's the message? And who's it for?'

'If I could figure out that last one it'd probably tell me who did it.' I told her we'd found out Gold got a call from a pre-paid phone around eight the night she was taken.

63

The conversation had ended at 8.19 p.m. after eight minutes and a couple of seconds. Gold had then left the house and gone to her office, checking with the call centre from there at 8.44, no messages. Her purse, snapped shut and apparently unrobbed, had been left on a corner of the receptionist's desk, the front office lights still on and Gold's green BMW parked unlocked in front of the office door.

'All they wanted was her,' LA said. 'Better bet they showed up in something like a utility van.'

'Right,' I said. 'Nothing unusual in or close to her car. No fingerprint results yet, but I doubt they even touched it – no reason to unless they were going to steal it. All the back rooms, Dr Gold's office included, were locked and dark when the secretary came in the next morning.'

'What about the husband?'

'He's younger than her, runs a computer and data-service company that's doing okay financially. Can you profile something like this?'

'Not like you see on TV,' she said. 'Even when you can, all you usually end up with is "white male, twenty-five to thirty-five, not good with relationships", yakkity-yak. Try getting a warrant with that.'

'Well, with you on the case we're takin' our game up a notch, right?'

She was silent for a few seconds, which I spent looking at the pictures above the mantel. Then she said, 'I'm coming to see you.'

'Hey, great,' I said. 'To what do I owe the pleasure?'

'Nothing. I'm signed up for a conference in Miami, and I'm taking a week off before that.'

'To do what?'

'Pay you a visit, what else?' she said. 'Horn-in on your cases – car chases, explosions, trading quips while you cuff the perps.'

'Where's all that coming from?'

'Prime time,' she said. 'Think you're the only one who's got a TV?'

'What if I signed you on as a consultant?' I said.

'Well . . . ' she said, like somebody looking a used car over, which told me two things: one, she was not going to need any more persuading, and two, she would now name her real price. 'Okay, here's the deal,' she said. 'I'll make it a week if you'll weld some bookends for my office – that credenza behind my desk.'

'Weld?'

'Yeah, with your blowtorch. Like that stuff you used to make with the ragged edges.'

'Acetylene torch,' I said.

'Okay, acetylene,' she said. 'If that's what flips your fritters.'

On a farm or ranch the number-two rule – number one being: never trust the weather – is that everything breaks, meaning that to be useful around the Flying S as a kid I had to learn basic cutting and welding. I still kept an oxyacetylene rig and an old Lincoln buzz-box in my backyard workshop where I sometimes roughed out odds and ends like makeshift trivets, doorstops, paper-weights – even a pair of candleholders that from a certain angle looked a little like the Grand Tetons – out of scrap metal as a way of clearing my head. Jana liked them and used them for bookends, garden sculpture or just general decoration.

'Your soul and your hands understand line and mass

better than you do,' she'd said with that quirky little smile of hers.

I visualised LA's office and the oak credenza, directly under a skylight, where she kept the leather-bound TS Eliots Gram had left her, held up by a few other volumes stacked as bookends. Rough-cut steel wouldn't look bad there.

'Done,' I said. 'But how about saying a few psychological words, just to convince me I'm not making a mistake here.'

She snorted. 'I'll see what I can do with your dead psychologist, Sherlock,' she said. 'But meantime, how about emailing me the stuff you've got so far – give me a chance to look it all over before I come calling.'

When we'd said our goodbyes I thumbed the phone off and dropped it in my shirt pocket, feeling like the guy who'd just closed on Manhattan for a sack of beads.

I grabbed a can of Dos Equis from the fridge, still gloating but a little bothered by a sense that I was forgetting something. But nothing came to me, so I sat back down to think some more about Deborah Gold. I wondered if she'd felt safe in the world. My theory was that only people who were definitely good-hearted or completely evil really did – you either expected the universe to abide by the Golden Rule in its dealings with you because that's what you'd do in its place, or, if you were bad enough, you didn't worry about it because you just didn't believe in consequences and expected fate to be as untrustworthy as you anyway. On the other hand, people of the middle ground, the best I could give myself credit for, were apparently doomed to a life of apprehension and doubt.

But it seemed to me Dr Gold's exit from the mortal stage had another dimension. It was like a scenario fast-forwarded through the bloody centuries from the ironically named Holy Land, the long arm of Caesar reaching across time to punish some unknown treason –

This stopped me.

Reaching across time –

The words repeated themselves in my mind, something in them buzzing with danger, somehow bringing back the stark image of Bragg Field at the centre of an infinitely cold darkness spreading away in every direction and to the ends of the earth.

If you believe the books, a criminal always leaves something at the scene of the crime and always takes something away. In this case the trade was a Roman coin for a tongue, but I couldn't put together any plausible explanation for either the coin's presence or the tongue's absence, much less figure out what the two had to do with each other.

Across time – why that? I had no idea, but all of it carried an irresistible feeling of meaning and connectedness. Vaguely remembering something I'd come across somewhere about Carl Jung and synchronicity, and putting that together with bits and pieces I'd heard about quantum indeterminacy, I wondered if it was actually possible, maybe down at the level of quarks and bosons, for causality to work differently in different situations or at different times.

Watching Mutt continue his grooming at the kitchen entry, I suddenly remembered what I'd been forgetting. Jonas. Checking the time, I decided it wasn't too late. Mutt strolled over to make a couple of figure-eight passes against my leg as I reached for the phone and punched in numbers. He was a cruiserweight of the housecat world but he jumped to my lap as weightlessly as Tinker Bell and gave me his chronically amazed expression. I stroked his thick black fur absent-mindedly, hearing and feeling the resultant rumbling purr as I waited for Jonas to pick up.

'McCashion,' said Jonas' voice.

We traded greetings, with no questions from him about Jana and the girls, then he said, 'Got a new one for you: student of mine's named Giles Selig.' Jonas spelled it for me. 'Middle name's got three letters – what is it?'

I thought about it for a minute, listening to the busy clicking of his keyboard as he worked on something, probably lecture notes.

'Asa,' I said.

'You son of a bitch!' he yelped. 'How the hell do you do that?'

'Nothing else came to mind but Bob and Gig. They didn't seem to fit.'

'Damn,' he sighed. 'So what's up, JB?'

'I want a consult. Can I buy you a drink?'

'Just me, or do I bring Abby?'

'Just you,' I said. 'This is business.'

'When?'

'Now.'

'Okay, let's make it John Boy's, but you've got to sell it to her. We were gonna watch *To Kill a Mockingbird* tonight.'

I heard him call his wife to the phone.

'Hey, crime fighter,' she said. I pictured dark intelligent eyes behind wire-rimmed glasses, her glossy chestnut hair and crooked smile. At this time of day I was sure she'd be wearing her old sweats and carrying a cup of apple tea around with her.

'Atticus gets the guy off,' I said.

'Yeah, yeah, I know, they all ended happy in those days, that's what I like about old movies. What's happening?'

'I want your husband.'

'You want him? Jim, this man is my only stuff. I need him. Where would I find a replacement at my age?'

'I'll cook the Special for you this weekend,' I said, meaning charcoal-grilled salmon fillets with caper and raisin sauce, one of the three real-meal recipes Rachel had taught me years ago based on her belief that a man had to be able to put at least that many different credible meals on the table if necessary. 'On the grill outside if the weather's good, otherwise I'll broil it in the kitchen.'

There was a silent pause, which told me I had her.

'Okay,' she said. 'But I want him returned in good condition.'

'No worries,' I said. 'It's only his mind I'm interested in.'

'His what?'

Beginning to feel that a little momentum might be building, I looked at the mantel again, the other end this time, where the watercolour caricature Jana had had done for me by a friend of hers a few birthdays ago leaned against the bricks: two charging tigers wearing jerseys numbered 39 and 22, the numbers Johnny Trammel and I had worn the year Bragg won State.

'Growl a little growl for me, baby,' she'd said as she handed it to me. 'And I'll show you what real tigers do in the dark.'

I'd brought it in here from the workshop last week in hopes of reawakening some sense of life in the place, but it hadn't done that, managing only to bring back the smell of the Bragg Field locker rooms vividly enough to send me on a reconnaissance tour of the house in search of missed laundry or forgotten cat food.

I decided on one more call before I left to meet Jonas, this one to Johnny over in Burnsville at the western end of the county, to see if I could get him and Li signed on for the cookout too. Not that you had to come up with anything special for him – he'd never been famous for turning down anything that came on a plate. He was still easy because in recent years he'd always seemed too preoccupied even to notice what he was eating, which I took to be a hazard of the legal profession. Some of the guys he represented would be hard on anybody's appetite.

The spring we graduated he'd tossed a half-dozen scholarship offers in the trash and started visiting recruiters, eventually ending up in Delta Force and being awarded two Purple Hearts and a Silver Star for his actions in places where hatreds a thousand years old ran like underground rivers, places whose names he would, along with what he'd done there, take with him to the grave. I shouldn't have known, but did, that his last mission was a so-called black op, a HALO – high altitude, low opening – jump from a C-130 in friendly airspace, he and his squad free-falling thirty thousand feet on a moonless night, five dark silences slanting like raptors down through the stars, nothing to be seen but the soft blue dots of the altimeters on their wrists as they vectored cross-country over a mountain range and a hostile border to pop their chutes a thousand feet above the last ground four of them would ever touch. Johnny made it out alone nine weeks later with a permanent limp and a never-explained tendency to gag at the sight of beets.

I took the best scholarship offer I got, the one from TCU, where I blew out both knees against Kansas State my second year and had no choice but to become an actual student, while Johnny eventually earned his law degree at Baylor and hung out his shingle in Burnsville, the county seat. He married a blonde former cheerleader named Alicia Meador and settled down to practise country law and watch his cows get fat on the little farm he and Li signed the mortgage on after he brought in his first big settlement. His medals were still gathering dust on his office wall along with his Chamber of Commerce and Rotary certificates and the team picture from our championship season, all of us standing forever shoulder to shoulder in sunlight that somehow seemed historical and heatless in the old print. Johnny himself looked like a dangerous but dapper Prohibition rum-runner or a tragic Irish poet, brick-coloured hair brushed casually to the side and face turned toward me with a small smile, as if I'd just cracked some dumb joke.

'Hi, Jim,' said Li's telephone voice.

I told her what I had in mind.

She said, 'Whatcha cooking?'

'The Special.'

'With that weird sauce?'

'It's the only one I know how to make.'

'Count us in. I know Johnny'll want to hear all about your hot case.'

I heard Johnny's voice in the background: 'Ask him what's going on with that. He got any suspects yet?'

'Tell him when I catch somebody I'll give them his number,' I said. 'If they're rich enough to afford a big-time lawyer.'

Hanging up the phone, I sipped beer, thinking about what Li had said. It resonated weirdly in my mind because, although the coin had felt warm to me, the case itself didn't at all. It felt cool, like old mausoleum air or the dank and unfresh stirring of the breeze off a swamp at night.

I put Mutt on the arm of the chair and stood up, thinking about what I wanted to ask Jonas and about the way things ought to be. 'Your watch, boy,' I said to the cat. 'Don't let any rats get by you.'

He just stared at me, looking mystified.

SIX

I took Border Avenue south, with Arkansas and its liquor stores on my left, Texas with its car dealerships and Baptist bookstores to the right, and a mile ahead, the Louisiana Quarter, which some said existed only to show the world just how much political corruption and fine cooking it was possible to cram into one medium-sized town.

Catching the light, I downshifted the F-250 around the corner onto Eastern and listened to the exhaust grumble and roar, a sound Jana called the 'Serengeti baritone'. It was probably more of an indication of my thinking than I understood at the time, but a few years ago when Jana and the girls were still with me, I realised I was tired of our number-two car, the Acura I'd been driving to work for the last six years. The first vehicle I'd ever been able to call my own had been a pickup, and after my time on the Flying S working for Dusty, nothing felt as natural under my feet as a truck. Which is probably why this one, parked under a huge oak beside the highway with a For Sale sign wedged behind one windshield wiper, had caught my eye. After a ten-minute test drive I bought it from the alcoholic mechanic who'd reworked it, a committed Jehovah's Witness until he came down with depression, started mixing his medications with vodka and fell from grace. He wasn't definite about exactly how it happened, but I got the impression it involved several counts of interrupting services at the Kingdom Hall to offer his opinions in favour of wholegrains and anal intercourse. Losing business, he decided to cash in some of his assets, starting with the big four-wheel-drive Ford. It had a heavy brush-buster and winch, oversized knobby tyres and a ceramic eyeball the size of a peach for a shift knob.

'Throw a hook down the well, you could turn the world inside out with this hoss,' the Witness said, his breath a weapon of mass destruction as he patted the brush-buster affectionately.

My daughter Casey's judgement had been, 'It suits you, Dad.' Later she had decided for some reason that the truck ought to be called Buford, and painted the name neatly in purple fingernail polish on the left fender just back of the wheel well.

Her sister Jordan had said, 'Mom keeps the van, right?'

'What does this thing eat?' had been Jana's first question as she did a walkaround of the vehicle.

'Scornful wives.'

'Knock yourself out, Thunderfoot,' she'd said, giving me a quick kiss and going back to her flowerbeds.

I found Jonas at a window table in John Boy's, staring at the screen of his laptop. He was dressed in faded jeans, sneakers and a red Centenary sweatshirt with the sleeves pushed up, and had a bottle of Corona at his elbow, but still somehow looking monkish with his prematurely white, close-cut hair and beard, and lean frame. I hung my jacket on the back of the chair and sat across from him, which gave me a view up into the split-level bar where most of the drunks and coloured neon were.

'Nachos coming,' he said, picking up the beer and taking a sip.

'What're you working on?'

'Exam for tomorrow. What's on your mind, JB?'

'Crucifixion.'

He cocked an eye at me and said, 'You trying out for Messiah?'

The waitress brought a plate of nachos piled high with cheese, refritos, chopped tomatoes, fajita strips, guacamole and pico de gallo, set a bottle of Corona with a slice of lime in front of me then disappeared back into the kitchen. I passed the lime around the mouth of the bottle a couple of times, shook some salt onto the rim and took a sip. 'This is about a case,' I said. 'I want to get your thoughts.'

He nodded. 'Always been your method: send you out for a bagel, you're not coming back until you find out who invented wheat. And *why*. But what are you doing investigating cases – aren't you supposed to be some kind of boss now?' He paused to sip from his own beer then studied my face for a moment. 'Wait a minute, I know that look,' he said. 'Like the time that little girl got kidnapped. You're on something big.'

He was talking about Joy Dawn Therone, the Girl Scout whose body had been found behind an old warehouse ten years ago. She had been raped both before and after her throat was slashed to the spine. I hadn't been one of the lead investigators, only one of the guys volunteering time, but I couldn't help thinking about the case, and had never believed it was a regular serial killing. I wasn't sure why, but I thought the murder more likely came under the heading of what the guy who kept the department statistics called HAMs – homicides of 'happenstance and

75

misadventure'. Nobody knew one way or the other, though, because no suspect was ever identified and no arrest ever made, but everybody at Three had kicked in to help pay for the giant angel she was buried under at Sylvan Memorial Park. Counting the marble plinth, it was over ten feet tall – big, but not nearly big enough to make up for us failing to protect her, or at least make the killer pay for what he'd done.

'Yeah, I'm on something,' I said. 'I don't know how big yet.'

Catching my tone, he said, 'Sorry, didn't mean to wake up any ghosts. What can I do for you?'

'You can start by telling me about crucifixion,' I said. 'Not the religious stuff. I mean who did it to who, and how it was done.'

'Interesting you should put it that way,' he said, wiping a little edge of foam from his upper lip with the knuckle of his left thumb. 'Because the actual procedure probably didn't look much like what you see in the stained glass at church. But it was nasty enough. The Romans got famous for crucifying people because of all the press Jesus got, but it had about a thousand-year run as a common form of capital punishment, probably starting with the Persians around the sixth century BCE, then the Egyptians, Carthaginians, Seleucids, even the Jews themselves. But a lot of them, including the Romans, tended not to do it to each other. Saved it for slaves and conquered peoples. Odd thing, though: the idea that Jesus was crucified – I mean on a cross – didn't crop up in any texts of known authenticity until a century or two after the fact.'

'So what did happen?'

'Oh, I'm sure they didn't let him walk,' Jonas said. 'But

what they actually did to him is anybody's guess.' He crunched a nacho and drank from his own Corona. 'Anyway, Constantine outlawed crucifixion in the Roman Empire in 330-something.'

'How'd it kill the victim?'

'Open question,' Jonas said. 'The leading candidates are things like exhaustion, shock, heat stroke, heart failure. On the other hand, I read a paper a few years ago to the effect that it was most likely asphyxia.'

'How would that work?'

'When they used a crossbeam, the arms were fixed to it, usually before it was put up on the stanchion, which more often than not was a tree, by the way, but probably never by just nailing through the hands. Then, whether it was a post or crossbeam, the weight of the body pulling down on the arms and restricting chest movement prevented proper respiration. The victim suffered progressive hypoxia leading to eventual death by asphyxiation.'

'What's the story on using trees?' I asked.

Jonas shrugged. 'Convenience, probably. Who's gonna hunt up a beam the size you'd need for a stanchion, drag it out there, dig a two- or three-foot hole for it in that rocky soil and plant it just to kill one troublesome Jew, when there's an olive tree or whatever right there?'

'Why not nail the hands?'

'Probably wouldn't have supported the weight of the body passively, much less with the victim struggling. What the Romans apparently did most of the time was drive the spike between the forearm bones just above the wrist, then add some kind of binding to prevent the nails from ripping out.'

'What about the feet?'

Jonas wiped his hands on his napkin. 'That's another deviation from lore, I think. If I'm not mistaken they usually drove one spike through both heels. In fact, there was a calcaneus found in the Holy Land a few years back – '

'Calcaneus?'

'Heel bone. This one still had part of the actual nail through it.' He stopped suddenly as he noticed the expression on my face. 'You look like a possum just walked over your grave,' he said.

'How long does it take to die by crucifixion?' I said, taking a blue crayon from the little clay pot next to the salt and pepper shakers and fiddling absently with it.

'How come you're not asking a doctor about this?'

'I am asking a doctor.'

'I mean a pill doctor.'

'Who can say where medicine ends and history begins?'

Jonas snorted. 'Count on you for the philosophical slant,' he said.

I waited.

'Okay, let's see,' Jonas said, picking up his Corona and waggling the bottle as he thought. 'Figure at the low end a few hours to, worst case, a few days. Among other things it would've depended on whether they broke the victim's legs, which supposedly was a common practice. If the guy was able to support his weight with his legs at least some of the time he'd last longer. Not sure why, but the story is they didn't do that with Jesus. There was also a time problem, because Jewish law didn't allow for the body to remain out overnight.'

Overnight. I imagined Deborah Gold hanging out there through a night that must have seemed longer than endless, dying one atom at a time. Maybe not as bad, minute for minute, as what was done to her beforehand, but bad enough.

I said, 'Did they ever crucify women?'

'Nothing to stop them, I guess, but I'd imagine it was fairly rare,' Jonas said. 'Kind of people we're talking about, they'd probably be more inclined to stone the women.'

'Was it a usual part of the procedure to mutilate the body, cut the tongue out, anything like that?'

Jonas shot me a strange look. 'Not that I ever heard of,' he said. 'Are you saying – ?'

'Hold on,' I said. I saw that as Jonas was talking I'd been doodling with the crayon on the brown wrapping paper that served as a tablecloth, producing a couple of versions of a flexed arm holding a heavy hammer, like the picture on a box of baking soda, and several of a figure with a wide base and drooping serifs:

T

'What's that stuff?' asked Jonas.

'I don't know,' I said. Looking at the shapes, I assumed the one that looked like a T must have been a cross, but something about the pictures felt wrong to me.

'What're they about?' Jonas asked.

'Nothing, as far as I know,' I said, dropping the crayon back into its holder. 'But it kind of feels like it could have a connection with a case we've got.'

'What kind of case?'

'A homicide.'

Jonas looked at me for a few seconds. 'This wouldn't be a homicide by *crucifixion,* would it?' he said.

'It would,' I said. 'Unfortunately.'

79

I looked down at my doodles, saying nothing, wishing I'd paid more attention in whichever of my two Psychology classes had covered personality structure and the unconscious mind.

Jonas said, 'And this also involved somebody's tongue getting cut out?'

I nodded.

'Jesus,' Jonas said. 'Pun intended.' He picked up his beer, looked at it for a second, set it down again. 'If you were anybody else I'd probably ask if you were kidding. You aren't, are you?'

Staring at my doodles, I didn't answer.

'Who was your murder victim, can you say?'

'Deborah Gold.'

'The psychologist? I'll be damned,' he said. 'And you're sure it wasn't just a display of the body? I mean, was it actually the crucifixion that killed her?'

'No autopsy results yet. But it was done pretty much the way you described. Why, is the big question.'

'No shit,' Jonas said. 'Pretty damn labour-intensive way to do murder.' He finished off his Corona. 'You thinking it was a hate crime of some kind?'

'You mean as opposed to a crime of goodwill?'

'The jock waxes jocular,' Jonas said. 'So who'd do something like this? And why?'

'That's more or less what I'm asking you,' I said.

'Well, okay,' he said, 'as for anti-Semitism, there's no news there. Besides pretty much the entire Islamic world, some of the survivalists, paramilitaries and Christian fundamentalists get their bad on against Jews. The skinheads tend to focus on blacks, but they're pretty broad-spectrum, talking about Jews controlling the TV networks, the banking

80

system, and so forth. But brainpower has never been their long suit. Way they'd have it would put us back at about the level of the Mongol warlords before anybody got them organised. And these assholes wouldn't like it if they had it because the first thing they'd find out is nobody'd salute them. They're always fatally ignorant of sociology and psychology, not to mention history. People just never behave the way these clowns think they would, especially themselves. I don't see players like that knowing enough to pull off a historically correct execution by crucifixion. Even if you throw in some personal animus to sweeten the pot, it'd be a hell of a stretch.'

'Could it be some kind of political statement?'

Jonas scratched his beard as he thought about it. 'Yeah, that would make a certain kind of sense, considering how easy it is to just shoot somebody if all you've got is a grievance,' he said. 'Kind of fits with the tongue thing too – like maybe it was about something she said to somebody. Or threatened to say. But except for the occasional Democratic fundraiser or something along that line, I never heard of her being particularly political. Was she involved in a trial, or had she testified somewhere recently? Some custody deal maybe?'

'Not that I know of,' I said. Maybe it was my unconscious mind at work again, but for some reason I decided to keep what Wayne had found in Gold's mouth on the list of things I wasn't going to tell Jonas.

'Or,' he said, holding up a forefinger, 'maybe all the philosophical stuff is trying too hard. What if it was something related to her profession – some disgruntled patient or some other psychologist she pissed off? Could be a better way of looking at it. The simplest explanation that covers the facts is usually the right one. Occam's razor and all.'

'They did her in for some ordinary reason, and all the drama is just to create confusion?'

He shrugged, found a couple of nacho fragments under some lettuce and ate them. 'Truth is not always in the distance,' he said.

Suddenly I remembered the morning Jonas and I had stood side by side flipping pancakes at the church, and the flour Father Joe had carried in. The round logo on the bucket had identified it as a Roman Meal product.

'Last question,' I said. 'Did any of the old Romans ever make it to this part of the world?'

He looked at me curiously. 'No,' he said. 'Are you gonna tell me what that's got to do with anything?'

'I don't know yet.'

SEVEN

I made it back to Lanshire a little before ten, got a bottle of beer from the fridge and a not-quite-empty bag of pretzel sticks from the cabinet, sat down and checked for phone messages. Nothing but sales calls. I clicked the TV on and watched a cheetah chasing a little gazelle of some kind across the tan plains. Mutt had taken up his breadloaf position on the arm of the couch next to me and seemed to be watching the screen.

The gazelle made a last hard cut to the left, causing the cheetah to overshoot and break off the chase, dropping to her belly in the grass and panting desperately.

I nodded off and drifted away into a dream of cheetahs and gazelles chasing each other the wrong way around a clock face –

– their speed increasing steadily, accompanied by a strange hum, until they merge into a blur, the numbers on the clock face transforming into the names of months, then years depicted in roman numerals, the numbers rapidly growing lower as time rewinds itself, the hum rising in pitch and volume until it becomes an ear-splitting shriek. Then all sound and movement instantly stops, the once-again-ordinary

clock face hanging silently in dark space for a minute, the gazelles and cheetahs gone. Now the clock face is a merry-go-round with a series of corpses instead of wooden horses impaled on the steel uprights, circling the carousel as they rise and fall in synchrony with the strange tuneless calliope music that fills my ears, their dead, empty eyes fixed on mine. I realise they are the eyes of Deborah Gold. Then one at a time the figures become LA, until her dead body is repeated at every station around the carousel, each one looking at me with the same indecipherable expression. Now the carousel lights suddenly go dark, followed by the lights of the fairground surrounding it, a spreading radius of darkness that reaches the horizon and continues into the sky, extinguishing planets, stars, galaxies. I know now that everyone I love, everything I care about, is gone for ever – know it but will not accept it. I am desperate to get away from here and find the girls and Jana and get them to safety somehow, wherever that is, maybe in some alternate universe, some other spacetime. But I can't move –

Suddenly I woke in a cold sweat, my heart hammering against my ribs as if I'd just run a hard 220. The late weather report was almost over. I clicked the TV off, stood and stripped off my wet shirt as I headed for the shower, the dream fading like the Cheshire cat, leaving behind a smile cruel beyond imagining.

EIGHT

The next day on my way to work I made two stops, the first at a grocery store for a chunk of salt pork and a meat thermometer, the other at a builders' supply where, after examining the faces of the different models, I bought a California framing hammer along with a half-dozen bridge spikes and a six-foot white pine four-by-four. I drove out to the murder site, tossed the timber on the ground, unwrapped the salt pork, laid it flat on the wood and used the hammer to drive a couple of the spikes through the pork and into the wood. It took at least a dozen hard swings for each spike, and hard swings at a nail generally guarantee a high proportion of glancing blows and complete misses, which is what I got now. But the chequering on the face of the hammer tended to bite into the metal and keep the force of the strike confined to the nail head. Looking closely, I saw an impressed waffle pattern that to my inexpert eye seemed identical to what I'd seen on the heads of the spikes pinioning Gold's wrists.

I walked over to the tree she'd been hung from and looked up at the abraded area where the crossbeam had been affixed to the tree. Standing close to the trunk, I reached up to touch the scraped bark. It was easy enough to reach, but too high for me to conveniently lash a cross-piece to the trunk. I carefully inspected the trunk farther down and eventually found a pair of barely visible horizontal indentations in the bark where something with hard, probably metallic, narrow edges at right angles to each other had been pressed forcefully against it.

I got out the meat thermometer, located the spot where Wayne had said the coin was found, and brushed away the dead leaves and litter to expose the bare soil, which I looked at carefully before pushing the probe a few inches into the ground. I watched until the temperature levelled off at forty-eight degrees, then pulled the thermometer up and repeated the process a foot north of the first spot and at about the same distance from the tree. The earth looked the same here, and after a few seconds the needle settled at the same temperature. I picked up the thermometer, stood looking at the tree a while longer, thinking about the height of the indentations in the trunk, then walked back down the slope to where I'd parked.

I was sitting at my desk studying my right hand as I flexed and clenched it when Wayne stuck his head in the door and said, 'Ready to hear what we got so far?'

I waved him in. He took the chair at the end of the desk and got out a pocket-size black casebook with D.G. and the date the body had been found printed on a square of yellow paper and taped to the front cover. Flipping it open, he started reeling off facts. Or maybe non-facts would be a better way of putting it. He hadn't found any usable fingerprints or organic material other than Dr Gold's on the bridge nails pinning her to the crossbeam and tree. They were ten-inch smooth spikes from GripInc, which he said didn't help either because GripInc was the second-largest manufacturer of nails, screws and various other kinds of fasteners in North America, meaning the nails could have come from just about any hardware outlet or construction supplier in the United States or Canada. The imprints left by the framing hammer used to drive the nails showed a couple of distinctive wear marks that could possibly be matched to the tool itself if it was ever found, but he wouldn't advise betting the doghouse on that outcome. The duct tape was a generic manufactured by KKL-Co and shipped out by the ton to wholesalers all over the country. There were no fingerprints on it, but a match of torn ends was possible if somebody was caught with the roll before using it again. The wood of the crossbeam was untreated and unweathered mill-cut southern longleaf pine, but that's all he knew about it at this point. The rope was general utility quarter-inch twisted sisal imported from Mexico by Jirem Corporation that had been cut with a sharp-bladed instrument such as a utility knife. It was also untraceable.

'What about the body?'

'Not much to tell from what we got before the ME's people – ' he cleared his throat ' – asked us to clear the room and leave the body in their capable hands.' What this amounted to was that nothing foreign was found where Gold's vagina had been, shooting down the outside guess that that was where her tongue might have ended up, but a tightly wadded yellow sticky note with one unevenly torn edge had been found in her right nostril. Somebody had written *glowen* on it with a number two pencil.

'Glowen?' I said. 'What's that?'

'No idea, Lou.'

Under the word, or letter sequence, whichever it was, was a line of numbers that somebody else – judging by the handwriting – had printed on an overlying sheet, leaving indentations that could be read in side-lighting:

4' 68 9172350

'What about this?' I said.

'Same answer,' he said. 'But we're still working on it.'

A balled scrap of brown paper probably torn from a grocery bag had been found at the base of the tree Gold was hung from, and a nose hair along with 'mucosal residue' found on it showed this wad had once been in the other nostril. No fingerprints or writing of any kind were found on it. Wayne's thinking was that the murderers, wanting to make sure Gold wasn't found alive in the morning, had stuffed the paper wads in her nostrils just to be on the safe side.

'But it looks like she woofed one of 'em out,' he said.

I pulled my keyboard into position to get online, but something stopped me. As I looked at the keyboard, the G, O, L and D seemed to grow slightly brighter and clearer while the other characters lost some of their definition. I took a deep breath and shook off the illusion. I typed in 'glowen' and pulled up a hotel, a town and a music festival in Germany, a collage and installation artist, an industrial planner, a college student and a hundred other people, places and things with no connection to the case that I could imagine. There were no Glowens in the yellow- or white-page listings for Traverton or the three-state region, and no towns, lakes, rivers or mountains by that name in my year-old road atlas.

Finally I gave it up, hoping LA had been right about my brain working behind the scenes. I asked Wayne to get a copy of his report to the chief, and signed out to pick up Casey and Jordan at school for the lunch I'd promised them.

NINE

The girls tossed their backpacks into Buford's bed, buckled in beside me and we drove the twelve miles down to Bullfrog Marina for catfish and shrimp at a wrought-iron table on the dock. The day was bright and cool, and there was a faint smell of shady water and faraway woodsmoke on the breeze. A couple of the year-round Canada geese that hung out at the marina glided past us toward open water, pulling long glassy vees behind them over the smooth surface.

I watched as the girls, angling for the best selection of side items, negotiated a sharing arrangement for fried okra, coleslaw, tomato relish and french fries, and for a few seconds felt like the luckiest guy in town. Casey, starting out as an only child, had always been energetic, disorganised and dramatic, noticing and reacting to everything, easy to piss off but just as easy to get forgiveness from. She had Jana's eyes and chin and quick emotion, but her toughness and creative power manifested itself in other ways – in her courage and originality and skill at colouring outside the lines.

Then came Jordan Jillian, who turned out to be a kind of anti-Casey, as she grew older becoming more and more like a little female Mr Spock minus the pointy ears –

logical, focused and even-tempered, with no nonsense in her. If anybody was ever born an engineer, or maybe a physicist, it was Jordan. She understood everything mathematical or mechanical without even trying. Her favourite force of nature was gravity, and she drove Jana and Casey nuts by dropping ping-pong balls, paper clips and buttons on them or the cat from the top loft of the A-frame and timing the fall with her little pink wristwatch. She was also tidy and green-minded – a rain-forest-and-public-radio girl.

'I think I'm gonna have this,' Casey pronounced. 'A virgin strawberry daiquiri.' She absent-mindedly pushed her hair back from her cheek in a way that was so exactly like Jana that it twisted my heart.

Jordan was disgusted. 'Five dollars for a six-ounce slushy,' she said. 'Good thinking.'

For some reason Casey let this go as she watched a grey-bearded man in a tan jumpsuit and faded camouflage boonie hat idling his green johnboat past us through the no-wake zone, a stack of bream tackle propped carelessly in the bow. Casey waved to him and he waved back.

I said, 'How are you guys really doing?'

Casey shrugged, and Jordan said, 'With what?'

'I mean sleeping okay, keeping up with schoolwork, no morale problems, that kind of stuff.'

Jordan looked off across the water, saying, 'Everything's okay.'

Casey selected a corn chip from the basket and bit off a corner. 'That's not really true, Dad,' she said. 'It's no good without you there. A house with only females in it is just so bogus, like a zoo without a gorilla. Everything's organised and quiet, and there's nobody to check out the garage monsters at night – all we can do is hunker down and hope that was just a possum we heard out there . . . '

'When did you hear a possum out there?'

'Night before last,' Casey said.

'How do you know that's what it was?'

'He left his card, Dad – how else?'

Jordan shook her head. I watched Casey.

'Anyway, Mom's always *taking care of us* now, fussing around about our clothes and stuff,' said Casey. 'I mean, it was better when she'd make us do our homework and then chase us off to our rooms so she could sit on your lap.'

I fiddled with my iced tea. 'I think so too, Case,' I said. 'But things are a little complicated.'

A couple of small frown lines appeared between Jordan's eyebrows, and she shook her head again. 'It's hard, but it's pretty simple. Mom is sick of you being a cop but you can't give it up.'

Casey crunched the rest of her chip. 'A gift for stating the obvious,' she said.

'You got that line from the movie we watched last week,' said Jordan. 'A good memory is no substitute for really thinking.'

'Hey, guys,' I said. 'It's not your job to worry about me, or your mom. She and I need to get this worked out, but – '

Casey said, 'Mom's like, you've lost your centre or something, Dad.'

Jordan snorted.

'She told you that?' I said.

'Not me. Grandma. They were on the phone, and I eaves-dropped. Mom was talking like it was some kind of karma deal.'

'There's no such thing,' Jordan said. 'It's a murder deal. Dad can't leave his job when people are doing that kind of stuff. What if all the cops did?'

'Yeah, Dad, what's happening with that?' asked Casey, already on the next page. 'Everybody at school is like, what's going on, y'all? Even the teachers. Like I'd know anything.'

Our plates came, and Casey picked up a shrimp, twisted the tail off and tossed it into the water, watching until a bream drifted up and grabbed it. She popped the shrimp into her mouth while Jordan stirred coleslaw around with her fork. I realised I wasn't hungry either.

Casey swallowed and said, 'Some of the kids think it was a cult. But I heard talk like, nobody'll ever catch whoever did it because they weren't flesh and blood.'

Jordan shook her head contemptuously but said nothing.

'Ghosts?' I said.

Casey shrugged. 'They're saying there were no tracks and no fingerprints or anything. Somebody even said people heard horses and the sound of marching boots out there that night. Is that true?'

'Who said that?'

'That's what I wanted to know, but it was kind of like, "I heard some kid's brother told his cousin about it".'

'I just wish I knew more about cryogenic suspension,' said Jordan without looking up.

'Cry-oh-what?' said Casey.

'Why, Jordan?' I asked.

'Well, one of the kids said his uncle told him Adolf Hitler and Martin Bormann didn't die at the end of the war. He said they had their heads cut off and frozen, and the Nazis have been keeping them in some kind of deep-freeze in Argentina. Now they've got them hooked up to machines and the heads are telling them how to fight the mongrel races and the worldwide Jewish conspiracy.'

'Gross,' said Casey.

Jordan stopped poking at the coleslaw and laid down her fork. 'The thing is, people do get themselves frozen, and there could be stuff going on that we don't know about. That boy who was talking about Hitler and Bormann said his uncle told the whole family to stay on their toes.'

'What do you mean?'

'I guess he meant for them to watch out. Like something bad might happen to them.'

'Why?'

'Because he said the government is getting totally out of control, and there's nothing they won't do any more. He said they burned up all those crazy people in Waco that time and – ' She stopped and frowned down at the coleslaw.

'And what, honey?'

Her eyes came up to meet mine. 'And this time there's gonna be hell to pay.'

TEN

Back at the office, I grabbed a few of the pink message slips that were piling up on my desk and looked at them. They were all call-back requests from reporters in Houston, London, Austin, Tel Aviv and Dallas. I picked up some more and in addition to duplications of the first handful counted three from Canada, one each from Shreveport, Bonn, Mexico City and Little Rock, and another that was hard to read but seemed to be from somebody named Ocaro at a shoppers' weekly in the Azores. By now Dr Gold's means of death was general knowledge, her killing touching some nerve that all the everyday murders missed, but the reporters had almost nothing to work with except the fact that Dr Gold had 'apparently been crucified'.

For local reporters the lack of hard information meant a lot of background coverage, opinion pieces and miscellaneous filler. Some of it was about me, one editor actually calling me a 'tragic figure' and a dogged nemesis of killers and rapists because of what had happened to my partner's wife and daughter six years ago. I tried to generate a mental picture of a dogged nemesis but only got an image of Snoopy in a trench coat.

But what happened to Bo's family – and what Bo and I

did because of it – was no cartoon, and there was no way to deny it had changed me. I still saw flashes of their faces everywhere, in mirrors and windows, or out of the corner of my eye, as if I couldn't completely agree with myself that they were gone for good. Jana said it had changed me, that I was less empathic and harder than the man she married.

'I'll take that at bedtime, baby,' she said. 'But when was the last time I got you to watch a female movie with me? You won't even eat eggs over easy any more.'

And it wasn't only Jana who saw something different in me.

'*That's* what I'm talkin' about,' Mouncey had said after watching through the two-way as I was questioning a high-school sophomore I'd brought in for shooting his stepfather through the heart with a crossbow. 'You gettin' to be some kinda bad po-lice.'

Bo had been one of only two long-term partners I ever worked with, the other being Floyd Zito, a story in himself, who had the kind of unpredictability and atmosphere of danger about him that made him interesting to women and kept bystanders alert. Bo, who'd partnered with me for six and a half years before he died, hadn't had quite that kind of star quality. He'd been tough and lanky, about my height, quick and coordinated enough to play shortstop but looking at first glance more like a beach bum, and he'd come closer than anybody I ever met to being a man without fear. He'd also been too much of a gambler, the kind of guy who ordered raw jalapenos with everything and saved the worm at the bottom of the mescal bottle for dessert.

But the night I got myself shot for the second time I'd come around long enough to hear him praying aloud and with no embarrassment beside my hospital bed: 'Lord, I know I've been out of touch for a while, but this fool here is my partner that I'm nearly used to by now and I need him out there with me because when it comes to having a guy's back he's not that bad, so I humbly beseech that you will see fit to keep his haemoglobin up and his white count down, and if you can do anything about his IQ now while we've got him in the shop, that'd be much appreciated too.'

His wife Lynn, from an old Arkadelphia family, was shy and thoughtful, had a magical touch with potted plants, flowerbeds, or anything else that grew, and loved opera and ballet. She had raised their daughter Kimberly to be a classical guitar player like herself, a thinker and an animal lover, and I enjoyed the serious way Kim talked with me, along with her spur-of-the-moment guitar recitals whenever she had learned a new piece.

Kim was eleven and her mother thirty-three when they died. A sidewalk drug dealer named Jeremy Tidwell carjacked their Kia when they stopped for a light on their way back from an after-birthday pool party some of Kim's friends had thrown for her. Sixteen hours later a family on a picnic found the Kia at Fox Lake, and an hour after that a reserve deputy found their nude bodies. Both had been raped, strangled and left posed in sexual positions.

'Oh Christ, no, Bis, no. No. No,' Bo whispered, his knees buckling.

Hugging him, holding him up, blinded by my own tears and choking on the rocks in my throat, I said, 'Hold on, man, hold on. I've got you. Just hold on.'

Tidwell was caught that afternoon at the back of the old cemetery on Spring Road. There were no civilians at the scene yet, and the uniforms who had run him down double-checked that their collar microphones were off and sent word back mouth-to-ear to ask if Bo and I wanted to come up. Bo should have been on leave by then, and he shouldn't have been carrying his weapon. Everybody knew it was a mistake for him to be here and armed, but it was a mistake everybody in the department was willing to make. Anyway, nobody had been able to look into his eyes and ask for his gun or try to make him go home.

'Suspect's right in there, sir,' a uniform said tightly. 'You want to take him?'

The killer, wearing a sleeveless T-shirt, old jeans out at one knee and ratty sneakers, stood with his back against the wall of the sexton's shed, trying to pull a couple of sprigs of chokecherry over in front of him as if they could protect him. He was thin, with jailhouse swastikas, skulls and dragons up and down his arms, SS lightning bolts on one side of his neck and a patchy beard that had never quite come in. As I registered these things I clearly saw what was going to happen, but too late, because in the same moment I was already hearing Bo's gun clear its holster.

'Give yourself time to think, Bo,' I said. 'That's all I'm asking – just think about where we're goin' here, partner.'

'Hey, man, I give up, okay?' the tattooed doper whined. 'I give up, man. Don't shoot. Jesus Christ, my hands are up, dig?' He cried and snuffled, a worm of snot tracking down his upper lip. 'Don't shoot me, man.'

But my attention was on Bo. The muscles and tendons in his hands stood out like cables under the skin as he gripped his Glock, sweat gathering in beads on his unshaven face. He was a man chiselled out of grey rock, not moving, disconnected from ordinary time and space, his reality now only himself, Tidwell, and the .40 he held dead on the bridge

of Tidwell's nose. The uniforms silently scanned the cemetery, the road and the edge of the woods, looking everywhere except at us, the energy of the moment so monstrous
that it filled the air with the smell of hot metal.

'Bo,' I said. 'Not like this.'

'Yeah, just like this,' Bo said softly, and I saw his will
build and converge and flow down his arms toward his
white-knuckled hands and the trigger of the Glock.

In some ways I knew Bo's reactions better than my own.
I screamed '*YOUR SIX!*', and in the half-second it broke
Bo's concentration and he involuntarily glanced back over
his shoulder, I was on Tidwell. I feinted a quick left and
then threw the best right I had, and he was down, me right
there on top of him, driving the right in again and again,
no skill or timing, only force, seeing Lynn and Kim lying
dead and posed like white dolls in the privet.

'*Like THIS!*' I screamed, now as disconnected from the
rest of the universe as Bo had been, my reality turning the
colour of arterial blood and time itself grinding silently to
a standstill as I slammed my fists again and again and
again into the murderer's face, until the broken bones of
my hands and Tidwell's face protruded in bloody splinters
through the torn skin. From somewhere came the sound of
hopeless sobbing in a voice like the hoarse bellow of some
scaled thing out of another age, but I had no understanding
then that the soul-sick, chest-ripping sound was coming
from my own throat.

Some unmeasurable time later the uniforms entered my
red dream and pulled me off the guy. They told me the next
day that it had taken five of them. Holding me back, they
turned their collar mikes back on. 'It's okay, sir, you got
him,' one of them enunciated. 'He's down, sir,' said another.

99

'You can take it easy now – we'll cuff him and get the meat wagon out here, get the EMTs to check out your injuries.' And, 'The suspect never should have resisted arrest like that, sir.' And, 'Lucky you were able to restrain him before he could injure any more officers.'

And Bo, braced against a black marble headstone, retching himself dry.

Tidwell survived to stand trial, where he was found guilty and condemned to death by lethal injection – a sentence that was never carried out because sixteen months after he cleared through intake at Huntsville another inmate shanked him in the neck over a cigarette.

But to Bo none of it seemed to matter. After the deaths he said less and less and began gradually slowing down, like a man moving underwater. And even though he became more like them every day, he didn't belong to the communion of the dead either. He wouldn't talk to me about it or let me make an appointment for him with Max, his belief in any world outside the darkness he now inhabited apparently gone for ever.

But eventually he started trying to talk a good game. 'I'm okay, man,' he said. 'I think I'm starting to pull out of it.'

It's amazing how being told what you want to hear can shut down your cerebral cortex. And, to be fair, Bo did seem to come back just a little, reconnecting with the world here and there. I noticed it as we sat on the deck behind my house drinking Dos Equis and keeping watch over a smoking brisket. I had just had the cast cut off my hand and wrist and was trying to get used to two-handedness again.

Bo said, 'See you still got Boat-zilla over there – '

'*Bufordine*,' I said.

'Okay, *Bufordine*. You gotta be the only guy in the world who'd name a bass boat – '

'LA named her,' I said.

'Well, that explains it,' he said. 'So, ever take that monster out to the lake any more?' There was a hint of life in his voice that I hadn't heard since before the killings.

'Not as much as Jana and LA say I should. Why?'

'Just thinking. I used to be so hot for it, but I haven't been out in years. Now I doubt I'll ever get the old mojo back.'

'I don't want to hear you say we're getting too old for it, Bo.'

He smiled. 'Too old? Naw, never gonna happen, bud.'

Eventually, he gave me all his gear, the Shimanos, graphite and boron rods and fancy Garcias, sonar rigs and trolling motors, a thousand dollars' worth of crankbaits, spinnerbaits and topwaters, stacking the stuff in a corner of my garage one afternoon after shift, the suspicion of bourbon on his breath just strong enough to make you think of looking at your watch.

'Somebody should get some use out of the stuff,' he said. 'Might as well be you.'

It wasn't until almost a week later that I got it. Leaning back in the recliner, thinking of nothing, I must have drifted back to some Psychology 101 lecture and connected it with other bits and pieces, including the ghostly calendar that floated up before my mind's eye, today's date circled in red. But not just any red – this was the red of still-wet blood. Today was the first anniversary of the murders.

'Holy Jesus!' I yelled, lunging up out of the chair, grabbing for the phone I knew would be useless, jabbing in the numbers for Bo's desk at Three, his apartment, his cell, his sister in Sugar Hill. No answer anywhere.

Clawing at my pocket for the keys, I made it across the lawn to the driveway in my best imitation of a dead run – what Jana called my *homo habilis* hustle – got the 250 started and burned out for Sylvan Memorial Park. I blew through the lights all the way out to the interstate and south on the bypass to 77, fishtailing through the gate at Sylvan, slewing past the great angel standing vigil over Joy Therone, jumping the curbs to cut across the orderly islands of dead on my way back to Lynn's and Kim's graves under the old willow oaks near the fence at the eastern edge of the cemetery.

I called in an Officer Needs Assistance when I saw Bo's dark blue Mustang up ahead on the gravel drive, driver's door open. Standing beside his wife's pink granite headstone, dressed in wrinkled white cotton shorts, a yellow golf shirt with food and coffee stains down the front, and unlaced sneakers, Bo waved carelessly to me as I slid to a stop. In his other hand he held his Glock loosely at his side, tapping it against his thigh as he watched me, a cockeyed smile on his face. He hadn't shaved in days, and his fly was open. He was well into the false-clarity stage of drunkenness.

'Wait,' I said as I got out. 'Just wait, Bo.' I was hearing the first sirens in the distance and thinking hard about the distance between Bo and where I stood.

'Hi, Bis,' he said, raising the Glock, jamming the muzzle up under his chin. 'And 'bye.'

The ten feet separating us looked like a light year to me, but our time was up. My knees grated with shards of glass as I charged. Bo knew all about the knees. But never in our years as partners had he seen me motivated like I was at this moment; maybe he'd underestimate me. Maybe he'd smell the cold breath of eternity and slow his trigger-squeeze half a second.

Something about his expression in that microscopic sliver of time told me it did surprise him to see how fast I was coming. But of course I wasn't fast enough. The automatic popped as I slammed into him, a pink spray of blood, brain and bone fragments fanning up and back from the crown of his head, his body collapsing through my arms as I caught hopelessly at his slack dead weight. Trying idiotically to break his fall.

Kneeling beside him, looking down into the now-vacant coolness of his eyes, I tried to see some hint, some microscopic reflection, of Bo and his family finally together again. I wanted them to be – willed them to be – and to know it. I couldn't make myself believe it, but neither would I ever let go of the hope.

I stared at the message slips in my hand for a few more seconds, but I had stopped reading them because I'd stopped caring what was on them. I had no heart for phone calls or reporters. There was nothing I wanted to say to anybody about the murder, the investigation, or anything else. I tossed the pink squares at my desktop, watching a couple of them catch the air and flutter across the desk and onto the floor.

Bertie appeared beside me carrying several sheets of paper and handed them to me, saying, 'Crime scene update. Wayne told me to tell you it's on the website, and maybe this would be a good time for you to say a little prayer for all the trees out there laying down their lives so we can have our hard copies.'

103

'Wayne said all that?'

'I'm sure he would have if I'd kept him on the line.'

I tossed the update sheets on my desk and started picking up stray message slips from the floor, thinking about what people pray for and what kind of answers they think they're getting.

ELEVEN

Zion Hope, lit from inside, looked like a Japanese lantern against the night woods of Elam Road as I pulled up to let Kat out. A dozen vehicles, most of them as old and beat up as mine, were clustered in the parking lot near the side door, a new passenger van sitting in their midst like a slice of wedding cake among corn muffins. I tried and failed to imagine what kind of meeting was going on inside and who might be there and how Kat fit into it all, watching as she slid out of the passenger seat and held the door open.

'G'night, Biscuit.' She blew me a kiss.

'Goodnight.'

When she smiled at me, closed the door and disappeared into Zion Hope, I suddenly knew this was an ending of some kind, one whose shape and significance were hidden from me, and the knowing left the night emptier than I would have imagined possible, the darkness denser and more absolute.

Less than forty-eight hours later, the telephone voice of Father Beane, edged with fear as jagged as torn steel: 'Have you seen Kat today?'

'No, sir,' I said, blood thumping in my ears as his mood

instantly invaded my veins like a nerve gas. 'Isn't she there with y'all?'

'I don't know where she is, Biscuit. No one's seen her since yesterday.'

In my mind I saw Kat again, smiling, blowing me a kiss, but suddenly my mental image of Zion Hope behind her was no longer a Japanese lantern against the soft, starry sky – it was a demonic face leering at me from a darkness beyond darkness, blinding, hellish flames roaring behind the eyes and grinning mouth. I wanted to ask Father Beane what he was going to do, and what I could do to help, but my lips wouldn't move and my tongue had turned to stone.

Later that night and into the next day, believing they were what they pretended to be and were trying to do what they said they were – and wanting desperately to help them find Kat – I talked to Jerry Casteel, the police chief, and Sheriff Morris Fellows at the police station in town, where the air was heavy with the smells of old smoke, gun oil, dirty feet and vomit. They asked me hundreds of questions, but as the hours went by these gradually condensed down to just a few coming over and over again, until it was obvious that they believed I was responsible for Kat being missing.

The sheriff said, 'Did you have sex with her?'

I hung my head, my ears burning. 'Yes, sir.'

They wanted to know how many times, where and when. Then they started asking questions that assumed none of that really happened, at least not the way I was telling it, that Kat had turned me down, that this had hurt my pride and made me angry. Maybe I forced her, even got rougher than I meant to. It was an accident. They could understand that. Hell, any man would. They guaranteed me the pros-ecutor would make allowances –

As I was beginning to think about the electric chair in Huntsville, wondering how many volts it was going to take to kill me and whether it was actually true that electrocution is a quick and painless way to go, Dusty, listening from his own chair against the wall, said, 'Hold it.'

The chief lifted a hand to silence him and started to say something else, but Dusty said, 'I told you to hold it and I meant it, Jerry.' He stood up. 'You too, Mo. Biscuit, don't you say another word.'

Dusty hired Lucas Fine, the richest lawyer in Rains County, a tall, thin, preacherly man with soft, blueveined hands and big white hair who never asked if I had hurt Kat or knew what had happened to her. Instead he talked about evidentiary rules, admissibility, arraignment, going to trial, the appeals process, the Supreme Court, until I finally understood that he believed as much as Jerry Casteel and Morris Fellows did that Kat was dead and I had killed her.

'Just relax, son,' he said. 'This is a long way from over.'

'But I didn't do anything.'

'That's right.'

It was hard enough to be wrongly blamed for doing something terrible, but it was a hundred times worse to be blamed for doing it to somebody you loved, and Kat's disap-pearance – along with what came afterward – wasn't just hard or terrible, it was impossible, and it destroyed some-thing inside me once and for all. I didn't understand exactly what it was, but I never went to church again except for occasions like weddings and funerals, instead spending Sunday mornings with Dusty in the training paddocks or

107

out on one of the stock ponds trying to catch enough catfish for supper while Aunt Rachel took off alone in her Volvo for the services at First Methodist in town – not because I necessarily stopped believing in what people called a higher power, but because I didn't trust higher powers any more. I didn't trust any power any more. I lost the ability to take anything on faith, and when human life was at stake I was no longer willing to make allowances for negligence and wrongheadedness on anybody's part, whether it was mine or God's. Or a police chief's.

And I realised for the first time that what was called criminal justice had nothing at all to do with justice, nothing to do with guilt or innocence, and most of all, nothing to do with the truth, but only with which story the lawyers and judges and juries liked best.

Meaning that my innocence didn't matter; they had me dead to rights. My life was finished. I was going to be executed for something I hadn't done. This new understanding uncovered a vein of stubbornness in me that I hadn't known was there, and I made up my mind to kill myself, by stuffing my socks down my throat if I had to, rather than let that happen.

But when the investigators had satisfied themselves about where I was when Kat disappeared they lost interest in me. Lucas Fine shoved everything back in his briefcase and drove away in his red Jaguar. The investigators talked to the whole Bragg football team and all the VISTA volunteers, Reverend Hooks and the members of Zion Hope, and everybody who worked at the Skillet. They kept coming back to Coach Bub, Father Beane and Reverend Hooks, but none of it did any good. For a while they took a special interest in Claude McCool, our defensive end, because he got stubborn and wouldn't say where he'd been during some of the time they were asking about. But that didn't help them either. The strict-looking men from Washington in dark suits and sunglasses, who said very little and went everywhere in pairs, had no better luck. Neither did the dowsers, reporters, photographers, the packs of slobbering bloodhounds or the two different psychic ladies with big straw hats and white gloves who bristled when they ran into each other.

As we watched Sheriff Fellows climb into the FBI helicopter warming up on the lawn beside the fire station, Daz, pale and obviously shaken up, said, 'This here's a sure enough cluster-fuck, ain't it?' The helicopter roared and lifted itself in a curling cloud of dust and grass clippings, tilted forward and thumped away over the trees.

Dozens of Rains County deputies and reserves, along with volunteers from as far as three counties away, fanned out across the countryside on foot, in cars and on motorcycles and horses, scouring the hills, woods and fields for any sign of Kat. A lot of them were riding horses from the Flying S, Dusty turning them over to the searchers only according to how the horse's personality matched up with the rider's skill, even though some of the animals were dressage stock or big-purse racers worth hundreds of thousands of dollars.

The horse I rode was called Mephisto, and I had never liked him because every time he sensed a lapse in my concentration he bucked me off, and he'd never liked me, maybe because no matter how many times he did it I always got back on. He had unbelievable stamina and intelligence, but what I picked him for was his vigilance. He noticed everything – a broken branch, a dead mouse, even the tracks of another horse in an unexpected place.

Every morning Dusty and I, and any of the Flying S hands who could be spared for the day, or for an hour, rode out as soon as there was light enough to see by, straggling back sometimes hours after dark to put up the horses and search each other out to ask if anybody had seen anything. But of course even before they could answer, it was obvious from the set of their shoulders and the bleakness of their eyes that they hadn't.

Little by little, I lost my sanity. Sometimes, far from the house, miles from any other rider, I could hear a strong, clear tenor voice softly singing 'Cielito Lindo' in the darkness. Other times I saw Kat, made not of flesh and blood but of pale light, floating in the air ahead of me, her eyes burning into mine.

Rachel got into the habit of meeting me at the back door when I came in at night to hand me a bread and meat sandwich or something rolled into a tortilla, which I usually took a couple of bites of before falling face-down on my bed, unwashed and without even kicking off my boots. I'd wake up in the same position an hour before dawn, fight off the stiffness and head for the door, Rachel there again with food and a bottle of water, probably knowing I'd drink the water but throw the food to the birds, her eyes filled with pain but steady and sober and registering no awareness of how I must have looked and smelled.

Once she found me trying unsuccessfully to gouge an extra hole in my belt with my pocket knife, my hands shaking and the knife slipping through my fingers. She brought a chocolate bar from the kitchen and made me eat all of it while she watched, waiting a couple of minutes to make sure I wasn't going to throw it up, then cut three neat new holes in the leather to let me cinch the belt tighter.

'There,' she said, her voice breaking as she helped me get it on and buckled. 'Now you're set.'

Kat's mother and father arrived from Shreveport International in a rental car and stayed with us at the farm for a week.

'Katherine writes such nice things about you, James,' Mrs Dreyfus said, dabbing at the corners of her tired eyes with a tissue.

In his business voice Mr Dreyfus said, 'Maybe when we get all this straightened out you can come visit us in Massachusetts, Jim. I know Kat'll want to show you around.'

'Oh dear God,' Mrs Dreyfus cried, pressing the tissue to her mouth.

Eventually deputies started dropping out of the search, riders had to get back to their jobs, Sheriff Fellows said things about the cost of operating the helicopter, and I could feel the world beginning to move on.

The sheriff's last press conference was about how the investigation was ongoing and every lead was being pursued, how justice would not rest until the answers were found, how Rains County was still a good and safe place for families to live and raise their children. Everyone understood that he was pronouncing the search a failure. Kat was gone.

I believed it was over.

TWELVE

Looking up from the forensics report, I saw Danny Ridout, wearing stacked Wranglers, Lucchese python boots and a turquoise Navajo shirt, walk into the conference room, drop into the first empty chair and flip his pocket notebook open. Mouncey came in behind him wearing a white track-suit with a gold accent stripe and silver Nikes, carrying a can of Sprite. She strolled past him to take the chair across the table from me, a half-sprung red wingback that had been knocking around the offices for as long as I could remember. She crossed her long legs and sipped from the can.

I held up a finger for time. According to the forensics update Wayne had just handed me, he hadn't found any identifying marks, foreign materials or 'adulterants', except for fibres from the victim's clothes and the rope, on the crossbeam, but the cut ends of the tree limbs showed two different tool signatures that could be seen in the close-up photographs – what he called macros. The biologist he borrowed from Domtar thought the crossbeam had most likely come from a tree that had grown in central or south central Arkansas, and the ring growth showed it had been cut down between eighteen and twenty-four months ago. I was impressed that she could tell all that from looking at the wood but couldn't think of any way it was likely to help us. Possible DNA samples and a partial cast of somebody's molar were recovered from a piece of bubble gum and two gobs of snuff and saliva found at the scene. Also found within fifty metres of the body were hairs from mice, rats, cats, squirrels, raccoons, opossums, even armadillos – which most people thought had no hair – deer, at least six different dog breeds and freshly shed hairs from three different human heads other than Gold's or any of the bystanders Wayne's crew had taken samples from. Two of the types were medium brown and the third was dark blond, all of them testing positive for various combinations of methamphetamine, opiates and marijuana. No useable footprints were identified. Dozens of cotton, wool and synthetic fibres were recovered, all apparently from clothing, but the fibre types and dyes were too common to be of much use. The whitesuits had also found a pewter button and a musket ball from the mid-nineteenth century, and both halves of a broken chert arrowhead that was probably a lot older.

As I laid the pages down, Mouncey said, 'Do he point out the murderer?'

'My job's the blueprint,' Wayne said. 'Framin' up is on y'all.'

'Perp's white,' offered Mouncey.

'How come?' Ridout asked, his shoulders and arms straining the fabric of his shirt as he reached across the table for the water pitcher.

'Brother chewing on anything, be a Kool,' she replied.

'Nothing tucked between cheek and gum?' said Wayne.

'Nothing he gone spit out, honey.'

113

I said, 'They're about my size, in pretty good shape – at least one's probably a rough carpenter, or was, and at least one's a deer hunter. They could have hauled Dr Gold out there in a crew-cab or four-door pickup, but I'd bet on a van.'

The room went silent. Finally Ridout said, 'Not questioning anybody's investigative skills, least of all yours, boss, but how the shit do we know all that?'

I summarised what I'd learned on my second visit to the crime scene – except for the results of my meat thermometer experiment – ending with the damage to the back of the tree trunk. 'The marks were from the bottom half of a climbing deer stand they used to reach the crosspiece – '

Wayne cleared his throat, his cheeks flaming red.

'We all missed them the first time,' I said. 'They were on the other side of the tree, behind the body – hard to see them at all unless you were already thinking they might be there.'

Wayne sketched a quick nod but stayed red.

'Nobody but a deer hunter owns a stand like that,' I said. 'He's gonna carry it around in a pickup or SUV, or possibly a van. But considering what they're up to, they're gonna throw it in the van if it's not already there. One with no windows on the side – '

'Be your Abduct-O-Matic special,' Mouncey said.

I said, 'What did you find out, Danny?'

He took a sip of water and said, 'First, cyberspace, the final, final frontier; I spent two and a half hours trying every keyword, combination and tag I could think of. Bottom line, I got ass lividity but I can say without fear of contradiction that nobody's ever done anything quite like this murder anywhere in the whole wide world. Unless

114

you want to count dead guys with their dicks stuffed in their mouths.'

'Uh uh,' said Mouncey, shaking her head. 'That god-father bidness a whole different tune.'

Ridout grunted, flipping a couple of pages in his note-book. 'So back to the here and now. The civilians who beat us to the scene were Michael Phillip Haber, 16; Joseph Neil Baines, 15; John Alan Haber, 41, the father of Michael; and Darryl Lewis Pascoe, 46. No dippers, no bubble-gum chewers, DNA pending.'

'Don't sound like no Romans to me,' said Mouncey.

'What would sound Roman to you?' I asked.

She shrugged. 'Thinkin' Alfredo Linguini, maybe Chef Boy-ar-dee.'

Ridout continued, 'Mike and Joey were out kicking around, looking for something to do, saw the body, freaked out and ran home to Mike's house south of the interstate, where they told his father and the next-door neighbour, Pascoe. All four returned to the scene after leaving instruc-tions with Mike's mother to call the police. No serious sheet on any of them other than a DWI Pascoe caught four years ago after a Christmas party outside Longview. No connec-tion I could find between Deborah Gold and any member, friend or neighbour of either family.'

'How them players feel about Jews?' asked Mouncey.

'My thought, about as much as they like lawyers and proctologists; not necessarily crazy about 'em but probably don't run into 'em at cocktail parties that often either. Just my personal take, there's nothing there.'

'I think you're right,' I said. 'Much as I hate it.'

'So,' he said. 'Forgin' ahead. Best guess, the doers ori-ginally approached the scene along the tracks from the north instead of from the road. Looks like three or four good-sized people scrambled up the bank about twenty-five yards back from the scene. Figure it was our guys, and they left their vehicle someplace up the way, out of sight. I'm them, I secure a perimeter and then detail a couple guys off to go grab the doc. They come back by way of the road to get as close to the scene as possible before they have to pull her back out of the vehicle. Three access points within a couple miles along the tracks north of the scene. The next one after that takes you almost halfway to Texarkana. Long way to hoof it along a railroad track in the dark and the rain, so I'm figuring the first or second crossing. It's all crushed rock at the crossings, so there's no tracks. Towsack full of cigarette butts and soda cans, but no useable prints left on anything, DNA pending again. There's plenty of access to the south and the track right-of-way is wooded most of the way down to the trestle, but in that direction the rails are never more than about thirty yards from the road. And that approach puts you pretty much in town except for the last hundred yards or so. Plus why approach from the south and walk past your site, then come back?'

Wayne said, 'Recon?'

'Could be, but I'm thinkin' characters like these would've already done that. And anyway, how much recon can you do at night in the middle of a storm? Assuming no night-vision gear.'

'Which we can't.'

'Can't what?'

'Assume.'

'Right. But it's still better logistics to come in from the north.'

I nodded.

'Nobody I talked to that lives around any of the accesses said they saw or heard anything unusual that night, except a couple of 'em said the thunder sounded a little funny.'

'Funny how?'

'Couldn't put their finger on it,' he said. 'Same hear-no-evil story for the doc's office. There's some houses not too far from there, and other offices in the complex, but nobody heard or saw a thing.'

I said, 'Any witnesses talking about horses or the sound of marching?'

A general turning of heads, all eyes finding me. After a couple of beats Ridout said, 'Not that I heard, but then I clean forgot to ask. Dast I enquire where that question came from?'

Before I could answer him the phone light flashed. 'Medical Examiner's on the line,' said Bertie's voice. Dr Huang Huang, the assistant examiner who'd done the autopsy on Gold.

'Lady have total hysterectomy, belly liposuction, also thighs and butt, different times. Gotta cellulite all over the place, pregnant one time, maybe more, tummy tuck, face and neck tighten up. Gotta five-eighths-inch gold ring through left nipple, looka like maybe fourteen-carat. Semen inna vagina say intercourse five-six hours before die when vagina where belong – no gotta DNA yet. Gotta old green-stick fracture right ulna, no other fracture, little bit of arthritis, not bad. Gotta lotta new scratch and bruise onna face, neck, hands, arms – '

I said, 'How close to the time of death did she get those?'

'Figga one-two hour bottom, maybe ten top.'

'What killed her, exactly?'

'Okay, we gotta dead heat here: lady die from shock and asphyxia, plus she drown – one don't getcha, other two will.'

'Drowned?'

'Buncha blood from her mouth inna stomach and lungs, lady strangle along with she not breathe worth damn anyway. Shock is ice onna cake.'

According to Huang, Dr Gold's septum and mucus membranes showed signs of regular cocaine use. 'Take-a cocaine less than twelve hour before she die,' he said. 'Plenty, but not gonna kill her. Also, we gotta little estrogen replacement here, we gotta little over-counter antihistamine, we gotta lotta THC. Guy who cut out her tongue and pussy, he pretty good, but don't think he surgeon.'

'Why not?'

'Way docta think. Certain places he cut, certain ways. This guy more like hunter.'

'Anything else?'

'Yeah, I say you gotta some kind crazy-ass case here, man.'

I thanked him and hung up, thinking about killers wearing gloves and long-sleeved shirts but probably not hoodies.

Ridout flipped to another page in his notebook, saying, 'We got two tip lines and the Crimestoppers lead sheet running, and so far ninety-eight concerned citizens have had enough civic spirit to pick up a phone and try to help us out. Sad to say – and naturally it comes as a shock to us all – it looks like most of 'em are clinically stupid, bad crazy or rattling our cage for one reason or another. Got one here thinks we ought to take a real close look at the husband, and while we're at it find out if Dr Gold had any enemies. Lady over on Beech suggests questioning local criminals with violent histories, see if they know anything.'

'Good plan,' Mouncey said. 'It pointers like that make us better investigators.'

'Et cetera, et cetera,' said Ridout. 'Other perpetrators: the FBI, the Trilateral Commission, a crew of seven or eight real small but well-conditioned and unusually vicious extraterrestrials, a conspiracy of the Mafia, the CIA and rogue elements of the Catholic Archdiocese of San Antonio, the Daughters of the Confederacy, the niggers, the honkies trying to get the niggers in trouble, the Jews trying to get the goys in trouble, Hell's Angels, the Dog Men of Arcturus, the offensive line coach of the Dallas Cowboys – which is who my money's on – somebody called the Chaplain, that Channel Ten weekend anchor with the maroon hair and – last but definitely not least – you, Lou.'

Imaginary headlines began materialising in my mind: 'POLICE INVOLVEMENT?', 'DEPARTMENTAL COVER-UP?', 'HOW HIGH DOES IT GO?'

'Don't know about the rest of y'all,' Wayne said, 'but that last one woulda clean got by me.'

I tossed the sheets on my desk.

'Least you be handy when we ready to make the collar,' noted Mouncey.

I looked at Ridout. 'You don't talk in your sleep, do you?'

'No, why?'

'Just thinking of your social life lately.'

He stared at me blankly for a few seconds before he got

119

it, then said, 'Don't worry, Lou, these irresistible lips are super-glued when I'm in dreamland.'

'Okay,' I said. 'Anybody have anything else?'

'Define "anything".'

'Define "else".'

'Haemorrhoids count?'

I stood up, stretched, and unclenched my teeth. LA had once told me that denial was the workhorse of ego defences, and I had no reason to doubt it. Ignoring the piles of message slips on my desk, I walked out of the office and across to the break room, got a can of tomato juice from the refrigerator and went to the bulletin board. Culling several dozen old notices, outdated memos and miscellaneous clutter, and dropping all of it into the wastebasket against the wall, I made enough free space to spell out 'glowen' in red, yellow, green and blue thumbtacks. I stood looking at it for a minute without getting any new ideas, rearranged the tacks to represent a drooping upper-case T, got no inspiration from that either, then tried the arm and hammer but ran out of tacks before it looked like anything at all.

The small TV on the counter caught my attention; all morning the news programmes had been running shots of the Tri-State Justice Building and the crime scene, but now there I was on the courthouse sidewalk, trying to answer some question about the investigation. I looked out of shape and discouraged, and I didn't like the way I sounded. I wondered if broadcasting schools actually trained their students in editing footage to make interviewers seem smart and tough and people like me dull and slow. I walked over to turn the set off, visualising plaid flannel shirts and leather work gloves. For a second I thought I caught an odd, unfamiliar smell – a mixture of hemp, tobacco, maybe something a little chemical – and looked around for the source, but the odour was gone so quickly and completely that I ended up writing it off as one of my useless little flashes of the so-called Sight.

THIRTEEN

Back at my desk I pulled up 'Psychologists' and found Dr Porfirio Benavides, with numbers for 'Off.' and 'Ho.' I dialled 'Off.'

'Professional offices,' said a woman's voice as calm and congenial as the one in space movies that announces the ship is going to self-destruct in eighteen seconds. A picture of the receptionist formed in my mind, but I couldn't retrieve her name.

I told her who I was and she promised to have Benny call me back between patients.

While I waited I read through the background information in Deborah Gold's file. In the last ten years she'd given media interviews on what I took to be standard topics like 'Beating the Holiday Blues', 'How to Talk to Your Teenager About Sex' and 'Recovery From Divorce'. She had also taught some undergraduate courses at the university as an adjunct, but not recently, and had had two clinical associates working for her, both with master's degrees, which in a psychology practice, going by what LA had told me, meant they probably did most of the actual work. Before that she'd had a psychologist partner, Mark Pendergrass, for two and a half years. Dr Pendergrass was originally from Houston, divorced with two middle-sized kids, who'd left the partnership this year and was now working in the federal prison system. I had met him but didn't really know much about him.

Gold's first marriage had been to a defence lawyer in San Diego, but after a couple of years of being single she'd married a former patient of hers named Andy Jamison.

I picked up a pencil and put a check mark next to this paragraph and another at the bottom of a yellow sticky note on the same page, which read 'Lawy's call Whore' in Ridout's handwriting. Then, after arguing with myself about it, I left a message on Ridout's phone asking him to run background on all the psychologists in town, with a little extra emphasis on the 'all'. I didn't like the feeling, but I knew going the other way would have been even worse.

I called Johnny at his office. 'Hey, Houdini,' I said. 'I've got a question.'

'Sure, what's up?'

'Exactly what do lawyers mean when they call somebody a whore?'

'What's the context?' he said. 'We talking about another lawyer, a witness, or what?'

'Expert witness, let's say.'

He said, 'If it's not an actual prostitute, or just somebody the lawyer doesn't like, the word means pretty much what it sounds like – an expert who'll deliver any opinion you've got the scratch to pay for.'

'Any difference between that and a hired gun?'

'Not much. I'd generally think of a hired gun as being a little farther up the food chain, not necessarily a liar, just more of a selective observer. Why?'

'Does "whore" sound like Deborah Gold to you?'

'Yeah, that was her rep. What've you got?'

'Nothing yet,' I said.

'You make her for something other than just being a victim?'

'No idea.'

'Yeah,' he said. 'Not hard to picture her on either side of that one. I hear she used to make noises about anti-Semitism – skinheads, latter-day Nazis and what-have-you. Wonder if that could've had anything to do with it?'

'Wish I knew,' I said. 'Anyway, I'll catch you up at the cookout if anything turns up.'

Getting back to the file, I saw that Gold had a son who'd moved to Israel two years ago after finishing a year at the community college, where he majored in History. Apparently he was living in Tel Aviv now, but nobody seemed to know what he was doing there. Her daughter had also left for Kansas City after getting pregnant and marrying a burglar named Dumarcus Shoe. This had caused a falling-out between mother and daughter, and they'd been out of touch for a couple of years. Andy Jamison had two teenage children, a boy and a girl, who lived with their mother and never visited the Jamison-Gold home if they could help it. Gold had a brother who'd drowned during a lake party when he was eighteen, and another who was now a real-estate broker in Austin. Her father had died of a heart attack ten years ago and the mother was in a nursing home in Hot Springs, where Gold saw her once or twice a year. Not a tight-knit family, apparently.

There was nothing wrong with Andy Jamison's alibi of being at the InfoMart in Dallas when his wife was murdered, except that it was an alibi. Other people said he was there, but so far there was nothing solider, like footage from surveillance cameras or cellphones that had a clear shot of him. He was still the victim's spouse, which meant he was at least a person of interest until something ruled him out absolutely. I tried to picture him swinging a framing hammer to drive bridge spikes through his wife's wrists and heels, then walking away and leaving her to die in the freezing rain. I couldn't get it to feel right, but I couldn't make it go away either.

Bertie, her reading glasses threatening to slip off the end of her nose, stuck her head in the door and signalled for me to pick up the phone.

It was Benny, and I told him he was in harness.

'This is happy news,' he said. 'How am I to be earning *mi avena?*'

'I need to talk to you about Deborah Gold.'

'Now, my friend, I am not so happy.'

'It's mainly for background right now, Benny. Whatever you know – personal, professional, gossip – anything could help.'

'If we must, then I will be doing my best.'

He told me he was taking his wife Irena out for dinner and a movie this evening. I recommended Mexican food.

'My personal favourite,' I said.

'Ai!'

They were headed out to Pier 27 for their famous All You Can Eat Catfish Nite.

We agreed to meet at his office the next day and I hung up picturing the two of them, like teenagers in love, their minds free of Roman horsemen and frozen heads, motoring out to the lake in his restored red and white '67 Corvette.

FOURTEEN

Signing the last of the reports Bertie had brought me, I took Cass Ciganeiro's call from the *Gazette*. She was an alpha wolf of a reporter with a reputation to live up to, one who never asked idle questions, and she was on the hunt. In spite of that, though – and not that I necessarily thought it would be a good idea to tell her so – I had always liked her, and trusted her as much as anybody in my job could trust a reporter. She was smart without abusing it, passably honest most of the time, and serious about doing her own job right. In return I think she trusted me as much as a reporter trusts anybody, at least partly because I tried never to stiff her if I could help it. This allowed me to tell her small temporary lies when I needed to, and get away with it about half the time. When she asked what was new, I told her there was next to nothing right now but she'd be the first call I made when I had anything.

She told me what to do to get her up on my monitor and me on hers, which to my surprise worked on the first try. When she was sure I could see her, she flipped me off, her usual fair warning that she was on the clock and we were on the record. She wore dark horn-rimmed glasses and a white, short-sleeved safari shirt, and still had that slightly horsy, sexy-looking, sceptical face that the paper sometimes ran next to her byline. She seemed to have lost a few pounds and done something different with her hair, both of which made her look more scholarly. I adjusted my position to centre my face on the screen.

'You're not getting enough sleep,' she said.

'You could be right,' I said. 'But there's something I need from you.'

'Better be gentle with me, darlin',' she said. 'I ain't in much of a mood.'

'Sure that's what you really want?'

'Ooh, a take-charge guy. That could be even better.'

'First of all, do you have anything on Dr Gold I can use?'

'Not much. She's had a lot of low-grade skirmishes with various folks over the years, other shrinks and what-have-you. Business-wise, I hear she was a great rainmaker. She gave us a few interviews for the Sunday supplement, and you know about the criminal cases she testified in here and there. I think that was thinning out, though. Judges had a tendency not to call her after they had her in their court a time or two.'

'What's the story there?'

'Just flat didn't like her, for one thing, and didn't trust her testimony. A few of 'em hate expert witnesses on principle, mostly the same ones you piss off – so take your pick. What's your angle on the investigation? Revenge? A lynching?'

'It's too early for an angle.'

'Cops always have angles.'

'Not me, at least not yet.'

'I'm writing this down: not a premature angulator. Anything else?'

127

'Yeah, what about hate groups, militias, income tax rebels and people like that who've made news lately? I mean anything you've got that didn't make it into print and we didn't get a call on.'

'You're talking about a lot of mouse clicks. I'll need some time, and you are most definitely gonna have to pay me back for this.'

Bertie held up three fingers as she dropped a fresh stack of reports, memos and requisition forms into the basket at the front of my desk.

'Hi, Bertie,' said Cass.

Bertie glanced at the monitor. 'Hello, Ms Ciganeiro.'

'Take all the time you need,' I said to Cass. 'As long as it's no more than ten minutes.'

'Fuck you.'

I punched line three. It was Casey, at the end of her rope: 'Dad*deee*?'

'Yeah, honey.' I shifted in my chair, reaching for the papers Bertie had delivered and searching for a pen that still had ink in it.

'It's *Mom*,' said Casey with a huge dramatic sigh. 'You know how she gets – '

I pictured those beautiful eyes rolling and thought about what it must feel like to know the universe can't hurt you, and everybody but you is a practising idiot. Which, now that I thought about it, was uncomfortably close to the mirror image of my own way of looking at the world.

'I think so,' I said. I pawed through the top drawer of my desk until I found a Bic. 'What's the problem?'

'I'm absolutely at my wit's *end*, Daddy.' I heard her flounce into the swivel chair by the phone. 'She's just so

128

retro! All I said was, like, I wanted to go to the Hat with Marlie and her brother this Friday, you know, for a Coke or something, and she's like – '

'Call me?'

'Uh huh.'

'To ask if you can go to the Neon Hat.'

'Just with Marlie, Dad. And her brother Jason.'

Marlie was Jana's helper at Kiln-Roi, and Casey's friend, a twenty-something who always had some kind of uproar going. The last I'd heard, she was divorced, and I happened to know she was an occasional customer of a pot dealer the area task force was watching. Jason was a blank, but I imagined jailhouse tattoos, a pony tail, maybe a tight black wife-beater with a white skull on the back.

'Don't they card?' I said.

'Oh, Dad.'

Okay, idiot question. 'Did you say Friday night, hon?'

'Yes, Dad, the day after Thursday.'

'Well, hey, come to think of it that's not such a bad idea. Some of the guys from the office are going to be there too. Maybe I'll tag along.'

'Uh.'

'Hell, the more I think about it the better it sounds. We can all get one of those big tables over there by the dance floor. See and be seen.'

'Well – '

'Friday's karaoke night too, right?'

'Uh, Dad – '

'Here's my end of the deal: you and Danny do "Whiskey River".'

'*Dad* – '

'Can Marlie and Jason sing?'

129

There was a silence. Finally Casey let out a huge breath and said, 'The thing is, though, Dad, I'm not really that sure I should go. Steffie and Sara wanted to have a sleepover here, you know, with pizza and everything. Anyway, Marlie's brother *is* kind of a freeze-frame when you get right down to it.'

'You sure, Case?'

'Um, yeah, I think so. In fact I'm positive. We can rent some movies and stuff.'

'Is Mom okay with that?'

'Yeah, she's good. She was like, we'll get some ice cream and Cokes to go with the pizza.'

'Well, if you're sure. We'll miss you, sweetheart.'

'You too, Dad – here, Mom wants to talk to you.'

Sounds of the phone changing hands.

'Looks like I owe you one, officer,' Jana said when Casey had moved out of earshot.

'Happy to protect and serve.'

Hanging up, I caught sight of Mouncey and Ridout crossing the squad room toward me on their way from the parking garage, Mouncey carrying her usual can of Sprite. They'd gone out to talk to Andy Jamison and were probably here to debrief.

'What have you got?' I asked when they were in range.

'Interview reports on your desk by a quarter to dark,' Ridout said, stabbing a stick of Juicy Fruit into his mouth, 'but I kinda like him for it. Guy with a perm's gotta have a guilty involvement someway or other.'

'Shee-ew,' said Mouncey. 'He nothing but a pussy. Want his woman killed, be hiring a bunch of college boys just like him to do it, wear they loafers without no socks. They fuck it right up and e'body go straight to jail.' She dropped

130

into the chair in front of my desk and popped the top on her soda.

I looked from one to the other. 'This is all you got?' I asked.

'Consensus so hard to find, troubled times like these,' said Mouncey, sipping Sprite.

FIFTEEN

I noticed the intercom light on my phone blinking and punched the button. It was OZ, calling me to his office.

'What've we got on Gold so far?' he said as I took the chair in front of his desk.

I told him what we knew and what we didn't, beginning with the forensics and ending with 'glowen' and the unexplained string of numbers, but leaving out my doodles.

OZ wrote the word – if that's what it was – on his desk blotter with his gold pen, then had me repeat the digits, copied them under the letters, and added the underlinings and other marks as I read them off to him. He looked at the blotter. 'Makes no damn sense to me,' he said.

'Me either,' I said. 'But we're working on it.'

'She had a husband, didn't she? Old harness mule like me, I'd have to take a hard look at the fella just on principle. You giving odds?'

'Not yet, but her dying was a windfall for him. She had control of his computer company. Now it's all his again.'

OZ's eyebrows went up a notch but he didn't speak. He picked up his coffee and took a sip.

'I had Mouncey and Ridout interview him,' I said, 'but

they came down on both sides of the fence, so I'm going to talk to him myself.'

OZ said, 'Any other ideas?'

'Too many,' I said. 'Somebody in the family, another psychologist, some anti-Semitic cult, a former patient, skinheads, survivalists, even the KKK. I'm working on whittling it down.'

With a distracted nod he set his cup down, saying, 'Heard from Dwight Hazen again this morning.'

'What did he want?'

'Talked like he had Karo for spit and never said anything you could really hang your hat on, but if I didn't misunderstand the sumbitch altogether he was saying if we don't get this Gold thing cleared toot-sweet, balls are gonna roll.'

He didn't waste any of our time explaining whose balls we were talking about. Not even Hazen had enough leverage to take OZ on directly, but I was another matter. It wasn't news that politicians, who liked to talk about making arrests, had a lot less to say about making sure you had the right guy.

'The elections are a year off,' I said. 'Could he be thinking that far ahead?'

'When's a politico not countin' votes?'

'So all he wants is somebody tagged for it,' I said pointlessly.

OZ nodded without comment.

I said, 'Did he have anybody in mind?'

'Not that he told me about.'

We thought about this for a minute.

'You suggesting I do it his way, OZ?' I said. 'Round up a fall guy?'

'Nope. You offering?'

133

'No.'

'How long'd you box anyway?'

It took me a second to change gears. 'Couple of years in school, then semi-pro for a while.'

'What division?'

'Light-heavy my last year.'

'Ever lose a fight?'

'One, on a cut. Fourth round, against a guy called Hammerhead Jones. He butted me, but the ref didn't see it.'

'Ever get paid for a fight?'

'Not much.'

'Let me see your hands. Both sides.'

I held my hands out palm up, then turned them over.

'Bunged up pretty good, especially that right one – looks like a sack fulla hickory nuts,' he said. 'How long you in a cast after that graveyard deal – five, six weeks?'

'Yeah, about that, why?'

'Would you've killed that fella?'

I saw again the naked bodies of Kim and her mother on the shore of Fox Lake. Saw Bo's brains spattered against dark green oak leaves a year later.

And saw the truth, like it or not.

'Yeah,' I said. 'Probably so.'

Another nod from OZ. 'One of the boys that pulled you off told me they meant to let you finish it, but a couple of 'em couldn't take it, watchin' what you done to him.'

I didn't respond.

He glanced through the glass panel beside his office door. 'Well, would you look here,' he said, his expression brightening. 'Must be some new rookies comin' in.'

I turned around and saw Casey and Jordan walking our

way across the squad room, plastic visitor IDs dangling from their necks.

'Ain't you ladies supposed to be in school?' OZ said as they came in.

'Hi, Mr Royal,' Casey said, getting her phone out. 'It's teachers' workday.' She took a picture of me and one of OZ, then turned and got a couple of shots of the squad room.

'What's up, guys?' I said.

'I've got something to report,' Casey said, grabbing quick shots of OZ's desktop and the pictures on his wall. 'But I get an A in Social Studies if I give a presentation.' She gave me a too-bright smile. 'You're it.'

'I'm your show-and-tell?'

'Perfect,' she said, snapping another shot of me, then holding the phone in front of my face to catch my response. 'Tell us, Lieutenant, how long does it take to learn to detect information that way?'

Jordan shook her head in disgust, then appealed to me. 'Mom said maybe you'd let me see the booking room.'

Casey's attention had moved on. Taking her line of sight, I saw a crew-cut patrol officer named Rick O'Reilly crossing the squad room carrying a blue folder and returning her smile. Yesterday he'd looked about sixteen to me, but now he was thirty-five if he was a day.

I waved him over. As he joined us, Casey took his picture. 'Yes, sir?' he said.

I introduced him to the girls and said, 'Have you got a few minutes to walk Jordan through the booking area, show her the cameras and fingerprinting stuff?'

'Be happy to,' he said like a gentleman.

When they were gone I asked OZ for a timeout and took

Casey back to my office. 'Yesterday I heard something – '
she said as she settled herself in the chair at the end of
my desk. 'This feels so weird – I heard something I thought
you guys might need to know.'

'I'm listening.'

'It's something my friend Lena told me – '

'The one whose mother owns the candy store?'

'Yeah. But the thing is, she really, really doesn't want to
get in the middle of anything – I mean like having to be a
witness or something – '

I nodded.

'Well, from the back of the store you can sort of see the
rear entrance to Jeff Feigel's office – there's just the one
little angle.' She cleared her throat, obviously uncomfortable
with the loyalty conflict: was she her friend's friend or was
she a Cadet Detective?

'Jeff Feigel, the lawyer?'

'Yeah, that's the one. He's got that silver Audi with the
licence plates that say "BIG LAW".'

'What did Lena see?'

'She says on most weekdays Dr Gold would go in the
back door of Mr Feigel's office and stay a half-hour or so,
then leave.'

'What time of day?'

'Around noon.'

'She notice anything else, like whether Dr Gold was
carrying anything in or out?'

Casey shook her head.

'Thanks, Case,' I said. 'This could really help us. And
I'll do my best to keep Lena out of it, okay?'

'Okay.'

I waited, feeling sure that more was coming.

'It's funny,' she said. 'I always picture you going places in a car or talking to some thug on the sidewalk – it's hard to imagine you working up here every day. But at least I'm used to the smell.'

'What do you mean?'

'It's how your clothes smell when you come home at night – ' Her voice broke. 'When you *came* home at night.' She brushed away tears.

'Hey, Case – ' I said as I stood to go to her.

But she cut me off. 'No, wait,' she said, holding up an index finger to stop me. 'I can do this.' She took a last swipe at her eyes, cleared her throat a couple of times and composed herself. 'Sorry I cried.'

'There's nothing wrong with crying. Your Aunt Lee is right – tears are a solution, not a problem.'

'I know. But Mom says it's unfair for women to control people by crying, especially people they love. She really means men, because it doesn't work on other women. Anyway, she says that's emotional blackmail.' Casey snuffled and swallowed hard. 'She cries all the time about you guys not being together – she just doesn't let you see it.'

I couldn't think of a response worth speaking.

'But that's not what I wanted to say,' Casey went on. 'I wanted to say – ' She found a tissue in her pocket and honked into it. 'I wanted to say, if Jordie or I did anything to cause this, I want to make it right. We both do.'

'What do you think you did?'

'I don't know – maybe being too attached to our friends here, or maybe talking too much about liking school. But that stuff's not important, really it's not. All we want is to be where you and Mom are.'

I considered this in silence for a minute, thinking the

137

last thing Casey needed right now was to feel that her offering was trivial or meaningless. I said, 'Thanks for letting me know about Dr Gold, Case. And don't worry, you didn't do anything to cause problems between your mom and me. However things turn out with us, we'll figure out a way to work around it, okay?'

She got up, took my hand to pull me up from my chair and hugged me, standing for a while with the side of her head resting against my chest. Finally she stood back and said, 'I love the sound of your heart.' She kissed the tip of her finger and touched it to my nose.

When the girls were on their way, and I'd given Patrolman O'Reilly one last hawk-like glare just to be on the safe side, I walked back to OZ's office.

'Cain't tell you who it was,' he said when I was settled in my chair. 'But a old boy I've known a long time put a bug in my ear about a Ranger's gonna be in town here in a day or two, if he's not already here – '

'He won't check in with you?'

'Not on a deal like this,' OZ said. 'I wouldn't either if I was him. He's gonna be lookin' at you mainly, but everybody's on his list until he crosses 'em off, and that don't disinclude me.'

This came as a complete surprise to me, but there was no question what it meant. The Texas Rangers is the oldest law enforcement outfit in North America, and Rangers are not regular cops. They had once patrolled the border country north of the Rio Grande, but now they got called in on things like old unbreakable murder cases, rogue cops and dirty departments.

'Looking at me for what?'

'It's the first time I ever heard any such of a damned

138

thing,' OZ said, 'but word is Hazen had the AG looking for a way to call your hands deadly weapons. Kick it up to a felony.'

No reply occurred to me. I looked down at my hands, wondering if what he was talking about was actually legally possible.

'How about the head doc that got hung up out there – what was your beef with her?'

'No real beef,' I said. 'I threw her out of my office once. Just before you came on board.'

'How come?'

'She basically offered to pass whoever I wanted on the psychologicals and eighty-six anybody I didn't like. That, and give me a blow job.'

'In return for what?'

'The Employee Assistance contract, guaranteed referrals, all the department business, family counselling for officers, that kind of stuff.'

'What'd you tell her?'

'I was pretty busy that day. I think I said something about not letting the doorknob hit her in the ass on her way out.'

'Bertie told me it was you got her contract cut. That the reason why?'

'The main one, but she gave me a bad feeling in general. It wasn't really my call, but Hank down in HR had the same impression of her I did. We went to a rotation with the other psychologists in town right after that.'

OZ took a sip of coffee and said, 'That don't sound like much to me, but I wouldn't be too surprised if the subject comes up again. There may be some noise about you being the wrong guy to investigate her killing, you having history with her and whatnot. We ain't gonna burn that bridge until we come to it, though.'

'You rather have somebody else on the case, Chief?' This was blowing smoke and we both knew it; if OZ had wanted me off the case I'd be off it already. I looked at my hands again, thinking about what he'd said earlier.

'No,' he said. 'You want off it?'

'No.'

'Well, then, how about you go ahead and do what you swore on to do, then come on back in here and have a snort with me?'

SIXTEEN

The last day of Deborah Gold's *shiva* was tailor-made for grilling hotdogs and throwing Frisbees around at the park, but I was on my way to talk to the widower, who'd told Ridout he'd be home because he wasn't going anywhere that he didn't know what he was supposed to say or do.

Winter was still on hold, the sky hard and bright and the air sharp-edged, as I drove up to the Jamison-Gold home near the top of Sterling Road. It was a two-storey in the style I had heard called 'faux Georgian', at least five thousand square feet, built on what looked like a triple lot, with a broad deck overlooking four levels of terraced flowerbeds, a fifty-metre pool with low and high boards, and clumps of weeping willows bending down to perfectly trimmed lawns. A green Hummer and a tan Lexus were parked side by side on the pebbled concrete driveway.

Background information on Andy Jamison was that he was a local, the youngest of three boys, who had given in to pressure from his father and enrolled in Business Administration at UT in Austin but quit in the middle of his junior year after both parents were killed in a plane crash outside Steamboat Springs, Colorado, using the insurance money to start his computer consulting and supply business. He'd been arrested once for cocaine possession when he was still in high school and gotten a DWI on Thanksgiving three years ago. His business was in the black, the house mortgage was current, both vehicles were paid for and he had never taken out life insurance on Dr Gold. There were rumours that he'd run around on both his wives right from the start but had never stuck with any romantic side-interest longer than a year or so. Nobody who was interviewed remembered him expressing any unhappiness with Dr Gold or the marriage, meaning that unless he was the one who killed her he was probably just a basic suburban cheater. The kind you hear on country music radio, whining excuses for themselves and their whisky-drinkin' ways.

My first impression of him when he met me at the door wearing only designer jeans and a gold neckchain was of a guy hitting his forties on the calendar but about twenty in his head. He showed me into what I took to be a professionally decorated den with an oversized fieldstone fireplace centered on the south wall and a bar with indirect lighting and swivel-mounted armchair stools across from it. There were built-in dark oak bookcases on both sides of the fireplace filled with classy old leather-bound volumes that somehow looked as if they hadn't been touched since the decorator put them there.

'The place is a mess,' Jamison said, running a shaky hand through his dark hair. He hadn't shaved lately and he gave off a faint suggestion of underarm odour. I watched him drop the gum he'd been chewing into the ashtray on the coffee table as he waved me toward the most comfortable-looking chair in the room, which was not a mess in any way I could see.

'Can I get you something to drink?' he said distractedly.
'No thanks.'

He found a pack of Salems on the coffee table, shook one out and lit it with a small white butane lighter. He took a hungry drag. 'So is there anything new?' he said. 'I've been kinda out of it.'

'It's still early,' I said. 'But this is getting all the priority there is to give it.'

'What's that mean?'

'Pretty much what it sounds like – everybody who can be spared is working the case one way or another, extra tip lines open, rush orders on lab work, that kind of stuff.'

'Priority over what – a dead whore? Some crack dealer down on Nolthenius?'

I spread my hands. 'Tell you what, Andy, the first guy you run across who doesn't have to answer to anybody, give me a call.'

'Yeah, yeah, I know, you're right. I'm sorry. Forty-eight-hour window, prominent psychologist, gotta look at the husband first, et cetera, et cetera.'

'What I want to do is follow up a little on your interview with Mouncey and Ridout.'

'Follow up how?'

'Do you know of any new people in your wife's life or any unusual involvements she could have had lately, any changes in her routine?'

He looked at me for a few seconds, something passing behind his eyes. 'They asked me that.'

'I need to hear the answer myself.'

'Deb wasn't that much of a socialiser,' he said. 'Not in the usual ways, at least. She had her circle.'

'What kind of circle?'

143

He shook his head. 'I guess that's what you'd call it. Certain people she got together with fairly often.'

'So she was seeing other men?'

He laughed oddly, ran his hands through his hair again. 'Is that the whole question?'

'What do you mean?'

'Deb had pretty catholic tastes in sex.'

'Okay, make it seeing other people.'

'Yeah, she was, and I knew it No big secret – that's what the group was about. That and coke. Jeff Feigel, Ben Frix, Mark Pendergrass, a couple of those girls who work at Ben's clinics. Not trying to get anybody in trouble here. I did a little blow with them once or twice, but I couldn't keep up.'

I wasn't quite sure how much of a surprise Pendergrass was, but I knew a little about the others. Benjamin Frix was a real-estate broker with offices here and in Texarkana. He had the reputation of being a Second Amendment bunker-builder-and-martial-arts kind of guy, tall, olive-skinned, all forehead, full lips and heavy-lidded black eyes, lots of dark hair on the backs of his long arms and hands, rounded shoulders. For the last twenty years he'd been getting himself arrested for everything from assault and battery to urinating on a police cruiser, which may have had something to do with his fourth wife divorcing him a year or so ago.

Feigel was a pudgy plaintiff's lawyer who specialised in going after doctors for what he could get out of their malpractice insurance. He had a reputation as a rotten litigator himself, and other attorneys sometimes called his practice 'Huff, Puff & Settle', but the story was he kept platoons of expert witnesses on retainer who, for enough money, would testify that the dead man committed suicide by stabbing himself in the back with a posthole-digger and then buried himself in a shallow grave. He generally left the local doctors alone, presumably because he couldn't be sure he wasn't going to come down with a ruptured appendix or a broken leg.

'Which was their main jones, would you say?'

'I'm not really sure how you'd pin it down with those guys.'

'Andy, you know it's all going to come out, don't you? No matter what it is. You sure you want to do this all over again when it does, maybe get pulled into it yourself?'

He blew out smoke and watched the plume, then answered as if he hadn't heard me. 'Mainly it was the sex games, I guess,' he said. 'Leather, fur-lined handcuffs, whips, boots, all that bullshit. It didn't appeal to me.'

'Where'd they get together?'

'Here, Ben's place. Deb designed-in a whole separate suite for herself when we built this house. I think Ben did something along the same lines. They were really into it.' He stubbed out the cigarette. 'I'm gonna get a beer. You sure you don't want something?'

'I'm good.'

He walked into the kitchen, where I heard the sound of the refrigerator door opening and closing, followed by the snap of a pop-top. He walked back into the room carrying a can of Bud, took a long swallow and sat down. He said, 'If you don't mind me saying so, I'd figure you for a jock back in the day.' He burped. 'No offence, man, but you're pretty busted up.'

I didn't respond.

'Anyway, you don't seem like the type for this kind of work.'

'What's the type?'

He shrugged. 'Y'know, a hard-ass like in the movies, tossing off lines, slamming guys up against the wall, all that shit. You look like you could be dangerous all right, but you're not really scary, just kind of ready-looking. You're married, right?'

'Yes.'

'I keep wondering if that whole idea isn't all a huge mistake, you know, like cigarettes. Millions of people telling themselves it's okay, but it's killing them. Us.'

'I'm the wrong guy to ask about marriage, Andy.'

He shrugged. 'Am I in trouble here? I mean, I got a hundred people can tell you I was in Dallas.'

'Nobody's a suspect right now,' I said. 'But there's a couple of things I want to know more about, like you being Dr Gold's patient before the two of you hooked up.'

He looked away. 'Yeah. I went in with Jackie when she asked me to. We were having some trouble and she thought counselling would help.'

'Did it?'

'Depends how you define it, I guess. It didn't help the marriage.'

'So you and Jackie saw Gold professionally for a while – how did it get from there to you divorcing Jackie and marrying Gold?'

He took another swallow of beer and looked thoughtfully at the can. 'That's the funny thing – I don't really know. There were a few sessions when Jackie and I went in for separate visits, then after a while Jackie kind of dropped out. Deb said she thought the marriage was over, counselling or no counselling. But I ought to keep coming, it might help me, I still had issues, whatever. I guess it started from there. Next thing I know we're going up to the Arlington or to Shreveport for dinner or down to the casino boats. Then we're talking about moving in together, rings, all that shit. I don't know, it just seemed to evolve its own momentum.'

'What was the age difference between you and Dr Gold?'

'Almost ten years.'

'Was that a problem?'

'Not really, at least not for me. Deb worried about it all the time, though. She was always implying she was younger than she was, getting things nipped and tucked, trying diets. You know how they are.'

'They?'

He looked at me. 'Women.'

'How'd you feel about your wife taking over your company?'

He blinked, and a muscle roped up in his jaw. 'Where's that coming from?'

'You know how people talk.'

'Well, I don't know what the hell anybody expects a guy to feel about getting his nuts cut like that. But it's true, she pretty much had it sewed up. Guess it's general knowledge by now.' He looked down at his tanned toes against the pale mauve carpet, belched quietly.

I said, 'I probably don't have to tell you what a weird story it makes, you signing off on something like that.'

He reddened, drained the Bud, looking at me. 'My signing off never had a hell of a lot to do with what happened between Deb and me, man. The deal with the business was, Deb busted me. Simple as that.'

'Busted you for what?'

147

He grimaced, reached for another cigarette, lit it and dragged down smoke. 'Little bimbo I was seeing. Deb walked right into the Lagniappe down in the parish one night and caught us with the bimbo's hand in my shorts.'

'So where'd it go from there?'

'It was funny, she didn't really blow up like you'd expect. Just went cold and tight. Lasers coming out of her eyes. Started throwing around words like "betrayal" and "violation". Said it was "an elephant in the living room", whatever the fuck that means. Made a mockery of our commitment to each other. So, cut to the shootout, now she didn't have any choice but to keep me in her sights. Take a more active role in the company, be around more, if she was ever going to rebuild her trust in me. Shit. Trust. Next thing I know, every other week here comes Jeff Feigel with more goddamn papers for me to sign, all this shit about laddered distributions and comp packages and no net loss of income, it's the only way I can hold on to anything out of the business, on and on.' He laughed harshly, shook his head again. 'Only night that year I took the girl down there.'

We thought about this in silence for a minute.

Finally I said, 'You're telling me you got set up?'

'What the hell do I know? All I can tell you is it'd sure as hell be Deb's style.'

'Now that she's gone, does control of the company come back to you?'

He crushed out the cigarette half-smoked and stared at it for a beat before looking up at me. 'What do you think?' he said.

Driving back to Tri-State, I got out the little plastic evidence sleeve containing Jamison's gum, made sure the slide lock had sealed, and dropped it back in my shirt pocket. I hardly ever got that lucky, but a match with the sample from the murder scene could save a lot of time and trouble, and you never know.

SEVENTEEN

The next body, burned too badly for immediate identification, was discovered that evening. Leaving Three, I'd made a U-turn outside my office door, taken the stairs to duck a clump of reporters hanging around the elevators, and driven out to the Hungry Gator to pick up a couple of crawfish pizzas for Jana and the girls. Dropping the food off with a two-litre bottle of cola, I got back to Lanshire in time to catch a re-run from an old series about a boy-girl team of FBI agents who seemed to be on the road all the time, never smiled and disagreed about everything – UFOs above all. Tonight they were on the trail of a serial killer who appeared to have super-powers, and conflict was brewing. I sat back in the recliner and crossed my ankles.

As the agents were moodily examining a mangled female corpse on a dark, completely deserted street that looked wet even though it wasn't raining, Mutt appeared from some-where, jumped to the arm of the chair and then to my lap, working himself into the shrimp position just above my knees. He sighed, closed his eyes, and in a couple of minutes was chasing dream-rats, or whatever was scurrying around in his neurons, his whiskers and feet twitching occasionally. But then suddenly he was wide awake, his head coming up sharply as he oriented to the driveway and gave a short trill with a questioning inflection at the end. He seemed to be staring through the wall just to the left of the door.

This was his standard reaction to hearing me fill his food bowl, but right now it could mean only one thing: LA was here.

I went to flip on the outside lights and open the door. She was already out of her white Nissan with a small commuter suitcase in one hand and a dark blue garment bag in the other. She wore jeans and red lacers and an old leather bomber jacket over a cream-coloured cotton sweater. In the entryway she set the suitcase down and laid the bag over it. Putting her hands on my shoulders and rising to her tiptoes to plant a kiss in the middle of my forehead, she said, 'I watched you on TV, Bis. You're a dogged nemesis.'

'Next time I'm going for catted.'

Ignoring the echoing emptiness of the house, LA closed the door behind her, tossed her jacket on the couch, said, 'Pee first, then talk,' and headed for the bathroom. As she walked away I noticed a couple of dust bunnies under the edge of the couch, bent down and grabbed them, then spent a minute or so trying to throw them in the wastebasket. Finally giving up on that, I went into the kitchen to wash them off under the tap.

When LA came back we brought the rest of her things in from the car and stowed them in the front bedroom. Then she sat me down on the couch and took both my hands in hers, gauged their temperature, gave them a visual once-over and looked closely at my eyes. 'Catch your crucifiers yet?'

'Working on it.'

She told me to stick out my tongue, looked at it critically, then placed the fingers of one hand against my left carotid. 'Still not smoking?'

'Nope.'

'How's your BP?' she said.

'One-thirty-five over eighty.'

'When?'

'Last month.'

She nodded, not entirely pleased, then picked Mutt up and set off on her diagnostic tour of the house, which would have to be completed and debriefed before we moved on conversationally. First the kitchen. Mutt hanging contentedly over her arm like a dish towel, she looked into the fridge, frowned, closed the door and checked the cereal cabinet. She glanced back at me. 'You actually eating any of this stuff?'

I said, 'Yes,' with a fairly clear conscience. I did eat cereal sometimes.

'Uh huh.'

She walked through my bedroom and into the adjacent bathroom, inspected the soap and shaving gear and the contents of the medicine cabinet. Emerging from the bathroom, she looked at the bed and what was on the nightstand, which included a squeeze bottle of nose spray, the Nick Cave novel I was halfway through and a little antique glass Coca-Cola ashtray containing a dozen or so coins.

'Still don't need an alarm clock,' she concluded, knowing from a lifetime's experience that if I was going to need help it would be getting to sleep, not waking up. Back in the living room she put Mutt down on the couch, checked to see what channel the TV was on and pushed her finger against my stomach.

'No real depression yet, but your serotonin's down about half a click,' she pronounced. 'Nothing we can't fix.' She brushed her uncontrollable hair back from her face with her hand and gave me a strict look. 'But there hasn't been a woman in here for months.' The unspoken 'you said three weeks' hung in the air like leftover smoke.

I started to protest but stopped myself when I saw the scorn in her expression. 'I usually go to her place,' I said.

She grunted, apparently satisfied for the moment.

'Hungry?' I said.

'No, thirsty.' She sat on the couch beside Mutt, who'd curled up on her jacket and gone back to sleep, and got out her cigarettes and a little gold lighter. She looked at them for a second, then laid them on the coffee table.

I went to the kitchen and reviewed my beverage stores. 'Coke, ginger ale, two-per-cent, apple juice,' I announced, leaving out the vodka, CC, Dos Equis and Shiner. I waited.

'How about some ginger ale over ice?'

Letting my breath out, I poured the ginger ale, grabbed myself a beer and returned to the living room. We sipped our drinks in comfortable silence. Finally I said, 'Things getting any better between you and Rachel these days?'

LA watched the bubbles in her glass, silent for so long that I began thinking about her wordless first weeks at Gram's when we were kids, and then about how little some things change with time. But finally she said, 'History can be a bitch, Bis.'

I took a swallow of beer, thinking about history, and about what a bitch LA's had been. 'Second that,' I said.

She glanced at me, saying, 'Yeah, you and Leah – the same but not the same.'

'Rachel's on a different road now,' I said.

LA shrugged. 'She ever tell you she tried to kill herself?'

'No,' I said. 'When?'

'That summer when I came to live with you and Gram. The year she bottomed out.'

'Before she got in AA I heard her talk a couple of times about being fed up with everything, everybody'd be better off with her dead, that kind of stuff. She said, "If my life was a fish I'd throw the fucker back."'

LA smiled crookedly into her ginger ale. 'Sounds like her, all right.'

'So what happened?'

'She finally told me about it when she was working the steps, doing amends. What she did was talk some guy into snuffing her.'

'Into *killing* her? How the hell do you do that?'

'He was some hardcore SM guy she found, into asphyxiation games or whatever. She more or less seduced him into taking it up a notch, but when the time came he couldn't make himself go through with it.'

'A notch?' I said. 'Jesus, that's a hell of a notch, LA.' There was a silence as I tried to assimilate this. I couldn't imagine Rachel surrendering to anything. I said, 'I'm having a hard time with the idea of her wanting to die.'

'She didn't.'

'Wait a minute, what are you telling me?'

'It was strategic – she made up her mind to get dead,' LA said. 'Not the same thing at all.'

'Then why?'

'It sounds crazy – actually I guess you'd have to say it was – but she found out somehow that with the right contacts a snuff film, a real one, would bring at least a million bucks in Bangkok. The split was going to be fifty-fifty. She auditioned a bunch of possibles until she found somebody she thought she could count on.' LA poked the ice cubes in her drink around for a minute with the tip of her finger, then said, 'He messed her up pretty bad, Bis.'

'How do you mean?'

'You sure you want to hear all this?'

'I'm sure I don't,' I said. 'But now I've got to.'

'There was a lot of localised tissue damage,' LA said. 'But the plan was for her to end up dead in a ditch somewhere, so the guy sees no reason to hold back, and he doesn't. The deal was for him to do anything he wanted to her, for as long as he wanted, but the finale had to be her dying. Then he loses his nerve and can't finish her off. She lost a lot of function, and she couldn't get pregnant after that, among other things.' She studied the rim of the glass for a minute. 'Kind of like me.'

'Lost what function?'

'Like the women in some of those African tribes, for one thing – not enough left of her to come.'

'Ever?'

'Yeah.'

I said nothing, trying not to imagine the scenario, the moment actually seeming to move and rustle with its own vile energy. Eventually I said, 'What happened to the guy?'

'Nothing. As far as she was concerned it was on her. Wouldn't tell the cops who he was. Called it a better deal than a lot of drunks make for themselves. "And I'm still here to whine about it", was how she put it.'

'She couldn't take the money with her,' I said. 'What was it for?'

'Me. For college and the dive training.'

We sat for a while, thinking about it, saying nothing,

my mental representation of Rachel slowly transforming itself like origami, unfolding into new dimensions.

Finally I said, 'It just doesn't sound like the Rachel I know.'

'It wasn't,' said LA. 'The Rachel you know is sober.'

I thought about Rachel and her life before Dusty and the Flying S, and about my office window at Three. About disconnects between realities. I said, 'You use hypnosis with your patients, right?'

'Sure, why?'

'Could somebody be hypnotised or conditioned somehow to set up their own murder?'

'A remote – I mean *really* remote – possibility if the circumstances were just right, say you were able to make somebody believe it was the only way to save their first-born's life or something like that. But in a situation like this I'd have to say probably no.'

'Any odds you can give me?'

'No, but call it ninety-nine to one.'

I picked up the phone, punched Danny Ridout's home number, LA watching curiously.

'Yo,' he said.

'It's me,' I said. I could hear the TV in the background. 'What are you watching?'

'Clint Eastwood. We're at the part where they paint the town red.'

'You buy that?' I said.

'Hell, it's a western, boss. What's not to buy?'

'Good point. But listen, I've been thinking – '

'Uh oh.'

'Right. Anyway, first thing in the morning I want you and M to run a check into whether Gold might have set up her own killing. I'm talking about insurance, depression, some kind of physical illness nobody knew about, stuff like that. And find out if she was seeing any kind of hypnotist.'

'You funnin' me, boss?'

'This is straight. It's an outside shot, but I want to eliminate the possibility. Indulge me.'

'Okay, you got it. But M's gonna think we're nuts.'

'I wouldn't call CNN with that,' I said. 'She thinks all white people are nuts. Most days, how are you gonna argue with her?'

LA set her glass down, got up and walked to the stereo cabinet to look through the disc caddies – rock in the middle, classical on the left, jazz and miscellaneous stuff like Leon Redbone and Bobby McFerrin on the right. 'When are you gonna put all this on a drive?' she asked rhetorically.

I didn't answer.

After flipping through discs for a while she settled on Puccini and slipped it into the slot. 'Un bel di vedremo' swelled to fill the room, and, as always with Puccini, I felt myself gradually relaxing, distancing a little from the day's entanglements.

'This stuff's good for the spirit,' said LA.

I swallowed the last of my Dos Equis. 'Does it really make hens lay more eggs?'

'That was Mozart.'

The phone rang and I picked up as LA turned down the volume.

It was Dispatch. 'Sir, we've got a deceased under suspicious circumstances, and Crime Scene said you'd want to know about it.'

EIGHTEEN

The 'circumstances' turned out to be a residential fire off north Sterling, half a mile or so from the Jamison-Gold place, one single-family dwelling completely involved, and one body so far. No ID yet, but the property belonged to Benjamin Frix.

I listened to the dispatcher's summary: the body found in the den, face-down, soft tissue too degraded for immediate identification. The 911 call had come from neighbours and an Oak Hill pumper had been on the scene inside nine minutes, units from Caddo Parish, the Tawakoni station and the Arkansas side arriving a couple of minutes later. With no hope of saving the house, the primary effort had been to prevent the fire from spreading to other homes.

I hung up and turned to LA, saying, 'Make a run with me?'

Her car was parked behind the Ford, so we took it.

On the way she said, 'That thing you do with your eyes when you're thinking makes you look kind of like a sleepy koala. What's going on in there?'

'Left at the next light,' I said. I told her about Frix, the sex group and the fact that I'd been planning to talk to him.

'He comes up on the radar and less than a day later he's dead, if this is him.'

'Gold and now Frix?' said LA. 'Another murder, you think?'

'Not if we're lucky.'

'This just keeps getting more and more interesting,' she said. 'I need to get out of the office more.'

'Then there's Gold's husband, if you need something to sink your mental fangs into,' I said. I described Jamison's apparent no-problem attitude over his wife's involvement with the group. 'How believable is that?' I asked.

'Any indication he's gay?'

I thought for a moment. 'Hard to say for sure. I'm guessing not.'

'Then I don't know,' she said. 'Passive guy, into his own reindeer games – not impossible.'

I told her the rest of what I knew about Frix, including all the stuff nobody had been able to prove over the years.

She heard me out, then said, 'Somebody whacked him.'

'I hope you're wrong.'

We found room to park the Nissan half a block down on the other side of the street and walked back to the smouldering remains of the house through a blaze of red and blue lights nearly as bright as day.

I held up my shield to get us inside the tape. By now nothing was left of the house but ashes and a couple of vertical structural remnants sticking up like long mummy fingers against a hellish smoke-filled sky. To our left the burned out hulks of a small convertible and a big off-road vehicle of some kind sat almost buried under the blackened debris of the garage roof. I saw the chief walking over to meet us, recognising him from a couple of conferences we'd both been to, a tall silver-haired guy named Earl Morning Singer, his eyes and teeth impossibly white against his soot-blackened face. After I introduced him to LA he said, 'We still got the body *in situ* over here if you want to take a look.'

'How come he's not bagged yet?' I asked.

'Tell you about that in a minute,' he said. 'Walk behind me through here; I'll try to keep y'all as clean as I can.'

The blue-black body lay prone in what looked like a comfortable sleeping position, the head lying on the left forearm, the mouth gaping wide in imitation of a yawn. The features were unrecognisable.

'If it's Ben Frix, I knew him,' I said. 'Did you find any jewellery on the body?'

'Didn't notice anything,' Morning Singer said. 'What are we lookin' for?'

I used the blade of my pocket knife to clear the ashes away from the right hand, exposing a gold signet ring with an embossed horseshoe wrapped around an engraved F.

'This is Frix,' I said. 'Or at least this is his ring. And have them check his collar bones. There was a piece in the paper a couple of years ago about him breaking one of them when he ran his four-wheeler into a tree or something out at the lake.'

Morning Singer bent down for a closer look at the ring, then got out a little notebook and scribbled something in it. 'Now, the reason the body's still here,' he said. 'Look over there at the back of the slab and tell me what you see.'

Under a crisscross of charred wall studs and other debris I could see a black cubical shape about four feet high and what looked like a low steel door still in its frame but leaning back at a forty-five degree angle.

Behind that were the blackened barrels and actions of a dozen or more guns lying at random angles, the stocks burned away and some of the barrels visibly warped by the heat of the fire.

'Some of those were automatic weapons,' Morning Singer said. 'And there was a lot of gold bars and other stuff that made us think we needed to get the feds out here for a look. Which means – '

'Zito,' I said.

'Right.'

'When's he coming?'

'By the dawn's early light, I imagine.'

I took a last look around, seeing nothing else I recognised as meaningful. LA and I shook hands with Morning Singer, thanked him for the walk-through and picked our way back out along the trail we'd come in on.

Back in my living room, I got Dispatch on the phone and told them to find out what kind of vehicles were registered to Frix, then listened as somebody whose voice I didn't know came on with the information. 'Okay, thanks,' I said when she'd finished. 'No, nothing new.'

Ending the call, I turned to LA. 'A Miata and a Land Cruiser,' I said. 'That must have been them in what was left of the garage. Only two spaces in there and nothing parked in the driveway. So it's Frix, and he was probably alone in the house.'

'What are you thinking?'

'Let's leave the whole group thing out of it,' I said. 'And forget the fire for a minute. Unfortunately for us that still leaves the kind of guy who gets murdered – never gonna be citizen of the year, has accomplices and enemies but no friends, doesn't trust anybody, keeps most of his money in

161

gold coins and bullion in a vault at his house. Along with his automatic weapons.'

'*Full* automatic? Real machine guns,' she said, bringing her index fingers into firing position, 'like Dillinger?'

'Pretty much. But he was a collector, not a hunter or competitor, hung out at gun shows and all that. Had an arrest for videotaping women in the restroom at his office with a hidden camera. He never went to trial for it, but I'm sure he was selling the tapes. I don't know what all that adds up to psychologically.'

'Adds up to a very hostile, undeveloped man.'

'What do you call a guy like that technically?'

'Narcissistic, paranoid. What Freud called a phallic character – overly competitive and vain, obsessed with status and power. Sexually immature, voyeuristic. Couldn't stand to be wrong.'

'Sounds like the ex of every divorced woman I know.'

LA shrugged, picking up her glass.

'I don't want this to be connected,' I said.

'Forget it.'

'A burglary that went wrong.'

'Put your money where your mouth is,' LA said.

I looked at her, trying to remember when I'd last won any kind of bet against her, if I ever had. Wayne hadn't thought this was an incidental killing either. Or a smoking accident or bad wiring. He wouldn't have asked Dispatch to call me if he had.

'What are we betting?'

'Dinner at whatchacallit, that place with the good chateaubriand.'

'The Chanticleer.'

'That's it.'

She was one of the few people I knew who still used a chequebook, and she brought hers out now. She wrote *Chanticleer* on the Pay To line, then signed the cheque in the same goofy way she always had, stringing the initials and last name together with no upper-case letters: *larowe.* I had asked her once why she did that but she'd just shrugged – another LA mystery. She tore the cheque out and smacked it down on the coffee table, saying, 'Ante up, cowboy.'

A brief pinprick of light flared somewhere out in the mental wilderness of things I should've realised but hadn't, then vanished without explanation. I got out one of the two debit cards I carried – the one I was pretty sure had two hundred dollars or so behind it as of today – and laid it on the cheque. 'Okay,' I said. 'But coincidences do happen, LA. You can't deny that.' My last desperate shot.

She hmm'd non-committally as she sipped ginger ale. I walked over to boost Puccini back up to therapeutic volume, LA watching me and thinking her own thoughts.

NINETEEN

Benny's offices were off Rockland, painted and carpeted in cooperative, cheery colours, nice ficus and umbrella plants in the corners, big Caribbean watercolours on the walls, comfortable-looking furniture. The magazines were slick, bright and mostly recent.

I heard goings-on in the small kitchen and break room down the hall, and smelled just-brewed coffee. A second later Benny appeared from his office and hustled out to greet me.

'Jim, it is very good to be seeing you!' He was round, kinetic and full of smiles but as always wore a serious suit and snugly knotted tie even at the end of a long day. He seemed to shake off an impulse to go for the *abrazo,* stuck out his hand instead and showed me back to his consulting office where we sat in big tweedy chairs arranged around a teak coffee table away from the desk. Andrea brought in coffee, tea and fixings along with three kinds of cookies.

'Hi, Lieutenant,' she said. 'I'm on my way out. If you need anything else, Dr B can show you where it is.'

Benny and I reassured each other about our health, disapproved of the weather and politicians, and traded generic family news. Then he tutted, saying, 'These terrible deaths that are happening.' He shook his head.

'Did you know Frix?' I asked.

'No, I have never met him personally, *pero que lastima* – he was anyway a human being. My friend, the world is too ugly.'

'Can't argue with that,' I said, picking up a cookie with something that looked like apricot jam in the centre. 'What about Dr Gold?'

'*En realidad*, I am not so sure how well I knew her. We never had the social relationships. Sometimes we consulted.'

'How'd that go?'

Benny looked pained. 'I would not be able to say she was very good with people.'

'Sounds unhandy in this line of work.' I drank some iced tea. 'Are you talking about talent, training or attitude?'

'Probably we should say it is the personality. Dr Gold was intelligent, no question at all, but she was very difficult and critical in her talking of her peers. Always the troubles, many chasings of the patients, many complaints to the boards. Many lawsuits.' He spread his hands. 'Nobody is resting at peace.'

'What do you know about her relationship with Mark Pendergrass?'

Benny rolled his eyes. '*Ai, Dios*, it is a mess. These two, they are having a boxfight over the schedule book, directly in the waiting room! They are screaming, the patients are screaming, the secretaries are screaming – *tal locura!* They sue each other from it!'

'What happened with that?'

'The judge, he throws them out. Each one keeps whoever

they are seeing. He lectures them, they are bad children, he will have no more of this nonsense in his courtroom.'

'She must have had a lot of patients,' I said. 'I'm wondering what they'd say about her.'

He examined his coffee for a while, then leaned forward and set it on the table in front of him. He seemed to be noticing that his clothes were too tight. He took in a deep breath through his nose. Finally he said, 'This is where it is becoming tricky. There is a problem of the confidentiality.'

'Hmm,' I said, then exercised my right to remain silent. I sipped tea and reached for another cookie.

He leaned back in his chair and thoughtfully put the tip of a manicured forefinger to his lips. 'But maybe I am thinking of something.'

I waited.

He picked up his coffee again. 'First, it is to know the general attitude from her ex-patients – '

'How do you know about that?'

'Some of them, they leave her and come to me. They are usually feeling she doesn't listen to them very much, she is taking the telephone calls all the time when they are there.'

'During the sessions?'

He nodded. 'This is what I am hearing.'

'Who is she talking to? And about what?'

'Everybody. Everything. Other patients, insurance companies, lawyers, they are all calling. If somebody cancels an appointment, she is calling the patient to complain, telling them they have to be there, they cannot cancel on her, the insurance will not pay.'

'Sounds like a confidentiality problem right there – '

'She is one who does not worry herself about that, my friend. A few years ago she loses a big lawsuit about it.'

166

A vague memory floated up. 'Was it something about a suicide?'

'It was, yes. A woman comes to her with a sexual problem. She is depressed, confused, doesn't know what to do. Dr Gold, she is always loyal to the money, she is calling the husband, who is rich, saying the woman is dangerous to her children, he should come in and see her, they will make a plan. There is a huge fee and then a divorce, and pretty soon the woman she kills herself. Her family, they sue Dr Gold and get a big settlement.'

'Did the settlement actually hurt Dr Gold financially?'

'Probably. If not then, later. We usually have one million or three million dollars of liability insurance. If the lawyers can make a settlement for less than that, she is off the hook, but then the insurance company is probably cancelling her and it is harder to get the coverage, and it will cost more. If the judgement is for more than the policy, she will have to be paying for the difference.'

'How able was she to do that?'

'She has some money, I believe. She is marrying the computer guy – ' Benny searched the air for a name, pinching his lip.

'Andy Jamison,' I said.

'*Si*, Jamison. And she gets her name on everything. It is a good business, so after that she can go to Israel whenever she likes.'

'What about that?' I said. 'I mean the way she ended up with Jamison. He's a patient, she picks him off when his marriage falls apart – isn't there an ethics problem there, a psychologist getting involved with a patient?'

'It is a maximum no-no,' Benny said, wagging a fore-finger from side to side. 'But maybe there is not a complaint

167

to the board, *no se*, but anyway nothing happens to her. Now I think it would be different, much more difficult to get away with this.'

'What about Jamison's wife? What's her reaction to Dr Gold poaching her husband like that?'

'I do not know from a direct certainty but I am sure she is angry, depressed. Maybe the marriage is already not so good, it is in the crappers anyway, I don't know. But I don't believe it is so.'

'Why not?'

'It is by a patient who knew her. I cannot say who she is. This person is believing the problems they are having are bad ones but not too impossible to solve, Mrs Jamison is willing to have a reconciliation, it is like so many marriages after a few years, usually there can be a resolution.'

'Who is the ex?'

'She is Jackie Milner. A high-school teacher for the twelfth grade, in the Terrebonne.'

'Could she carry enough of a grudge to have Gold killed?'

'*Quien sabe?*'

'Did she get married again?'

'I do not know. I think she cares for her work. I believe her students love her pretty much for being a good teacher. They are bringing her flowers, candy, tickets for the movie. She is being made Educator of the Year.'

'Who loves her, the boys or the girls?'

Benny seemed surprised by the question. He thought for a moment. 'I believe it is mostly the boys, you know, now that I am thinking of it. Why is it that you ask?'

'Just trying to get a picture of her in my head. She and Jamison had kids, didn't they?'

168

'Yes, two. One is a girl, twelve, the other is a boy who is fourteen.'

'How are they doing?'

'They are not seeing their father very much. Dr Gold is not making them feel welcome, I think.'

'What's the boy like?'

'His soul is of the artist. He studies the dance. A very kind boy.' From the way Benny said this I knew the boy was his patient.

'You're saying he's gay?'

'I am not believing it is for me to say.' He shrugged.

'Okay, Benny, I appreciate this,' I said. 'I think it's going to help us a lot.'

'The other thing is a certain patient I am thinking of,' he said. 'I will ask if she would be agreeing to talk with you. I believe her judgement is good to decide this. I am sure she would not suffer harm to do it.'

'Good,' I said. 'Thanks. If she agrees, just let me know when and where. What the hell would we do without you?'

He smiled broadly. 'You flatter me too much. We are after all on the same side together, no? Please let me help in any way that I can.'

'By the way,' I said. 'Does the word "glowen" ring a bell with you?'

'*Como?*'

I wrote it out on a sticky note from his desk and handed it to him.

He studied it a moment. 'I do not like this word,' he said.

'Why? Do you know what it means?'

'No, I do not, but it has a feeling that is not good.'

'What feeling?'

'*Un sentimiento de maldad*,' he said. 'Here.' He placed his hand over his heart.

'Okay, can we go back a little bit? I'm wondering if you know whether Dr Gold had sex with any other patients.'

'Yes, I am hearing that this is so.'

'What about underage patients?'

'*Me temo que es tan*, I am having pains to say.'

'Would that be with males or females?'

He shrugged. '*Quien sabe?*'

When I described the interview to LA later, she asked for details of phrasing, body language, pauses, respiration rate, eye movements. When she'd heard it all she said, 'He's not hiding anything important.'

Jana said, 'He's required to report that stuff about kids, isn't he?'

'Not necessarily, when it's just rumours,' LA said. 'Kind of a fine line there sometimes.'

We'd just finished dinner at Haddad's, prime rib medium-rare and baked potato for me, a smidgen of haddock with steamed carrots and zucchini for LA, a veggie plate with portobellos, broccoli and red potatoes for Jana. The wreckage of all that had been cleared and we were having coffee while we waited for dessert. Casey and Jordan were overnighting with friends.

'What about Jamison's ex?' I asked LA.

'Not a good suspect.' She sipped coffee.

Jana nodded, picking up her tea cup. Female consensus. Case closed.

'Why not?' I asked.

'This wasn't a woman's crime,' said LA.

'Anyway, how does somebody like her put together a

crew to do it?' said Jana. 'Does she troll the Harley shops, KKK meetings, tattoo parlours?'

'Okay, point taken,' I said.

'Second place, she wouldn't have waited this long,' said LA. 'When women kill, it's usually an affair of the heart and it's usually impulsive, or else it's surreptitious stuff like slow poisoning.'

Our crème brulees came, LA eyeing hers suspiciously. Jana pushed her own across to me and asked the waitress for melon. I drifted off into reflection about the murders. I was sure Jana and LA were right. There was nothing about the Gold operation that seemed at all feminine, impulsive, hesitant or haphazard. In fact it had an almost military feel: focused killers who'd acted cold-bloodedly and with coordinated precision, each one knowing exactly what to do at every stage of the mission.

Operation? I thought. *Mission?* Why was I calling it that? I didn't know, but the way they'd planned and pulled it off – being ready with camouflage netting, timber, spikes large enough to nail a human being up to die, carrying a framing hammer around – made them sound to me like blue-collar guys, working stiffs but not necessarily career thugs, vets maybe, enlisted or low-level non-coms, knowing all about tools and timbers, guys who were agile and fit but not kids, working like well-drilled soldiers.

'Or legionnaires,' I said.

'What?' said LA, glancing at me.

'He does that all the time when he's on a case,' said Jana. 'Thinking out loud.'

I realised I hadn't told Jana about the coin. I described it to her.

'Are you kidding me?'

171

'Jay's got a point,' LA said. She took a tiny bite of crème. 'You're definitely dealing with something strange here, Bis.'

'It *is* spooky,' said Jana. 'Like a Sherlock Holmes mystery.' Her order came, half a dozen chilled cantaloupe and honeydew balls in what looked like a margarita glass, and she spooned one into her mouth.

'You didn't let the press have this, did you?' LA asked me.

'You know I didn't.'

She nodded. 'Bet our bad guys wanted them to get it, though,' she said. 'Assuming they actually are twentieth-century crooks instead of real Roman soldiers risen from the sand.'

It was my turn to nod. I took a bite of crème, which was sweet enough to make me wonder how long it had been since my last visit to the dentist. I laid my spoon down.

'Why would they want that?' asked Jana.

'Because unless they dropped the coin there by accident, which is hard to believe, it was a message.'

'So what are they trying to say?' asked Jana. 'And who are they saying it to?'

After a few seconds of silence LA said, 'Gonna have to wait for the third act to find out, huh?'

TWENTY

I cleared the last of the swipe-locks at the federal prison north of town in time to catch Dr Mark Pendergrass just as a slender kid with shaved head, spade-shaped goatee and at least three dozen tattoos was being escorted away in shackles.

Long-term lockups are tireless engines of rage, despair and insanity that unspecifiably foul the air, and nothing about the bright prints and soft carpet in Pendergrass's office or the Donald Duck tie he sported did anything to lighten the impression. He dropped a little bottle of hand sanitiser back into his desk drawer as he stood to shake hands.

He was not quite my height, with a roundish face and light brown hair that tended to fall onto his forehead, giving him the look of a tassel-toed preppie hitting middle age while still in the grip of denial, a little soft in the middle but not really fat, still boylike in some way that was hard to pin down.

He gestured toward a couple of comfortable-looking orange chairs set in conversational proximity across the room and said, 'Can I get you something to drink?'

'No, thanks.'

'You're investigating Dr Gold's death, you said? I'm surprised to see you out doing it yourself.'

'I try to stay busy,' I said. I glanced over his desk, which was a little less cluttered and military-surplus-looking than mine but about the same size. Walking in, I'd seen the usual stuff on it: blotter calendar, pen and pencil cup, stapler, black four-line phone, tape dispenser, picture of the kids, couple of yellow legal tablets, a tear-off memo pad. If it were my desk there'd also be doodles on sticky notes, paper clips bent into various abstract shapes, a mystery key or two and at least one orphan stick-pen cap, maybe a forgotten coffee cup in which early Cambrian evolution was starting over. I didn't believe the tidiness quotient of a man's workspace meant much about his character, but I mentally recorded the observation anyway.

'So how can I help you?' asked Pendergrass.

'I'm still trying to fill in the blanks, Mark – figure out who Dr Gold really was and why anybody'd want to kill her. What can you tell me about her?'

He picked up a pencil that had been lying on his blotter calendar, re-squared the calendar and leaned back in his chair, idly twiddling the pencil. 'Other than on the street or across the supermarket, I think I've seen her twice since we ended our association – dissociated, you might say.' A brief smile at his own little shrink joke. 'Both times were at the monthly psychology meetings.'

'Talk is, the two of you had some personal history.'

He made eye contact briefly, then looked away. 'What can I say? We came to a parting of the ways.'

'Style or substance?'

'Not sure how you'd break it down, but one thing I

wanted was more control over who ended up on my case-load.'

I said, 'She was a cherry-picker.'

He shrugged. 'I guess you'd have to expect it from the senior clinician in any group practice, but yeah, that was my perception.'

'What about the billing?'

'All done jointly. But unless it was a contract situation the patients pretty much paid as they went. Either way, you got a cheque at the end of the month for whoever you saw that month.'

'Any adjustments based on ability to pay? Any kind of sliding scale?'

'No.'

'So when cases were assigned, you ended up with what?'

He tossed the pencil back onto the calendar, saying, 'More no-pays and slow-pays than I wanted, that's for sure. More HOUNDs.'

'Hounds?'

He waved this aside in the air with his hand, saying, 'Nothing, just an old grad school saying – hardest patient for a therapist to get anywhere with: homely, old, unassertive, non-verbal and dumb.'

I looked up at the diplomas and certificates on the wall behind him. BS, Master's, PhD. 'Where'd Dr Gold train?' I asked.

'She didn't have her paper up anywhere that I ever saw, but I understand she went to one of those schools of professional psychology in southern California. Design-your-own-curriculum or whatever, I'm really not sure.'

'Know of any connection between her and Ben Frix?'

'I never heard of one.'

175

'Any idea who she did socialise with?'

'Not really. I'm not even sure how much socialising she actually did. We didn't have a lot of friends in common.'

'How did you hook up with her originally?'

'When I first came to town they put an announcement with a little headshot of me in the paper, the Business Focus column. I was just starting work at the mental health centre in the Louisiana Quarter, and she got in touch and offered a part-time deal at her offices. That eventually evolved into full-time, and I left the MH centre. I was with her about two years before the split.'

'What happened with the appointment book?' I said. 'I've heard stories.'

A muscle jumped in his jaw. 'Yeah, that. I picked it up to copy my appointments before I left, and she tried to grab it. Next thing you know, we're wrestling for it across the receptionist's desk.'

'Who won?'

'I ended up getting the pages copied, but things were pretty hectic there for a few minutes. The way she looked at it, all the patients who came through the door were hers, and if I was going to leave I could find my own. But as far as I was concerned, my patients were mine, therapeutic relationships established, ongoing issues, all that.'

I waited until I was sure nothing else was coming. 'So that was the end of it?'

'No, she got the lawyers involved. Judge Gaither obviously didn't like either of us, but he basically ruled in my favour, and I kept all the patients I was seeing.'

'Why do you say Gaither didn't like you?'

Pendergrass barked out a sour little laugh. 'He a friend of yours?'

'No.'

'The sneering old fart made faces at us, called us ridiculous.'

I said, 'Where did things go from there?'

Pendergrass shrugged. 'I don't know how you'd put it except to say it went from there to her butchered and hung up to die.'

I watched him without speaking for a beat. 'Why do you say butchered?' I asked.

Another silence, Pendergrass glancing at his phone. 'Do I need a lawyer?'

'You're not under arrest.'

'Am I a suspect?'

'I think you know how homicide investigations work, Mark,' I said. 'How about answering my question?'

He studied me for a moment, then said, 'I know a couple of the reporters who were out there. One of them had telephoto gear.'

Trying to remember the angles and distances and wondering what might have been visible through good photo-optics from beyond the yellow tape at the crime scene, I decided to move on. I said, 'How about Dr Gold's marriage – you know anything about how that was going?'

He brushed absently at something on his desk blotter, then looked up. 'Not really,' he said. 'But there's always talk.'

'Talk?'

'That Andy wasn't happy but couldn't get out. Deborah put some money into the business and got Jeff Feigel to do the paperwork, and by the time they were through there was no way for Andy to leave her without losing everything, or maybe ending up on salary or something with her signing his paycheque. No idea how true that was, but it'd be a hell of a tight collar for a guy to wear.'

'Are you saying it could be motive enough for murder?'

'Professional opinion?'

'Any kind of opinion.'

'Why not?'

An old-time homicide detective I once knew had had a tendency to comment on situations like this by saying, 'So much bullshit, so little time,' and I could understand his thinking. I said, 'Mark, I've got information that you were more socially involved with Dr Gold at one time than you're saying.'

He looked down at his hands, jaw muscles tightening again. 'Where'd that come from?' he asked.

'Sources close to the investigation.'

He looked at me, his eyes hardening with calculation. 'How far is this thing going, Jim?' he said. 'I mean, I've got a lot on the table here.'

'So did she,' I said. 'The thing is, being in the middle of a murder investigation is like sleeping with an elephant – you kind of lose your bargaining power. Tell me about the group.'

'Group?'

Another voice from the past came to me. It belonged to Gram, my grandmother, who'd actually been better than a dictionary because she not only knew the meaning and spelling of every word ever invented but could tell you where it came from, what it used to mean, who brought it to America, and about a thousand other things you didn't want to know. In this case her remembered voice was patiently explaining to me the meaning of 'disingenuous'.

'You can do better than that, Mark,' I said. 'You're too

178

smart to think I'd ask if I didn't already know about it. What we're looking for here is a story that fits the facts and doesn't leave you in the crosshairs.'

He inspected his nails as he processed this. Finally he cleared his throat, and his eyes came back to me. 'All right, the group,' he said. 'It's not easy to explain, but I guess it just sort of evolved. Deb had always been an experimenter. Several of us got talking at a hot-tub party one night, everybody's high, getting off on the music, and before long we were trying a group scene once in a while – '

'What kind of music?'

'Not live, if that's what you mean – digital stuff, rock oldies mostly. Why?'

'Idle curiosity,' I lied. 'Was everybody in the group on board for the tub parties and blow?'

'I got the feeling it was a bigger thing for Deb and Ben than it was for the rest of us. For sure it was those two, and especially her, who were always pushing the envelope, "opening ourselves up to new things", moving into weirder and weirder stuff until it all started getting a little too surreal for me. Anyway, I drifted out of it around the time I started getting pissed off at Deb over the office stuff. I don't know where the whole thing went after that.'

'Who all was involved?'

'The only other regular I knew of was Jeff Feigel, but there were always at least half a dozen people there. We had day-trippers sometimes, people just checking out the scene. A lot of times Ben would show up with some girl who worked for him, or even two or three of them, and Deb was always bringing in her practicum students, interns and miscellaneous kids – '

'Kids?'

179

'What? Oh, no – I don't mean *kid* kids. I'm just talking about somebody under twenty-five. Anyway, none of them stuck.'

'What about Andy Jamison?'

'I have no idea what he was thinking, but to me it was obvious this was Deb's thing, not his. He was around quite a bit at first, but less and less as time went by, and eventually he just kind of faded away.'

'Any patients involved?'

'Not as far as I know, but with Deb there's no telling. She married a patient, of course, if that proves anything.'

'Was he ever actually into the scene in a big way?'

'Just the chemical end of it, enough to try a little blow once or twice. The rest of it didn't seem to interest him. He bailed too.'

'Ever hear of anybody in the group involved with drugs at the wholesale level?'

'Dealing? No. Is that your theory – this could be drug related?'

'I'm just asking the question, Mark. I don't know enough yet to have a theory.'

'I was never aware of any drug connection other than for personal use. Do you think Ben Frix's death was connected with Deb's? I mean, are we talking about some kind of vendetta against the group?'

'I don't have any reason to think so,' I said. 'On the other hand there's no evidence the other way either. Do you know of anybody who could be carrying that kind of grudge?'

'Not a clue,' he said. 'What I want to know is whether I should expect to see my name in the media over this?'

'You know how these things go,' I said. 'The longer it takes to clear the case, the more digging the cops and reporters are going to do, and they're not going to prioritise anybody's privacy ahead of that.'

He looked at me as if he thought I might say something to take the edge off this. I didn't.

Finally he shrugged, saying, 'I guess there are worse things that can happen to a guy than bad publicity – you take what you can get.'

I ended the interview on that note and drove back to Three thinking random thoughts about sex, drugs and rock and roll, and wondering where in this puzzle a piece of work like Mark Pendergrass was going to end up fitting.

TWENTY-ONE

It wasn't quite full dark, and the air drifting in through the open sliding doors to my back deck was fresh and just cool enough. The cookout. Total relaxation. I looked around at LA, Johnny, Li, Jonas and Abby, all holding drinks and looking amused, comfortably seated in various chairs and a loveseat in my living room. They seemed to be watching me expectantly.

'How are you feeling?' asked LA.

'Great,' I said truthfully. I wiggled my toes and stretched. I'd never felt better, in fact. All was right with the world, my usually stiffly painful knees like well-lubricated bearings. Same with my right hand. The sensation was weird but beautiful.

Johnny smiled ironically as Li whispered something in his ear. LA raised her ginger ale glass, delicately pinged its rim with her fingernail.

'To arms!' I blurted.

Laughter all around, happy applause.

'Wait.' I held up my hand for silence. 'To arms – '

More laughter. But I wasn't going to let that stop me. 'Just hold on,' I said. 'The Redcoats are coming!' I completed the rhyme, then looked around at everybody in satisfaction. For some reason they were all still laughing.

182

Then it began to come back to me: LA's hypnotic induction, the pain management suggestions, asking if I'd allow a gag for entertainment in return for the therapy. She'd always found me a good subject, a 'somnambulist', who could do all sorts of stunts while in trance.

'Okay, you got me,' I said, shaking my head, reaching to pick up my beer. 'Am I going to embarrass myself any more, or are we done?'

'You know my rule: one party, one parlour trick,' said Dr LA, the ethical prankster.

Remembering the induction took nothing at all away from the effect of the suggestions; I still felt terrific. I could have danced the Nutcracker. The only cloud in my sky was that Jana and the girls weren't here.

Later on the patio, the charcoal settling back down to cooking temperature after a session with the leaf blower to get it started, Jonas and Johnny pumped me about the case. I told them what I could, including a description of the city manager's attempts to pressure OZ.

'Any conclusions?' asked Johnny, sipping Dos Equis, interested but looking tired. A midnight-oil lawyer who worked all his cases hard.

'Just that I may have to look for a new job if I don't get these killings off my calendar pretty soon.'

'Hazen's always had his head up his ass,' observed Jonas.

'Maybe you ought to buck this to somebody else,' said Johnny. 'Get the heat off you.' He took a pack of cigarettes from the pocket of his green Viyella shirt, slid one out and lit it with a Bic lighter. 'Maybe even get out of Dodge for a while.'

I shook my head. 'Probably good advice, but I'd be bullshitting you if I said I was going to take it.'

183

'What's OZ's thinking?'

'He knows what I know,' I said. 'He'll probably do the usual – give me all the rope I need to hang us both, then sit back and see what happens.'

Johnny nodded, took a drink. 'You decide you want to spend a few days out at my place to let things cool down a little, just say the word. I could probably use some hands-on advice about running a farm.' Li came over and asked him some question she'd just thought of about the new well pump they'd had installed last week out at their place. Jonas wandered off toward the bathroom.

When Li was gone Johnny said, 'So, you liking the idea of the survivalists or what?'

'They're as good a bet as anybody,' I said. 'But there's been some buzz from another psychologist about things going on out at the federal prison – gives us a couple of other angles to look at.' I took a sip of my own beer. 'What do you think, Johnny?'

He considered for a few seconds, swirling his beer around a couple of times. 'If you can rule out the usual love-money suspects, yeah, I'd like the paintball and camo guys for it,' he said. 'Aren't they pretty much all anti-Semitic?'

'I just hate thinking about it,' said Abby. 'I hate it that something so ugly could happen here. Did you hear that asshole on NBC talking about the Blight on America's Soul while the camera panned down Border Avenue? Like, "Here it is, folks, the home of the Blight".'

'That's what's so heinous about the whole thing,' said Jonas as he returned to his chair. 'A life is lost, and the smugness of the network anchors ratchets up another notch.'

'I'd rather think about food,' said Li.

'I'll second that,' said Abby. 'Why don't we have an inter-vention or something, see if we can get Jim cooking?'

Beginning to feel hungry myself, I walked into the kitchen to get everything ready, Mutt monitoring every move. As I blended the sauce and assembled the fillets, condiments, utensils and side items – green salads, foil-wrapped ears of corn and thick slices of fresh pineapple and plantain; basically whatever I'd seen at the supermarket that looked good to me – Mutt purred roughly and butted at my leg with his big head. I sliced a small corner off the biggest fillet and dropped it in front of him. He grabbed it, ran to the far end of the counter, shook it viciously to make sure it was dead, then ate it.

After everything was on the grill Johnny showed us a couple of his new card tricks. When Mutt pawed at the palmed diamond queen in Johnny's left hand, Johnny tried to wither him with a fierce glare, but he only licked his chops. LA, kicked back in the chaise longue with crossed legs, sipped ginger ale and took it all in with an absent little smile.

After the card tricks Abby, watching Mutt groom himself, mused, 'In another life I was a mouse.'

'You were a mongoose,' said Jonas. 'And I the hapless cobra.' Locking his beady gaze on her, he began to hiss and sway in his chair. She snorted. Johnny raised a lawyerly eyebrow and took another swig of Dos Equis. Li went to the stereo I'd set up on the potting table against the back wall of the house and found an old collection of dance-friendly numbers from the seventies and eighties about love, loss and yearning. Seeing fire and seeing rain. Seeing sunny days that never end.

Johnny stubbed out his cigarette, stood and held out his

hand to LA, inviting her to dance. I watched them for a minute, even after all these years half-stunned by LA's absolute possession of her physical being. It was one of the things that had made her a world-class diver, and as always conveyed a sense of the warp and woof of the universe somehow ordering itself around her as she moved, even Johnny's limp almost completely lost inside the force field of her grace.

Li, a terrific dancer herself, slid her arm around my waist, said 'You okay for a turn?', and fell smoothly in with me as I swung us across the deck and into the music, the two of us weightless as a couple of shadows, my knees so free of pain that I actually forgot about them. It reminded me of how much I had liked dancing before TCU and the injuries, and of the lessons with LA and her girlfriends back in Oak Cliff a thousand years ago, the summer they'd recognised that it was time for me, a male and therefore in need of remediation, to learn the essential skill of slow dancing. Li wore a slightly flowery, after-the-rain scent that suggested green spaces and clean air.

But then suddenly the flow of time seemed to ripple and double back on itself, and I was dancing with Kat Dreyfus, her image brighter and clearer than anything real could be as she gazed at me across the years. 'Soon,' she said softly.

'Ooh, *Dancing With the Stars*,' Abby said.

Kat faded, to be replaced by a surreally brilliant image of the dead-black crosshairs of a mil-dot sniper reticle against a featureless grey background.

I closed my eyes, taking a deep breath, my heart slamming in my chest. When I opened them again Li was back.

The number ended, Li curtsied and I applauded her,

swallowing hard against the sensation that I'd just ingested a bellyful of angle iron. Trying my best not to look the way I felt, I made my way back to the grill, scooped the browned pineapple and plantain slices onto a plate and turned the fillets for the final moments of cooking, which I knew to be the make-or-break point. Rachel had taught me the skin-on, whole-fillet method with salmon, doing most of the grilling with the skin side down so the lime juice, butter and cilantro could do their work with the flesh, then flipping the fillets for a couple of minutes at the end for a crisp top.

'JB, that aunt of yours must be a fucking *witch*,' said Abby, forking up another bite of fish. 'This is almost as good as away-from-home sex.' She cocked a wicked eye at Jonas. 'I guess.'

Watching Johnny pick at his food, I thought about Jana and the girls, the vision of Kat, and the image of the cross-hairs, then when that took me nowhere I thought about the Gold case, now the Gold-Frix case, telling myself what I usually did at this stage of an investigation: the bad guys could run – they could even hide – but only until we came for them. And Hazen's interest in the case was a loose end. I didn't understand it, and for me that made it unignorable.

And then there was Johnny himself. Having once been grilled for six hours in a really nasty homicide trial, every word potentially a matter of life or death, I knew that being cross-examined by a good lawyer was not an afternoon at the park, and I wondered whether Johnny might end up representing the killers in court.

By now the changer had moved on to some vintage CCR, a bad moon rising, trouble on the way. Listening to it, I thought about how Jana, always a fan of swamp rock, and Fogerty in particular, talked about him as a fellow artist.

187

Suddenly her absence became an impossible weight on my chest, a sensation of suffocation and loss and an almost physical need to talk to her the way I used to, about the case, the girls, our marriage. The National League standings. Corn futures. Anything. Any damn thing at all.

I tried to reorganise my thoughts, recognising this for what it was – the kind of useless raking over of the past that had never led me anywhere except the twilight country of depression. I needed to stop worrying about getting hammered in court by my oldest friend and focus on what this case might do to the people who mattered most to me.

TWENTY-TWO

The ex-patient of Gold's Benny put me in touch with was Heather Obenowsky. I collected LA after her mid-morning AA meeting and we drove up to meet Heather at Muggs for cappuccinos. She was sixteen or so, dressed in tight black pants, high-heeled boots and denim jacket over a red T-shirt – a sharp-faced but pretty girl with dark spiky hair, untrusting brown eyes and seven silver rings in her ears, right eyebrow and left nostril. I didn't doubt there were others I couldn't see. She'd agreed to the meeting on the condition that I wouldn't ask any questions about why she was in therapy.

When I introduced LA, and the two made eye contact, I felt something happen between them that at the time I didn't understand, though I realised we'd just crossed an invisible line of some kind.

After asking what we wanted, LA walked over to the counter, eventually returning with three cups.

I said, 'Thanks for talking to us, Heather.'

'Dr B told me you're a good man,' she said. 'Coming from him, I think that means you tell the truth and you don't let people down. And he said I could trust Dr Rowe too.'

LA said, 'Please call me Lee.'

I said nothing.

Heather gave LA a brief nod, held her eyes for an extra microsecond, and returned her attention to me. 'So I guess that'd make you kind of like, what, king of the good guys?' she said.

Checking to see which cup was mine, I picked it up and took a cautious sip to gauge its temperature. 'Not yet,' I said. 'But I'm workin' on it.'

'How'd you get your nose busted?'

'Not ducking in time.'

Almost but not quite smiling, she seemed to be thinking me over. I waited.

'I'm trying to figure out how you do that,' she said.

'Do what?'

'Look like you're' – she searched for the words – 'I don't know, I guess like you're seeing and hearing more than other people. Or at least like you could if you wanted to. Kind of like my cat.'

LA said, 'What's your cat's name?' She took a sip of her latte.

'Smackie. She's a girl, a calico.' Heather glanced around the room, saying, 'All calicos are girls.'

'So I've heard.'

'Do you have a cat?' Heather asked me.

'In a way,' I said. 'Mostly I think he's got me.'

'What's his name?'

'Mutt,' I said.

'How'd he get a name like that?'

'That's what the kid next door called him.'

'Doesn't that confuse him?'

'With him, I'm not sure how you'd tell,' I said.

The half-smile came back. 'You seem pretty tough for, uh – '

190

'For an old guy?'

An actual smile this time. 'I was gonna say for a guy who has good manners,' she said. 'You're not even that much older than me, really – just kind of in the middle there somewhere, like Dr B.' The smile went away. She looked down. 'Sorry. I try not to say stuff like that, but – '

'Like what?'

'Just dumb shit,' she said. 'Talking like a kid.'

'That's not how it sounded to me,' LA said.

'Do you have any? Kids, I mean.'

'No,' LA said, then nodded toward me, 'But he does.'

'Two daughters,' I said, drinking cappuccino, this time feeling the sugar and caffeine parachute all the way down, hit bottom and begin deploying among my red cells.

I saw a brief shadow pass in Heather's eyes. She swallowed with a small dry sound, and after a minute said, 'How old are they?'

'One's close to your age, the other's a little younger.'

Now her expression took on a kind of dullness, something about the look catching at me.

'What are their names?'

'Casey and Jordan,' I said, experiencing a strong sense of déjà vu but having no idea where it was coming from.

She looked away, gazing through the window toward the mall, took in a deep breath and let it out. Her eyes –

I glanced at LA's expression as she watched Heather, and it came to me. It wasn't in the eyes, it was deeper than that. I'd grown up seeing it in LA, and still sometimes caught glimpses of it in Rachel, a thin fracture line running through the centre of the soul. No matter how far these women moved beyond the past, no matter how strong they became, the discontinuity would always be there, and none

191

of them would ever be completely present in my universe. They belonged to a sisterhood whose reality was closed to me.

'Heather,' I said. 'I get it that bad things have happened to you. I'm not going to ask you about that, and I'm not going to pretend to understand what it's like. But please listen to me here, because there's something I need for you to know. I love my daughters very much, but to me they're kids, not women. And there's no way in hell I would ever let them be hurt like you were. Do you understand what I'm saying? There's nothing I wouldn't do to protect them. Nothing at all.'

She watched me for a long moment, then glanced at LA, something gradually relenting in her expression. Finally she nodded. 'What do you want to know about Dr Gold?'

'How long did you see her?'

'About six months. She was on Mom's insurance plan. I didn't want to go, but Mom made me.'

I said, 'What did you think of her at first?'

'I guess I thought she was okay. She talked on the phone a lot when I was there, like with other patients and stuff. She was weird, but then I didn't know how those kind of doctors are supposed to act.'

'Weird how?' asked LA.

'She had these big old bugged-out searchlight eyes that seemed to look right through you, and she asked funny questions, like did Mom's family have money and how big was our house, stuff like that. Then later on it got stranger and stranger until finally I quit going to the appointments.' She swallowed again.

'Can you tell me a little more about that, Heather?'

She fiddled with her cup. 'Uh . . . she wanted to know

192

if I was having sex with anybody and what it was like, whether I, you know, touched myself, how I did it and how it felt. How much I liked it. Did I think about *him* when I did it.' She looked away at nothing that I could see, her eyes spiking invisible fire.

'But you still didn't know if that was how therapists are supposed to talk?'

She nodded once. Looking at LA, she said, 'I mean, it isn't, is it?'

'No,' LA said, her own eyes hard.

Heather nodded again. 'Then she, um, she said I was beautiful, made a lot of comments about my figure and had me show her my breasts.'

'What do you mean?' asked LA.

'She made me take off my shirt and bra. I sat like that for the rest of the session. She just kept looking at my chest.'

'Did she touch you?'

'No. But it was obvious she wanted to. I could tell by her eyes and the way she was breathing.'

Silence for a few beats as we all thought about this.

Then Heather said, 'She kept talking about these friends of hers that she wanted me to meet. She asked me if I'd been introduced to submission, if I understood that pain was only another kind of pleasure, if I knew what bondage was and did I like being restrained, things like that.' Heather glanced down at her breasts and quickly pulled her jacket over them. 'Sorry,' she said.

LA, who never missed anything, somehow made it clear, without saying or doing anything at all, that she'd noticed nothing.

I said, 'Is that when you stopped going?'

Heather cleared her throat. 'Sort of,' she said. 'You know how sometimes when people talk on the phone you can hear the person on the other end real clear? Well, one day she was talking to this official-sounding guy who called a lot – '

'Official-sounding?'

'Yeah, a voice kind of like somebody making a speech or something. Like with microphones in front of him. So she's talking to him and she says, "We may have to consider an increase in your fee. I have expenses, you know, and there's a lot involved. These girls have ideas, they watch TV just like we do, they think about things – it's a constant issue whether they might talk to somebody, say something irresponsible."' The corner of Heather's mouth twisted.

I said, 'And you knew what that meant.'

She looked out the window again. 'Oh, yeah. I knew what it meant. That was when I made up my mind not to go back.'

'Was Dr Pendergrass working there when you were seeing Dr Gold?'

'Uh huh, for a while.'

'Do you think he knew what was going on?' LA said.

'If he had eyes, he did.'

Later I asked for LA's impressions.

After thinking about it for a minute she said, 'In a lot of ways Heather's who I once was. Does that tell you anything?'

Now I took some time to think. Finally I said, 'Yeah, enough.'

TWENTY-THREE

Looking disgusted, Mouncey sat in the chair in front of my desk, sipping Sprite as she finished outlining her alibi findings so far.

' – Feigel in San Antone doin' a deposition,' she said. 'Talked to a couple lawyers down there where he at, look like that one gonna hold up, so he clean for the crucifyin'. Last one, Pendergrass, tole me he at the movies – maybe we call in a alibi professor, tell us what that one worth.'

'Not much help there,' I said. 'But you're right, I think we can at least cross Feigel off our list for Gold. Now all you've got to do is run them all over again for Frix. And we need to find out what they knew about any kids getting involved with the group. Also, let's go ahead and track down Pendergrass's ex, see what she can tell us.'

'You startin' to like him for Gold?' she asked.

I shrugged. 'Pretend we're beagles,' I said. 'No theories – we just follow the trail.'

'Getting to be a smelly trail, Lou.'

I looked at my watch. 'Truest thing I've heard all day,' I said. I stood up and stretched. 'Quitting time for me. I've got a date.'

Up went her eyebrow, the left one, which usually meant a combination of curiosity and disapproval.

'With my wife,' I said.

Down came the eyebrow. 'Time you seeing to that,' she said. 'Good woman like her ain't gone wait for ever.'

Driving north on Border, I visualised the three-storey A-frame – built in the sixties by a truck-stop millionaire and the biggest I'd ever been in – seeing on the low-definition screen of memory the furnishings and wall art, the girls, Jana herself. Even the cat, a semi-runty, white, notch-eared female who'd adopted them and who roamed all night, yowling and fighting like a welterweight tomcat. The girls called her White Trash, and she seemed to like me, but she always sniffed my shoes and cuffs suspiciously whenever I showed up, collecting no-telling-what intelligence about Mutt with that blunt little nose of hers.

Standing on the welcome mat at the front door of the house, fifteen yards or so behind the gallery, I took a deep breath, lifted the brass butterfly knocker and rapped twice. Thirty seconds later Jana opened the door, her glasses on her forehead and her short auburn hair sprigging untidily up like a woodpecker's topknot. She wore red workout pants, orange flipflops and a white pullover studio smock smeared and spattered with several shades of clay and bisque. Behind her the studio end of the house was lit up and in working mode, with several pigs of clay out and the wheel wet. The girls were obviously not here, and I didn't see any sign of White Trash either.

'Jim,' she said. 'Shit, come in.'

'Make up your mind,' I said, stepping in onto the nubbly Berber rug.

'Idiot. You don't have to knock. It made me think you

were another reporter.' As she stepped aside to let me in I caught the spicy scent of the cinnamon sticks she chewed on as she worked. 'Did you catch those horrible people yet?'

'Working on it,' I said.

'I just don't understand who could do such a thing. People are saying it was because she was Jewish – can that be true?'

'Maybe,' I said. 'Nobody knows yet.'

She looked at me closely. 'You look tired,' she said. 'Want anything while I get cleaned up?'

'I'll get it.'

She locked the door behind me and turned off the outside lights. 'Lee Ann took the girls down to spend the night at the farm,' she said. She disappeared into the bedroom, and I walked into the tiled kitchen, which was green with potted herbs, chives and peppers and gleaming with copper cookware hanging from overhead racks. Beside the refrigerator was a cabinet stocked with chips, salted nuts, beef jerky and other health-destroying snacks, and in the freezer a whole shelf stacked with sirloins, T-bones, boudain, kielbasa, bratwurst, hot links and fajita steak, all of it mine.

Opening the fridge door, I reached in past the carrot juice and tofu on the top shelf for a bottle of Corona, uncapped it and walked over to sit on the couch near the Swedish fireplace. There were several magazines on the coffee table: *American Art Review*, *Southwestern Art*, *American Artist*. I leafed through one as I sipped beer, noticing a reproduction of a Frederic Remington I remembered from the Amon Carter in Fort Worth. Farther into the journal I found an ad for a gallery in New York that was showing several Van Goghs from the Arles period. Feeling a twinge in my ear, I flipped ahead to a full-page layout for a one-man show by John Hanna at Whistle Pik in Fredericksburg. To my innocent eye his paintings looked strong, deep and alive.

A couple of pages later I learned the Charles River Plein Air Society was sponsoring a week-long retrospective in Boston. Still lifes, pastorals, seascapes, harbour scenes. I felt a chill and looked around for any source of a draught but saw nothing. I flipped a few more pages and was looking at a painting of a Polynesian girl in a topless outfit with red flowers in her hair when I heard the faint sound of the shower off the master bedroom coming on. Instantly a vision of Jana under the hot spray replaced the island girl. After thinking about it for few seconds, I got up and went back to cover the exposed clay and flip the switches that shut down the studio, then walked into the bedroom, kicking off my shoes and shedding my clothes as I went. In the huge orchid and cream bathroom I saw Jana's naked shape through the frosted glass door of the shower as she washed her hair. She said, 'Come in.'

Jana had designed and built the shower herself out of Italian marble and tiles she'd glazed and fired in the kiln out back, and it was big enough to park a jeep in, with six adjustable shower heads and a seat built into one wall. I stepped into the hot water and steam behind her, took the glycerin soap from her hand and began lathering her neck, shoulders and arms. Then I worked my way down her back, massaging the muscles, then over her breasts and stiffening nipples, under her arms, across her stomach. Having finished her hair, she turned around, put her hands on my shoulders and stood with legs apart, breathing harder as I soaped her gently between her legs, then knelt to lather and wash her thighs and the rest of the way down her legs to her feet and finally her toes.

Then it was my turn. She washed my hair with a shampoo that smelled like cut green grass, taking her time, letting her breasts brush against me as she worked. Then she lathered me all over with the glycerin soap as I had done for her, finally motioning for me to sit on the shower seat, touching the bullet wounds under my left arm and just above and to the right of my navel with her fingertips, taking a lot of time gently washing my knees, lightly tracing the knotted surgical scars with her thumbs and fingers. When she was finished she pushed my shoulders back against the tile, kissed me deeply and moved forward to hold my hips with her thighs as she let herself smoothly down onto my erection. I shifted to accommodate her, but she said, 'Don't move.'

I obeyed. She remained motionless for a minute, holding my face in her hands and looking into my eyes, then began moving her hips slowly. Watching my reactions closely to pace us both, she had to remind me twice more not to move as she patiently, expertly brought us to climax together, pressing her open mouth down on my shoulder and screaming softly against my skin as she came.

Later as I dried her off she sighed deeply and said, 'Nothing like a hot shower at the end of a hard day.'

Neither of us said anything more that night. We slept back to back between unbleached, organically-grown cotton sheets, and I tried to imagine waking up in this bed every morning. I had a toothbrush here, along with everything else needed for an overnight, even two at a stretch, but Jana and I had never made it to the second night. We hadn't been able to stay clear of the issue of my job and the Flying S that long. And I knew better than to think my coming here meant anything in terms of our basic relationship. We'd become what I once heard called 'enemies with benefits'. I wanted to believe 'enemies' was overstating it, but there was no denying that marriages could sometimes go up in smoke while leaving the spouses' sex life standing, like the brick chimney of a burned-down house. And where my job was concerned, I knew nothing had changed in Jana's heart.

'For God's sake, Jim, don't you get it?' she'd screamed at me the last time I was here. 'Nobody likes cops! They're like morticians and laxatives – you don't want anything to do with them if you can help it. This fucking job is going to be the end of you!'

'That's overreaction, Jay.'

'Oh really? You've already been shot twice! Who's zoomin' who here?'

'I'm off the street now.'

'Are you? What's so terrible about running the farm, Jim? About peace and quiet and safety for a change? You've told me a thousand times how much that place meant to you. How can you let Dusty and Ray just sell it and go tripping off to see the world? Watch it broken up into trailer parks and salvage yards while you stay here and let a bunch of sister-fucking frecklebacks blow your brains out in the street?' She angrily swiped at the tears on her face. 'Where does that leave the girls and me? Can we prop that goddamn macho pride in your chair at the table when you're dead and gone?'

'Frecklebacks?'

She'd snatched a tissue from the box beside her, honked into it, and said, 'Don't patronise me, dammit!'

Now, as we worked our way through a breakfast of yogurt, melon balls and chilled guava juice, I said, 'OZ's always said he wants me to replace him when he retires. But Dwight Hazen's making noises about firing me.'

'Firing you?' she said. 'What's *that* about?'

I took a deep breath. 'He's talking about the Gold case and maybe some old stuff, but I'm not really sure what he's thinking.'

She watched my eyes for a moment. 'So what is it, Jim? What in God's name keeps you stuck like this to that tar baby of a job?'

I didn't have an answer for her.

TWENTY-FOUR

On the way downtown from Jana's place I convinced myself that because I had struck a blow for sound nutrition at dawn I was now entitled to do something about my hunger. I stopped for a couple of sausage-and-egg biscuits and coffee at the first drive-thru I saw.

The stuff actually tasted pretty good, prompting me to think I might be on an upswing. I drove south, leaving the residential stretch of the Boulevard behind and cruising through the commercialised lower end, past a couple of insurance agencies, RCS equipment rentals, the big Glen Lawrence & Owen Contractors complex, Hardin Autoglass, an old Texaco station born again as a body shop. I rounded the long curve at West 30th and continued down into old Traverton where the three states came together and the layout and numbering of the streets got crazy, arriving at Tri-State a couple of minutes behind schedule.

As I walked past her desk Bertie handed me a printout detailing the possibly case-related items found in the remains of Benjamin Frix's house: thirty-six gold bars, almost two hundred pounds of gold and silver coins, five Colt and Springfield .45 slabsides with six cases of ball ammo, an X-Frame in .500 Smith and Wesson with a ten-and-a-half-inch barrel – a massive, unwieldy revolver of almost uncontrollable power and recoil – four MAC-10s with several cases of ammunition, half a dozen AK-47s and ammo, an M1 carbine modified for full-automatic fire along with ten thirty-round magazines, sixteen live hand grenades from different military eras, and a Claymore mine. At the bottom of the page was a notation that around a dozen rounds of pistol ammunition had cooked off unnoticed before firefighters arrived, but all the grenades and most of the ammo had been stored either in the insulated safe or in fire-resistant canisters.

The first call I returned from my desk was Cass Ciganeiro's, and as I waited for her to come on I grabbed the notepad from the top drawer, its margins filled with doodles of Ts and hammer-wielding arms.

'Here's some stuff for you,' she said. 'Starting back maybe twenty years ago there've been some protest-type groups operating in this area, holing up in the Ouachitas and Ozarks, stockpiling automatic weapons – ' I took another look at the printout as Cass went on: ' – these characters are usually anti-government, anti-Semitic and white supremacist. Any one of them could be a candidate.'

'Haven't the feds slowed those guys down at all?'

'You mean by shooting women, children and dogs, setting fire to religious loonies, wiretapping everybody and just generally wiping their ass with the Constitution?'

'Well . . . '

'If history is any guide, it probably had the opposite effect,' she said. 'The only thing I can imagine these characters doing is circling the wagons a little tighter, maybe going deeper underground. They're still pretty hooked up to the religious far right.'

'That's another thing I don't get,' I said. 'The holiness connection. Whatever happened to the Prince of Peace?'

'Honey, try to stay focused; around here they throw lions to the Christians. And don't forget that guy Lummus who got the needle in Arkansas a while back. He and his buddies wanted to kill most of the rest of us and overthrow the government, bulldoze the universities, jail the press and make America a whiter and better place. Before he died he said we'd better watch out because justice was coming and it was going to be terrible swift.'

Something in this started a tingle at the base of my brain. I said, 'Like in "His terrible swift sword"?'

'What do I know? At that point he was out of the loop on Xanax or something anyway, so no telling what he had in mind. But I think most of us took it as a generic threat on behalf of his brothers up there in the hills.'

'The Sword of the Lord, something like that, wasn't it?' Another tingle.

'Yeah, that's it exactly. Ties to the Klan, Aryan Nation, Posse Comitatus and some of the clandestine militias. Usually it's just a bunch of redneck dropouts with bad teeth playing war, but they're serious and they're pretty organised. The women and children sometimes tag along, and let me tell you, when you talk to them, they're scarier than the men.'

'Cass, you know I read the paper front to back every day, especially your stuff – '

'Yeah, right.'

'But if there's been anything on these groups since Lummus's execution, I don't remember seeing it.'

'There really hasn't been much,' she said. 'Naturally we get hate mail all the time, every kind you can imagine, like the stuff you guys probably get. A lot of it's just incoherent and scattered, and there's been no connection with any reported crime that I know of.'

'Or we'd have heard from you.'

'Damn better believe it,' she said. 'So what've you got for me? I bent over for you on this, Jim, and I better at least get a reach-around here.'

'Ask away.'

'Any weapons used?'

'None found.'

'I said "used".'

'No comment.'

'Don't jack with me, Bonham,' she said. 'Never forget – I know your nickname.'

'Okay,' I said. 'Gold wasn't shot or stabbed. She was nailed up alive, and there were no immediately lethal wounds on the body. Also, there are no suspects yet.'

'A quote, by God,' she crowed. 'You're confirming death by crucifixion?'

'That's how it looks.'

'Dying of crucifixion – what's that mean exactly?'

'Hanging there the way she did, she couldn't breathe right, so along with going into shock, she asphyxiated.'

'Sounds nasty. They do anything else to her?'

'Yeah, they cut her tongue out while she was still alive.'

'Holy shit. How the hell do you get somebody to open their mouth for that?'

'The only thing I can think of is brute force and something to pry with.'

'Anything else?'

'Not for publication.'

'On background?'

205

I described the mutilation and transposition of organs. There was a silence.

Finally Cass said, 'Jesus Christ, Jim. That's fucking sick.'

'No argument here.'

'How did they grab her?'

'It looks like they overpowered her at her office.'

'What about the husband?'

'There are no suspects.'

'Has he been questioned?'

'Nobody's been questioned. Right now it's interviews.'

'So, off the record, did he have anything to do with it?'

'Who knows?'

'What's your best guess?'

'I don't see him in on it.'

'What about Frix?' she said. 'That a murder yet?'

'Awaiting the autopsy.'

'You see a connection?'

'There's no evidence of one.'

'What's your best guess?'

'Off the record, Ben Frix is a murder, and if I had to bet I'd put my money on there being a connection.'

'I can imagine how happy that makes you.'

'Right.'

'Have you talked to any of Gold's patients?'

'No comment.'

'Will you?'

'Pursuing all avenues.'

'I'm not gonna warn you again, Jim,' she said. 'Next time I get strict.'

'Sorry, best I can do on that one,' I said.

'Did Gold have money problems?'

'Apparently not.'

'Was she into drugs?'

'Still looking into that. There's no known connection to her death, though.'

'That sounds evasive.'

'Sorry again.'

'Some reports said she was raped – that true?'

'No "scientific certainty", but I don't think so.'

'Any semen found?'

'No comment.'

'So you're not ruling out sexual assault as the motive?'

'Don't use those words to me,' I said.

'What, "sexual assault"?'

'"Ruling out".'

'Anything about the cross itself or how she was affixed to it?'

'It was a six-foot four-by-four lashed to a tree. She was nailed to it.'

'What's a four-by-four?'

'Common lumber size, like a couple of two-by-fours stuck together, a little under four inches to the side. Used for posts, heavy framing, bracing.'

'What's the significance of the length?'

'Probably nothing because it's one of the standard lengths they come in. Six, eight, ten feet – like that.'

'Any way of tracing the source?'

'Ninety-nine per cent against.'

'Where does the other one per cent come in?'

'Always the possibility we might catch a weird break.'

'What kind of break are we talking about?'

'If I knew that I wouldn't have to wait for it.'

'How about the nails?'

'Big.'

'Geez, Jim.'

'That's all I've really got on the nails, Cass. They're not going to help us anyway, unless we catch somebody with the rest of the boxful and match them.'

'Why not?'

'Too generic to trace.'

'Had Gold received any threats?'

'Not that I know of.'

'How many perpetrators?'

'Had to be more than one.'

'Then how many?'

'Consensus, more than two, less than five.'

'That works out to three or four.'

'So girls can learn math after all.'

'Exactly how do you know she was alive when she was nailed up?'

'Condition of the body.'

'That's pretty vague.'

'You're right.'

'How long did it take her to die?'

'Conjecture, several hours.'

A silence. Finally Cass said, 'And I thought it couldn't get any worse – '

I said nothing.

Cass said, 'Anything at the scene point you anywhere?'

'Can't comment. Sorry.'

'Tight-ass.'

'I would hope.'

'I didn't say virginal.'

Bertie came back, this time carrying a car key on a ring with a little zodiac-symbol medallion, which she dropped on my desk.

'Just a minute, Cass,' I said. Then to Bertie, 'What's this?'

'Lee Ann's car key. She traded vehicles with you to go shopping for a desk.'

I checked my pocket, finding my key ring with the Ford's key still on it. 'She's driving the truck?' I said. 'How'd she know where to find the spare key?'

Accurately diagnosing this as unworthy of a response, Bertie just gave me a pitying look and walked away.

'Lee's here?' said Cass's telephone voice. 'Is she consulting? I could use some conversation with a chick as smart as me. Can I interview her?'

'You'll have to ask her,' I said. 'But I wouldn't get my hopes up. She handles your kind with the greatest of ease.'

'Yeah, that's what makes her fun. What else have you got?'

'Nothing right now,' I said. 'I'll have more for you, at least off the record, when all the primary interviews are in. There are two tip lines open on this, and there's a mountain of stuff from Crimestoppers, lead sheets, informants and so on. Anybody's guess how good any of it'll be, but you'll be the first one I call, Cass.'

She settled for that, though not gracefully.

'Say hi to Lee for me,' she said. 'And tell her she gives me a quote or I'm unfriending the shit out of her.'

TWENTY-FIVE

I cleared out most of my day's accumulation of dead trees by scribbling my name eleven times, returned a call from a high-school counsellor who wanted me to speak to a couple of classes – happily bucking it to Ridout – then noticed what I'd drawn on the legal pad in front of me while talking with Cass. There were several more versions of the arm and hammer logo, but it was obvious they were changing, the hammers looking less and less like hammers and more like something else, though I didn't know what. The heads had become narrower, closer to the fist, the tops of the handle shafts now looking pointy and projecting through and past the heads. I felt another brain-tingle, but couldn't connect it to anything. I balled up the page of doodles and tossed it at the basket. Off the wall and in. I dialled LA, and she picked up on the fifth ring.

'Your truck rides like a log wagon,' she said.

'Any luck?' I said.

'Not yet,' she said. 'But I ran into Zito and Hotfoot.'

'Hotfoot?'

'His sniffer dog.'

'I thought his dog's name was Diggity.'

'Diggity's retired,' she said. 'Bad hip.'

'Where'd you find them?'

'At a fire – I heard him on your scanner and drove over there. He showed me around.'

'That's Zito for you,' I said. 'Did he show you his trick?'

'What trick?'

'He can juggle three quarters with his one hand. He shows it to all the girls.' Zito was now rich because of the faulty detonator that had cost him his right hand and forearm, but in my opinion it hadn't improved his character.

'Is that the only trick he knows?' she enquired unmercifully.

'Unfortunately, no,' I said. 'Gotta watch him – he's always on the prowl.'

'Does he give good prowl?'

'Don't even ask.'

'I bet he does. I might prowl with him a little just to see.'

'That's disgusting,' I said. 'Anyway, we've already got a one-armed man in the family. Another one would be way too Freudian.'

'Don't get ahead of me, Bis. Right now we're just talking prowl.'

The next evening, with LA and Zito out line-dancing at the Neon Hat, I finished a supper of microwaved beef stew and sesame breadsticks and decided to walk out to my workshop to start on LA's bookends. But, for whatever reason, I couldn't stop thinking about Zito, remembering how over the years we'd worn out the horse tracks in Hot Springs and the dog tracks in Shreveport, the casino boats at Bossier and all the waterholes in between. Something was sticking in my craw about Zito and LA seeing each other.

Of course I knew how Max would react: he'd look at me

over his little glasses and say, 'What's the beef? You and Zito have been friends for years.'

'Maybe that's part of the problem,' I'd answer. 'Zito and I crowed the sun up together too many times for me to have any illusions about him.'

'I think I can put your dilemma on the half-shell for you, my friend,' Max would then say. 'You're worried about LA getting involved with a guy like you.'

A guy like me.

The words took several odd bounces around the inside of my skull, which left me wondering how close to the truth my imaginary conversation with Max had gotten.

I looked around the shop, trying to appreciate what I saw, everything that was supposed to be out here still in place, tools put up more or less where they belonged, the bench workably clear, the floor swept no more than a week ago. Things could be worse.

But something felt strange, and I thought I felt a faint stirring of the hair on the back of my neck. I stood for a minute trying to figure out where the feeling was coming from. Taking another look around, I couldn't see anything that seemed wrong, but the feeling persisted. I went back out and checked the yard around the shop. For a second I thought I caught the hint of an odd smell in the air, the same one I'd thought I smelled at Three, but it was instantly gone. Finally I put it all down to imagination and walked back inside.

'Okay,' I said aloud to my personal space. 'Let's do this.'

I cleared the junk off the firebrick table, brought up the pressure on the acetylene and oxygen gauges, put on the welding apron and goggles, pulled on my gauntlets and used the striker to pop a flame on the cutting head.

As I opened up to working pressure, checked the oxygen jet and began to rough out a couple of oblong bases from a scarred and pitted chunk of half-inch steel plate, I tried to steer my mind away from bad guys and their deeds, toward stillness and peace. Toward the place I knew Jana was in when she was working – somewhere far from the razor-edged everyday world, a zone where things flowed, came together and fit right, where she was able to become almost more spectator than artist as the clay came to life in her hands.

But it didn't work. My thoughts just stupidly and tiresomely kept plodding back to the separation, to seeing Casey and Jordan only a couple of times a week – admittedly more my fault than anybody else's – to the memory of Dr Gold's grey face beaded with icy rain, the milky lifeless eyes, made sharper somehow by being fixed and vacant, lancing into mine.

A guy like me . . .

Suddenly aware that anger had muscled aside everything else in my head, I realised I was no longer cutting the steel but attacking it, slashing at it with my knife of blue-white fire. I stopped working for a minute, lifted the goggles and took a couple of deep breaths, forcing myself to visualise LA's credenza and the volumes of Eliot under the skylight. Settling the goggles back in place, I heated and bent pieces of old rod stock, welding them to the base, shaping random chunks of rail plate to add to that, responding to the shape and mass and gravitational pull of the steel, trying to avoid thinking altogether.

And I must have succeeded somehow because two and a half hours went somewhere as flame spewed from the steel in rivers of stars that bounced brilliantly across the concrete of the shop floor, and my hands did what they did with no interference from me. Finally I stood back, raised the goggles and took a long look at the two pieces in normal light: they felt finished to me. Or not. The eye of the beholder was going to have to be the judge of that.

With my left hand I used the tongs to plunge the pieces one at a time into the water bucket beside the table and dried them with the torch. I purged the acetylene line, shut down the tanks, hung up goggles, apron and gauntlets, then wire-brushed the slag and scale off the metal and took down its sharp edges with the stripping wheel. I used a cold chisel and maul to cut my initials into the base of each piece, knowing LA would never let me get away with not signing them. Finally I lacquered the metal to rust-proof it and glued on and trimmed a couple of green felt bases.

When that was done – and since I was out here – I browbeat myself into getting on the stair-stepper for fifteen minutes, now thinking about the only thing I possibly could while doing this, which was dialling out the firing of the sensory neurons in my knees. Then, having come this far, I decided to work out on the heavy bag for another few minutes, keeping the sweat coming, this time doing something that felt good, finishing with a combination hard enough to rattle the rafters and numb my wrists and forearms. Then I tossed my gloves onto the bench, double-checked valves and switches, grabbed my still-warm artefacts and went in to shower.

I had finished the newspaper and was slouched in my chair with a Corona, watching a documentary about the mortally wounded *Bismarck* steaming in circles until the Fairey Swordfish got the range, when LA came in. She was

decked out in tight Wranglers, red lacers and a bright
yellow western shirt, with a saucer-sized silver buckle on
her belt that I hadn't seen before. She was sober as a church
mouse, but happy. Zito had that effect on women.

'Go to your room, young lady,' I said. 'We'll talk about
this in the morning.'

She laughed, a sound that had never been much more
than a theoretical possibility when we were growing up.
Showing me her Cotton Eye Joe step, she said, 'Top that if
you can.'

'Forget it,' I said. 'I'm a stiff on the dance floor.'

'False modesty,' she said. 'You've still got a move or two
left in you.'

I reached down beside my chair to retrieve the bookends
and handed them to her. She took them carefully in both
hands and examined them thoroughly, turning them one
way and then the other, soaking them in. Finally she looked
up at me. 'My God, these are perfect,' she said. 'And I know
exactly what they are – it's from "The Waste Land" – the
ragged claws.'

'Just tell me one thing,' I said.

'Sure.'

'Did you make the deal because you really wanted these,
or to get me busy?'

She studied me for a couple of beats. 'Yes,' she said. She
leaned down and kissed me on the cheek. 'And thanks, Bis.'

'You're welcome,' I said. 'Just don't forget the days you
owe me.'

'You're at the top of my to-do list,' she said, setting the
claws on the mantel and tilting her new buckle up for a
closer look. 'Would you believe this has the Alamo engraved
on it?'

'No longhorns?' I said. 'No map of Texas? What the hell were they thinking?'

'Minimalists, I guess,' she said. 'So what's on the programme for tomorrow?'

'Talking to Max about the case, for one thing,' I said. 'Maybe he'll have some ideas about the inner workings of Gold's psyche.'

'Hmm,' she said. 'Interesting.'

'What?'

'How easy it is to think the answer could be there, in something that doesn't exist any more.'

'In where?'

'Her mind.'

That night in my dreams:

I am standing alone and in darkness on an empty plain, the world filled with a rhythmic booming that shakes the ground under my feet, an immense heartbeat. But then it is thunder, and I am watching as glowing human bones rise one at a time out of the dark earth in the flashing lightning of a terrible storm spreading across the sky. The bones assemble themselves into a luminous skeleton that curtsies to me, executes a smooth glide and turn, swings weightlessly onto the back of the tall white stallion that is suddenly there between us, and rides silently away into the heart of the rumbling storm, leaving behind a vision of lightning that slowly transforms itself into a wide T with drooping arms, burning bright with unknowable meaning for long seconds before flickering, dimming and finally vanishing.

TWENTY-SIX

The next morning I got up a few minutes ahead of the sun, made myself put in ten minutes on the stair-stepper, then showered, shaved, got dressed and went out for the newspaper. Looking around in the horizontal dawn light, I noticed a slight dusting of frost on the grass and caught a glimpse of what I took to be a coyote disappearing between two houses a block to the north. Along this stretch of Lanshire I could see three other newspapers lying on the lawns of fellow tree murderers.

Back inside, I rummaged around among the cereal boxes, remembering that as a kid LA had generally favoured corn flakes. I found some instant oatmeal and four different kinds of sugar bombs in various shapes and colours that must have been abandoned by the girls, but only an old corn flakes box with a spoonful or so of cereal at the bottom that looked and smelled like it was over the hill anyway. I tossed the box and its contents in the recycle bin, mentally adding replacement flakes to the imaginary and soon-to-be-forgotten grocery list in my head. I set out shredded wheat and raisin bran along with some granola that looked to me like forest litter, and got the coffee going.

As I was trying to make up my mind which of my

cereals I disliked least, LA, wearing the almost knee-length Bigger Bang tour T-shirt she'd slept in, walked into the kitchen, yawning and scratching her head. She stopped, stared at the cereal boxes and other stuff on the table for a minute, then padded over to the counter to get coffee. On her way back she grabbed an orange from the fridge. Sitting across from me, she gave me the blank, wide-eyed morning gaze that told me she was only provisionally conscious at this point and wouldn't be conversational for at least another couple of minutes. She sipped coffee, ignoring the orange. I dumped raisin bran into my bowl and reached for the milk, watching her. She took another sip of coffee. Mutt showed up, circled her chair and butted at her shin. She didn't react.

Then, as I was reaching the halfway point with my cereal, she set her cup down, glanced at Mutt and reached down to ruffle his fur. A minute later she said, 'Tell Max you're grinding your teeth in your sleep again.' She set her cup down, yawned once more, looked at the orange for a while and went back to ignoring it. 'Tell him I said you're at seven and holding.'

I was about to ask what she meant but, looking at her expression, recognised from long experience what a waste of time it would be.

Then, as I was carrying the dishes to the sink, she said, 'I finished off your apple juice last night. What was that funny smell by the back door?'

TWENTY-SEVEN

Driving to Max's Oak Bluff office, my mind replayed what LA had told me.

'It was more than one smell, something like – I don't know – maybe a combination of pine sap, burning rope, wet paint, sweat, stuff like that, but really faint. Reminded me a little of the smell when they had crews working on the new wing of my office building. I wondered if it was something in the trash you'd just gotten rid of or something in my hair from the club. What's the deal, Bis?'

'Probably nothing. I'll explain later.'

I parked in the lot next to Max's office, took the three steps up to the door and walked into his waiting room. Looking around at the familiar, comfortable furniture, big thriving jungle plants and restful art, I had a sense of time slipping silently away, leaving faint afterimages of the tangle of feelings I'd come here once a week for a year trying to sort out.

Max came out to meet me dressed in his usual khakis and a plum-coloured twill shirt with sleeves rolled up to the elbows, and we walked back to his office, where a little stereo in the bookcase was playing *The Magic Flute* at low volume. From his walk it was obvious he had a bad back, but he was a good-sized man with strong arms and big, square, clever hands. His semi-grey beard was trimmed close and he had a little less hair on his head than I did, brushed casually and without any attempt at subterfuge.

He grabbed the red mug I always used and poured coffee for me, then made himself a cup of tea at the credenza where the electric hot-water carafe stood on a green plastic cafeteria tray with sugar, creamer and other paraphernalia. He squeezed a little honey from a bear-shaped container into his tea, stirred it with an ebony letter-opener carved in the shape of a medieval sword, and sat down. I took my usual chair.

'LA says to tell you I'm grinding my teeth again and I'm at seven and holding.'

'Ah.'

'What does "seven and holding" mean?'

'Just a little shorthand we worked out,' he said. 'It means you're at seven out of ten, ten being one hundred per cent depression-free. And you're not losing ground.'

I grunted irritably and drank some coffee.

'So, all this craziness – what's going on? Can you enlighten me?'

'That's what I was thinking of asking you.'

Max said, 'Which do you want enlightenment about, the case or Gold herself?'

'Let's start with her.'

'Well, as I'm sure you've found out by now, she was the worst kind of bitch imaginable,' he replied.

'Don't pull your punches.'

'Certainly not.'

'You're saying she had enemies?'

220

Max's eyebrows went up. 'My God,' he said. 'Show me her friends.' He shook his head. 'It almost seemed necessary to her to be insufferable. I can't think of anyone who didn't dislike her.'

'Personal or professional?'

'Both. It pains me that she was a psychologist; she was an embarrassment to us all.'

'You think the killer could have been another psychologist?'

'Most of us don't deal with our anger that directly or violently, but I suppose anything's possible. What about the husband?'

'Out of town,' I said. 'Always the possibility he contracted it out, but nothing pointing that way so far. Ever hear of her being into SM, bondage, that kind of stuff?'

'No,' he said. 'With whom?'

'Ben Frix, for one,' I said.

'Wasn't that the insurance broker – died in a fire at his house?'

I nodded as I picked up my coffee. 'You know of any connection between Frix and Gold?'

'None at all. But in your place, given the circumstances and timing, I'd certainly be wondering about that.'

I gave him the basics of what I knew, ending with the anatomical shuffle the killers had performed.

'Good God,' he said.

'What's the psychology of something like this?'

Max scratched his chin, thinking it over. 'Well, there's all the obvious stuff like the assumption of rage against women, sexual sadism, revenge, that kind of thing. But the savagery of it doesn't seem to fit with the implied level of calculation. I'd say there's a confounding of purposes here.'

221

'Multiple killers with different motivations?'

'As strange as it sounds, I think you have to consider the possibility. Any suspects at this point?'

'It looks like it's between the skinheads, her fellow psychologists, her former playmates and pretty much everybody else in the world. Just about the only people we can definitely rule out are the ones in the cemetery, and I'm not so sure about them any more.'

'What do you mean?'

I told him about the rumours of cult involvement, the talk of freshly-thawed heads in Argentina, the hints of supernatural legions warped forward in time and marching in the night. 'And you can imagine how much Frix's death adds to the fun.'

He smiled slightly. 'What would life avail us without mystery?'

I shrugged. 'So, what am I missing here?'

'Well, let's think about it,' he said. He sipped tea. 'Take the skinheads, meaning everybody from the neo-Nazi, KKK and Aryan Nation characters to the radical tax resisters, ultra-right survivalists, abortion clinic bombers and what-have-you – what you've got are mostly frustrated, marginal characters, Christian extremists in a lot of cases, obsessed with weaponry and so forth, looking for phallic potency and the unconditional love their mother was supposed to give them but didn't. Take it all together, you could get a pretty unholy stew of sexual frustration, misogynistic rage and violent religiosity. That might be enough to explain a murder like this.' He set his cup aside.

'What would you say if I told you the crucifixion was done by the numbers, the way they did it two thousand years ago?'

'How so?' he said.

I summarised for him what I'd found out about old-time crucifixion so far. 'Then there's the Roman coin we found at the bottom of the tree they nailed her to.'

Max shook his head. 'Truly bizarre,' he said. 'But it just doesn't sound much like our friends with shaved heads. Religious extremism and atheism are the natural habitat of lower-level and mediocre intellects, so if the motive wasn't specifically religious in some way, and assuming the skinheads were involved, you'd almost be forced to think in terms of some intelligent manipulator behind it all. And if the killing was a racial or ethnic gesture, wouldn't you expect some sort of accompanying manifesto? Some thumbing of the killers' noses? A note, a Star of David, a swastika in spray paint, a letter to the editor, something like that?'

'I would.'

'So, since the killing makes no sense as a plain murder, a religious statement or a terrorist gesture, and unless ancient Romans actually were involved, I think you're after someone who's very clever, someone Dr Gold injured or threatened in some profound way. An individual who has the ability to recruit and control the worst kind of thugs imaginable.'

I didn't reply.

He sat thinking for a minute, then picked up his cup and took a last sip of tea, grimacing slightly at its coolness. 'The motive and the act just don't go together,' he said. 'Drama and overkill on the one hand and cold efficiency on the other.' He scratched his chin. 'Do they still publish journals for mercenaries?'

'Yeah, but the ads are written in a way that doesn't tell

you much, and then it's almost impossible to get back to the guy who placed the ad and connect him with whoever answered it.'

'Are the feds getting into it?'

'Not yet,' I said. 'If somebody yelled "hate crime" loud enough they'd probably show up, but it's hard to see how a bunch of black-boots kicking down doors is going to help.'

Max nodded.

'What about Mark Pendergrass?' I said. 'Is he the kind of guy who could do something like this?'

'Mark? I don't know anything directly, but there's always been talk about him, so I suppose anything's possible – '

'What kind of talk?'

'That he was whisked out of town to an all-male military school after some kind of rape allegation when he was in high school.' Max shrugged. 'I can't vouch for that, though.'

'Any legal consequences for him?'

'None that I heard of,' Max said.

'How much violence was involved?'

'No idea. Evidently he's stayed out of trouble ever since – but there again, don't quote me.'

'Is he any good professionally?'

'Not bad, from what I've heard – no superstar, but at least competent.'

'How much do you know about his showdown with Deborah Gold?'

'Almost nothing, really, other than the secondhand talk that went around,' he said. 'The two were pretty close at one time, but I don't think he had any higher regard for her than the rest of us in the last few years. Still, it's hard to imagine him out in the middle of the night doing something like this.'

'You're not saying everything you think,' I said.

'Well, I'm thinking – just between you, me and the wallpaper – that Mark is a sex addict. And the heart and soul of addiction, besides insatiability, is generally escalation – always chasing newer and better thrills. Any addict gravitates toward the kind of people who reinforce each other's drive to notch it up, generate more excitement. With sadomasochism, where's the limit?'

'You're saying – '

'I'm saying in the minds of some, the ultimate thrill would be death for the submissive participant. It's a more common fantasy than you might imagine.'

I thought of what LA had told me about Rachel, and about snuff films worth a million dollars. Things like that seemed to belong anywhere in the galaxy except here in Max's office, but now I pictured him walking me through it like a tour guide, pointing out the significant sights. I looked at my right hand, the third finger more crooked than the rest, and said nothing.

Max watched me. He said, 'Do you ever wonder about yourself?'

I flexed the hand. To me it looked too scarred and inelegant, but at the same time too commonplace, to be called a deadly weapon. I said, 'Yeah, Max, I guess I do. I mean, the reason I hated the guy my mother hooked up with was that he solved things with his fists. He was violent toward her. And me. When he got beaten to the point he couldn't get violent with a wet Kleenex any more, I was walking on air.'

'So?'

'So I wonder how different I really am from him.'

'Kids who are abused don't have a hell of a lot of options. One is to pass it on, become an abuser yourself. Another is to try to lower your profile so much you fall off the radar, give no offence to anybody, try to avoid ever becoming a target. And then we have your solution.'

I looked at him. 'My solution?' I said.

'You learned to channel your aggressions in mostly constructive ways, and made up your mind never to let yourself, or anybody else for that matter, be a victim again,' he said. 'Whatever the cost.'

'You think I'm cold-blooded?'

'Anything but. Why do you ask?'

'Jana once accused me of it,' I said. 'She asked me if I was scared the night I got shot in Roosevelt Courts. I said no, and it was the truth. I just don't know if that's good or bad.'

'"Every man has his secret sorrows which the world knows not,"' Max said. '"And often times we call a man cold when he is only sad."'

'What's that, Shakespeare?'

'Longfellow.' Max studied me for a minute. 'I can tell you that a man who's incapable of violence isn't worth the wind he sucks,' he said. 'I'm just hoping that stays hypothetical in this case.'

'Hypothetical?'

'Maybe I'm jumping at shadows,' he said. 'But I'd hate to see this thing get upside-down on you.'

'What are you saying?'

'I'm saying you're used to being the hunter, not the hunted,' he said. 'I think you need to watch your back, Jim.'

TWENTY-EIGHT

Jana confronted me at the threshold when I dropped by the A-frame with a handful of mail for her. It was just after school and the girls' backpacks still lay against the wall by the door.

'I found one of those damn reporters behind the gallery this morning!' Fresh from the wheel in her clay-spattered T-shirt, Wranglers and chukkas, she was almost vibrating with anger. 'Some snotty kid with a gold ring in his eyebrow, going through the magazines in the recycle bin!' She glared at me, jaw set. The girls appeared from somewhere in the house.

'Why don't we all sit down and talk about it?' I said. I laid the mail on the counter, loosened my tie, undid the top button of my shirt. 'Case, I'm getting a little dehydrated. Think you could maybe find us something to drink?'

As Casey brought root beers for everybody, Jana seemed to be cooling off a little. She said, 'I think they actually camp out there in front of the gallery. They're already there when I open the doors, standing around eating Egg McMuffins, cracking jokes and drinking coffee.' She kicked at a microscopic kink in the corner of the throw rug in front of her chair. 'You'd think they were waiting for the space shuttle to lift off or something.'

'I bet having fleas feels a lot like this,' said Casey, wrinkling her nose.

'I swear, if I get another microphone shoved in my face, I'm shoving it back,' said Jana. 'And it's not going to be in the guy's face either.'

Jordan rolled her eyes.

'I mean, our home isn't our home any more, it's a *scene*, for God's sake! I can just imagine what the customers think of all this.'

'We've seen reporters before,' I said. 'This'll blow over, Jay. It always does.'

'The guys aren't even cute,' griped Casey. 'They look like computer-lab nerds. Or social studies teachers.'

'Some of them,' said Jordan.

'One of them even asked me if you and I had plans of getting back together any time soon,' Jana said hotly.

'What did you tell him?' I asked.

'It was a her. I said, "Excuse me, may I get through please?"'

'That's not what it sounded like to me,' noted Jordan.

We all looked at her.

'You said, "Make a hole, Miz Britches."'

'Well, just what are you supposed to say to someone who wears green cargo pants and patchouli?'

'They're mostly just doing their job – try not to take it personally,' I said, sipping root beer. 'They're probably nice people when they're at home.'

'They weren't all reporters,' said Jordan.

Again all eyes went to her.

'What do you mean, honey?' I said.

228

She shrugged. 'One of the guys watching the house wasn't a reporter.'

'Why do you say that, Jordan?'

'He didn't have a telephone or a camera or anything, and he never talked to the others. All he did was drink coffee and stare at us.'

There was a silence during which I became aware of the pulsing of blood in my neck and hands and the weight of the Glock on my belt. Jana looked at me. 'Jim,' she said, her voice tight.

I set my root beer on the coffee table. 'Is he out there now?' I said, standing up.

'I don't know, but I saw him yesterday.'

'What does he look like?' I scanned the lawn and shrubs through the blinds. For the moment no one was visible, but I couldn't see the front of the gallery or the street from here.

'He was big and he had bad teeth. His hair was brown and he had it tied back in a pony tail. He was wearing a jacket with one of those motorcycle eagles on the back.'

'Harley-Davidson,' said Casey.

'How old was he?'

'I guess about as old as you, Daddy,' she said. 'Maybe older. I'm not sure.'

'Any tattoos, scars, anything like that?'

'I didn't see any.'

'Did he come near you? Say anything to you?'

'No, he just looked.'

I stepped outside and began to work my way around the perimeter of the A-frame, kiln and gallery. When I rounded the hedge that bordered the sidewalk I saw a van marked with the Channel Three logo parked across the street. In it sat two bored-looking guys in their twenties, one clean cut, the other with an uneven goatee and long, ratty hair, watching the front of the gallery. I crossed to the driver's window and flashed my badge. 'Hi, guys,' I said. 'You got any ID you can show me?'

I thought I recognised the passenger, the one with short hair, as a junior Channel Three anchor, one of the faces you saw filling in late Saturday or Sunday night, and he clearly knew me. The driver was probably his cameraman. They both produced driver's licences and press cards. 'Is everything okay, Lieutenant Bonham?' asked the reporter, whose name tag said he was Geoffrey Dean.

'So far,' I said, handing back the licences and cards. I described the Harley-Davidson man. 'Either of you guys seen him, or anyone else who wasn't media, hanging around out here?'

'Yes, sir,' said the cameraman. 'The guy you're talking about was here for a while yesterday. We made him for a neighbour or maybe just a looky-lou.'

'Can you tell us how he figures into the case, sir?' asked the reporter.

I gave him a look, wondering how far he could be trusted. 'Here's how I'd like to work it, Geoff,' I said. 'There may or may not be a connection, but I'm very interested in this guy just the same. And it'd be a big help to me not to catch anything on the late news about a "mystery stalker" or "potential suspect". If you can keep your eyes open for this guy or anyone like him and hold off on the kind of coverage I'm talking about, the minute I get anything I can release I'll give you an exclusive – on-camera, real answers, and I won't say "no-comment" unless I absolutely have to. Does that sound like a deal you could get interested in?'

230

'Not just on this guy?' said Geoff. 'On the whole case?'

I nodded, handed him one of my cards. 'This is my private number. Got a card for me?'

He brought out a bright, cleverly designed business card with his name and number printed along one of the short edges, and just like that I was in bed with another reporter.

I finished my tour of the perimeter and went back inside. 'Okay, guys,' I said. 'It's probably nothing, but here's what I think we should do. Let's be really careful about keeping the doors locked and the blinds pulled, and move the chairs around a little, just enough so you aren't sitting in the same places you usually do. Try to stay away from the windows as much as you can.'

From their expressions I got the feeling I might have crossed the line between not enough information and too much by a step or two. Trying to cut my losses, I summed up: 'If you see this character again call me right away, whatever time of day or night it is. I'll talk to Patrol and get some extra drive-bys – '

'Police protection,' said Jana.

'It's only a precaution, Jay.'

'Brushing our teeth under armed guard – '

A snort from Jordan, who was never an easy laugh, or an easy scare. But Casey seemed to be warming up to the drama.

'Will actual cops come here to protect us?' she said. 'I mean, maybe some young guys? Can we have them in for coffee or something? Let them loosen their ties and hang their guns on the backs of the chairs and make bad jokes and all that stuff?'

Jordan said, 'What about the doughnuts?'

'Now we're feeding them,' said Jana through her teeth.

'The guy was probably nothing but a bystander,' I said. 'But just to be on the safe side let's take it a little bit seriously, okay? In fact, I'll drive you girls to school and pick you up for the time being, or get somebody from downtown to do it.'

'Oh, sure,' said Jana. 'Holing-up like Mafia witnesses. What's next, a bomb in the pizza box?' She was genuinely pissed, but I knew her anger was the kind that functions as an insulation against fear.

'Relax, Jay, this'll all be history before you know it.' Contradicting my own words, I got up to check the rear deadbolt, windows and outside lights, telling myself I'd damn well better know what the hell I was talking about. But now I had no choice – I had to think not only in terms of catching Deborah Gold's murderers but of them, whoever they were, becoming the hunters, as Max had said. Bringing the fight to me and my family. Which suddenly made all my objections to Jana's idea of leaving this life behind seem unbelievably brainless.

On my way back across town I saw somebody at a construction site that I recognised. His name was Harold something-or-other, the husband of one of Jana's regular customers, and a couple of times we'd stood around shooting the breeze while his wife was shopping. I pulled over, parked and walked over to where he stood giving orders to a couple of guys applying something to a finished foundation slab.

'Hey, how you doing?' he said when he caught sight of me, sticking out his hand to shake.

After we'd exchanged some small talk I asked him about the smell of the stuff his guys were laying down.

'We use a couple different things for sealing these slabs,'

he said. 'What you smell is mainly acrylic and epoxy. The odour gets in your clothes and hair sometimes. Why?'

'I'm hoping it'll help with a case I'm working on.'

As I pulled back onto the street, having now answered at least one of the questions that had been plaguing me, I was thinking about the admissibility and credibility issues involved in the Gold case, and trying to remember if I'd ever heard of anybody identifying a suspect by smell.

TWENTY-NINE

OZ was big on fish fries, and every year since taking over as chief he'd sponsored one for the entire department at the lake. He sometimes picked the day as much as six months in advance, without worrying about the weather, and whatever his system was it worked infallibly for him. The day always turned out to be a perfect example of Indian summer at its best, windless and mellow and golden. The saying was that not even the sky would try to buck OZ, and there was nothing about today that made me doubt it.

A dozen men had shown up early this morning with fryers the size of oil drums, barrels of peanut oil and tubs of catfish fillets. Huge quantities of potato salad, baked beans and coleslaw appeared, and giant coolers of iced beer and soft drinks multiplied like wire coat hangers. By early afternoon the party was up to speed, with pickup softball games and football scrimmages, three-beer conferences about oil temperature and cooking times and expert exchanges about breast sizes, the Series, the Middle East and the NFL playoff picture. A steady stream of on-duty troops from all the divisions and firehouses, along with a few poachers from the Arkansas and Louisiana departments and the various sheriffs' offices, came by to check out the brisket and ribs. Kids chased each other, squealed and rolled in the grass, and the women, with no cooking responsibilities, gossiped, laughed, put on sunblock, listened to music or read paperbacks.

I looked around at the scene, feeling good about it, breathing easy, a weight off my chest, but not able at first to put my finger on the reason. Then I got it: it was because I knew Jana, Casey and Jordan were as safe here as they could be anywhere.

The three of them and LA took over a picnic table under an old lightning-struck pine, Jana sipping a beer as she sat on the table, LA and the girls fishing out Cokes and Sprites from a sea-chest-sized cooler we'd filled with drinks and ice at the E-Z Mart just after breakfast.

LA and I took a walk. 'Not a bad way to decompress,' she said as we wandered past a pair of cookers attended by a half-dozen guys hooting over old cop stories and watching the younger studs, one of them being Ridout, run pass plays on the nearby grassy flat. Mouncey and a couple of the other women had wandered off along the shore, but her husband Demond and their nine-year-old son Jarad were kicking a soccer ball around with a flock of other boys about Jarad's age.

'Yeah,' I said. 'The job really tightens you down if you let it. I doubt it's what OZ had in mind, but this is probably good therapy.'

'Mmm,' she said, taking a sip of Sprite.

Knowing the Harley-Davidson man would never show up here, I still couldn't help scanning the crowd for any sign of a pony tail, a biker's jacket or a face I didn't know. A couple of the undercover drug guys came close appearance-wise, but the bad-guy feel just wasn't there. What I did see was a man in boots, jeans, faded denim jacket and a white Stetson, leaning against a tall sycamore a hundred yards away on the far side of the gathering, eyes hidden behind mirrored sunglasses but apparently looking in my direction. He was lean, and even at this distance looked as hard as saddle leather. I put him at forty-something, definitely not a local but a guy with a cop look.

LA, standing with me, saw him too. 'Hmm,' she said. 'A guy like you.'

A nasty little tickle ran like a cold-footed lizard up my spine. 'Why do you say that?' I asked. 'He doesn't look anything like me.'

Reacting to my tone, she glanced at me and shrugged, saying, 'Different on the outside, kind of like you on the inside. What's the rub?'

I didn't know how to answer that, but I thought I knew who the man was. I decided to go have a talk with him, but LA derailed my attention. Looking at the chief standing alone on the point gazing off toward the dam like a ship's captain spying out whales, she said, 'So tell me, what did Max have to say?'

'You guys all bark up the same tree,' I said. 'His thinking was pretty much the same as yours. And he told me depression can look like cold-heartedness.'

'So listen to the man.'

When I looked back toward the sycamore, Stetson was gone. 'Seems like Jana and the girls are having a good time,' I said.

'Yeah,' LA said, glancing back toward their table. 'Look at Casey – she's already as tall as Jana. Word is, the boys are showing a lot of interest lately.'

'Yeah,' I said. 'I've been meaning to get around to that.'

'To what?'

'Selling them into slavery.'

'Daddy?'

I looked around to see Casey catching up to us, pink and a little breathless, her golden hair loose and shining, modest breasts bouncing under her white sweatshirt.

She said, 'Officer Harnes wants to know if you and Aunt Lee want your catfish cajun or wuss.'

'Cajun,' said LA.

'Same here,' I said. 'Hey, uh, Case – '

But she was already running back to deliver her message.

Suddenly I smelled Clubman aftershave and breath mints, looked around and saw Dwight Hazen at my elbow, watching Casey run and giving me his jawy, clear-eyed Captain America profile. He wore what I took to be a carefully chosen guy outfit: black tracksuit, brand new Adidas cross-trainers and a fresh-off-the-shelf Longhorns cap. He turned to me with a bright smile and stuck out his hand.

'Lieutenant Bonham,' he said. 'Good to run into you.' He transferred his smile smoothly to LA. 'And you must be Dr Rowe.' Handshakes all around. 'We've certainly got a beautiful day for it, haven't we?'

'Haven't seen you out for one of these before, sir,' I said.

He looked around the scene as he drew in a hearty breath through his nose and blew it out. 'Fresh air, changing leaves, great fellowship – it's a lot to be thankful for. And let's not forget the chow.'

LA gave me a look. I said something non-committal as Jordan came up to us, decked out in jeans, a red pullover and her beat-to-hell Sea World cap, but looking like a serious little corporal delivering a battlefield dispatch.

'Aunt Lee, Mom says can you please help her put up the volleyball net?'

'Sure, hon,' LA said, and arm-in-arm they were off.

'Those are lovely girls you have there,' said Hazen.

Saying nothing, I looked at him until his smile wavered and broke and his eyes slid away.

'Chief Royal tells me we may be making a little headway on the Gold case,' he said, gazing off across the lake.

'We'll get them, sir,' I said.

'Any idea at this point when we might look for an arrest?'

'No, sir, not really. I tend to think in terms of finding out who did it and getting the evidence to make an arrest before we talk dates. It's not always easy to go at it from the other end.'

Hazen watched the chief make his way back toward the crowd, longneck Bud in hand. 'Look at him. He's a dying breed, isn't he? I mean a slice of the old West right here in our midst. I don't care if it is going against the grain, I think he's a tremendous asset to the city, and it's going to be tough to see him go when he retires.'

'Against the grain?' I said.

Hazen looked at his shoes, cleared his throat. 'I don't mean to talk out of school here, Lieutenant,' he said. 'It's just that the chief's style isn't everybody's cup of tea, know what I'm saying?'

'No, sir.'

'Well, I guess it's like anything else – results are the bottom line for all of us, aren't they? OZ's a legend, you could even say an icon, and he's been above question or reproach ever since he stepped in. That was before my time, but I don't think anybody'd deny he's done a great job. That covers a multitude of sins, I'm sure you'll agree. And everyone knows he wants you for his replacement.'

'Hard to imagine a higher compliment, coming from him.'

'Amen to that. And personally I can't think of a better choice under normal circumstances. But we've got a situation on our hands here, Lieutenant.'

'Situation?'

'To say the least. When the networks start booking hotel rooms down here, people get nervous. I have to answer to the council, and nobody over there wants to be on the ten o'clock news trying to field questions about hate crimes in Traverton. What I'm concerned about is whether we can show the world we're able to clean up our own mess. I just had a conversation with the attorney general, and he wants to know why we don't have anything more substantial for the press on this Gold thing. Frankly, I was at a loss to answer him.'

'You mind if I ask whether you called him or he called you?' I said.

Hazen examined the back of his hand and his manicured nails. 'I think the point is, Jim, everything's contingent on our getting somebody in custody on this Gold thing. I'm sure you understand.'

'Yes, sir, I think I do,' I said, watching a Channel Four reporter and cameraman approach us from the direction of the parking lot. 'But let me ask you another question.'

'Shoot,' he said.

'It's about punishment fitting the crime,' I said. 'Take a child molester, let's say – you think prison time is the way to go with a guy like that, or maybe some kind of rehab?' I glanced back toward my daughters, then met his gaze and

239

held it. 'Or would it be best to just cut off his balls and see how far down his throat you can shove them?'

Hazen opened his mouth but nothing came out. By this time the news crew was on us.

The reporter said, 'Lieutenant Bonham – '

I held up both hands, nodded my head at Hazen and walked away to join my family as the guy handling the camera started setting his tripod up for the interview.

THIRTY

LA and Zito walked into the mid-morning situation briefing at Three, Zito decked out in black western pants, ropers, white shirt with pearl snaps, a tan cord blazer with its lower right sleeve tidily folded and pinned, and LA somehow looking equally tarted up in faded jeans, a rugby shirt and an old pair of boat shoes. Zito shook with, shoulder-chucked or hugged pretty much everybody in the room, then threw me a crooked little smirk as he grabbed a chair.

But I don't think this stuff even registered on LA. I was guessing the Miami conference was off the table by now, because she was clearly in the zone. Several times I'd seen her going over some document or listening to somebody with the little *High Noon* squint that told me she was one hundred per cent engaged: no matter where this trail led, she was in for the kill.

What really brought out the predator in her was Dr Gold's PC, now sealed and gathering dust on a shelf in the evidence room. It engaged LA because as a source of evidence it was the blue-ribbon pig – but, even more importantly, because she couldn't have it. We weren't even free to plug it in without a judge's order.

People tend to treat the computers on their desks almost

like provinces of their own minds, confiding in them like sorority sisters, baring their souls, even believing in the security of their firewalls, filters and passwords, so that the computer eventually becomes in effect a window into the user's brain. LA was immune to this kind of self-delusion but she knew other people weren't, and she kept eyeing Gold's CPU like a fox casing the barnyard. Off and on over the past couple of days I'd seen her head to head with Bytes, the contracted digital geek, a tall skinny straight-backed guy whose actual name was Kevin Hauser, about what they'd do first with the unit if they could get their hands on it.

Settling in his chair, Zito eyed me and said, 'Say, sport, I came to watch the dogged nemesis at work, see if I can pick up a trick or two.' He produced a small dog biscuit from his shirt pocket and tossed it to me. I caught it.

'Good idea,' I said. 'But that kind of puts us in a corner, old timer, because I'm gonna be using some two-syllable words here. All I can say is, try to follow along as best you can.' I looked at the biscuit and took a bite. 'Needs salt,' I said.

'What's new with the Frix fire?' asked Ridout.

Crossing his legs, brushing something invisible off his pants, Zito said, 'Not much to tell. The accelerant was plain old kerosene. Looks like the bug split about five gallons of it between the body in the den and the stairwell, then touched it off.' He shook out a cigarillo and lit it with his Marine Corps Zippo.

'No smoking in the building,' somebody said.

'Right,' Zito said, drawing on the cigarillo.

'Sounded like the fire took off pretty good,' said Ridout.

'Yeah, went up the stairwell and involved the second

storey by the time the first floor was going good. Guy was no pro, but he did what it took to send the place up.'

'So your theory would be the bug was the killer?' I said.

'You got it, hombre.'

'How bad was the body?'

'Standard crispy-critter,' said Zito, blowing out smoke. 'Same as you'd get with napalm. ME's crew broke him in two places bagging him.'

'Any sign of what killed him?'

He nodded his head. 'Sifted out a couple of shell casings. Forty-four Mag.'

'Wayne's got them?' I said.

'Yeah, he's got 'em. What's the connection with your shrink case?'

'Frix had an involvement with Gold,' I said. 'Somebody does her, then a couple of days later he gets it.' I spread my hands.

He nodded. 'Hard to laugh off, all right,' he said, triggering a small grunt of agreement from Mouncey. LA pointed her finger at me, dropped the hammer of her thumb, then found some change in her purse and headed toward the soft drink machines in the hall.

Chateaubriand on me.

Down at the other end of the table Wayne finished the conversation he'd been having with one of his techs about something and looked up at me. 'I finally gave up on finding a perfesser to tell me about that coin and looked it up for myself, Lou.' He consulted his notes. 'It's Roman, all right. The face on the front is Apollo. Them little curls are supposed to be pigtails, by the way. The other side's Diana, goddess of childbirth and the forest. Romans decided she was the same deity as Artemis, who was the Greek goddess of the hunt. That's why she's got a bow and arrows on her shoulder.'

'What's the coin made of?'

'Silver, mostly.'

'And it's never been in the ground?'

'No telling, but for sure not recently. Under the microscope it looks like it's been laying around in a drawer somewhere, a little of the tarnish polished off, couple of green felt fibres and whatnot.'

'How about a date?'

'Best I could do is it's from the reign of Augustus.'

'So, any reason to think it wasn't our killers who dropped it there?'

'Not really, because our information is Gold didn't collect coins and neither did her husband,' he said. 'Beats the hell out of me what the bad guys were doing with it, though.'

No one offered a comment on that.

Next we all looked at his enlarged reproductions of the note found in Gold's nose. Nobody had any new ideas about the mystery numbers or the 'glowen' inscription. Early on, thinking the word sounded vaguely Teutonic, I'd checked a couple of translation sites to see if it meant anything in German. No good. Likewise, since I was at it, French, Spanish, Portuguese, Russian and Latin. No luck there either.

'An anagram?' Somebody said.

'Of what, "wongle"?'

'"Legwon"?'

'"Newlog"?'

'How about an acronym?'

'Let's see, "Good-looking old women eat noodles"?'

'"Gina lifts old willie every night"?'

244

'Somebody trying to write "glowing"?'

'Who the fuck knows?'

'Nobody the fuck knows.'

'Speaking of that, how about the numbers?'

'Yeah, will somebody please tell us what the hell they mean?'

'Four feet something?'

'Counting something by twos?'

'Measurements?'

'Who the fuck knows?'

Trying to figure out what the numbers meant, I had tried a substitution cipher based on the ordinal positions of the letters of the alphabet, but all I got was gibberish. I'd also looked for a connection with decimal notation in library classification systems, navigational and mapping coordinates and the criminal codes, but got nowhere. None of the combinations of digits seemed to connect to any emergency call code, area code, telephone number, ZIP code, radio frequency or address anybody could think of. The spacing of the digits and the underlining of some of them looked like they should mean something, but I had no idea what. I stared at the sequence, massaging my forehead:

4' 68 9172350

Four groups of digits, three short and even, the fourth long and odd. None of the groups was a prime number. Was it significant that no digit was repeated? I picked up a pencil and wrote the numbers in reverse order:

0532719 86 '4

The underlined numbers could then be read as March 27, 1986. I made a note to myself to check the media files for that date.

I turned the page upside down and looked at the numbers, but they didn't mean anything to me that way either. Borrowing Mouncey's compact mirror, I looked at them in reflection. Same story. I clicked the pencil against my teeth, wondering if this could be part of a longer string of numbers. Was it possible the writer had failed to finish the series?

Somebody was saying, 'Oughta have a national database of bite marks. Ever' perp, give him a bite of cheese, make a cast of the marks and file it – '

Out of the corner of my eye I saw LA walk back into the room, diet DP in hand. Noticing my expression and the page on the table in front of me, she stopped beside my chair and rested her hand on my shoulder, saying, 'What are you doing with that?'

'Mainly going nuts,' I said. 'This has got to mean something, but I don't know what the hell it is.'

'I do,' she said.

THIRTY-ONE

'It's Welsh code,' said LA.

'Say what?' said Ridout as everybody gathered around. 'Welsh code.'

'They got they own codes?' marvelled Mouncey.

'Ever see anything written in Welsh?' said Wayne. 'The language is a code all by itself. Takes the whole alphabet to yell at a cat.'

'This Welsh is a man's name,' said LA. 'The numbers are the old way of summarising an MMPI profile.'

'What's that?' said Wayne.

'It's that big old test you have to take now before you hire on,' said Ridout. 'Prove you ain't crazy.' He looked to LA for confirmation, got a nod.

'The one they're using now is the MMPI-2, and most psychologists just file the profile itself in the chart,' LA said. 'If they use any kind of summary it's usually no more than a three- or four-point code. This is kind of a fossil.'

'Any current uses for it at all?' I said.

'I don't know. Maybe to retrieve archived records or maybe in some system that requires it, which I think the VA used to.'

'Would anybody but a psychologist be able to read it?'

'Not likely. A few counsellors and psychiatrists, maybe some medical records and research people. That'd be about it.'

'What does it mean?' I said.

LA took the page, studied the numbers. 'This is a pretty bad one, actually. Antisocial and paranoid traits along with atypical thinking and a lot of energy. Unstable, probably sadistic. Could be a dangerous person.'

'Criminal?'

'Yeah, especially at a lower level of intelligence. Going up the IQ scale, you'd be talking about an unscrupulous manipulator, maybe a white-collar criminal, lawyer, politician, something like that.'

'How you tell that from them little numbers?' asked Mouncey.

'The numbers and markings and spaces, and the order they come in, give you the shape of the profile, and that gives you the personality structure.'

'Any idea what all this might have to do with anything?'

She shrugged, saying, 'Just that it's connected with psychology and Gold was a psychologist. Otherwise, who knows?'

Bertie stepped into the room, pale as death, thumbs and forefingers pinching the corners of a sheet of notepaper and an envelope in the dead-rat carry. Beyond her in the squad room I could see a couple of curious faces following her progress.

'Acetate,' she said tightly.

Wayne found a couple of clear plastic page-covers in

one of the cabinets, held them open as she laid the sheet and envelope gingerly inside.

'I handled these before I knew what they were,' she said. 'My prints are going to be all over them.'

We all gathered to look at the envelope and the letter, which had been scrawled on cheap drugstore tablet paper.

Lt J Bonum
Tri-State Justice Bldg
TTN USA

'It was in with the rest of the mail,' said Bertie. 'Postmarked downtown.'

Wayne disappeared down the hall to get his photo and print gear. I held the letter up to read it aloud.

To Lt Bonum
For without are dogs and Sorcerers but I am the root and the offspring of David and the bright and morning star I am the flaming sword at the east of Eden that turns every way and keeps the way. Behold thy days approach that thou must die.
from the Chapel

'Well, kiss my sweet pink ass,' said Ridout.

'What all that preacher talk about?' said Mouncey.

'It's Scripture,' said Wayne as he rejoined us. 'That first line's something Jesus said, and the other about dying is from the Old Testament. The sword part's from Genesis.'

'How you know that?' said Mouncey.

'Used to teach Sunday School. Here, let me shoot that, Lou.'

'Suppose this has anything to do with our case?' asked Ridout, watching Wayne prep the letter.

'Naw,' said Mouncey. 'This about the Lindberg case, darlin'.'

THIRTY-TWO

The next day LA was standing by the bookcase in my office flipping through some of the old Highway Patrol journals that came to the office unordered, and stayed there by the year unread, when Ridout and Mouncey showed up to report on what they'd learned about the possibility Gold might have engineered her own death.

Consulting his notes, Ridout said, 'My end, I didn't find anybody who ever heard Gold talk about killing herself, she didn't buy any insurance, no big debts. Her internist and her ob-gyn both say as far as they know she didn't have any life-threatening disease. Swung by for another chat with the husband. He says nope, she never said anything about killing herself and if I knew her I'd know that was never gonna happen.'

'I could've told you that,' LA said without looking up from the five-year-old article about police pensions she was skimming.

Ridout eyed her. 'So how come you didn't, doc?'

'You didn't ask.'

'Oh.' He cleared his throat and continued. 'Also,' he said, 'still no findable connection with any of the kind of guys we've been talking about that she might've hired to do her in.' He shrugged. 'In other news, Wayne says to tell you there's no match on the gum you got from Jamison's place and what we picked up at the scene.'

'How about the other people in Gold's office?' I said.

'I'd say we got zip on that one. Secretary's a twenty-one-year-old lawyer's daughter named Jessica Destin who belongs to a riding club and takes accounting classes at night, which is where she was the night Gold got it. She just replaced the old secretary, a church lady with a dying husband, name's Earlene Cutchell. The counsellor's a Margaret Ailesworth, been with the practice about four months. She's almost retirement age, plays bridge with some other old ladies or goes birdwatching with her husband John in her free time. Played bridge, then went out with a few of the other players for coffee. That broke up a couple hours later, putting her on the road too late to be nailing anybody up in a tree. No indication she knows anybody that might've done it for her. The psych associate who worked for Gold is a guy named Peregrine Espy, and no, I ain't shittin' you, so don't even ask. He's a flaky gay kid who probably weighs one-twenty with rocks in his pockets and is into TV shows about old crockery and dancing. Seemed worried mostly about where he's gonna find another job. Home with Mom on that fateful night, watching *Antiques Roadshow*, no connections with Gold outside the office, no involvement with extremist groups, no sheet on him or Mom, yada yada yada. Jackie Milner, Jamison's ex, didn't have much to say except she's pretty happy with her life now and Dr Gold was probably right about the marriage being a horse with a broke leg – said after the first week or so she wouldn't have taken Andy back even if she could've had him. Hated Gold in a quiet kind of way, but her day planner stays pretty full with her job and the kids and the guy she's dating now, real-estate developer named Chuck Aiken. Background on both of them pretty much dittoes Ailesworth and Espy. My take, put 'em all in a bag, shake 'em up real good with some flour and you still got nothing to fry.'

'Thanks,' I said. 'And stop looking so damn cheerful about it. M, have you got anything?'

Leaning forward to set her Sprite on the edge of my desk, she found the notebook page she wanted and tapped it with a long purple nail. 'First off, Pendergrass's ex, like you ast for. Name Laura, she a cosmetologist, live in Houston. Say Pendergrass a sure enough asshole, anything sit down to pee, he got to nail it. Don't know about no group sex or butt-whuppin' or any that other stuff, but come to him, nothing gone surprise her. Said let her know if she be any help lockin' his sorry ass up.'

Another dry hole. 'Moving right along,' I said.

'Next thing, her shrink. Name Runnels. He a Oreo.'

'A what?'

LA said, 'Black on the outside, white on the inside.'

'Co-rect,' Mouncey said. 'Got the tweeds and the pipe and the Porsche, belong to the country club, golf trophies on the shelf – he got the whole possum-trot goin' on. Probably a Republican to boot.'

'Ain't all doctors Republicans?' said Ridout with a glance at LA.

'What did you get out of him?' I said.

'He not too happy talking to me at first so I tell him that be fine, he right, best we do it by the numbers, I be back in thirty minutes with a subpoena for him and all them files he got, bring along the U-Haul, prolly no need shuttin' down

253

his practice more'n a month or two while we go through ev'thing with him, he figure out something to tell the medical board when they come sniffin' around, and maybe I get to meet all them *Dateline* folks up in here doin' they interviews. He rethink it a little and pretty soon he see his way clear to help me out. Say the doc been seeing him a year and a half, mostly for drugs. Say she got a "mixed personality disorder".'

I looked at LA. 'Earn your salt,' I said.

She said, 'He didn't mean they were actually mixed – it's more like stacked. He was saying she had more than one personality disorder, or more likely traits from more than one. Did he say what they were?'

'Uh huh. "Paranoid and antisocial with narcissistic traits." Also say she agitated. Now and then he give her some Oxy and whatnot for that.'

'Nothing about depression?'

She shook her head. 'Ast him if she be the kind to kill herself. Say that about the last thing he be lookin' for.'

'He say anything else?'

'Tole me she got no friends, don't trust nobody, use people, see the world divided up between predators and prey, naturally she prefer to be on the predator side. Seem like we talkin' about hawks and rabbits there.'

'Ugly picture,' said Ridout.

'It get better,' said Mouncey. 'Doctor Oreo say she got "sexual compulsions".'

'Such as?'

'In addition to she SM all the way, she "polymorphous perverse" too.'

'What the hell's that?'

'She gets it on with anybody,' LA said. 'Male, female,

old, young, somewhere else in the food chain – wouldn't matter much to her.'

'You got it,' said Mouncey. 'She a equal-opportunity ho.'

'That fit with the Welsh code?'

LA nodded.

'Must be easier to get dates that way,' I said.

'Best part, the doc like pee parties. Call it the golden shower.'

'Holy shit,' said Ridout.

'You not listenin',' said Mouncey. 'We talkin' whiz here.'

'Who whizzes on who?'

'Don't know, darlin'. Might be you want to research it a little deeper.'

'What about the coke?' I said.

'Look like she snorting about a eight-ball a day. Don't run it or smoke it. Her connection that lawyer Feigel, like you say, Lou. He Jewish too, by the way.'

'Sayin' he's next on the cross?' asked Ridout.

'Cain't never tell,' said Mouncey. 'Top of all that, I got something else might be good.'

'Do tell.'

'Talkin' to that snitch down on the stroll, got the disease make him bark and cuss all the time – '

'Tourette's?' LA said.

'Yatzee,' Mouncey said. '*Too*-rets.'

I'd run into the guy myself. He worked at a car wash, knew a lot of people in the life and liked to think of himself as a spy.

'So anyway, we talkin' little this, little that, he telling me about some kinda scam they running out the fed prison, getting stuff on other people's credit cards and what-have-you, then he off about some old white guy they got out there used to be a math professor or something. But he a preacher too. Name Jaston Keets. Say he real smart, he some kind of guru for them fat honkies dress up like soldiers, run around in the woods.'

'But he's been on the inside for a while?' I said, wondering where this was going.

'Went up six years ago. He one them Sword of the Lord guys had they camp on top the mountain, takin' potshots at the feebs when they come round.'

'Lummus's group,' I said, feeling the beginnings of a small mental buzz. 'Hey, didn't those guys have some kind of sign up at their compound, a logo or something?'

'Uh huh,' she said, producing a dog-eared leaflet denouncing America's godless ways and the Jewish-black-immigrant-unChristian government's "goon squads", the kind of flyer that occasionally showed up on windshields in parking lots around southwest Arkansas and into north-east Texas and northwest Louisiana. I'd seen them without seeing them for years, but I sure as hell saw this now, and I couldn't believe my eyes. I said, 'This logo – '

'Seen them little doodles you been drawing e'where,' Mouncey said as I was pawing through my top drawer. Finally I found what I was looking for – a sticky note with my latest rendition of the baking soda figure I had been drawing, a flexed, muscular arm holding what I now real-ised was a short, thick sword. I held it next to the flyer. The two drawings were almost identical.

'This where the plot get thick,' Mouncey said. 'Snitch say e'body call Keets the Chaplain.'

THIRTY-THREE

When I'd set up a meeting with Keets at the prison, LA said she wanted to come along.

'Tell him I'm a secretary or something – maybe I can detect a clue,' she said. 'By stealth.'

'Great idea,' Zito said. 'You still got your secret-agent licence, right?'

The only prints found on the 'Capt Bonum' letter and envelope belonged to Bertie and a couple of post office workers, and the envelope itself was the self-sticking type, meaning it didn't need licking and therefore gave up no DNA. Something tying Keets to the letter would have been a good hole card for the interview, but even without that I thought we might get some use out of the letter when we talked to him.

When the day came, a skinny redheaded corrections officer led LA and me back to a dingy, low-ceilinged conference room that smelled like mice and looked even bleaker and more desperate than the prison in general. Except for a square, grey metal table and a few hard-used military-looking chairs, there was no furniture in the room, which was brightly lit by the kind of fluorescents that give human skin the colour of dead amphibians.

'Homey,' I said.

LA glanced around the room. 'No place for a claustro-phobic, but I guess we've seen worse.'

The heavy metal door fitted with a reinforced glass observation window opened and the redheaded guard brought Keets into the room. He was unshaven and looked seventy or so, outfitted in standard jailhouse-orange scrubs, ragged-out carpet slippers and thick horn-rimmed glasses over small blue eyes. He leaned on an aluminum quad-cane, a pale man, not really obese but heavy and soft from prison food, with oily, iron-grey hair lying in long discrete hanks across his shiny scalp.

'Rap on the door if you need anything,' said the guard. He gave his prisoner a final glance and let himself out.

I shook hands with Keets and introduced LA, saying, 'This is Lee Rowe. She works with me.'

'Why don't we all sit down?' he said. 'These old shanks aren't what they used to be.'

We took chairs on three sides of the table, LA briskly opening a steno pad and producing a stick pen, looking clerical and well-organised.

'Forgive me, Ms Rowe, but I am something of a student of human taxonomy,' Keets said. 'You appear to me to be of partial northern Mediterranean extraction, possibly Greek. May I ask if that is so?'

LA, whose long-gone biological father, or sperm donor if you listened to Rachel, actually had been Greek, said, 'I'm mostly who-knows-what.'

'Ah, the Greeks,' said Keets as if she had confirmed his speculation. 'Among the most estimable of races until their eventual debasement. Of course with your height and noble features I would suspect yours must be the old, true blood

258

of Pericles and Pythagoras.' He watched her print the date neatly at the top of her page.

'Yes, sir,' she said neutrally, drawing a line under the date.

I said, 'I appreciate your willingness to talk to us, Mr Keets. Or is it Reverend Keets?'

He smiled. 'We both know you could have compelled me, at least to meet with you. And you may call me whatever you like.'

'And we both know how long that would have taken and how little good it would have done.'

A nod of acknowledgement. 'How can I serve you, Lieutenant?'

'We're here about the murder of a psychologist – '

Keets shifted in his chair and leaned the cane against the table. 'A Jewish woman psychologist, I believe,' he said. 'We're not allowed use of the internet here, but we do have day-old newspapers and a certain amount of television access.'

'You're right about Dr Gold,' I said. 'And your name came up as someone who might have information that would help us.'

'My name?'

'Actually, what came up was a reference to "the Chaplain".'

'And it came up how?'

'An anonymous tip to the hotline.'

'Ah.'

'I thought being as familiar as you are with the survivalist and Christian Identity groups might give you some insight that would help me figure out who killed Dr Gold. And why.'

Another smile. 'Nicely put, Lieutenant. What you mean

to say, I believe, is that you hope I might be able to finger someone for you.'

I turned to LA. 'Ms Rowe, would you call that a – what's the term?'

'Semantic quibble, I believe.'

'Right,' I said. 'So let me ask a different question: you acted as chaplain to the Sword of the Lord faction in Arkansas, didn't you?'

'Yes, proudly.'

'And I understand you were a mathematician.'

'I have taught mathematics, yes. It is, I believe, the purest of the many languages of God. But I am also an ordained minister of Christ.'

'What denomination would that be?'

'There can be only one true church.'

'Are you still involved with the movement?'

'Jaston Lawrence Keets, Chaplain, Army of the Sword of the Lord.'

'No serial number?'

'You are accustomed to command, Lieutenant?'

'It's not exactly everything it's cracked up to be.'

'Have you experienced combat?'

'A few minutes at a time.'

'Ah. Then you have taken human life?'

'That's not all it's cracked up to be, either.'

'But in principle you have no objection to killing when circumstances warrant?'

'There's not always a choice.'

'Indeed. You are no doubt a good officer. By the way, do you, as they say, believe in our government's wars, the ones they keep telling us are fought to preserve our freedom?'

'Not enough to think that's what they're really about.'

'But as a soldier you would have served as ordered?'

'Yes.'

'My wars were a long time ago. Look at me now – I have arthritis, diabetes, kidney disease. My liver's no good any more. I have no family to return to if I leave here. Assuming I knew who executed your Zionist quack, what inducement do you imagine might cause me to inform on good soldiers for doing as they were ordered to do?'

'Interesting way of looking at it. Do you think the killers were somebody's soldiers, acting on orders?'

'As it happens, no.'

'Why not?'

'I do not think those men, whoever they were, believed in anything beyond themselves.'

'How do you mean?'

'The killing clearly was not exigent, nor did it strike effectively at the illegitimate occupation forces of Washington, either of which might have justified the effort and risk of such an undertaking. Of course I applaud the death of any Jew, but in this case the target was merely a symptom, one of millions. She was neither an important agent of the occupation nor an immediate threat. Her death was an empty gesture, serving only to bring unnecessary pressure on the liberation movement. I think your killers, Lieutenant, were ad hoc mercenaries.'

'And none of your own?'

'And none of my own.'

'Excuse me, sir,' said LA deferentially. 'Would you mind telling us how you would have responded if you actually had ordered the killing?'

Keets looked at her a long moment. 'That's a remarkable question.'

LA waited politely.

'I imagine I would have simply denied all knowledge of the situation and advised you to go to hell,' he said.

I caught what may have been a faint smile from LA.

'So you probably don't think much of the NBA?' I said.

He grunted dismissively. 'Ten niggers leaping, and a partridge in a pear tree. If jumping makes civilisation, let's elect a parliament of jackrabbits. No, sir, the hope of humanity on earth has never rested in any but white hands, and it never will.'

'Mr Keets, do you know Benjamin Frix?'

'No, sir,' he said. 'I do know that you are using the wrong tense for a reason, and that Mr Frix was recently found dead in the ashes of his home. No doubt that is regarded as a suspicious circumstance. For all I know, you are proceeding on the theory that there is some connection between his death and Gold's. Are you prepared to tell me why you asked if I knew him?'

'No, sir,' I said. 'What can you tell me about this?' I pushed a copy of the death threat across to him.

He picked up the paper, tilted his head back to get the best benefit of his trifocals and read the letter, LA watching him closely. 'The Revelation of St John the Divine,' he said when he'd finished. 'Along with snippets from Genesis and Deuteronomy. An interesting juxtaposition. It's possible the reference to the flaming sword is a nod to the ZOG's dastardly adventure in Waco some years ago.'

'Excuse me – ZOG?' said LA, her pen poised.

'Our Zionist Occupation Government,' replied Keets. 'Usurpers of the mantle of Jefferson and Jackson. At any rate, the letter is an interesting document. What do you make of it, Lieutenant?'

'That's my question to you.'

'And I am persuaded by it that you derived no identifying evidence from this,' he said, glancing at the letter again. 'Thank you for having the sense not to try to bluff me in that regard. May I assume that because of the reference to a chapel you thought of me as the author?'

'No.'

'Why not?'

'For one thing, I don't believe you would've misspelled my name.'

He smiled. 'Even as subterfuge?'

I said nothing.

'Unable to assume the guise of ignorance even to avoid prosecution? That's quite an indictment.'

I waited.

'Ah, well, you're probably right.' He shook his head. 'Vanity is certainly master to us all.'

'And if you had misspelled my name to throw us off, what would be the point of the chapel reference?'

He glanced at me sharply and nodded. 'You're clearly an intelligent man, Lieutenant.'

I said, 'Make a note, Ms Rowe.'

She jotted something on the pad.

Keets said, 'Many people think of athletes, which I believe you once were, as dullards, but the reverse is more often true. In any case, you're correct, I didn't write this. Or have it written. But I'm sure the misspelling of your name was an attempt at deception. I dare say the entire letter was intended as a red herring.'

'And not a warning to back off?'

'Please, Lieutenant. Who would be asinine enough to expect something like this to stop a police investigation? Or deter a man such as yourself? Only an idiot, surely. But it is a threat to you personally. The address and salutation tell us that whoever wrote them knew the correct abbreviation of "captain" and the airport designation and common shorthand for Traverton, and was aware that you were investigating the killing, none of which would be particularly consistent with the implied subliteracy of the document. And the author was erudite enough to locate and correctly quote several biblical passages, as well as put them together in a coherent way. It's clear no ordinary criminal wrote this. But I believe it suggests something further.'

'What's that?'

'I think it's likely the person you're looking for is actually someone who not only knows who you are and how to spell your name correctly but is in fact someone quite close to you. Someone with a very specific reason for targeting you.'

'So what do you think?' I asked LA as we drove down Border through the light mid-afternoon traffic toward Tri-State.

'Well, Keets takes a kind of offbeat pride in his affiliation with the Sword movement, but it's not his natural element. He's much too bright for that.' She fiddled with the radio, settling on one of the Shreveport classic rock stations. A Beatles single from '67, 'All You Need Is Love'. She adjusted the volume. 'He's a man who'll never be at peace with himself,' she said. 'Think about it – all that mental wattage, but he's permanently stuck with a bunch of guys who think higher education means getting a GED. His involvement with them was probably a reaction to some trauma he experienced. And he's ashamed of something about his military service.'

'How do you know that?' I said.

'His expression when he mentioned it, the fact he didn't elaborate, the way he jumped immediately from that to his health problems, as if they were a judgement on him in some way. My guess is he either feels he was a coward under fire or he did things over there that he still has guilt about. Maybe both.'

'Then he's not a sociopath?'

'No. If he were, he'd have spent more energy trying to flatter and manipulate us.'

'He gave it a shot with you.'

She shrugged. 'That was nothing – just male reflex. He was much more interested in showing us how smart he is.'

'So what did you write when I told you to make a note?'

She held the pad up for me to read: *Note to self – check definition of 'intelligent'.*

'Okay, got me,' I said. 'If Keets had been right about me I would've known better than to ask. So, back to the reverend – you were talking about how you know he's not a sociopath.'

'Right,' she said. 'The other thing is, with a sociopath you don't get a lot of signs of autonomic arousal.'

'You're saying he had them.'

'Yeah. Especially when he read the letter.'

'What were you watching at that point?'

'Heart rate, blink rate, respiration, pupils.'

'How the hell did you watch his heart rate?'

She touched her finger to the side of my neck the way she had the night she arrived. 'Looked right here,' she said. 'Carotids are just under the surface.'

I visualised my throat constantly pulsing out my thoughts for all the world to see, my irises semaphoring every emotion, my mind naked as a pole dancer. No wonder I could never beat her at gin rummy.

'So what did all that tell you?' I said.

'I don't think he knew anything about the letter at all before you showed it to him. But in the abstract it interested him very much, juiced him, gave him something to think about. A puzzle, a new angle on the world. Guys like him are bound to get pretty bored in prison.'

'Yeah, that's another thing that's never made a hell of a lot of sense to me – how a character that smart ends up in the joint in the first place.'

She opened the window a couple of inches, lit a cigarette with her slim gold lighter, took a drag and blew out smoke. She said, 'Short answer?'

'Please.'

'Smart is probably the wrong word. Keets is intelligent all right, but the thing is, IQ scores don't really have much to do with how smart you are or how well you're going to do in life. About the only thing they're good at pre-dicting is what kind of scores you'll make on your next IQ test.'

'You're saying Keets is intelligent but not smart. Why do you think he got himself locked up, exactly?'

'I think in his case it's self-punishment. He probably wasn't raised to hate people, or do the kind of things he's done, but he got pushed around somehow in his life and ended up grabbing for any kind of strength he could find. Hate looks strong, so he signed on and never looked back. But the boy his mama tried to raise right is still in there somewhere, and the little guy keeps sabotaging the adult's agenda. Bright as he is, Keets has probably always been basically a schmuck who shoots himself in the foot every time he goes for his gun.'

'So you don't think he knows anything about the killing?'

She looked at the ash on her cigarette. 'I didn't say that.' She watched a white Taurus full of teenage girls passing us in the outside lane. 'I'm sure he knows exactly who killed Dr Gold.'

I stared at her.

'Watch the road,' she said.

'Do I dare ask why you say that?'

'I think at first he figured we were there about the credit-card scam M told us about, which he's probably running. He was ready for that, but when you said we were investigating the murder, it caused an adrenaline dump. No way that happens unless he's at risk somehow. At risk means involved. Involved means he knows something.'

'LA, are you ever gonna stop jerking rugs out from under me?'

'Hah.'

'So what else does Keets know?'

'That's what we've gotta find out, Mr Dillon.'

I dropped her off at Kiln-Roi, then drove the half-mile to Three, where I found Mouncey and Ridout in my office, Ridout playing solitaire on the computer, Mouncey flipping through the fattening Gold file. Ridout closed the game and cleared out of my chair.

'How'd it go?' he said.

While I was summarising the interview for them Zito stuck his head in the door. 'Hey, grunts,' he said. 'Say, Bis. Seen LA?'

'Naw,' said Ridout.

"Spect she hiding,' said Mouncey. 'Kind of riffraff we get around here.'

'She's at Jana's place,' I said. 'Come on in and provide us with a federal presence.'

'Sure,' he said. 'Suffer the little locals is my motto.'

'You gone enjoy this,' said Mouncey. 'We fixin' to study up on the sex group Gold and Frix in.'

'Order of the golden whiz,' said Ridout.

'Butt-whup of the month,' added Mouncey.

'Say what?'

'Masks, whips, boots,' I said. 'The Freakers' Ball.'

'Now y'all have gone and made me imagine Frix nekkid in high heels,' Zito said, shaking his head.

'Happy to share,' said Ridout.

'Any way he could be good for Gold's killing?' asked Zito. 'Then an accomplice turned on him?'

'That be good,' said Mouncey. 'Be like a Bogart movie.'

'Yeah,' I said. 'That way it's a two-fer murder. Makes for more challenging police work.'

'I sense a nasty streak of laziness developing in you, old buddy,' said Zito. He looked over at the folder Mouncey held. 'Hey,' he said, grabbing a sketch of a framing hammer Wayne had apparently made earlier. 'What's this about?'

'It's probably what drove the nails that crucified Gold,' I said. 'A California framing hammer. Ever seen one?'

He looked up at me, saying, 'Seen it? I got it in my evidence locker, hoss. We found it at the Frix fire.'

'You what?'

'It was laying in the ashes a couple of yards from the body. Some of the handle's gone, but it was this puppy all right. Seemed a little out of place to me so I tagged and bagged it.'

'Well, shee-it,' said Mouncey.

'Line three,' Bertie announced from the doorway. 'Lady named Earlene Cutchell says she's got something you need to know about Dr Gold's killing.'

A quick series of images from *Saturday Night Live* – stained glass, Dana Carvey in drag – flitted through my mind before I clicked on Earlene Cutchell as the name of the church lady who'd been Deborah Gold's secretary.

THIRTY-FOUR

The sky was November classic, hazed at low altitude and streaked with high cirrus mare's tails, as I drove out to the Cutchell place. Turning up the driveway, I glanced in the rearview and saw the third of three vehicles that had been behind me, a completely anonymous black Ford sedan, flash by, giving me a strobe shot of the guy behind the wheel. His posture, the set of his shoulders and his general look seemed somehow out of sync with his scruffy flannel shirt. He didn't even glance my way as he passed, but I saw his Stetson and caught the flash of sun on his shades.

He was the man I'd seen watching me at OZ's fish fry.

The Cutchells' house was a square white pier-and-beam on an acre or so of land off Buckner, a World War Two-era structure shaded by mature native pecans, sweetgums and turkey oaks. It was flanked by forsythias, pyracanthas and spireas, and a camellia surrounded by a white fall of curled petals stood by the walk. Parked under one of the big oaks in front of the house were a red five-year-old Corolla and a dusty black Ford stepside that looked closer to fifteen years old. A composed-looking tortoiseshell tabby sat on the hood of the Toyota, watching me with cautious amber eyes.

Mrs Cutchell answered my knock almost instantly, as if

she'd been watching the driveway through her front window the way country people do when they're expecting company. She was a tall, plain woman in her early fifties, a Pentecostal wearing wire-rimmed glasses, no makeup, a simple print dress hemmed below the calf and sturdy shoes, her hair pinned in a bun at the back of her head. She invited me into a small, organza-curtained front room that smelled like floor wax and mothballs, and introduced me to her invalid husband and Brother Ritchie – 'our pastor', she said in a slightly hushed tone. With his wavy slicked-back hair, orange polyester pants and wide white belt, he looked like Jerry Lee Lewis in his prime. Holding a well-thumbed bible in his left hand, he stood and offered me his right, which was warm and moist.

Mr Cutchell was a collapsed, angular grey man in clean, pressed denim overalls and railroad shirt, with oxygen tubes in his nostrils. Without getting up from his worn easychair he gave me a cool bony hand and a small nod, and waved me to the couch. A multi-coloured braided rug covered most of the dark pine floor, and what looked like a hundred-year-old grandfather clock stood in the hall, its darkly gleaming brass pendulum sweeping out a slow, back-and-forth arc behind the etched glass. Brother Ritchie returned to the caned rocking chair beside Mr Cutchell.

'Can I get you something?' said Mrs Cutchell. 'Some tea or coffee?'

'No, thank you,' I said, bringing out the small notebook I carried in my shirt pocket.

'Lieutenant Bonham, I want to say something about why I decided to call you.' She looked at the other men. 'It was Raymond and Brother Ritchie who convinced me I needed to tell the truth about this.'

271

A wisp of a smile lifted one corner of the pastor's mouth, his expression shifting, vulpine.

'But before I called I asked people I trust about you, people who know who you are, and I prayed about it.' She sat in the mate to her husband's easychair, knees and ankles tight together in front of her. 'Can I ask you one question?'

'What do you want to know?'

'That man you injured several years ago, the drug dealer – I was told you did that to keep your partner from shooting him. Is that true?'

'Yes, ma'am, it is.'

'Something else I was told was that you conduct yourself like a true Christian, that you try to do what's right even if you have to break rules and even if you get hurt doing it. I felt led to you.'

Not knowing how to respond to this, I didn't try. I said, 'Mrs Cutchell, are you aware of how Dr Gold died?'

'Mercy, can there be anybody above ground who isn't?' she said. 'And now that Frix man. It's all just so horrible! Have you learned anything about who's responsible?'

'Not much. I appreciate your offering to help and being willing to go over all this again.'

She looked down at the backs of her hands. 'I'm sure the detective who came out was a nice man.'

'Danny Ridout?'

'Yes, I think that was his name.'

'He's a pretty good investigator,' I said. The oxygen tanks hissed faintly. Brother Ritchie cleared his throat.

'It's me,' she said, looking at Ritchie, who gave her an encouraging little nod. 'Mr Ridout was fine, very polite, but there were some things I didn't tell him.'

I waited again.

'It's not an easy thing for me to admit, Lieutenant Bonham, but I'm afraid I strayed from the light a long time ago.' She lowered her gaze. 'I was raised in the Lord. There's no excuse for it.' She met my eyes again. 'I gave in to pride-fulness and envy and greed. And worse. I denied the Lord and turned away from Him to follow my own desires. I fell short of His grace. But when Raymond got sick it brought me to my senses, and Brother Ritchie led me back to the light. That's what the church is, you know, a light unto the world – '

I said, 'You worked for Dr Gold a little over six years, didn't you?'

'Yes, sir. Six years that I'm not proud of. I guess I once thought I was.' She shook her head.

'What was it you had trouble with about those six years?'

'Well, I didn't have trouble at the time. While I was working for Dr Gold I thought, maybe the Devil led me to think, that her way of doing things was the right way.'

'What was her way?'

'Oh my goodness. Her way. Well, her way had a lot to do with it being the only way. With lying and cheating, and with hating anybody who might take a patient away from her or get more attention than her or beat her in court. She never forgave anybody for anything, and when she had it in for somebody, getting revenge was all that mattered to her. She thought everybody had it in for *her*. She was just so needy.'

'Needy?'

'I don't know. Is that the right word? I guess what I mean is she could never be satisfied. Not with anything. If she had three school contracts she wanted five, ten. If she saw twelve patients a day she wanted it to be eighteen.

273

More. If somebody in town was getting forty-eight per cent from one of the insurance carriers she wanted to get sixty.'

'Forty-eight? Is that typical?'

'Actually that's probably a high figure. The insurance companies are the worst thieves you can imagine. They're even beginning to extort money from treatment providers just to be on their so-called "panels", meaning you have to pay to be allowed to treat their patients.'

'How much money are we talking about?'

'Oh, say a thousand dollars or so a year for each network. If they aren't stopped it'll eventually be a lot more, of course. Then when you file, they "lose" a certain percentage of the claims, say they didn't receive them, or some trivial piece of information is missing, or you used the wrong forms or codes. Mostly lies of course, and if you call them on it, usually they'll eventually "discover" the error, and maybe even apologise, but payment is delayed at least until the next billing cycle. Usually longer. And by then they'll be denying something else for no good reason. It's just an endless battle.'

'What went on between Dr Gold and Dr Pendergrass about this?'

'Oh my, they were constantly at odds, especially there near the end. I believe Dr Pendergrass felt he was being cheated. But he wasn't, or at least not by us. I know because all the billing went through my hands.'

'Is this related to what you said you needed to tell me?'

'In a way. With Dr Gold of course everything was about money. She was as dishonest with the insurance companies as they were with us, and I'm sure if anyone wanted to really look at the records they could make some kind of case against her. Probably against me too, as far as that goes.' She touched a tissue to her eyes. 'I'm not saying I deserve to be delivered from what I've done,' she went on. Another glance at Ritchie, who again nodded reassuringly. 'I'll render unto Caesar what I must.'

'Mrs Cutchell – '

'And whether I am punished or not, I'll never work in an environment like that again, I can promise you,' she said. 'But what I thought you should see was this.' She picked up a printout from the side table and handed it to me. It was a column of letter sequences, in caps, and beside that a column of number/letter combinations:

ALK	00800M
CR	01200M
FB	01400Q
FJJ	00150W
FO	02000Q
LNF	00400M
LNR	00600M
MR	01000Q
PSF	10000Q
VBM	00300M
ZK	00500M

'Where did you get this?' I said.

'From Dr Gold's computer. I printed it out the day I was fired. In fact, it's the reason she let me go. She caught me with it on the screen, but I'd already slipped this into my purse.'

'I get the idea you knew exactly what this was,' I said.

'Yes, sir, I know what it is. Earlier I said all the billing went through my hands. I should have said all the regular billing did. This list had to do with a special account Dr Gold kept. I found out about it when the bank mixed up the statements one month and I opened the wrong one.'

'Then the letters on the left would be people's initials – ' She nodded.

'And the numbers on the right are dollar amounts?'

'Right. Four hundred, a thousand, twelve hundred and so forth. Regular payments.'

I glanced up at her. 'Did you know who the payments were for?'

'Dr Gold. Her private account.'

'What about the letters on the right?'

'That tells you whether the payment was to be made weekly, monthly or quarterly.'

'You know these patients?'

'No. At least I don't recognise the initials, but Dr Gold called them patients when she walked in on me.'

'What else did she say?'

'She screamed that this was privileged information, that I had no right to be snooping in her computer, things like that.'

'How did you get into her files?' I said. 'Wasn't this password protected?'

'Oh, yes, it was. Dr Gold thought she was smarter than everyone else, but she had a habit of using the names of constellations as passwords. Signs of the zodiac, I guess they're called. Brother Ritchie thinks it was part of an overall pattern of evil. And that what happened to Dr Gold was a righteous judgement on her.' She glanced at the preacher again and got another thin smile and a hint of a nod. 'Anyway, I got in on the third try. Leo.'

'Mrs Cutchell, what did you say Dr Gold's hourly fee was?'

'A hundred and ninety-five dollars an hour. More for going to court or testing.'

'How often did she see the patients?'

'Usually once a week.'

I looked down the list of figures, all of them round and tidy sums. What did anybody sell – or buy – for such nice even amounts like these? 'That fee doesn't match up with these numbers,' I said. 'Did she charge anybody by the month for their visits? Or by the quarter?'

'No.'

'So – '

'So these entries have nothing to do with treatment, Lieutenant Bonham.'

Of course they didn't. No one spoke for a few seconds as the only plausible explanation buzzed silently around the room a couple of times and came in for a landing.

'Because they're blackmail payments,' I said unnecessarily.

With this much at least off her chest, Mrs Cutchell, then her husband and finally Brother Ritchie, nodded.

THIRTY-FIVE

When I called District Attorney Rick Hart for an appointment, I didn't mention his younger brother Robert, or the fact that I had managed to steer him into rehab instead of jail the year before. Rick didn't mention my troubles with the city manager. On this don't-ask-don't-tell basis we met at his office and got down to business.

'There's got to be some way we can at least get the names,' I said as we sat on opposite sides of his busy-looking mahogany desk.

'Files are out, names are out, billing records are out,' he said, shaking his head tiredly. 'You know this stuff as well as I do, Jim. It all comes under the statute.' He tossed his pencil onto the yellow pad on his desk and blew out his breath. Touched by the afternoon sun angling through the window, his kinky red hair glowed like incandescent filaments around the edges. 'I don't like it any better than you do,' he said, 'but there it is. Inge's gonna toss anything he thinks we developed from those records – it's all fruit of the same fuckin' poisoned tree.' He took a clove from the small cut-glass candy dish beside his desk calendar, bit it in half with savage precision.

I said, 'What about the Cutchell list?'

Hart stood and walked to the window, staring abstractly into the pale sky, five and a half pudgy feet of disgust in pinstripe worsted. Finally he said, 'Considering how you came by it, I think we can dance our way around that. As far as it goes. What the hell good it'll do us is the real question. No way to decipher the initials or connect them to anything. Same for the numbers.'

We both knew our best hope for finding out who planned and ordered Gold's killing was her patient records, either in her computer files or as hard copy. All the records had been in custody and under seal at Three since the day the body was discovered, but without a court order they might as well have been on Phobos. If Rick's office used the information anyway and got caught, it would blow the entire case. Even physical possession of the records put the police and prosecutors at the dark end of a grey area.

'Okay,' I said. 'Forget the names. How about just initials?'

He turned to face me. 'What do you mean?'

'LA tells me psychologists are supposed to make arrangements with somebody, a master I think they call it, to handle their records if something happens to them, they die or whatever. My guess, Gold would never do that – she was too paranoid. If I'm right, maybe you can get Judge Inge to appoint a master, another psychologist, to oversee the files and have the names converted to initials. We look for matches with the Cutchell list. Find them and you've got probable cause, even with Inge.'

Hart stared at me. He went back to his desk, tapped his teeth with his fingernail. 'By God,' he said. He scribbled a couple of lines on the pad. 'By God, we might just make that work.' He leaned back in his chair and thought for a minute. 'Give me the rest of the day,' he said. 'I'll pull up some case law and talk to the judge.'

Under the deal he eventually worked out with Inge, a psychologist master – Max, as it turned out – was appointed by the judge to supervise the preparation of the list. The final roster came to 582 sets of initials representing all the cases in Gold's active and recent files, and it was in Hart's hands before lunch on the day it was finished. I got OZ on the phone and told him what we had.

There was a silence as he thought about it. Finally he said, 'How good does it eyeball?'

'First look, the initials on Earlene Cutchell's list don't seem to match any from Gold's files, so it's probably going to take some decoding, but it's the best shot we've had so far.'

'Then run with it,' he said. 'The council's still leaning on us hard to chase these yahoos out in the woods, so I'll do-si-do 'em a little to keep the heat off. Hazen's jaws are gettin' pretty tight. He keeps asking me where you're at. I still haven't heard anything about a subpoena for you but it could be out there, so look sharp. Meantime, there ain't no point in getting anybody else hung out to dry until we know something for sure.'

My phone rang. It was Dispatch.

To tell me LA had been shot.

THIRTY-SIX

'What's her condition?' I asked the dispatcher, my chest tight. 'Where was she hit?' The light around me seemed to pulse with invisible colour, my own voice hollow and distant.

A hesitation. 'Uh, the responding MTs advise it was a, uh, head wound, sir. We don't have any other information right now.'

I pictured LA's defiant hair, her dark sceptical eyes, her rare but beautiful smile. *A head wound?* That couldn't be right. There had to be some mistake. Head wounds killed people, and LA couldn't be dead. That couldn't happen; the universe couldn't do anything so terrible without some kind of forewarning.

But it could.

The universe wasn't the responsible party here, though, and I knew it. It wasn't the universe that had brought LA into this and put her directly in harm's way. Gotten her killed. This was my fight, not hers; her work had been healing broken minds and hearts, not chasing murdering assholes to whom her life meant nothing at all.

It was at this moment that I saw my own selfishness and stupidity more clearly than ever before in my life. I'd been unforgivably blind, bringing this horror down on us, inviting disaster with open arms and sacrificing LA's life on the altar of my own fucking brainlessness.

On my way to St Vincent's I got Dispatch again to tell them where I was. 'Let Patrol know,' I said. 'And if there's anybody out there who doesn't know this truck, give them the description and tell them if they want to see their kids again, don't get in my way.'

'Roger that, sir.' He told me the shooting had been called in from Burnsville Road and 59 South, where somebody in a passing vehicle had apparently fired at least one shot at LA from the next lane as she drove north toward the interstate. No reports of anybody hearing shots. Her unsteered vehicle had then drifted into the median, where it had bogged down in the soft soil of a drainage swale and come to a stop. Nobody had gotten a plate number or description of the shooter's vehicle. No witnesses to the shooting itself had been located.

I managed to get Mouncey on her cell and asked her to get to the scene and take control of the investigation, but there was nothing else I could do. And there was no excuse for not seeing that something like this was coming. I should have given more weight to the threat sandwiched into Keets' words. I should never have underestimated him like this. I should have taken all the precautions that hadn't occurred to me then but were so obvious to me now.

What I couldn't stop hearing and re-hearing in my mind was Dispatch telling me LA had been shot in the head, and what I couldn't stop seeing was a parade of images of the head-injury victims I'd seen over the years: faces shot away, skulls blown apart like melons, bodies gone slack and pale. And finally a mental picture of LA lying on a hospital gurney, what was left of her face covered by

282

a bloody sheet. I caught myself flexing my right hand again and again, remembering what Max had said about a man's capacity for violence, and understood finally that this was what it took to blow away ten thousand years of civilisation in half a second: the murder of your own flesh and blood. I realised now how absolutely wrong I'd been to stop Bo from killing Tidwell. If I'd just let him pull the trigger that day, he'd still be alive and telling dirty jokes and yelling at the Cowboys on the TV screen, whether he was still carrying a badge or not. His instinct had been the true one, not mine.

It was a mistake I was never going to make again.

As if I weren't the cause of what had happened, I served notice on the heavens: the world was now a free-fire zone. There was no hole deep enough to hide LA's killer, not anywhere, and no mercy imaginable for him. I struggled to beat back my nausea and keep my thoughts focused. I had to maintain clarity and control for what I was going to do.

I slammed through the ER entrance, blew past the clerk and a nurse in pink scrubs who actually ran away when she saw me, looked into Room 1 where I saw a grass-stained teenager with a swollen ankle, into Room 2 where a kid was screaming about a bug in his ear. I ripped the curtain to Room 3 aside but it was empty.

I found LA in Room 4. She was sitting on the edge of the table as a young oriental doctor in blue scrubs carefully stitched a cut above her left eyebrow. There were other, smaller cuts on her cheek and up near her hairline. Bunched bloody towels lay on the table beside her and on the floor, and a couple of nurses were re-kitting the cranial trauma gear. There was blood all over the front of LA's white pull-over shirt.

Catching sight of me from the corner of her eye, she said, 'I'm okay, Bis.'

'Is she, doc?' My own blood was roaring in my ears.

'Yes, she is. There is a small artery here, and all the blood caused a little hysteria with the onlookers, but the bullets did not strike her at all. These injuries are from flying glass. This one will make a small scar, but a cute one. She is going to be fine.'

THIRTY-SEVEN

Two hours after getting LA through the discharge hassle and driving her back to Lanshire, I was out of a job. I'd gone to Three with the idea of catching up on the dailies and updating OZ, but he had checked out right after lunch and still wasn't back. I was telling Ridout about the Cutchell interview when I looked up and saw OZ walking across the squad room from the direction of the elevators, his jaw tight. He caught my eye and nodded toward his office. I caught up with him and closed the door behind me as he was bringing out a fifth of Jack Daniels and a couple of jelly glasses from the bottom drawer of his desk. He poured three fingers of whisky into each glass.

'Just got back from a meeting with a bunch of them egg-suckers on the council,' he said, tossing back his whisky. 'They're gonna call a special session as soon as they can get a quorum together.' He rapped the glass down on his desk.

'About what?'

'You. They're calling you a headcase, re-openin' the investigation on that old collar at the graveyard, even talkin' about you having something to do with Gold's killing. Bastards say they'll be looking at termination and maybe even some kind of charges. Sounds like they think they can get you behind bars.' He shook his head in disgusted disbelief.

'Hazen's behind it?'

'Like shit behind a goose. And for now you're off the job, so I gotta have your sidearm and tin. Got your hideout piece?'

'Yeah, I do.'

'Good.'

As I tossed my Glock and badge case on OZ's desk, I tried to imagine how the investigation was going to play out with me gone. I didn't see how just taking me off the board could be enough to derail it, and without that there didn't seem to be much benefit to Hazen, the council or anybody else in getting rid of me. But maybe I was overestimating my own importance. Maybe there was no connection between my heading the investigation and the sudden interest in bringing me down. I remembered Jaston Keets scoffing at the idea of death threats deterring me or the department, and he was right, because after me the next guy they'd have to get past would be OZ. It was hard to imagine anybody thinking that was going to be a better deal than keeping me.

I said, 'What exactly is Hazen's angle, OZ?'

He shook his head. 'Damned if I know, Jim, but this ain't over. Not by a long shot. You still got that hellacious boat?'

'Yeah, I've still got her. Why?'

He told me what he had in mind.

The next day's *Gazette* coverage of my firing – which I knew wasn't Cass's because she only wrote under a byline – turned out to be worth about seven column inches above the fold, far right:

Decorated TX-Side Cop Out; Inquiry Pending

From Staff Reports

TRAVERTON, Texas -- Noted Texas-side police lieutenant James B. Bonham was today indefinitely suspended without pay, an action tantamount to firing, by city officials after City Manager Dwight Hazen announced an official inquiry into the near-fatal beating of a suspect in an earlier investigation. The suspect, Jeremy Gage Tidwell, who had been wanted for questioning in the murders of the wife and daughter of Bonham's then partner, the late Robert 'Bo' Jackson, was critically injured while being taken into custody, requiring extensive plastic surgery of the face and jaw. According to Hazen, Bonham, who he says has a history of mental health problems, assaulted Tidwell in retaliation for the murders.

The rest of the article was more of the same, Hazen promising an arrest 'when circumstances warrant'. I tossed the paper into the recycle bin and shrugged at LA, who sat across the kitchen table from me. She had changed the bandage above her eye, and the visible nicks and cuts on her face seemed to be healing well.

She took a sip of coffee from her mug and said, 'Fuck 'em if they can't take a joke.'

287

'OZ wants us to take *Bufordine* up to DeGray,' I said. The boat had belonged to a Shreveport dope dealer before he got busted, after which it went through forfeiture proceedings and came up for auction in Traverton in the middle of a sleet storm. Realising nobody else was in the hunt, I bid two thousand dollars, all the disposable cash I had. Under normal conditions it wouldn't have been enough to buy the trailer the boat rode on, but on this day it put me in possession of a bass rig worth more than my house, a Merc-powered 20-foot Allison capable of a hundred knots on flat water.

Looking the boat over, LA had said, 'This is a phallic flip-off that can't be topped, Bis. We'll call her *Bufordine*.'

I would never have thought of christening a bass boat, but LA had liked Casey's name for my truck and – probably thinking I needed more continuity in my life – decided to extend the theme.

'Hey, that's a great idea, Bis,' LA said now. 'Hell of a lot better than sitting around the house grinding your teeth and feeling sorry for yourself.'

'Yeah, just the thing for a disgraced cop,' I said. 'Fresh air and sunshine. A last taste of freedom.'

'What was OZ's thinking?'

I sketched out the plan for her. 'He said the only disgrace would be letting that shorthorn son of a bitch Hazen get the drop on me.'

'Just what Matt Dillon would've said.'

As much as the idea of being off the case galled me, I had to admit OZ was probably right. The last thing he needed was Hazen dragging me in front of the council and the grand jury, and my getting out of town would pull most of the media pressure away from the Gold investigation.

But my real interest was getting Jana and the girls out of the line of fire.

'What about the Ranger who's supposed to be investigating you?'

'No telling. Nobody seems to have any idea where he is, but those guys are a force of nature and a law unto themselves. Nothing anybody can do about him. OZ says at least he's not talking to Hazen or any of the council members, whatever that signifies.'

LA shrugged philosophically and lifted her cup in salute, saying, 'Okay, troop, *que sera sera*. At least we've got ourselves a plan.'

As it turned out, Jana had scheduled a major buying trip to Dallas that I couldn't talk her out of, which almost caused me to change my mind about leaving town. But I couldn't do anybody any good if I was in jail.

Jana's idea was that distance and anonymity were her best protection. 'All those miles over there, nobody knows anybody in a town like Dallas – how're they gonna find me?'

Thinking about this, I didn't answer her immediately, which she rightly took as a sign I wasn't convinced. She watched me for a minute, then said, 'How about if I take the girls with me?'

'Where would they be staying if you didn't?'

'The usual – Casey with Sara McLemore, Jordie with her friend Lindsey down the street.'

'Where they've stayed a hundred times before,' I said. 'And everybody knows it.'

'Well, not a hundred, but yeah, plenty of times.'

'Take them with you.'

Calling in a personal marker, I got T. Jack Frost, the

Patrol supervisor, a bad dog of a man with three daughters of his own, to agree to give Jana and the girls an unmarked escort out of town, hand off to the Highway Patrol to take them at least as far as Mount Pleasant, and keep an eye on Kiln-Roi and the A-frame until we all got back.

'On it,' he said. 'When you coming back to work, Lou?'

'I'll check my horoscope and find out,' I said.

Next I got hold of Ridout and Mouncey, told them where I was going and asked them to keep me posted if anything happened.

'You got it, boss,' said Ridout. 'Hey, these council assholes are just barkin' at the moon, ain't they?'

'I guess we'll know soon enough,' I said. 'Meantime I'm counting on you guys to keep the wheels on, okay?'

'You believe it, Lou,' said Mouncey.

THIRTY-EIGHT

I did a last walkaround of *Bufordine* in the driveway, made sure we had all the drain plugs and checked that the hitch chains were in place, the trolling motor locked back and the fishing seats snapped down. I reached over and turned the key to confirm fire in the deep-cycle batteries and pushed against the massive lower assembly of the motor with my toe, finding it firmly seated in the transom-saver. The Raker aftermarket prop felt solid.

The day was cool and bright, with a photographic quality to the light, as we pulled out and headed north-east into Arkansas on our way to Lake DeGray. The off-hour traffic was fairly light on I-30 and we were making good time, the big boat tracking smoothly behind us, when my phone buzzed. It was Wayne, and he had apparently just gotten the news.

'This sucks, Lou,' he said. 'What're we gonna do?'

I was beginning to get the early buzz of a familiar feeling – a sense of things being connected in some way that I needed to see but couldn't. I tried and failed to pin it down.

'Nothing,' I said, distracted and unable to shake off the sense of something at the back door of my awareness, patiently trying to pick the lock. 'I'm going fishing.'

'Gotta be some way to turn this around,' he persisted. 'Maybe we could go to the AG.'

'Forget it,' I said. 'But I'm curious about what you've got. As a citizen.'

He downshifted grudgingly from indignation, reporting that the semen recovered during Gold's autopsy positively matched Frix's DNA, and the 28-ounce Gibb Yeoman framing hammer Zito had found in the ashes of Frix's house was definitely the implement that had driven the spikes at the crucifixion scene. Frix had already been dead when the fire started, with two gunshot wounds and massive blunt trauma to the head that was consistent with the framing hammer. The bullet fragments they had found were from .44 Magnum Federal ammunition, but they were too damaged for ballistic matching.

'For whatever good any of it's gonna do us,' he said.

'Anything else?'

'Word is, Hazen's pushing for us to basically start rounding up rednecks and sweatin' 'em until somebody breaks. It ain't happening, though. Chief says he'll damn well let us know when the gad-blasted city manager starts running our gad-blasted investigations. He kind of left it hanging in the air that if any of us happened to talk to you and if you happened to have any thoughts about how we ought to proceed, it'd be a good idea to follow up on that and keep him advised.'

Imagining Dwight Hazen, or anybody else, trying to stampede OZ actually made me smile. I told Wayne I'd give him a call back if anything occurred to me and thumbed the phone off.

'What's funny?' LA asked.

'Hazen thinks he's going to make OZ dance to his tune on this deal.'

She snorted.

When I outlined for her the other side of the conversation, she said, 'Told you it all hooked up. Gotta pick up on the gestalts.'

'The whats?'

'Patterns,' she said. 'Foundation of perception.'

I looked at her over my sunglasses. She opened the window a crack, got out a cigarette, lit it and fiddled with the radio until she found a Springsteen number she liked. We watched the passing countryside and listened to the Boss for a couple of miles as I thought about being out of work and maybe even headed for jail. I was surprised at how little the unemployment part bothered me, and it might have been wishful thinking but the idea of going to jail seemed too far-fetched to worry about.

In the rearview mirror I could see a couple of news vans in tandem hanging back a few hundred yards behind us. One of them looked like the Channel Three rig I'd seen in front of Kiln-Roi, and they both seemed to be full of people – reporters and cameramen, I assumed.

We pulled in at DeGray a little sooner than I'd expected but didn't get on the water right away. First came the reporters, swarming on us like hounds on a boar when we stepped down from the truck. I half hoped to see Cass with them, but I really knew better; she didn't do this kind of legwork any more. As the media crews were bringing out their microphones and firing up their cameras I drew my fingers across my lips in a zipping motion and said, 'Anybody who can't stay off the record for this conversation raise your hand.' Nobody did. I located Mallory Peck among the reporters, made eye contact with her and said, 'Do I lie?'

She gave me a crinkle-eyed smile and said, 'Not if you can help it.'

'Ever keep you out of the loop without a good reason?'

'No.'

'So okay, guys,' I said to the group at large, after a small nod to Geoff Dean to acknowledge our pre-existing deal. 'The bandages Dr Rowe here is wearing are for glass cuts, and they are connected to the Deborah Gold case, but the injuries are not life-threatening, and we're really, truly not going to say anything else on the record about that or anything else while we're up here – '

'Lieutenant Bonham, what about – '

I held up a palm just as Geoff said, 'He means it, Rob.'

'So if you have to have quotes you've got to get them from Three,' I said, 'but take all the footage you want. And since we're going to be up here a day or two, why don't we just kick back and enjoy the weather?'

LA and I walked over to the lodge dining room and ordered an early lunch – blackened catfish, jalapeno hush-puppies and fried apples – from a friendly, freckled Texas waitress who was homesick for Vernon, a feeling I wouldn't have thought was possible. Outside the windows of the dining room the lake stretched away between the hills, with little timbered islands here and there that looked like the tall ships of another century. Some of the reporters had settled in twos and threes at other tables around the room, checking out the menus and occasionally glancing our way, probably to make sure none of their colleagues was poaching.

I decided to call Ridout and ask if he'd pulled together the background I'd asked for on the local psychologists. He had. Thinking ahead to the hours I was going to spend on the boat, I waved away another coffee refill. I didn't expect Ridout's news to amount to much, and I was mostly right. There were no felonies, because that would be a licence-killer, but a misdemeanour popped up here and there, along with several traffic tickets and a few lawsuits by disgruntled patients.

And one revoked licence. Mark Pendergrass.

'How's he working without a licence?'

'Prison system doesn't require it. He's got a counselling licence in Texas, but at the prison he doesn't even need that. Out there he's still a psychologist by job title.'

I thought back to the paper I'd seen on Pendergrass's wall but couldn't remember seeing anything there with the word 'Psychologist' on it. I said, 'What happened with his licence?'

'Messing with women patients,' he said. 'They tell me that's the usual reason.'

'Who filed the complaint?'

'Care to guess?'

'Deborah Gold.'

'Ten-ring,' he said. 'How'd you know?'

'Shot in the dark,' I said.

'I got one left, Lou – you want it?' He'd saved Max Karras for last.

'Anything there that connects to the case?' I asked.

'Don't look like it.'

'Shred everything but Pendergrass,' I said.

THIRTY-NINE

At the dock LA said, 'Let me run her, Bis?'

I saw a couple of reporters hustling out along the rental dock down the shore, cameras and gear swinging from their necks and banging on their hips.

I considered *Bufordine* fairly intimidating, but that wasn't a concept that had a lot of meaning to LA. I helped her get her lifejacket on and the kill switch snapped into place, watching as she stowed her Braves cap under the dash and captured her hair with a yellow elastic headband. Then she put on her sunglasses, zipped her peach-coloured tracksuit up to her chin and settled into the captain's seat behind the wheel. Slowly backing the boat clear of the ramp, she eased us out the channel through the no-wake zone to open water, swung the bow toward the centre of the lake and started bringing the throttle forward.

There were no medium settings in LA's personality, but today for some reason she gave the boat only enough gas to get us up on plane and running at a decent clip. Behind us a couple of boats were already pulling away from the rental dock. LA glanced back, then returned her attention to the water ahead of us. We were cruising at low revs, the following boats by now almost half a mile back but no longer losing ground. LA seemed to forget about them.

But a few minutes later as we were passing one of the little uninhabited, heavily wooded islands that dotted the lake, a couple of other bass boats travelling in opposite directions crossed in front of us about two hundred yards ahead, just beyond the island, the occupants tossing each other friendly waves as they passed.

By this time LA's course had taken *Bufordine* past a small promontory of the island, temporarily blocking the view of the trailing boats, and now her eyes narrowed as she swung into the churned water left by the other bass boats, cutting hard to starboard and throttling up. *Bufordine* jumped forward, and LA took her in a tight curve around the tip of the island, the low rumble of the motor rising to a murderous roar, the tach needle bouncing at the redline. She trimmed the boat out and with one hand on the wheel, the other on the power bar, took us back along the far side of the island, intently scanning the bright water ahead for other traffic, debris or birds. I held on. At five hundred miles an hour in an airliner it's possible to be bored. At a hundred miles an hour in a bass boat, it's not.

A pair of ducks flushed ahead of us, redheads as it turned out, open-water divers; birds that, unlike mallards and other puddle ducks, tend to put their money on horizontal velocity instead of altitude when spooked. LA ran in under them, throttled back to match their speed, then reached up to point her finger like a six-gun at the drake beating frantically in the air above her head and dropped her thumb. She blew the smoke off her fingertip, made a holstering motion with her hand and throttled back up.

As we rounded the downlake end of the island LA

came back on the power bar, re-entering the main channel and falling in line a few hundred yards behind the pursuers. I thought I could pick out somebody crouching on the foredeck of the lead press boat, fumbling with what was probably a camera bag as all the vessels now continued single file up the lake at about the thirty knots the rental boats could manage, *Bufordine* now bringing up the rear of the procession. The reporter who had been digging in his bag was now peering ahead through his telephoto lens trying to spot us, but none of the reporters thought to look back.

When we reached the point north of the Yancey Creek channel LA slowed and brought us around, prospecting back along the shore for promising water. The sun was past zenith when she found a deep cut next to a raft of lily pads. She swung in and brought the throttle all the way back, and the boat wallowed down into the water as the reporters' boats gradually lost themselves in the distance, still in search of us.

I walked forward to tip the prop of the trolling motor into the water, checked the battery connections and the foot control and used the silent little motor to position us off the lily pads. Unstowing the rods from the gunnel racks, I glanced at the fishfinder but decided to go primitive and leave it off.

'Best fish buys dinner,' I said.

LA shook her head as she got out of the chair and unsnapped the rear fishing seat. 'First fish.'

Which was no surprise. Wanting to see all the action, she was going to fish topwaters, which except at dawn and dusk are slow producers but can bring in some really good fish. On the other hand, wanting immediate results, I intended to work the bottom along the cut with a plastic worm, which is usually the quickest way to get a take.

'Figuring out why Hazen got me canned is one thing,' I said, handing LA the lighter of the two casting rods. 'But I keep coming back to Gold. I mean, what the hell was it that got her out of her house that night? Going by the lab results, the party was just getting hot. What would make her bail out at that point?'

LA stuffed the headband back in her pocket and put on her cap before tying on a green floating frog and making a practice cast into open water to get the feel of the outfit. 'Gotta figure it was the call of the coin,' she said. 'I don't know what else is going to be enough of an incentive.' She adjusted the reel's inertial brake and cast again. Satisfied, she reeled in and turned to square off against the pads.

'How about fear?' I selected a six-inch grape worm and Texas-rigged it on a 1/0 hook.

'Of what?'

'Blackmail, let's say. Suppose she had dark secrets? I mean darker than we already know about.'

As LA thought about this, she lightly caught one side of her lower lip between her teeth, her oldest concentration-enhancing technique, and whipped out a cast to drop the frog weightlessly onto one of the pads. She shook her head again.

'Everybody's got dark secrets,' she said. 'But if it was blackmail she'd have to be sure they had something or she wouldn't have gone out to meet them. Considering her profile, I don't think they could've bluffed her. She'd be way too suspicious – not to mention too smart – for anything like that. Plus, I doubt they'd actually have had anything on her. Look at the elaborate killing they were about to do – who's gonna go to the trouble of putting together a real blackmail package just to set up a murder?' She glanced at me. 'Anyway, do blackmailers do homicide?'

I dropped the purple worm next to a stickup and after a few seconds felt the bullet weight touch bottom. 'I guess it could happen,' I said. 'But you kind of look for it to be the other way around: victim murders blackmailer.'

'In the movies, anyway,' she said.

There was a tentative double bump on my line. I waited a second, then set the hook. It turned out to be a smallish bass, a pound or so, and I unhooked and released it.

'Gotcha,' said LA.

'Crackers and water on me,' I said.

She ignored this, her eyes on the frog.

Trying out various scenarios in my head, I said, 'Okay, say Gold gets a call at home – '

'How do we know it was at home?'

'Her purse. Not that it necessarily tells you where she was coming from, just that she wasn't already at her office. If she was, it would've been behind her desk or in a cabinet or somewhere else in her personal office.'

'Okay, so she gets the call, some kind of hot case, big up-front fee, hearing scheduled the next day maybe, can she meet to discuss it, et cetera, et cetera.'

'No, not to discuss it, that doesn't work,' I said. 'They'd have had to do that on the phone to get her to interrupt what was going on with Frix and her other playmates and get her out of the house. It had to be to meet the callers and collect a fee, let's say, or to look at some kind of evidence, maybe files of some kind.'

I heard the distant sound of outboards approaching from uplake.

300

LA twitched the frog off the edge of the lily pad, and it immediately disappeared in a swirling splash. She snapped the rod back and the fish was on. Fearing for her line, I cranked my own lure in as fast as I could and ran to get my foot on the trolling motor control. I steered us over as far into the pads as possible, hoping to get on top of the fish. It made a couple of hard runs under the heavy cover, then broke water and shook its big head. It was a good bass, deep-bellied and putting on weight for the winter, probably five pounds, maybe even six. The fish jumped twice more before LA got it alongside and I leaned down to lip it and hoist it clear of the water for LA to see, thinking now more along the lines of seven pounds.

By this time the boats carrying the reporters, some hoisting cameras onto their shoulders, had closed to hailing range.

As LA watched me twist the frog free of the bass's lip a reporter in the first boat, a stocky young guy with a bushy black moustache, apparently holding no grudge over being ditched, yelled, 'Hey, can I get a shot of that?' I held the dripping green-gold fish up for the cameras, then bent down and slipped the fish back into the water and watched it swim away.

The media boats eased in as close as they could without getting in the way of our fishing and dropped anchor.

'No way I'll ever beat that one,' I said. 'I'm calling it quits.'

LA didn't care. Already back in her casting chair, she sailed the now slightly bent frog out at about two o'clock from her first cast, this time dropping it into a narrow lane of water between the pads, then settled back to wait, her

301

eyes locked on the tiny bump of the frog's back on the smooth water.

I stowed my rod and sat back in my casting chair. Neither of us said anything. With the lulling sound of waves lightly slapping the hull and the warmth of the sun, I began to drift into daydreams, remembering the strange images I'd been drawing compulsively all week. The muscular bare arm holding a hammer that was actually a sword made sense to me now; the squatty-looking T didn't. But I'd noticed that in my mental representations it was changing too, becoming less like a letter of the alphabet and more like a gallows or a stanchion supporting a cross-piece with something hanging like fruit baskets from either end.

Then suddenly these images were replaced by an impression of LA writing her name on something somewhere, her signature – all in lower case – stringing her initials and last name together into one word, *larowe*, the way she'd signed it as long as I could remember. And near her hand on the desk or counter or whatever it was lay her key ring with its round medallion bearing an embossed emblem, an initial, some kind of logo maybe. No mental picture of what it was, just a strong sense that there was something significant there.

'Hey,' I said. 'What's the shape on that little medallion you have on your key ring?'

My tone roused the reporters, and LA looked at me questioningly as they began grabbing for their cameras and microphones.

'It's my birth sign,' she said. 'They had a whole book full of symbols you could choose from – the clerk asked what my birthday was, looked it up, and sold me this one.'

'You're a Libra, right? What's the logo look like?'

'Sometimes they draw it like a little igloo, but mine's more like this.' She drew it in the air with her finger, and I gaped at her.

'Let me see that again,' I said.

This time her fingertip almost seemed to leave a faint smoke trail as she traced the figure in space.

It was the drooping T I'd been drawing for days.

FORTY

I got the rest of my brainwave as we were winching *Bufordine* up onto the trailer. No fireworks, no blinding flash of epiphany, not even a bottle-rocket, just the answer. My mental representation of the scribbled *glowen* that nobody had been able to interpret merged smoothly in my mind with LA's signature, and like a mirage, separated from it vertically Then both images slowly spaced themselves out horizontally: *l a rowe* above, *g l owen* below.

GL Owen.

Glen Lawrence & Owen, Inc, the biggest home and general construction contractor in Traverton, whose offices I drove past every day on my way to and from work. The kind of business where framing hammers and the guys who use them would be everyday sights.

I called Mouncey from the restaurant as we were waiting for our burgers and suggested setting up interviews with Owen site supervisors about their crews. Guys like we were looking for talked a lot, and not always soberly, leaving behind a trail of people who knew all about them and their politics, their sex partners, and everything else from their favourite beer to their boot sizes. Even their lost framing hammers.

'I'd ask about rough carpenters, people with .44 Magnums, guys who move from job to job together and talk about blacks and Jews a lot. Or guys who are Aryan Nation or Klan-connected. And pay special attention to guys who work on concrete slab crews.'

'Why we doin' that, Lou?'

'The nose knows,' I said.

'We run it down,' she said. 'Good to know you still out there thinkin'.'

'I hear OZ's holding the line for now.'

'He okay. You know how he talk, like we in a cowboy movie. Say keep our nose in the wind, whatever that mean.'

'Thanks, M.'

'But what about the big man?' said LA when I ended the call. 'If you're right about the GL Owen thing, that probably means construction bums, or at least not high-level planners. They didn't think this up on their own. Gotta be an evil genius mixed up in there somewhere.'

'I don't know – maybe Keets could be the guy after all,' I said. 'If Mouncey and Ridout collar the grunts who actually did the killings, they'll probably sweat a name out of them.'

She shook her head. 'Maybe,' she said. 'It's not that big a jump from knowing who the killers were to actually being the mastermind, which says Keets. But then I would've thought he'd dance us around about it a little more if he was involved, just to entertain himself. And Frix notches up the confusion. You didn't find any connection between him and Keets, did you?'

'Nope.'

'Okay. Frix was in Gold's sex club. Maybe he pissed off the same people she did. What if it was about kids or short-termers in the group? Some parent or husband finds out about it, decides to make an example of them instead of going through a trial that would at least embarrass his family and might even end with an acquittal.'

'And crucifies her? Pretty resourceful daddy,' I said.

'If somebody used Jordan or Casey that way, couldn't you get something like this done, Bis? If your mind worked that way?'

The question gave me a short, unwanted inner look at what I might do if the same thing had happened to Casey or Jordan, what I'd tried to do to Jeremy Tidwell, and what I'd intended to do when I thought LA had been killed. Not a pretty picture, but whether I wanted to face it or not, it was exactly how my mind worked. The one glimmer of redemption I could see was that LA, who probably knew my mind better than anybody, including me, didn't seem to find me scary.

A man who's incapable of violence isn't worth the wind he sucks . . .

The waitress refilled our glasses, asked if we needed anything else and glided away.

'And who knows more bad guys than a cop?' LA said. 'Who's got more leverage with them?'

Someone close to me, Keets had said. *A guy like me*, Max had said. I shook my head, the faces of all the cops I knew flashing through my mind in mugshot format. 'It just doesn't compute for me,' I said.

LA picked out a slice of radish between thumb and forefinger, ate it in two thoughtful bites. 'What about Feigel?'

'Besides his involvement with the group, he was the guy supplying coke to Gold.'

'Not a suspect?'

'For Gold, no.'

'Jana said Casey was worried her friend Lena might get pulled into the Feigel thing.'

'No need. There's a task-force roundup scheduled next month, and it turns out they've already got enough to hook him up then.'

The waitress brought out the burgers, mine with bacon and cheese, LA's a veggie with organic onion dressing, topped up our iced teas again, smiled and vanished into the kitchen.

'So what happens next with Jana?' LA asked.

'I'm still going in circles about her,' I said.

LA said, 'No, you're not,' and took a sparing bite of soyburger.

'What do you mean?'

'I mean you're going in circles about yourself. Why do you think you haven't taken the deal on the farm?'

'I'm not a rancher,' I said. 'This is all I've ever really done.'

'Bullshit,' she said. 'You do what you do because that's how the cards fell. But don't forget you managed the Flying S at a profit for a whole year while Mom and Dusty were chasing around Europe to all those fertility clinics, right after you got back from TCU. And Dusty knows you can do it again or he wouldn't have made the offer.'

'So what are we saying here?'

'I'm saying you're never going to find anybody who loves you more than Jana does, but she's not great at showing it, and she's damn near as prideful and stubborn as you are. And she can't turn back the clock for you, Bis. She can't repair history and she can't be the wife who only watches and waits.' LA ate a bite of snow pea and said, 'Not living up to the Flying S has never been your problem, Bis.'

'What, then?'

307

'It's the stories you live by. The endings you believe in.'

No answer that seemed worth the breath occurred to me.

'Do you really want to know the beginning of this story? I mean enough to pay the price?'

'What price?'

'Beginnings cost almost as much as endings.'

'Are you hypnotising me again?'

'Think you need that?'

'I don't know.'

'Then it doesn't sound like anything to waste any worry on, does it?' LA said. 'Try to clear your mind, relax, focus away from here and now.' She pinged the rim of her glass with her fingernail. 'It's the week after Homecoming. Let yourself remember. Where are you? What are you doing?'

'Aleha ha-shalom,' Kat said softly, touching the glass covering Dr Kepler's image. *'Baruch dayan emet.'*

Before I could ask what this meant she pulled my mouth down to hers and kissed me again, her breath coming faster.

'Five minutes,' she said, and disappeared into the bathroom.

I heard the shower come on, and a second later the bathroom door opened and she stuck her head out. 'When I come out of here I'm going to be naked as a baby,' she said. 'I hope you won't make me feel all alone.'

Undressing and sliding between the sheets, I lay waiting, my heart slamming in my chest. When Kat said, 'Ready or not,' and stepped out of the bathroom in a cloud of steamy air that smelled of Lifebuoy soap, nipples darkly erect, looking slim and white and perfect as a dream, my throat constricted almost to the point of asphyxia. I held the covers back for her, and after striking a little pose for a second she smilingly joined me, saying, 'I used your toothbrush – I'll get you a new one.'

Then her mouth, sweet with Pepsodent, was on mine and she was tight against me, her hands almost hot where they touched my skin. I slid my own hand down the long smooth curve of her side and pulled her leg over mine as we kissed. She reached between my legs, saying, 'You're so ready. Come on.'

But I couldn't let it be over that soon.

I moved down to kiss her breasts and her navel and her stomach, then gently pulled her sideways to the edge of the bed, spreading her legs and slipping off the side of the bed to kneel between her knees.

'Oh God,' she said, her hips lifting to meet my tongue. Moaning softly, she locked her legs behind my shoulders, and I held her thighs with my hands. Swimming down deep under a silent sea older than time, I kissed her and kissed her until finally she said tightly, 'Oh, oh my God,' her back arching, her heels digging into my back. I didn't stop, just slowed down, letting it happen, holding her tight as she climaxed, tasting her salty wetness, staying with her until her body finally relaxed and her gasping breath returned.

A minute later, lying beside her again, I touched her nipples lightly with my thumbs as she turned on her side to kiss me. 'Your turn,' she breathed. She smoothly pulled me over, onto and into her. We found an easy rhythm, as natural as the dancing, and I began to lose my awareness of everything but the feel and taste and smell of her. Knowing I couldn't hold back much longer, she took my face in her hands, blew softly against my skin and whispered, 'Come in me, baby, come in me now.'

* * *

I heard a tiny crystal bell somewhere far away and felt my chest being crushed by an unbearable weight of grief and loss.

LA said, 'Just give yourself a minute – it'll pass.'

Struggling to catch my breath, trying to fight back the tears, I said, 'What the hell am I supposed to do?'

'You think your job is where you were meant to be,' LA said. 'But belonging is much bigger than that. You're lost, troop.'

'Lost?'

'Lost in your own story,' she said. 'And stories don't end until they end.'

'I don't get it.'

'I know. But you will.'

'When?'

LA spoke, but I heard the voice of Kat Dreyfus: 'Soon.'

FORTY-ONE

The next day, buzzed and restless, agitated – by being so far from the action, I told myself – I paced around the docks while LA sat drinking lemonade with Matt Jory and Dan-something, a middle-aged veterinarian couple from Little Rock, on the rear deck of their houseboat, the *Dog Star*. She'd run across the two animal doctors in the gift shop and hooked up with them on the grounds that they were both TS Eliot fans, had wicked senses of humour, had been in therapy and liked shrinks.

I turned for my fifth trip past the boat as Dan was launching into a story about a schizophrenic Jack Russell terrier. I glared at my phone and wondered about the cell coverage in this part of the Ouachitas. I had between two and three bars, but for some reason that wasn't always a reliable guide up here. I gave the phone an experimental shake, and the ringer sounded. It was a patrol officer named Jenns who'd been detailed to let me know if the GL Owen lead had paid off.

The signal quality was lousy but the news was good: '. . . tenant, Investigator Mouncey tried earlier but . . . the voicemail cue so she told me . . . eep trying until I got . . .'. In short snatches he gave me a rundown on the suspects:

two brothers, Bobby Wayne 'Nature Boy' Jewell and Rayford Dougliss Jewell, the latter a motorcycle outlaw known variously as 'Matt,' 'Bone' and 'Catfish', and a skin-head fall partner of theirs by the name of Stonewall Jackson Merritt. The latter two were army vets who'd been associated with Aryan Nation prison gangs during stretches for methamphetamine manufacture and distribution, commercial burglary and armed robbery, and Jenns' description of Rayford Jewell convinced me he was the Harley-Davidson man. All three had extensive work histories in commercial building construction, usually on slab crews, where they routinely handled concrete hardeners and sealants.

With all the media attention and so many people working the case, things were coming together fast. A pad of sticky notes matching the sheet on which the lab guys had found the word *glowen* and the Welsh code impression had been found in Nature Boy's pocket. Dr Gold's earrings turned up in a jewellery box that belonged to the elder Jewell's girl-friend. The Ruger .44 Magnum that had killed Frix had still been in the glove compartment of Merritt's pickup. The Crime Scene crew found traces of DNA that turned out to be Gold's in a low-end home food hydrator from his garage.

I said, 'Where'd you bust them?'

' . . . arrested . . . off north Rockland working on a slab crew . . . Hart wants to arraign Thurs . . . '

Then I lost the call altogether. I tried a couple of times to get Jenns back but had no luck. Jamming the phone in my pocket, I walked back toward where LA and the vets were sitting, gave her a small fist-pump and refocused on the dog story at the point where the terrier had just stolen a hooker's push-up bra from a laundromat. A minute or so

312

later, as Dan was setting up the punch line, my phone rang again. It was Jana.

I said, 'You ready to sleep in your own bed again, Jay?'

'I sure as hell am,' she said. The reception had improved, but not much. 'Does that mean you caught them?'

'Just got the call,' I said. 'How're the girls?'

'Getting . . . little antsy by now. Not unlike their mother, if you want to know the truth . . . get them back to . . . as long as you're sure it's safe, Jim.'

This was when I spoke possibly the most mistaken words of my life: 'Everything's fine, babe,' I said, smiling across at LA, who was laughing along with the other vet at Dan's story. 'Come on home.'

As LA and I walked back to the marina office to settle our bill, my attention wandered off over the river and through the trees.

But kept coming back to what hadn't happened.

There was a small television on the shelf behind the counter, and it was displaying a file shot of Mark Pendergrass's puckish face against a scholarly-looking background of bookshelves and certificates. An ugly coldness took possession of my chest, and I looked at LA, who shrugged. The voice-over from the TV reported that the Traverton psychologist, forty-one and a divorced father of two, had been found dead this afternoon in the den of his Lakewood townhouse on the Arkansas side. The face of Joe Holder, a homicide detective I knew from task-force conferences, appeared on the screen. Someone off-camera said, 'So it was definitely foul play, Detective Holder?' and stuck a microphone in Holder's face.

Holder, evidently not trying out for Public Information Officer this year, gave the reporter an odd look, saying,

313

'Yeah, I'd say when you got a man butchered like a beef it's fair to call that foul play. Most definitely.'

'Cause of death?'

Holder shook his head, and I heard a distant male voice in the background. I thought it said, 'Jesus Christ, Larry, did you get a look at – ' before the sound was cut off.

FORTY-TWO

Back in Traverton I met Wayne at John Boy's. He was carrying copies of the preliminary reports the Arkansas guys had sent him on Pendergrass's death.

'Got all this on my phone,' he said as he handed me the folder, 'but you can't make out half of it on that little screen.'

I flipped through the pages, learning that the psychologist's body had been discovered by his golf partner, bound spread-eagle and face-up on his pool table with sisal rope and duct tape. He'd suffered a number of cuts, contusions and abrasion, but the cause of death was unrelated to that. He'd died as the result of brain trauma sustained when a ten-inch bridge spike had been used to nail a 'foreign object' to the centre of his forehead, the spike penetrating to the rear of his skull.

'Cold bastards,' said Wayne. 'Do that, then show up the next morning for work like nothing happened.'

I tossed the folder back onto the table. At this hour John Boy's was nearly empty, and we had the back corner of the dining room to ourselves. I'd decided to come back to town right away, not because I was stupid enough to think the arrests would put an end to Hazen's campaign against me but because separation from Jana and the girls and the action was getting less tolerable by the minute. Thinking like perpetrators and fugitives everywhere, I imagined that even though I could feel the hot breath of the process-servers on the back of my neck, I understood how they worked well enough to stay clear of them.

Making it back from Dallas half an hour behind me, Jana had called from the outskirts of town to tell me they were going straight home to the A-frame, but she wanted to see me a little later after she'd had time to shower and change. With the bad guys, particularly the Harley-Davidson man, locked up I was beginning to relax.

'"Foreign object"?' said Wayne. 'What're they talking about?'

I was thinking about the rope, spike and tape the Arkansas detectives had recovered. There was no doubt in my mind that they were going to match the samples Wayne had taken from the Gold scene. I drank some of my iced tea and set the glass down, thinking of something else I had no doubt about. I said, 'It was Deborah Gold's tongue.'

Wayne looked at me quizzically, saying, 'Damn. Where'd you get that, Lou?'

'I don't know,' I said truthfully. 'Just picking up the gestalts, I guess.'

I looked up into the bar at the neon beer signs, remembering the photograph of Mark Pendergrass's family I'd seen in the psychologist's office. They'd probably been notified by now. I wondered how they'd taken it.

I said, 'Did you offer Feigel protection?'

'Happenin' even as we speak,' said Wayne.

Wayne took another sip of coffee. 'Hell of a way to do police work, ain't it?' he said. 'Playin' hide and seek with

316

ourselves. Hope them two heroes we got coolin' off down-town get talkative before too long.'

There was an ice-cold silence.

'Two?' I said.

Nature Boy and Merritt had been picked up without inci-dent but the elder Jewell had somehow gotten word of the arrests and hit the wind before the investigators made it to the commercial building site where he'd been working. This fact had been lost in one of the gaps in Jenns' report.

The Harley-Davidson man was still out there.

I reached for my phone to call Jana. There was no answer.

Wayne was saying, ' – job-site supervisor told me Jewell'd been talkin' for days about "the asshole that got his baby brother killed".'

I said, 'What baby brother?'

Zito had wandered in and now joined us at the table.

'Let me pull it up,' he said, flipping open his laptop. 'We talkin' Texas, Louisiana, or what?'

'Start with Texas.'

He worked the keyboard and cursor. 'Okay, here it is,' he said. 'The Jewells did have a half-brother, quite a bit younger, different last name. He died in the joint a while back, I think, name was Jeremy Tidwell. *Hey*, wasn't that the guy – ?'

My expression must have been answer enough.

Zito closed the laptop and looked at me.

'Jewell say anything else?' I asked Wayne, standing up, redialling Jana's number.

'Just something about hitting the son of a bitch where he don't live. Then he jumped in his van and blasted out toward town. Don't know what that's supposed to mean.'

I knew exactly what it meant, but I made it to Jana's place a few minutes too late anyway. Slaloming through the traffic and blowing through lights with the bubble flashing, I tried Jana's landline, the gallery and her cell again, getting no answer anywhere. I threw the phone down on the seat beside me. The street ahead was jammed both ways, and I angled between parked cars and bounced over the curb as I took to the sidewalk, mowing down half a dozen parking meters with the brushbuster. A few seconds later I had to cut back left to avoid a barbershop customer who'd stepped out in front of me and frozen, causing me to hit a couple of shopping carts someone had left in front of the Dollar Store. From the corner of my eye I caught a glimpse of one of them spinning insanely through the air as it cleared the roofs of the passing cars and crashed through the display window of the Auto Zone across the street.

Reaching Border, I swung south toward Kiln-Roi with the accelerator jammed to the floorboard, veering from one side of the roadway to the other as I dodged vehicles, screaming insanely at their drivers to get the hell out of my way. As I approached the gallery I wrenched the wheel over, jumped the curb and smashed through the hedge, finally sliding to a stop between the gallery and the A-frame. Jewell's white GMC van sat at an angle across the flagstone walk near the front door.

Jana's silver Odyssey was in its usual parking place just beyond the walk, the side door wide open as if she and the girls had been unloading their luggage. But there was no sign of life anywhere that I could see – no talk or laughter, no wrangling over suitcases, no sound but the ticking of the cooling engines.

Knowing I was out of time and unwilling to concede

even another second or give any warning by trying the knob, I drew my backup SIG, forced out of my mind the white-hot pain from my knees and without breaking stride kicked the A-frame door off its hinges, bursting into the room while splinters were still flying.

What I saw was one of the scenarios I'd been praying for: Jana alive, but gagged and bound with duct tape in a side chair. Her eyes were wide and unblinking, the pupils dilated by fear as she looked at me, breathing hard. My own senses seemed to have sharpened supernaturally, so that every detail of the A-frame's interior stood out razor-edged and brilliant, even the smallest of the wood splinters and flecks of white paint from the door frame scattered across the floor and the individual dust motes drifting slowly in the shaft of sunlight coming through the side window. The house was dead silent except for the tap-tap-tap of the battery operated clock on the wall to my left as it parsed time into seconds that seemed to stretch out like minutes. There was no other sign of life at all, no Jordan, no Casey, no cat, no Jewell.

I looked at Jana again, seeing fear and desperation in her eyes, a sheen of sweat forming on her forehead and cheeks, but no sign that she'd been injured physically. But her stress level had not come down with my arrival; it was still rising.

Suddenly I caught a whiff of sweat, tobacco, stale marijuana smoke, and concrete sealant, all of it combining to create the smell I'd noticed outside my shop the night I'd made LA's bookends, the same odour LA herself had smelled at my kitchen door. I could tell it was coming from the kitchen. I moved as soundlessly as possible to my right to get a better angle on the kitchen entry, holding the SIG

319

in both hands and at low-ready, the muzzle directed toward the floor a few feet in front of me, trying not to think about how in a few more heartbeats Jana's position would probably have led me to turn my back on the kitchen.

At that moment Rayford Jewell and Casey appeared from behind the dividing wall, Jewell wearing the Harley-Davidson jacket Jordan had described and holding Casey in front of him, one hand clutching her right breast under her sweater, the other holding a short-barrelled Taurus revolver, a .38, with the muzzle against the side of her neck. He was grey, sweating and weeks past his last shave, his hair bound with a filthy red bandanna, his meth-ruined teeth like an abandoned graveyard. Looking at his drug-shot eyes, I saw a feral hog at bay, a thing long past fear and completely devoid of reason.

'Where's – ' I said before something in Jana's eyes stopped me. I glanced back at Casey. Same look.

Jordan was in the house, but Jewell didn't know it.

Having no idea exactly where she was, I began mentally reviewing the walls, appliances and other obstacles that could be concealing her, trying to calculate which ones could be counted on to stop a bullet, and visualising trajectories on the other side of the ones I knew wouldn't.

'Say, po-leece,' Jewell croaked. 'If I'd known you was comin' I'da baked a fuckin' cake.'

I said nothing, watching him closely and trying to control my own breathing. His hands shook slightly with a fine amphetamine tremor, but he had a solid, white-knuckled grip on the revolver.

'We fixin' to have us a little party before I head out for the coast,' he said. 'I'm thinkin' this little coochie-mama here might wanta come with me. Kind of a payback for Jerry, right? Daughter for a brother.' He leaned down and nibbled at Casey's ear. 'Bet I can make her last a whole week.' Shuddering, she stared at me with huge eyes.

'Can't see that working, Bone,' I said. About two-thirds of his head was behind Casey's. The SIG's grip was solid in my hands, the three tritium dots steady on Jewell's exposed eye. I had put more than three thousand rounds through the weapon without a jam or misfire, and I'd never picked it up without making sure the magazine was full and there was a round in the chamber. At the training range this was a dead-certain shot. But what was outside the ten-ring here was not white paper but my daughter's skull.

'Better hope it does, *Lieutenant*,' hissed Jewell. 'Only other way we go is I finish this little trout here, and then we find out how quick I can get to you and take that piece-of-shit gun away from you while you're trying to shoot through her.'

Looking at Jewell's expression, I saw no weakness, no indecision, and no doubt. He was going to do exactly as he threatened.

No options left now. No more decisions to make. Right here and right now the entire justification for my presence in the universe came down to what I did in the next second. I shifted my weight invisibly for better balance and began my trigger squeeze.

But at that moment I suddenly understood with absolute clarity where my other daughter was. And what she needed from me. I gently eased the pressure on the trigger, trying to keep the SIG completely motionless.

Jewell's expression and body language didn't change; he hadn't seen my reaction. Careful not to look up, I stared

321

hard at Casey, cleared my throat and waited a second to be sure I had her full attention.

Then I said, 'Hairball,' as sharply and authoritatively as I could.

Jewell looked at me in confusion but said nothing.

Casey's wide eyes blinked a couple of times, and a moment later her beautiful, delicate, mortally endangered throat began to convulse.

The gagging sounds caused Jewell to look down.

'Hey,' he said.

Casey vomited noisily down the front of her sweater, over his arm and onto the polished wood floor.

'Shit!' cried Jewell, reflexively pushing her away.

I glanced up in time to see the thirteen-pound, 3,000-page *Illustrated Encyclopedic Dictionary* Jordan had saved up her allowance for months to buy, tightly bound shut with the neon-pink laces from her sneakers, falling in deadly silence through the three storeys of air above Jewell's head. With the sound of a slamming car door it struck the crown of his skull and collapsed him bonelessly in his tracks, where he lay motionless, his eyes vacant and a trickle of saliva starting from the corner of his mouth. I grabbed the Taurus, checked its cylinder, and stuck it in my belt.

'Daddy!' cried the fouled Casey as she scrambled up from the floor. 'He caught us! He was gonna kill us!' She looked down at Jewell as she wiped her mouth with her clean sleeve. 'But you came!'

Outside, the sirens of half a dozen cruisers wailed as they closed in from different directions, and from overhead I heard the loose, flapping thumps of Jordan's sneakers coming down the stairs as I ran to free Jana.

Mouncey burst through the side door, weapon at low-ready. 'How many we got, Lou?' she said tightly, taking in the collapsed Jewell and scanning the upper floors.

'He's it,' I said, stripping away tape from Jana's mouth.

'Ow!' yelled Jana. 'Shit!'

Mouncey put up her gun.

'We clear in here,' she said into her radio as I handed her the Taurus. 'One bad guy, he down. Look like the Lou kilt him with a book.'

She bent to frisk Jewell and check for a carotid pulse, shaking her head once at me when she didn't find one.

FORTY-THREE

Mouncey had taken Jana and the girls to CiCi's for thera-peutic pizza and Cokes, and LA had just gotten here to Lanshire to meet me. Trying to fight off the acid edginess that for me always came after the wrong kind of adrenaline rush, I looked at her sitting across from me on the end of the sofa. 'Hypnotise me again,' I said.

She raised her unbandaged eyebrow.

'Why?'

'There's something I've got to know.'

I explained what I wanted.

She was silent a moment.

'Okay,' she finally said, getting up to adjust the lights. 'Go ahead and start your breathing routine – '

– I'm weightless and moving without effort or sensation over the springtime landscape of Rains County, drifting along above the quarterhorses and cattle herds of the Flying S, the long brown box of Braxton Bragg and the green rectangle of the football field beside it.

Now it's Sunday. Daz, Johnny and I are going to the antique car show at the fairground, and I'm here at Johnny's house to pick him up. Johnny's mother saying her son is in the shower and telling me make myself at home. Would I like something to drink? A Coke?

Yes, ma'am, thank you.

The house is open and airy, the pine floors clean, bright pictures on the walls, comfortable furniture. Mrs Trammel is glad to see me. She thinks I'm a good influence on Johnny, who was getting a little wild before I came along and Johnny got into football. You were like the cavalry, she has said. She is a schoolteacher, fourth-grade.

You can wait in his room if you like, she says.

Sipping Coke, I stroll into Johnny's bedroom. On the inside of the door there is a poster from some vampire movie, featuring a woman in black lipstick, black nail polish, a torn black dress, with two black fang-marks on her neck. The room is messier than I could get away with, the bed unmade, Johnny's blue jeans and sweater on the floor where he dropped them on his way to the shower, a couple of soft drink cans and a half-finished Baby Ruth on the dresser. The radio is playing 'I Remember You'. The window is open and the white muslin curtains gently lift and fall in the warm breeze. I can smell the asters in the flowerbed outside the window.

I wander over to the little table Johnny uses for a desk. Among several magazines I notice a collector's album, drab green canvas backing, with a hand-lettered label reading:

I.

Republican

II.

Imperatorial

III.

Imperial

I have always known Johnny is a coin collector. He uses these coins for his magic tricks. But the hobby doesn't interest me, and until now I've never seen the whole collection. Idly flipping through it, I find an array of lopsided, roughly struck coins, some with serrated edges, others worn almost featureless or with cracks and cuts in the rims. A weight too heavy to bear grows in my chest. I want to turn away but movement is impossible. I can't look at what I'm seeing, but neither can I look away –

' – three, two, one – wake up, Biscuit,' said LA.

I looked at her and wiped my eyes.

'Why were you crying?' she said.

FORTY-FOUR

LA and I made it to Rick Hart's office without seeing any Texas Rangers or warrant-servers. Bytes had been called in again, this time on the state's dime, and had set up his laptop and a few peripherals on a table in Hart's law library. Now he was looming like a mantis over the keyboard, watching the monitor with unreadable, long-lashed eyes as he worked to get his systems talking to each other. He was wearing a green Rice sweatshirt and baggy khaki chinos, boat shoes on long sockless feet despite the season. The way his reddish hair spiked up reminded me of a cartoon character who has just been surprised, and it looked like he hadn't shaved this week. I saw his Adam's apple travel to the top of his neck and back down as LA and I walked into the room. He looked up as we joined him. 'Hello again, Lieutenant. Hi, doc,' he said, doing a quick double-take as he saw my expression. His face was open and innocent, and if he felt the weight of what he was doing, it didn't show.

Somebody had brought coffee for LA and me, and I waved mine off with thanks while LA accepted hers. We stood back as Kevin worked, his face expressionless and still but his fingers dancing like insane spiders over the

327

keyboard, the screen images coming and going so fast I couldn't tell what I was seeing.

Trying not to sound impatient, I said, 'Anything?'

He transferred his attention back to me. 'No, sir, but I've been working on the list. Let me just get this started – I wrote this program myself. It should help.' He manipulated the mouse, typed in a command and clicked a few more times. 'Okay,' he said. 'What you see here is Dr Gold's actual total caseload.'

A column of initials, all the As and the first few Bs, appeared on the right side of the screen.

'And over here we have the ones you gave me.'

On the left another column of initials flashed on, short enough that all of it fit on the monitor screen.

'Now what we've got to figure out is how they match up, if they do.'

'If the initials on the short list had showed up on the long one, you'd already know that?' I said.

'Right. Therefore we assume some kind of encryption.'

I thought about this for a few seconds. I knew from an FBI workshop I'd once sat through that almost unbreakable codes did exist, but they were mainly research algorithms requiring complicated keys or decryption devices to read and were much too tricky and time-consuming for any ordinary use.

I said, 'For this kind of stuff people are going to use a system they can keep in their head.'

'Right,' he said. 'But nothing too simple either. Dr Gold wouldn't have been worried about somebody like Homeland Security or the CIA – she'd know it wouldn't take them three seconds to bust anything she could ever come up with – but she would have been serious about keeping out the casual snoopers and light-duty hackers. That gives us a ballpark idea how deep to look.'

I said, 'What are you doing now?'

'Trying a few obvious transformations, like substituting adjacent letters in the alphabet, B for A, Q for P, and so on. Plus I've tried converting the initials to digits based on their position in the alphabet and then looking at the numerical positions of the patient initials on the master list, that kind of thing. I got a hit or two, but nothing above the level of chance so far.'

'Okay, staying with simple but not too direct,' I said. 'It's got to be something she can convert without any hassle, but tricky enough that nobody's going to stumble onto it. Try reversing the initials and moving up a letter.'

'You bet.' A burst of keystrokes and mouse clicks. On the screen all the initials on the Cutchell list changed but nothing happened on the right-hand list.

'Now try going back one,' I said. But as I looked at the screen, thinking of cryptograms, word jumbles, acrostics and finally chess, the image of Coach Bub materialised in my mind. His expression was mischievous as he wagged his finger at me the way he always did after I'd missed a read in scrimmage or some chess ploy with the knight that he thought was obvious. It stopped me. The knight. The 'mystic knight'. The piece that struck obliquely, moving in any direction, over any intervening man, in a combination of one and two squares at right angles to each other . . .

'Wait,' I said. 'Look at the keyboard, Kevin. Just the letters. Try going ahead or back one letter on the keyboard, then forward or back two letters in the alphabet from there.'

He looked at me for a few seconds, the idea gradually coming into focus in his mind. He nodded, stared at his keyboard a moment, typed in the revised commands and worked the mouse. When he tried the first combination, two ahead on the keyboard, one back in the alphabet, the array on the monitor changed. A set of initials in the left-hand column brightened and a corresponding set on the right began flashing. He let the display scroll all the way up, then default back to the beginning of the list.

'Couple hits,' said Kevin. 'That's not it.'

'Seven combinations left,' I said. 'Run another one.'

He tried again, with no luck, then once more with the same result. On the fourth combination – two back on the keyboard, one ahead in the alphabet – the master list scrolled as usual, but now with randomly spaced sets of initials on the right flashing brightly one after another as they moved up the screen.

'Whoa,' said Kevin, letting go of the mouse. More flashes. 'Whoa, whoa, whoa.' He watched the screen intently as the display scrolled to the bottom of the list and went back to the beginning. 'Bim-bada-boom,' he said.

'Is this what it looks like?' I asked.

He turned to me with a smile. 'It's exactly what it looks like. The flashes are hits, one on the patient list for every entry on the Cutchell list. One hundred-per-cent match. In other words, slam-dunk-a-roonie. You figured it out, sir.'

'Can you print it out for me?' I said.

'I can put it on your phone if you want.'

'Paper'll work fine,' I said. 'Indulge me.'

'You're the boss,' said Kevin, the printer swishing softly. 'Dead trees coming up.'

He handed me the sheets, LA watching me as I scanned the pages, and I felt her becoming aware of my breathing and my heart rate. Of course I knew, or at least knew of, some of these people. A car dealer. A bowling alley owner. A noisy schoolboard member. A husband-and-wife doctor team from the Hebron Clinic. Dwight Hazen, the city manager who'd canned me and was now trying to get me locked up.

Forcing myself to continue down the list, I thought of the stylised T I'd been obsessed with, the T that turned out not to be a T, or a cross. The only meaning it had for me right now was as the seventh sign of the zodiac. The Scales, symbol of justice, the legal profession, balance and harmony.

Ninth on the list in my hand was an encoded set of initials I didn't need Kevin's translation to recognise: PSF.

The mastermind.

FORTY-FIVE

I drove west on the interstate under a cold, dull sky, not seeing the miles as they passed, trying not to think or remember. But of course I did think. I thought about who lives and who dies, about betrayal, and about whether anything that was good about being human could ever really be enough to offset the pain and loss and sorrow of it. I wondered how many people went on living and feeling not because life is sweet but because they believed they owed it to somebody – their loved ones, God, their karma. I remembered other autumns I'd seen, the sunlight of other times, and faces I was never going to see again. I remembered a life when I'd thought I understood the world and what to expect from it.

Exiting at Highway 14, I crossed the overpass and turned back along the access to take Houston Road down to the house-sized red-brick office building centred on a half-acre of lawn west of the county courthouse. A dark green Suburban I knew well was parked near the front door next to an oldish grey Beemer and a white four- or five-year-old Corolla.

Inside, I walked past the tasteful-looking furniture, generous plants and slick magazines in the waiting room, past the receptionist's desk – .

'Uh, Lieutenant Bonham, he's – '

Ignoring her, I opened the heavy, brass-furnished mahogany door and stepped into Johnny's office. He looked at me for a beat, his coat off and his sleeves rolled up, then set his pencil down at the top of the blue legal pad in front of him as if it were a blasting cap. His client, a balding middle-aged hustler with gold chains winking in the thick black hair at the opening of his collar, more gold on his wrists and fingers, blue goombah chin, the kind of guy who'd own a low-end used car lot or a titty bar, turned to get a view of me.

'Excuse us,' I said.

'Just a minute,' he said, cranking farther around in his chair, puffing up a little, starting to get dangerous.

'It's going to have to wait,' I said, the guy looking at my eyes and subsiding after a beat or two.

'Go on, Mike. It's okay,' said Johnny, his expression registering the terrible magnitude of the lie he'd just told.

Physically he looked great, belly still tight, no more than fifteen pounds over his playing weight. But there was a darkness in his face, a deadness in his eyes that I now recognised for what it had always been.

The gangster grumped out, deflated. With a weak, lopsided smile, Johnny invited me to sit. I did.

'You always had brass balls,' he said.

I didn't answer.

'I mean, here you are empty-handed, fronting a guy who's supposed to know ninety-nine ways to kill you with a paper clip.'

I still said nothing.

He drew in a deep breath and let it out. 'Thanks for not sending somebody else, Bis,' he said.

333

'I'm unemployed, Johnny,' I said. 'But you've got to know they're coming.'

Johnny nodded absently and looked down at his red foulard tie. 'Why do I wear this fucking thing in my own office?' he said. He loosened the tie and opened the collar of his white oxford buttondown. 'It's all a costume drama anyway, man. You ought to be able to just dress for comfort wherever you are, worry about stuff that really means something instead of this kind of bullshit.' He flipped the tie. 'Hey, remember when we used to go deer hunting, back in the day? Down on White Oak? Remember how some mornings it was so quiet you could hear a falling leaf ticking down through the branches fifty yards away?'

I remembered that, and I remembered an icy dawn when a ten-point buck, supernaturally alert, suddenly and silently appeared thirty yards in front of me, his breath pluming from shiny black nostrils as he surveyed the brown bottom-land hardwoods around him. Raising my .308 a millimetre at a time, moving only when the buck looked away from me, I finally settled the crosshairs behind his tawny shoulder and held them there for a few seconds.

Squeezing the trigger smoothly, dropping the firing pin on an empty chamber, I whispered, 'Bang', and the animal bounced away through the trees, the white flag of his tail held high.

'Remember those hogs that treed us that Thanksgiving?' said Johnny.

'I remember.'

'Tusks like fucking sabre-tooth tigers. Thought they were gonna eat us alive.'

I watched him.

'How'd you know?' he said.

'Got her casenotes,' I said, 'after I saw the blackmail list from her computer. Depression, PTSD, insomnia. Forty thousand a year.'

Johnny sighed. 'Her computer. Brilliant.' He shook his head. 'Ain't it a bitch? And the forty K wasn't all of it. She was always after something, constantly wangling introductions, pumping me for dirt on people. The worst part was having to listen to her. "You're carrying a lot of guilt around, Johnny, you're going to need my help. This is a long-term thing. You'll need to keep me on retainer."' A short laugh. 'For ever. My psychologist for life. I tried to wiggle out of it. I had a PI dig up some shit on her, even got her psych records from the counselling service where she went to school. According to Mark it was pretty bad, especially her MMPI. But she just laughed at me.'

So the Welsh code LA had translated for us was Gold's. It fit. I imagined Pendergrass jotting down the code as he and Johnny talked on the phone, on the notepaper that had been stuffed up Gold's nose. Jewell at some point swiping the pad and adding the reference to GL Owen on the next sheet, probably after getting a lead on a job.

'Was that the reason for the tongue?'

Johnny looked away, nodded briefly. 'Having them cut it out, yeah. I was that angry. But drying it out in their fucking jerky oven? Jesus, what pigs. The other shit was ad-lib,' he said. '*Lagniappe.*'

'There was something else, Johnny,' I said. 'A couple of things you didn't do.'

'Didn't do?'

'When I asked you about lawyers calling a witness a whore, you didn't show any interest in who or what I was talking about. And when I told you I was hearing interesting things from a psychologist about what was going on at the prison, even with all your curiosity about the case you didn't want to know which psychologist it was or what he was talking about. Or she. The only way that makes any sense is if you already knew.'

Johnny sighed, shook his head. 'I should've known I'd make a dumb slip like that sooner or later. It's been weird, man. When you're a litigator you think you're good with words and stories and details, good with lies, but then when everything's a lie there's just too fucking much to remember.'

'Why Pendergrass?'

'He had to go because I knew y'all would break him down, and that'd be the end of me.'

'Was it you who called the shot at LA?'

Johnny pinched the bridge of his nose. 'No, Bis, not that. Never. Believe it or not, I almost decided to call you and turn myself in when I heard about it. Picked up the phone, even punched in the number, but then I lost my nerve. Told myself that'd be their last move, that you'd get her and Jana and the girls clear.' A bleak smile. 'Fucking morons thought killing LA was gonna improve their situation? Shut you down by shooting at your family?' He hacked out a sour laugh. 'I can pick 'em, can't I?'

'Where'd you get them?'

'Through Mark. They were all out there at the prison at one time or another and knew that Sword guy, Keets. He must have known about them having a hard-on for you over that doper that killed Bo's wife and girl.'

'What about Frix?'

'He knew what Gold knew. Decided to try blackmailing me after she was dead.' Johnny ran a hand through his hair, saying, 'By then there was just no stopping-place for me, Bis. He had to go too.'

'You sold a lot of people on the idea of the survivalists, Johnny.'

'I know, man. It was a pretty good story, wasn't it? The perfect bad guys.'

'Why the coin?'

He shrugged. 'Smokescreen, same as the letter. Tabloids get hold of it, CNN, the net, who knows, maybe we get a California situation, the case derails, a fall guy shows up. I didn't count on you running the investigation yourself.' He took in a deep breath and blew it out. 'It was actually the coin that gave me the idea how to do her. Thinking of the Romans, y'know? Money got a little tight one month, what with the payments to Gold and all, and I sold off most of my collection. Saved a few for mementos. I didn't think you'd remember them after all this time.'

I said nothing.

'I'm really sorry, Bis. About all of it. All of it except Gold. Her I'd do again. After Delta Force I didn't think I had any killing left in me, but there're just no words to tell you how much I hated that bitch, man.'

'You know why I'm here,' I said.

'You mean other than to bust me?'

I took the folded sheet of paper from my inside pocket and pushed it across the desk for him to read. It was a copy of a progress note from his own file, isolated at the top of an otherwise blank page. The entry, seeming to throb with malignant heat, read:

JQT9/2
<u>kld bst frnds grl</u> wh HS snr, nv cau

337

Wh HS snr. When high-school senior. The year we won State. The last year of Kat's life. *Nv cau* of course was shorthand for never caught.

'You're going to tell me what happened to Kat and where she is, Johnny,' I said. 'I'll do anything it takes to get that.'

A crooked smile from Johnny.

'Anything?' he said. 'Even kneecap me?'

After a silence I said, 'You really think I'd stop at that?'

Johnny gazed out the window, and in the slatted year-end light I could see the fine tracery of veins in the whites of his tired eyes, the radiating crow's feet at their corners.

'No,' he said. 'Any more than I would in your place.' He stared blankly through the glass a while longer, then said, 'On the field you and Daz worked together like a couple of wheels in a fucking watch, Bis. I've never seen anything like it. It was you and him that took us to State, pure and simple. But I don't think you ever really understood him.'

I waited.

'He was blind-jealous of you, buddy. Jealous of the girls you got, jealous of that place you lived on. Even jealous of your folks. You know what his were like. He figured you'd have gotten picked way ahead of him in the draft, and he knew you were smarter than him too. Hell, you were smarter than any of us. And didn't even know it.'

'Why are we talking about Daz, Johnny?'

Johnny rubbed his eyes with his fingertips, saying, 'Why are we talking about Daz?' He swivelled back to face me. 'Because it was Daz who had the idea of grabbing Kat. I was there, but it was Daz who – ' His voice failed him, and he swallowed dryly before continuing. ' – who strangled her.'

A long, unmeasurable moment passed, the earth grinding silently on its cold axis.

'Were you jealous too, Johnny?' I said.

'Of you? Yeah, I guess so, Bis. I finally realised you really did think you were just an orphan with nothing of your own. But back then all I saw was that great family you had, the ranch and those horses, the way you could carry a football, the way nothing ever kept you down. The way the chicks came to you like moths to a candle. But Kat was the most beautiful girl I'd ever seen, Bis. I have to admit I wanted her as much as Daz did.'

'Did he rape her?'

Johnny breathed for a while, his jaw tight, then nodded shortly. 'Yeah, he raped her.'

'And you?'

Johnny hung his head. 'Have you ever done anything bad, Bis? I mean really, truly, go-to-hell bad?'

I didn't speak.

'It's incredible what it does to you,' Johnny said. 'The way it closes in on you. It's there every day, every minute, every second, the noose tightens a little at a time, and you know there's absolutely no hope, no way of fixing anything. It doesn't get better with time, it gets worse, and you know eternity could go by, and then a thousand more like it, and still nobody's ever going to forgive you, not ever, not your-self, not even God, if there is such a thing. I got so I saw all of it every goddamn time I closed my eyes. Still do. I think that was the real reason Daz had his wreck – there was no way he could live with it any more.' Johnny looked up at me. 'I did my best to let 'em cap me over there, Bis, I really did, but I guess Delta taught me too damn well. The assholes would pop up with those ratty-ass AKs, I'd react before I could stop myself – ' He shook his head. 'Then there we'd be, man, my goddamn heart still pumping away and theirs not.'

'Where is she?'

He stared at the desk blotter for a few seconds, seeming fascinated by whatever he saw, like a biologist discovering some new form of life.

After a while he said, 'By that big pond on your place out there. The one that's way the hell and gone out in that wide valley where the old cabin was, with all the willows and cottonwoods around. West side, where the big rock is, about six yards back from the water. We took her out there in Daz's jeep after she told us about the place. We said we were going to meet you there. It just drove Daz nuts thinking about you and her. He wanted to take her out there and fuck her. I guess he convinced himself she'd go for it once we were there. She trusted us because we were your friends – '

His voice broke.

Taking a few seconds to get back on track, he said, 'But she fought us like a goddamn tiger, man.' He closed his eyes tight but opened them again almost instantly, as if what he was trying not to see had been even harder to look at behind his eyelids than in the light of day. 'When it was over we buried her there and took off.' He hung his head. 'There's no words to explain how bad it hurts, Bis.'

'Don't try.'

He looked at me, nodded once.

I said, 'I want you to testify against the guys you used in the killings, Johnny.'

Another nod. 'Already done,' he said, holding up a red flashdrive. 'It's all here.' He tossed it back on his desk and looked at me with an expression I couldn't decipher. 'I made love to Li twice last night, Bis. First time I've done that in fifteen years. I wonder if it told her something. You think it did?'

I watched him.

Johnny slid a cigarette from the pack on his desk, patted his shirt pocket, pawed around a little on his desktop, then reached into the pocket of his trousers and – still the magician he'd always been – produced a Walther .380.

'Oops,' he said, levelling the little pistol at my chest. 'Thing is, I can't take the needle, Bis. And I'm not doing life, either. Not saying I don't deserve it.'

He brought out a lighter, lit the cigarette and took a long drag. He blew smoke out toward the ceiling and watched it mushroom. 'I think what we need here is to clear the board.'

'So let's clear it,' I said. 'What would it be worth to you to sleep again?'

Johnny looked at me for a couple of seconds. 'That was pretty good, Bis. You always did have a certain gift for the apt phrase. You'd have made a hell of a trial lawyer.' Eyes on mine, he laid his cigarette in the small cut-glass ashtray, carefully laid the Walther down on the blotter, opened a side drawer and brought out a pint of Wild Turkey.

'Little snort?' he said.

I didn't answer.

'Hope you don't mind if I do.' He uncapped the bottle and took a long swig, then wiped his mouth with the back of his hand. 'Custom o' the country,' he said. 'I love you, Biscuit. Is it okay yet for a guy to say that?' Eyes still locked with mine, he set the Wild Turkey on the blotter next to the .380.

I was thinking about the comparative clumsiness of my

own hands, and trying to remember exactly how my jacket had bunched on the right side when I sat down.

'I really do love you, Bis. But – '

He picked up the automatic, aimed it at the third button of my shirt and snapped the safety off.

The butt of the SIG was exactly where it needed to be, behind one fold of my jacket. In some mental zone that had nothing to do with thought or even conscious intention, I came out of the chair with the SIG up and bucking in my hand, the shots somehow sounding soft and far away, Johnny jolting back in his own chair with each round as the Walther slipped from his hand.

I stopped firing, hearing the last shell casing clatter against the baseboard across the room.

Johnny, his shirt already drenched red, whispered, 'Bang.' He bent slowly forward and laid his cheek on the blotter beside the bottle of whisky, the cigarette still burning in the ashtray, its blue ribbon of smoke rising smoothly until it began to ripple and fold on itself.

With Regina screaming behind me, I picked up the cigarette and stabbed it out in the ashtray, then reached across the desk for the weapon whose trigger Johnny had never pulled. As I picked it up carefully by the chequered grips, its weight told me it wasn't loaded. I left it on the end of the desk away from Johnny's dead hand.

Which was procedure, every bit as useful as the meat wagon that would respond to the 911 I was punching in.

FORTY-SIX

At trial Johnny's confession, long, lawyerly and airtight, turned out to be damning for all three of the defendants, as if at the end Johnny – skilled litigator that he was – had done the only thing he could to clean up his mess by leaving out no detail of the crimes and closing every loophole any of his accomplices could possibly have slipped through.

Stonewall Jackson Merritt pleaded guilty to all three murders and turned on his co-defendants, admitting that he and the Jewells had killed Dr Gold for the late attorney John Trammel in return for twenty-five thousand dollars each, luring her to her office that evening with the promise of a huge fee for a custody-related court appearance the next morning. Frix, who'd known for years about Gold's relationship with Johnny, had been murdered for another twenty-five thousand, divided three ways, after trying to blackmail Johnny. For killing Pendergrass, Merritt, acting alone this time, had doubled his price.

The court gave him consecutive life sentences for the murders of Deborah Gold, Benjamin Frix and Mark Pendergrass.

Bobby Wayne Jewell's lawyer, gambling on a plea of not guilty by reason of mental disease or defect, acknowledged his client's participation in the crime but argued that he was an honorably discharged combat veteran suffering from post-traumatic stress disorder sustained in defence of his country, and that his criminal actions were a product of that disorder. He got the needle. He'd avoided my eyes during the trial, but when the sentence was read he looked at me and shrugged. At a press conference on the court-house steps after the trial his attorney said something about 'kangaroo justice by association', but he mentioned no plans for an appeal.

Against all odds and everybody's expectations, Rayford Dougliss Jewell hadn't died of his head injuries after all, or at least hadn't stayed dead. The EMTs had managed to jump-start his heart on the third try, bringing him back to the world of trouble he'd briefly left behind.

It had been Ridout who called me with the news about this particular Jewell.

'He's bad fucked up, Lou. But the docs say he's probably gonna live, if you can call it that.'

Bone was tried in the Gold and Frix murders after a hot courtroom debate over his competency to stand trial. According to expert witnesses, the haemorrhaging in his brain caused by the impact of Jordan's massive dictionary falling from the third-storey loft, and the resulting cardiac arrest and oxygen deprivation, had left the elder Jewell with intractable seizures and traumatic dementia. His attorney, moving for dismissal, argued that Bone couldn't understand the charges against him or assist in his own defence.

'He may not be as smart as he used to be, counsellor,' said Judge Gaither, 'but I've watched you down there asking him questions and listening to the answers ever since we went into session. Motion denied.'

Jewell was found guilty and given concurrent life sentences. He sat slumped in his wheelchair and gave no sign that he heard the verdict or the sentence.

Hearing about his condition, Jana had said, 'Jesus! Not that he didn't deserve it, but that's horrible. I hope Jordan's going to be all right about it.'

Jordan settled that question for me when she said, 'I don't know what he expected, going around capturing people with a gun that way.'

Casey only wrinkled her nose and said, 'He smelled like roadkill.'

Without Dwight Hazen's pressure, the case against me evaporated overnight and the council offered me my job back with a raise and a service commendation. I turned them down.

FORTY-SEVEN

I was off the job, but for me the story wasn't over. Dwight Hazen was indicted on four counts of sexual contact with a minor and three of sexual assault based on information provided by three victims, all former patients of Dr Gold. They had come forward after Geoff Dean's 'Lateline Special Report' and the publication of Cass Ciganeiro's articles in the *Gazette*, all the coverage well salted with references to the fact that Hazen had been making blackmail payments to Gold. Heather Obenowsky didn't want to testify unless absolutely necessary, but she agreed to be there in court with the other girls for moral support and to help Benny with a group for sexually abused girls.

By the time Hazen's indictments came down he'd vanished like smoke. The cameras then turned to a series of public officials – not including OZ – who were eager to share their disappointment and outrage as well as their sorrow for the victims and the community, referring repeatedly to the huge personal, philosophical and political differences they'd always had with Hazen but hadn't acted on, out of respect for both the sacred will of the people and the requirements of due process. It turned into a time of advisory panels, investigations and blue-ribbon committees, and there was even some loose talk of a morality czar in Traverton.

Then came an anonymous tip to Dispatch, relayed to me by Mouncey, that I had a personal pickup waiting at Sylvan Park. Politely declining offers of police backup, a bomb squad sweep and secret surveillance by the FBI, I drove alone out to the cemetery in the cold, coppery late-afternoon sunlight. On the way I met the black rental Ford I'd seen in front of the Cutchell place. This time it was headed toward the airport, the driver now dressed in a tan western suit and bolo tie. His mirrored shades prevented me from seeing his eyes but he offered me a small nod and touched the brim of his white Stetson as he passed.

I had no idea what I'd find when I got to the cemetery, but I had a feeling it would relate to the Gold case. And it did.

Without thinking about it, I turned left as soon as I was through the gates, toward Joy Therone's grave. From a distance it looked as if the monumental angel standing watch over her was holding out a big sack of garbage for inspection. As I got closer I saw it was Dwight Hazen, wearing a black bouffant wig and dressed as a pregnant woman, cuffed to the angel's wrist and grimacing with the effort of standing on his tiptoes. Several thousand dollars in Mexican pesos and a street map of Ciudad Miguel Aleman were later found stashed in his girdle.

On later questioning he refused to say where he'd been and what he'd done between the release of the indictments and his arrival at Sylvan, and I resigned myself to the likelihood that I was never going to know all of what happened, including the whole story of how he ended up at the cemetery, in the angel's custody.

347

But I saw him twice more. The first encounter came when he was in court to challenge the legality of his capture. I was there to testify at an appeals hearing in an old case and ran into him in the hallway outside the courtroom. Despite his lawyer's efforts to steer him away from me we came face to face for a couple of seconds, long enough for him to sneer contemptuously at me, and for me to develop an unaccountable but absolute certainty about something.

I tracked Rick Hart down in the third-floor men's restroom. I said, 'Zip and listen, Rick – Hazen killed Joy Dawn Therone. Don't ask me how I know. I know. All you've got to do is prove it.'

The investigation that followed uncovered enough evidence for an indictment, leading to, among other things, a desperate battle by Hazen's lawyers to keep him from having to provide DNA samples in the Therone case. They lost.

The second meeting came when I made the trip to Tri-State to visit him in his cell on the fourth floor, where I found him pale and unshaven but still defiant.

'I suppose you think you pulled one off, don't you?' he asked.

'You tell me.'

He watched me for a few seconds, breathing hard. 'What did you come here for?'

'I'm not sure,' I said. 'To get a good look at you, now that I know who you really are. Maybe to hear what some-body like you says when he's busted once and for all. Or maybe just to look you in the eye and tell you what you already know – you're through with little girls. The DNA's going to be the end of you.'

'What makes you so sure I'll get the needle?'

'I'm not,' I said. 'But there's always hope.'

'Funny talk, considering the source,' Hazen said, trying for a cynical smile. 'You always said you were against the death penalty.'

'That's true,' I said. 'On the other hand, sometimes a man's got to show a little flexibility.'

'You know, I've always hated jocks like you, Bonham – grabbing all the girls and headlines. God's gift to the fucking world.' He slammed his fist down on his thigh. 'Who the hell do you think you are?'

'Nobody, really,' I said. 'But just the same, I'll be there with the Therones when the techs stick you. Look for me. I'll be the guy in Joy Dawn's chair.'

FORTY-EIGHT

Dusty, looking as fit as he was when I was in high school, had been waiting for us at the front gate of the Flying S on the day the story ended – by becoming another story – leaning back against the grille of his old tan Dodge four-by-four in the thin wintering sunlight with a steaming mug of coffee in his only hand, legs crossed at the ankles. In his blue flannel shirt, faded jeans, boots and weather-beaten black Resistol he looked completely at home on the range, the perfect image of what he was – a horseman in his element. At his side Knuckleball, the yellow Lab, pink tongue hanging out, watched with him as the caravan gradually slowed and turned off the highway.

Tyres crunching in the gravel, the vehicles rolled one by one through the wrought-iron arch and drew even with him: two sheriff's department cruisers full of deputies, the coroner's Blazer, *Buford* with me at the wheel and LA and Zito on the seat beside me, a couple of official county pickups, one a four-wheel drive pulling the backhoe on a double-axle flatbed trailer. When we'd all eased to a stop Dusty spoke briefly to the drivers of the two cruisers, then, with Knuckleball at his heel, walked along the line of vehicles, nodding and trading a few words with the occupants as Knuckleball gave three polite wags of his tail at each stop. After concluding his inspection of the trailer, Dusty walked back to my window.

'Hi again, Dusty,' said LA.

'Hi, girl.' Now Knuckleball's tail waved continuously as he grinned from ear to ear.

Dusty said, 'You holding up okay, son?'

'Yeah, I guess so, thanks,' I said. 'Dusty, this is Floyd Zito, an old sidekick. Zito, Dusty Rhodes.'

Zito reached his one hand across to shake, and Dusty eyed his empty right sleeve, set his coffee on *Buford*'s roof and took Zito's hand. 'You and me together might make a piano player, Floyd.'

'Yeah, if you can tell me what the hell all those little black and white keys are for,' said Zito.

Dusty smiled. He said, 'Bis, I told those boys in the cruisers they'll need to leave their vehicles at the house. Guess I'll let 'em ride in the back of my truck, the ones I can't get in the cab.' He nodded at the backhoe. 'Dry as it's been, we might get that rig across the creek. Can't make it, I'll come back for a tractor.'

Rachel met us on the drive behind the house. 'I guess I wish you luck,' she said, hugging me hard.

Overhead, barn swallows looped and dived in the clear air.

As we bumped along behind the trailer, over trails I had for most of my life associated with hooves, not wheels, LA tuned the radio at low volume to an oldies station out of Texarkana, a long-ago ballad about seeing a sunrise in a lover's eyes.

351

I said nothing, gazing blindly off into distances I'd once thought were beautiful.

LA said, 'When did you know Johnny's gun wasn't loaded?'

I hadn't expected the question, though I probably should have. I wasn't sure of the answer. I hoped it was after I fired the first round.

'Not soon enough to let him live,' I said.

'It was the way he wanted it, Biscuit. Once he knew it was over. It was you he chose.'

I looked at her, not speaking, the sour sickness of that moment churning in me like hot slag.

'He thought he owed you that,' she said.

I still didn't answer. I turned off the radio.

Finally I said, 'It didn't buy him anything.'

'He wouldn't have wanted it to.'

Forty minutes later we stood watching the men offload the backhoe beside the pond.

'Can he dig careful enough with that thing?' asked Zito.

'He's done it before,' said one of the deputies.

LA glanced at him.

'Dug up bones, I mean.'

The operator, a freckled old farmboy with calloused hands the size of catcher's mitts, extended the hydraulic arm over the site I had marked out for him and brought it slowly back, a uniform three-inch layer of soil and bracken curling gracefully into the bucket.

'Hey,' said Zito. 'Guy knows what he's doing.'

Another careful pass, then another, all of us watching like student surgeons as the earth slowly gave up its truth.

'Did he say anything about how deep?' asked LA.

I shook my head, saying, 'I don't even know if he was telling the truth about her being out here.'

'Might ask the bastard again, if we knew the area code for hell,' said Zito.

I looked down at my shoes.

'Sorry, bud,' he said. 'I just meant why would he lie, right there on the verge of dying and all?'

LA, losing interest in the conversation, wandered in closer to the point of excavation and stood where she could see the new earth as the bucket uncovered it. The lulling regularity of the machine's movement, the perfect sameness of the cutting strokes and the cough and roar of the diesel seemed to enclose us in a kind of bubble of isolation, a dimension where the meaning of ordinary time slipped away.

Suddenly LA signalled the backhoe operator, and we all moved forward. No one spoke as we stood looking down at the ivory curve of bone exposed by the last pass of the bucket – the visible edge of a long-gone world and a story that was finally ready to end.

When the almost-weightless body bag had been loaded into the coroner's wagon, we still stood in silence, because there was nothing to be said. LA stood apart from the rest of us and watched in silence, her eyes brimming, haunted by her own sorrows, old and new.

Finally, she came over and hugged me. 'Now, Biscuit,' she said softly. 'Now you can come home.'

Acknowledgements

Some of my early sources of inspiration were benign, real credits to the universe, while others, including many of the more valuable ones, were wildly dysfunctional, irredeemably mean or just flat out crazy. I'd like to take this opportunity to express my appreciation for all of them – the innumerable friends, enemies, acquaintances, accomplices, soul-takers, teachers, abusers, miscellaneous kin and others who by walking with, or near, me through significant stretches of our lives filled my head with a wonderland of stories.

And as for the here and now: along with the many others who richly deserve acknowledgment for their kind patience and direct or indirect support, proofing with the vision of eagles, feedback and general cheerleading in getting *Blackbird* aloft – like my great friends in Portugal as well as those across the rest of Europe, Australia and North America, not to mention my long-suffering family, office staff, daily associates and patients – I'd especially like to thank my editor at Canongate, Francis Bickmore; my agent, Victoria Hobbs of A.M. Heath in London; my manager and good friend, Dr. Marshall Thomas of 7Arts Foundation and Colossal Concepts Management, a polymath who never calls himself that but occasionally bestows the title upon those who have won his invaluable regard, and who keeps a garden in which he attempts to grow others of his kind; and the Honourable James Edmund Byng, Force of Nature.